PUBLISHING
REPUBLIC OF

STUDIES IN THE HISTORY
OF IDEAS IN THE LOW COUNTRIES

SERIES EDITORS

Hans W. Blom, Robert von Friedeburg, Siep Stuurman
and Wijnand W. Mijnhardt

Amsterdam – New York, NY 2005

PUBLISHING IN THE REPUBLIC OF LETTERS

The
Ménage-Grævius-Wetstein
Correspondence
1679-1692

RICHARD G. MABER

Colofon: Richard G. Maber / Publishing in the Republic of Letters: The Ménage-Grævius-Wetstein Correspondence 1679-1692. - Amsterdam-New York : Rodopi

The paper on which this book is printed meets the requirements of "ISO 9706:1994, Information and documentation - Paper for documents - Requirements for permanence".

ISBN: 90-420-1685-x
©Editions Rodopi B.V., Amsterdam – New York, NY 2005
Printed in The Netherlands

CONTENTS

ILLUSTRATIONS

(after page 79, *infra*)

ACKNOWLEDGEMENTS

The letters edited in this volume are held in the manuscript collections of the Kongelige Bibliotek, Copenhagen (letters from Ménage to Grævius) and the Universiteitsbibliotheek, Amsterdam (letters from Wetstein to Ménage). I am very grateful to these libraries for permission to publish them, and also to the Department of Rare Books and Special Collections of Princeton University Library for permission to include a letter from Ménage to Toinard. The specialist staff in these libraries have been unfailingly courteous and generous in their advice and help. I owe a particular debt of gratitude to Dr Erik Petersen of the Department of Manuscripts in the Kongelige Bibliotek, Copenhagen, who first informed me about the Ménage correspondence there.

Much of the material in the annotations has been gathered in the course of my work on Ménage's correspondence in libraries in many parts of Europe. The extensive investigative research involved has been supported by grants from the University of Durham Central Research Fund, and the Staff Research Fund of the School of Modern European Languages. I have benefited immensely from the specialist advice of staff in the departments of manuscripts and printed books of a considerable number of libraries, in particular, for this edition, from the following: Bibliotheek der Rijksuniversiteit, Leiden; Universiteitsbibliotheek Utrecht; Koninklijke Bibliotheek, Den Haag; Bibliothèque Nationale de France; Bibliothèque de l'Arsenal; Bibliothèque de la Sorbonne; Biblioteca Medicea Laurenziana, Florence; Biblioteca Nazionale Centrale, Florence; Princeton University Library; the Bodleian Library, Oxford; and the British Library. I have been fortunate in being able to draw extensively on the rich library resources available in Durham, and to profit from the friendship and learning of their custodians: in particular I must thank Mr Roger Norris of the Durham Cathedral Chapter Library and, above all, Miss E. R. Rainey, Dr A. I. Doyle, and all the staff of the Special Collections of Durham University Library.

Many academic colleagues, in Durham and elsewhere, have responded generously to requests for assistance. Dr Volker Schröder of Princeton University gave invaluable help with the resources of the Department of Rare Books and Special Collections at Princeton. I am grateful to Professor Peter Rhodes of the Department of Classics and Dr Robert Carver of the Department of English in Durham, and to Professor David Levine of the Department of Classics in the University of Leeds; and, especially, to Dr Hans Blom of Erasmus Universiteit, Rotterdam, for his advice, support, and patience throughout this project.

Some passages in the Introduction have appeared in a different context in articles published in *The Seventeenth Century* and *Seventeenth-Century French Studies*, and are reproduced by permission of the editors.

INTRODUCTION

In the early summer of 1692 the seventy-nine year old Gilles Ménage, one of the most celebrated scholars in Europe, recounted to an admiring audience the adventurous printing history of his greatest work of classical erudition. His vast commentary on Diogenes Laertius's *Lives of eminent philosophers* had been first published, with an edition of the text in Greek and Latin, in London in 1664. In the course of preparation there was a dramatic episode: the copy that Ménage sent from Paris to the printer Octavian Pulleyn was lost in transit, and only found again after a period in which it seemed that many years' work had gone to waste. When it came to the expanded and much improved second edition, published in Amsterdam by Henrik Wetstein, things went no better. Instead of the quick publication that Ménage had anticipated the printing dragged on interminably for year after year, until he despaired of ever living to see the completed work. However, there was a happy ending: he announced that he had at last received two copies of the finished edition, by a tortuous route, and declared himself delighted with the result:

> Quelques années après on me parla de le réimprimer en Hollande, et je fus sollicité d'y ajoûter beaucoup de choses. Il sembloit qu'on l'allât imprimer sur le champ, tant on marquoit d'empressement pour cela . . . Enfin toutes mes augmentations étant achevées, je les envoiai en Hollande. Cependant il y a près de neuf années qu'il est sous la presse, et je n'en ai reçu que deux exemplaires que M. Wetstein m'a fait tenir de Hollande par Strasbourg. C'est une route bien longue; mais la guerre est cause de ce desordre. Je suis bien satisfait de l'impression. Tout le monde la trouve belle. Je ne croiois pas voir cet ouvrage avant que de mourir.[1]

The copies arrived just in time: Ménage died on 23 July 1692.

Ménage's comments immediately arouse the reader's curiosity. While long delays in the publication of scholarly works are a familiar occurrence, in the seventeenth century the fault was at least as likely to lie with the procrastinating author as with the printer; yet Ménage claimed that he sent off his final copy some nine years before the book was published. Again, while the periodic states of war did severely disrupt the international book trade they scarcely seem a complete explanation for the delay, and in any event would only seem to account for about half of the time that Ménage waited for his work to appear. One wonders exactly what did happen during those nine years 'sous la presse'.

By remarkable good fortune, two sequences of letters have survived which tell the complete story of Wetstein's printing of Diogenes, and the background against which this took place. They are all the more interesting in that they tell it from the very different perspectives of the strong-minded old scholar in Paris and his equally forthright printer in Amsterdam. These sequences consist, firstly, of forty letters from Ménage to his scholarly friend Johann-Georg Grævius in Utrecht, the first being dated 19 May 1679 and the last 8 February 1692, now preserved in the Kongelige Bibliotek Copenhagen, MS Thott 1263, 4°; and secondly, thirty letters from the Amsterdam printer

Henrik Wetstein to Ménage, which extend from 25 October 1683 to 8 May 1692, preserved in the Universiteitsbibliotheek Amsterdam, MSS Gm 8a-8ae. In addition, a letter of 11 December 1683 from Ménage to the French scholar Nicolas Toinard includes extensive quotation from a further letter from Wetstein to Ménage, the original of which has not survived. This letter, which is now in Princeton University Library, has been included in the present edition as Letter 14A.[2]

The two sequences interlock and complement one another precisely. Their interest is further heightened by the fact that in each case we have the first letter, opening the correspondence, and the last; while there appear to be a small number of letters that have not survived, both sequences are very substantially complete. Grævius was helping Ménage to get his works published outside France, acting for him first in connection with an edition in Leipzig, then providing the initial contact with Wetstein, and subsequently often acting as an intermediary in a sometimes fraught relationship. Thereafter we have essentially two sides of a triangular correspondence. Only a very few of Grævius's Latin letters to Ménage appear to survive, five in rough draft form (KB Copenhagen, MSS Thott 1268, 4° and Fabricius 104-123, 4°) and one as a copy in one of Grævius's letter-books (Universiteitsbibliotheek Utrecht, Hs. 7. C 30, pp. 57-59), but the contents of the others can easily be inferred from Ménage's replies and the correspondence of mutual friends; and while none of Ménage's letters to Wetstein are extant, he expresses himself freely to Grævius on the state of his relations with the printer and the progress of his works. Similarly the nature of the third side of the triangular relationship, the correspondence between Grævius and Wetstein, is clear from the many references in the two principal sequences.

These letters share a strong narrative thread in the endless complications attending Wetstein's printing of two of Ménage's works: the small-format definitive edition of his poetry (finished in 1687), and above all, of course, the edition of Diogenes Laertius. This enterprise is first raised in Ménage's fourth letter to Graevius (12 August 1680), and at last brought to a triumphant conclusion in Wetstein's final letter to Ménage of 8 May 1692. The result, as Ménage noted with such pleasure, was rightly acclaimed as a magnificent achievement of both scholarship and publishing. The importance of the edition is discussed in detail below. The present correspondences throw a completely new light on the origins of the work, and its slow evolution to its final form; they also make clear the crucial role played throughout by the interrelationship between the three correspondents.

As we shall see, though, the interest of these correspondences is by no means confined to the history of the Diogenes edition. Revealing portraits emerge of the correspondents themselves, and there are vignettes of a wide range of other figures in the world of literature and scholarship, seen through their eyes in the mood of the moment: obliging friends such as Emery Bigot, Pierre-Daniel Huet, and Nicolaas Heinsius, evoked in terms of the warmest admiration; Pierre Bayle, ever curious, refusing to pass on a book intended for someone else until he has read it first (Letter 53); the magnificently learned but infuriating collaborator Marc Meibomius, who drives Wetstein to distraction and, ultimately, a spectacular row; the dilatory biblical scholar Nicolas Toinard; or the printer Étienne Foulque who enrages Ménage by, the old savant is convinced, perpetrating an 'insigne friponnerie' on him (Letters 45, 46). Ménage's letters usually each contain a number of items of news, both general information from Paris and the latest developments in the world of scholarship; while the correspondences bear witness to the practical effects of the great political events of these years, the wars and the Revocation of the Edict of Nantes.

All the way through, there is the running story of the slow progression of the Diogenes edition and, as one setback follows another and Ménage advances in his old age, increasing doubt as to whether it will ever be published in time for him to see the long-awaited work. The two correspondences reach diametrically opposite emotional conclusions at almost the same time. Ménage's last letter to Grævius is a sad note of consolation on the death of his friend's son; while shortly after, Wetstein ends with his delight at the publication of Diogenes, at last, and the universal acclaim with which it has been greeted.

Ménage's two correspondents, Grævius and Wetstein, are figures of exceptional interest in their own right. Nevertheless the dominant personality and prime mover in their respective relationships is undoubtedly Ménage himself, and to appreciate the full interest of these letters they must be situated in the context of his life.

Gilles Ménage, 1613-1692

Gilles Ménage is a unique figure in seventeenth-century French intellectual life. He was one of the most remarkable scholarly polymaths of his time, yet in important ways he did not at all conform to the patterns of behaviour expected in such a role. He has always proved impossible to categorise, both for his contemporaries and for subsequent commentators. In large part this is a result of the exceptional variety of fields in which he was influential, but it is also a product of his strong, unconventional, and sometimes provocatively independent personality.

Ménage was born in Angers in 1613, into a distinguished legal family: he was to write biographies of his father and maternal grandfather, and of a fifteenth-century forebear, which feature in his correspondence with Graevius (see Letters 20, 29).[3] After coming to Paris in 1632 he began by studying law and pleaded a number of cases with success, but gave up practising in favour of literature and scholarship, while always keeping up close contacts with the legal world. He established his financial independence by taking minor orders in 1648 in order to enjoy the revenues from two abbeys; while he never showed much sign of a religious vocation, he cultivated friendships in ecclesiastical circles and indeed lived the last forty years of his life in a house in the cloister of Notre-Dame, behind the cathedral.

Most unusually, Ménage's growing fame as a scholar was matched by his social success. He was handsome, witty, and entertaining, with a taste for satire and *médisance* that must have added to his attraction. He was a leading personality in the Hôtel de Rambouillet and other salons, and he conducted his own prestigious salon on Wednesdays, his celebrated 'Mercuriales'. In Madeleine de Scudéry's romance *Clélie* there is a detailed, and highly favourable, portrait of him under the name of the character Anaximene, showing him as he appeared in the mid-1650s. The portrait emphasises his appearance, charm, and attractiveness to ladies, as well as his intellect and the more serious sides of his personality; although apparently flattering in the extreme, it is worth noting that the young Madame de La Fayette recognized him from the description immediately, even though she was in Auvergne at the time and had had no idea that he was going to figure in the work.[4]

It is, in fact, for his particular friendships with intelligent and cultured ladies that Ménage is often best remembered; not only Mlle de Scudéry, but most famously Mme de Sévigné and Mme de La Fayette, two clever and charming young ladies who went on to become, in the eyes of posterity, the two most distinguished women writers of the century. His reputation as the 'pédant galant' was immortalized in Molière's creation of Vadius in *Les Femmes savantes*, Act 3 Scene 5 – the egocentric scholar whom the ladies queue up to kiss – which is quite obviously based on Ménage (the character was originally called *Magius*), just as the much more unpleasant and fraudulent Trissotin is clearly a satirical portrait of his enemy Cotin. But Ménage is recorded as having taken Molière's satire in very good part;[5] he clearly liked and admired Molière, and there are several anecdotes of his defending the playwright against his critics. He was certainly always particularly responsive to women of intelligence and distinction. In old age he wrote his *Historia mulierum philosopharum* (1690) and dedicated it to Anne Dacier, the distinguished classical scholar, outspoken champion of the Anciens, and daughter of his old friend and correspondent Tanneguy Le Febvre: he then insisted on reprinting this work in his edition of Diogenes Laertius as a supplement (and perhaps corrective) to the Greek work, a matter much discussed in his correspondence with Wetstein. This unusual aspect of the great scholar's personality is well summed up by Pierre Bayle in his *Dictionnaire* (article on Ménage): 'Après tout, les liaisons de Mr. Ménage avec les Dames de beaucoup d'esprit lui ont fait honneur dans le monde, et lui en feront à l'avenir; car il est si rare que tant de Grec, et tant de Grammaire, n'étoufe pas les talens qu'il faut avoir pour être d'une conversation polie et galante auprès des femmes de qualité, que c'est une espèce de prodige.'[6]

Unlike most scholars, Ménage played a distinctive role in the world of *la littérature mondaine* through his salon contacts and his many literary friendships. He produced an important edition of the works of Malherbe, with a commentary, and also edited the works of his friend Jean-François Sarasin. He was a successful poet in his own right, composing a considerable body of well-turned, if frequently derivative, verse in Latin and Greek, in Italian (complemented by a prose volume of *Mescolanze italiane*, 1678), and in French. He produced verse in a considerable range of forms, much of it addressed to his cultivated lady friends and very frequently amorous; but there is, too, an irrepressible vein of sharp satire in his verses, and more than once his mordant wit threatened to get him into serious trouble. He also, in the vigorous French intellectual tradition, engaged wholeheartedly throughout his life in literary and scholarly controversies. There are echoes in his correspondence with Grævius both of the first of his *querelles*, dating from 1640 – with the abbé d'Aubignac, over the action of Terence's *Heautontimorumenos* – and of the last, provoked by Adrien Baillet's *Jugements des savans sur les ouvrages des principaux auteurs*, which extended from 1685 until his death.

The impossibility of categorizing Ménage too neatly is exemplified – not least in this correspondence – by his ambiguous position in the Querelle des Anciens et des Modernes. As a learned scholar of classical literature one might have expected to find him on the side of the Anciens, and as we have seen he admired that great defender of the Anciens, Anne Dacier. But at the same time he appreciated 'modern' literature and was very friendly with Charles Perrault, the leading Moderne, even though he did not share his viewpoint,[7] just as he had earlier championed Molière; Perrault even designed the frontispiece of the Diogenes edition for him (see the Wetstein correspondence, Letters 55, 57, 59, 62, 62A, 63, 64). As Mme de La Fayette had once written to him, in a quite different context, 'L'on peut bien dire que vous estes de ces gens qui avez des amis en paradis et en enfer'.[8]

It is no surprise to find that reactions to Ménage's complex personality are equally diverse. He had the reputation among his enemies – mainly jealous rivals – of being vain and quarrelsome; he certainly had a most unusual independence of spirit, and an intense dislike of external constraints of any kind. On the other hand a contemporary was able to call him 'le plus affable, le plus honnête, et le plus communicatif de tous les hommes',[9] and his life is marked by a considerable number of close and exceptionally long-lasting friendships which are often evoked in his letters.

As a scholar, Ménage established a European reputation with his immense erudition and intellectual versatility: he was regarded with respect by the leading Italian scholars of his time, and was elected a member of the Accademía della Crusca in Florence; he was greatly admired by Queen Christina of Sweden; and Leibniz wrote of him as 'un homme d'une érudition profonde'.[10] He owed his fame as much as anything to the exceptionally wide range of his achievements. The subjects of his major scholarly works can be divided into no fewer than five distinct categories.

Firstly, his greatest achievement in the eyes of posterity is undoubtedly his fundamental contribution to the development of linguistic scholarship and etymology. He published outstanding works on the evolution of the French and Italian languages (*Origines de la langue françoise*, 1650, revised as *Dictionnaire étymologique*, 1694; *Observations de Monsieur Ménage sur la langue françoise*, 1672; *Observations ... , Segonde partie*, 1676; *Le Origini della lingua italiana*, 1669), and he also extended his researches to include the development of Spanish and Greek. The second category consists of his works of Latin and Greek literary scholarship. These include his controversial study of Terence's *Heautontimorumenos*, 1640; an edition of Guez de Balzac's Latin poetry; notes on Lucian that Graevius included in an edition of 1687; and above all of course his remarkable commentary on the text of Diogenes Laertius, first published with the London edition of 1664, whose revised edition of 1692 forms the principal subject of the present correspondence. The third field in which he achieved distinction was legal scholarship. His compilation on civil law entitled *Juris civilis amœnitates*, first published in 1664, was an influential work which was repeatedly reprinted in the seventeenth and eighteenth centuries, and inspired a complementary volume on canon law by the leading German jurist Johann Strauch (*Amœnitatum juris canonici semestre*, Jena, 1674: see Letter 1, note 4). In a fourth category one can group his works of history and biography, written in both French and Latin. These include his *Histoire de Sablé*, 1683

(=1686), a very substantial and formidably erudite history of Anjou; the three biographies of members of his family, *Vita Mathæi Menagii*, 1674, *Vitæ Petri Ærodii et Guillelmi Menagii*, 1675, all of which are packed with fascinating digressions and annotations on the most diverse subjects; and a relatively slight and late work on the lives of the women philosophers of antiquity and the Middle Ages, *Historia mulierum philosopharum*, of 1690, which nevertheless has the great merits of establishing a new field of enquiry, and putting together a body of references never previously assembled. Finally, one can class together his editions of the works of modern authors, in both Italian (editions of Tasso's *Aminta*, 1655, and Giovanni della Casa's *Rime*, 1667) and French (editions of the works of Sarasin, 1656, and the poetry of Malherbe, 1666).

A striking feature of Ménage as a scholar, a poet, and even as a letter-writer is his apparent lack of real creative literary imagination; in all these fields, he had a tendency to work principally by accumulation, and was inclined to blame his phenomenal memory for the fact that he found it exceptionally difficult to have what he felt were truly original ideas. On the other hand his intellectual versatility is genuinely remarkable. He astonished his contemporaries by his ability to work in several quite different fields at the same time: when giving an account of his current activities in a letter to Huet of 1663, he noted that he was simultaneously publishing his *Poésies* (written in four languages, French, Italian, Latin, and Greek), the first edition of his commentary on Diogenes Laertius, and his legal work *Juris civilis amœnitates*; completing his edition of Malherbe; and working on his latest enterprise, a study of the Greek dialects.[11] The same dazzling multifaceted intellectual vigour is no less evident in his old age throughout his correspondence with Grævius, as he reports on his typically diverse current works in progress, and sends copies of the new editions of an impressive variety of his earlier publications; for example, no fewer than five different works are mentioned in his letter of 25 February 1689 (Letter 42) .

Ménage's correspondence is uniquely important for understanding his complex personality and the place of his diverse activities in his life. But in this, as in so many things, Ménage was unconventional. He had the reputation of maintaining a particularly rich and valuable international correspondence, and yet at the same time his correspondents themselves frequently complained that, despite all his many admirable qualities, he was a hopelessly inefficient epistolary partner.[12] The fact is that he wrote regularly – perhaps once or even twice a week – over periods of many years to a small group of his most intimate friends (Louis Nublé, Emery Bigot, Pierre-Daniel Huet, Mme de La Fayette), while to a much wider circle of friends, despite the often very warm feelings between them, he would write simply as occasion demanded, with gaps of months or even years between letters, but with the assumption that the friendship continued unaffected in the meanwhile.

Ménage's principal correspondents can be divided into six different categories, each of which has its own typical characteristics. These groups are: his family; figures prominent in French literary life and the salons; the world of French erudition; Italian scholars; French Protestant refugees in the Netherlands; and Dutch and German scholars in the Netherlands and Germany.[13] Of these groups the last, his connections with Dutch and German scholars, has been investigated less than any other. Among the many valuable features of the interlocking correspondences with Graevius and Wetstein is the fact that they form by far the largest sustained sequence of letters between Ménage and the Low Countries to have survived. They have the further advantage of being in French and not Latin, unlike most of Ménage's correspondence with Northern scholars. This not only makes them more accessible to the modern reader, but gives them a more immediate appeal than much Latin correspondence. Wetstein's letters in particular are strikingly idiosyncratic and personal in tone, and give an impression of spontaneity that no doubt reflects their place in the busy life of the famous scholar-publisher. Ménage's letters to Grævius are, inevitably, in general relatively more formal and even at times formulaic; and yet they too are also full of personal news and comments of all kinds.

Ménage in 1679-1692

Important as they were, Ménage's scholarly activities during the period of this correspondence did not by any means fill his whole life. Although his movements were restricted by his age and his increasingly frail health he maintained a diversity of activities that are sometimes scarcely hinted at in his letters to his learned friends. For example, in his letter to Grævius of 17 December 1681 (Letter 6) Ménage mentions the recent death of his brother and the serious burden of work involved in taking responsibility for his brother's children. No fewer than two hundred letters survive from Ménage to his nephew Pierre Ménage de Pigneroche, all written in the years 1681-1692, which show not only how seriously he took his role as head of the family and advisor and guide to the younger generation, but also, more surprisingly, that he engaged in substantial purchases of land and property in the Angers region during this last phase of his life. A quite different aspect of his life is revealed in his close friendship with Mme de La Fayette, which once again became particularly important in the later part of this period: although only ten letters from Ménage to her survive from the years 1690-1692 as against 36 from Mme de La Fayette to him, it is clear from her letters that he was writing to her at least twice a week, and often once a day.

A favourite maxim of Ménage's was: 'Il faut mourir la plume à la main',[14] and he kept vigorously active to the end in undertaking new enterprises. The scholarly publications of the last twenty years of his life include new works of philology, biography, French history, classical erudition, intellectual history, and learned controversy, and a collection of literary writings in Italian.[15] However, in his last twelve years he also devoted a great deal of effort to organizing the publication of revised editions of all his principal works, generally considerably augmented. His editions of Sarasin and Malherbe – in each case, the most important collected edition to date – were both republished in Paris, in 1685 and 1689 respectively, while his *Origines de la langue françoise* (1650) appeared posthumously as *Dictionnaire étymologique ou Origines de la langue françoise* (1694).[16] Six more works were republished outside France: four in the Low Countries, and the others in Frankfurt/Leipzig and Geneva; a new work, his *Anti-Baillet,* was also published in the Low Countries after being refused a *permission* in Paris.[17]

The task would have been impossible without a great deal of help from Ménage's friends abroad, principally in the Netherlands. It is a measure of Ménage's status that he never lacked for willing, and generally much younger, helpers; indeed, it is apparent from the *Mémoires* of the Huguenot émigré Jean Rou, who oversaw the printing of *Anti-Baillet*, how pleased and flattered he was to be asked to undertake the task.[18] The help that Ménage received from French Protestant émigrés such as Rou, Jean Le Clerc, Jacques Basnage, and Pierre Bayle, complemented his networks of friendship and mutual assistance among the leading Dutch scholars, including Gisbert Cuper, Nicolaas Heinsius, and, most important of all, as this correspondence shows, Graevius in Utrecht.

Ménage had not originally intended to ask Grævius to look after the Diogenes edition; it seems clear that he intended each of his publications outside France to be overseen by a different collaborator, where possible to be printed in a different place, and where this was not possible at least by a different printer. Thus the new edition of *Juris civilis amœnitates* (1680) was to be supervised by Carpzovius (Friedrich-Benedikt Carpzov) in Leipzig; the *Origini della lingua Italiana* (1685), by Minutoli in Geneva; the *Poésies* (1687) by the poet Petrus Francius, helped by Grævius, in Amsterdam; the *Discours sur l'Heautontimorumenos* (1690) by Grævius and Michel Janiçon, in Utrecht; the *Mescolanze* (1692) by Pierre Bayle in Rotterdam; and the *Anti-Baillet* (1692) by Jean Rou in The Hague. Although Carpzovius offered to take responsibility for a new edition of Diogenes in Leipzig, Ménage hoped to have it published in Amsterdam, and also hoped that it would be overseen by Nicolaas Heinsius. Although Grævius had been involved with Ménage's plans from the start, it was only after Heinsius's death in 1681 that he came to act as Ménage's principal intermediary in the long publication history of the work.

The stimulus that prompted Ménage to set in motion the new edition of Diogenes seems to have been the news, in 1679, that a Leipzig printer was proposing to reprint the 1664 London first edition. Ménage felt that this edition was in urgent need of revision, and mobilised his scholarly friends to stop the reprint. At Bigot's request, Heinsius wrote from Holland to Carpzovius in Leipzig on 22 January 1680; Heinsius subsequently reported the success of the mission to Ménage; and on 27 June 1680 Ménage wrote to express his thanks, and explain his plans for a revised edition of the great work:

> J'ay reçu la lettre qu'il vous a plu m'écrire; par laquelle j'ay appris avecque bien de la joye qu'on avoit arresté à Lipsic à vostre priére l'édition qu'on y fesoit de mon Diogéne Laërce: cette édition se fesant sur celle de Londres, qui est toute pleine de fautes d'impression, et de si considérables, que je les ay appelées dans ma Préface *portenta Typographica*. Outre toutes ces fautes que l'Imprimeur de Lipsic n'ust pas manqué de représenter, il n'ust pas mis dans leur lieu les Additions et les Corrections, qui sont en grand nombre. Il y a un mois que je ne fais autre chose que de copier ces Additions et ces Corrections à la marge de mon Exemplaire: et j'en ay encore pour un mois. Quand cet Exemplaire sera en estat d'estre imprimé, si nostre ami Mr. Carpsovius le veut faire imprimer à Lipsic, je le lui envoieray volontiers. Cependant, Monsieur, je vous rens mille tres humbles actions de graces de la peine que vous avez prise de lui écrire pour faire cesser cette Edition de Lipsic.[19]

In his turn Heinsius passed this on to Carpzovius, who wrote on 30 August to express his pleasure at the prospect of the revised Diogenes Laertius being printed in Leipzig.[20] However, already in his letter to Grævius of 12 August (Letter 4) Ménage was expressing a firm preference for the work to be printed in Holland if possible, and in his next letter, of 14 November 1680 (Letter 5) he asked Grævius if he could induce the Boom brothers to print it.

Nevertheless it was at first principally to Heinsius, Grævius's close friend, that Ménage looked for help in having the Diogenes printed in Holland, often communicating through the intermediary of Bigot. An early problem was the format and number of volumes of the new edition, both questions which were to feature prominently in Ménage's later discussions with Grævius and Wetstein. He wrote to Heinsius on 10 March 1681:

> Vous avez écrit à Mr. Bigot que les Libraires d'Amsterdam vouloient bien imprimer mon Diogéne Laërce in 8° mais qu'ils ne le vouloient pas imprimer in folio. J'ayme mieux qu'il soit imprimé en 8° à Amsterdam qu'in folio à Lipsic. Mais je ne comprens pas bien comment on le pourroit imprimer in 8° estant un tres gros volume in folio, imprimé à deux colonnes: car en ce volume, il feroit du moins quatre volumes. Je vous prie, Monsieur, de faire représenter cet inconvenient à ces Libraires, et de me faire savoir ensuite leur pensée là dessus.[21]

With Heinsius's death in 1681 Ménage turned definitively to Grævius. In the same letter in which he responded to news of the death, he wrote: 'Je persévére toujours dans le dessein de faire imprimer mon Diogéne Laërce en Hollande. Et je vous l'envoieray pas la première commodité qui se présentera pour vous l'envoyer' (Letter 6, 17 December 1681). Without Grævius's help, the great work could never have been brought to its conclusion.

Johann-Georg Graevius, 1632-1703

Johann-Georg Gräfe, or Grævius, was born in Naumburg, Saxony, in 1632 and undertook his first studies at Leipzig. While still a young man he visited Holland, and was profoundly impressed by the advanced state of classical scholarship there compared with the training he had himself received. He became a protégé of the famous scholar Friedrich Gronovius, changed from Lutheranism to Calvinism, and, after two years at the university of Duisburg (1656-1658), was appointed to succeed Gronovius at Deventer. He was appointed to the chair of history at the University of Utrecht in 1661, and found the atmosphere so congenial that he was never seriously tempted to move, despite extremely favourable offers from universities as diverse as Amsterdam, Leiden, Heidelberg, Berlin, and Padua.

Grævius was celebrated as a lecturer and orator and left a considerable number of *Orationes* which Pieter Burman, his own protégé and devoted admirer, published after his death (*Johannis Georgii Grævii Orationes quas Ultrajecti habuit*, Leiden, 1717). He was particularly proficient at composing *Orationes funebres*. When Heinsius died, Grævius's first reaction was to produce an 'Oraison funèbre' for his friend and he had to be persuaded by Ménage to undertake a proper biography, which he never managed to complete (Letter 7 and note 3). He had an outstanding reputation as a scholar, based at this stage primarily on the large number of learned editions that he produced. These included editions of Hesiod (Amsterdam, 1667), Lucian (Amsterdam, 1668; with also an important contribution to the Amsterdam edition of 1687, which was probably principally undertaken by Jean Le Clerc), Justinus (1669, much expanded 1683), Suetonius (1672), Catullus, Tibullus and Propertius (Utrecht, 1680), Florus (Utrecht, 1680, expanded 1702), Cicero (*Epistolarum libri XVI ad ... Atticum*, Amsterdam, 1684; *De officiis*, Amsterdam, 1688; *Epistolarum libri XVI ad familiares*, Amsterdam & Leiden, 1676-77), and Caesar (Amsterdam, 1697). Among more modern writers he edited the letters of Isaac Casaubon, Junius's *De pictura veterum*, a number of works by Meursius (Johannes van Meurs, 1579-1639), and Huet's Greek and Latin poetry. Inevitably, many of Grævius's editions feature in his correspondence with Ménage; particularly noteworthy is Ménage's considerable contribution to the 1687 edition of Lucian, as shown in this correspondence from Letter 25 onwards.

By the later 1690s Grævius had achieved a position of European pre-eminence, particularly among Latin scholars. This position was definitively established by his massive compilation of Latin inscriptions, the *Thesaurus Antiquitatum Romanorum*, which came out in twelve folio volumes at Leiden from 1694 to 1699. At the time of his death he was engaged on the even more remarkable compilation of the *Thesaurus Antiquitatum et Historiarum Italiæ, Neapolis, Siciliæ . . . atque adiacentium terrarum insularumque*, which was completed by Pieter Burman and published in 45 folio volumes from 1704 to 1725.

A particularly noteworthy feature of Grævius's later years was his friendship with Richard Bentley, unquestionably the outstanding classical scholar of the next generation. When Grævius's promising son Theodor Georg died at a tragically early age in 1692 (see Ménage's letters 61 and 68 in the present correspondence), his father completed and saw through the press the edition of Callimachus on which the young man had been working. Touchingly, he did everything he could to make the publication a landmark of scholarship, incorporating important contributions from his learned friends Ezechiel Spanheim and, above all, Bentley. The edition finally appeared in 1697. Bentley provided an extraordinarily extensive compilation of fragments of Callimachus, corrected and edited with a skill and insight that far superseded all previous work on the poet.[22] Despite their radically different personalities, the close links of respect and friendship between the two great scholars continued until Grævius's death.[23]

Grævius's eminence, and the sense that he could prove useful to France as a famous orator and scholar, resulted in his being awarded a generous 'gratification' from Louis XIV in 1685 (see Letters 26, 28, 29); but, although he did the expected thing and expressed his gratitude appropriately, the gift failed to buy his political allegiance. He later caused dismay in Paris by publicly celebrating the achievements of William III, with whom he had excellent relations (*Oratio de auspicatissima Expeditione Britannica: cum Guilielmus, Arausionensis Princeps, Angliæ, Galliæ et Hiberniæ Rex inauguraretur*, London, 1689, published also in the same year in English and Dutch). Ménage is recorded as voicing the French reaction although, typically, it did not in any way affect his own relations with his friend:

Je suis fâché de ce que mon ami M. Grævius à qui M. le Duc de Montausier a fait donner une grosse pension de la Cour, a fait un Panégyrique du Prince d'Orange. On dit que ses Maîtres l'y ont obligé: mais il devoit s'en exempter. Cela lui fait tort. (*Ménagiana*, II, 128)[24]

Far from holding this against Grævius, Ménage sprang to his defence at what he perceived as a lack of proper respect in a reference in a published work:

Mais je ne puis pardonner à M. Dubois d'avoir mis à la tête de sa traduction des Offices de Ciceron, *faite sur l'Edition de Grévius*. L'honnêteté vouloit qu'il mît *de Monsieur Grévius*. M. Grévius est un homme qui vit encore, et très-connu à Paris. Je suis son ami et il en a quantité d'autres. (*Ménagiana*, III, 393)

As this comment suggests, Grævius was known for his likeable and obliging personality, maintained a wide correspondence, and had a large number of friends and admirers whom he was glad to help in a variety of ways: he even saved the life of one scholar, the dashing soldier-poet Jan van Broeckhuizen (Janus Broukhusius), by interceding on his behalf when he was condemned to death under military law for acting as a second in a duel (see Letter 43, note 5). He had expressed his admiration for Ménage by sending him copies of his works before they entered into direct correspondence, and would undoubtedly have been delighted to be able to be of service to the older scholar: indeed, he often went to a good deal of trouble to give all the help that he could. It is clear from Ménage's letters that their epistolary friendship was firmly based on mutual respect as well as mutual assistance.

It would not, of course, have occasioned any surprise that two such eminent scholars as Grævius and Ménage should be in correspondence; what is noteworthy, though, is that the fact should be considered significant enough for Bayle to allude to it in a polemical work as a matter of common knowledge. In his *La Chimère de la cabale de Rotterdam* of 1691, written in reply to the attacks of Jurieu, Bayle defends himself against the charge of corresponding with French Catholics (and hence the enemies of the Dutch state) by citing Grævius's correspondence with Ménage and two other famous French scholars – both of whom figure in Ménage's letters – as obviously admirable and important enterprises: 'Ce seroit peut-être le dernier effort du Fanatisme que de prétendre que si l'illustre Mr. Grævius avoit commerce avec Mr. Ménage, ou avec Mr. Dacier nouveau Converti, ou même avec le P. Hardouin, il correspondroit avec les ennemis de l'Etat'.[25]

The principal themes of their correspondence will be discussed below in a consideration of the light that it casts on the practical working of the international Republic of Letters. One might note, though, how, despite the relative dryness of Ménage's style, these correspondences are not without personal feelings. The passing of time, and the increasing age of the two scholars, is movingly marked by their sharing the news of the deaths of their friends and family: Ménage's brother, Daniel Elzevir, Nicolaas Heinsius, Emery Bigot, and finally, in the last letter of their correspondence, Graevius's son (Letters 4, 5, 6, 47, 68). Above all one retains a sense of the underlying warmth and congeniality of these scholarly relations, as memorably embodied in the 'commémoration ... le verre à la main' with which Ménage and six learned friends toasted the absent Heinsius and Grævius, and the 'savante débauche' with which the pair in Holland returned the compliment (Letters 3, 4). Finally, on a more practical note, one connection of Grævius's proved in the event to be of particular benefit to Ménage: this was his established friendship and regular correspondence with Henrik Wetstein, the celebrated scholar-printer of Amsterdam.

Henrik Wetstein, 1649-1726

Henrik Wetstein (born Johann-Heinrich) was a member of one of the most distinguished families in Basel. His father Johann-Rodolph II had held the chairs of Greek and then theology at the university of Basel, and his brother Johann-Rodolph III followed in his footsteps as first professor of Greek and then New Testament theology (see Letter 55). The social and intellectual distinction of his family, allied to his own qualities, no doubt gave Wetstein the confidence that was essential for dealing with famous but often extremely difficult scholars in establishing his press as one of the principal scholarly printing-houses in Europe.

His correspondence with Ménage was certainly one of dramatically changing moods, unlike the consistent friendliness and admiration expressed in Ménage's letters to Grævius, and one of the pleasures of reading it lies in its varied and lively tone. He could speak his mind with a straightforward lack of deference to Ménage and, clearly, to others, when the occasion arose. The first occasion in this correspondence was in 1684, when Ménage lost patience with Wetstein's slowness and asked Grævius to withdraw all the materials for the Diogenes edition and look for another printer (Letter 17 of 2 June, and Letter 21 of 8 December). On 16 December Wetstein wrote to report that he was sending everything to Grævius that day, and added a blunt comment in which there is also a subtle mixture of praise for Ménage's work, and for the quality of the edition that he would have produced had he been allowed:

> ... je voi bien qu'il sera envoyé en Allemagne. Aussi je suis trespersuadé que Vous serez le premier à Vous en repentir, & bien plus-tot que moi. Bien que je ne nie pas, que je serai tres-fasché si cet excellent ouvrage ne se doit pas faire comme il faut. (Letter 22)

In his next letter, of 25 December, he was even more outspoken in his reproof to a distinguished man of more than twice his age – although here too he gets in a well-judged, even if highly oblique, compliment over how much a good edition of Ménage's Diogenes (i.e. one published by Wetstein) would be a matter of 'l'utilité publique':

> Et je Vous demande excuse si je ne me puis empecher de Vous dire ici, que je suis tout etonné de Vous trouver à Votre age un feu de jeune-homme de 20. ans, & qu'à 72. ans Vous ayez encore tant de passion pour une poignée de fumée, preferant une petite satisfaction de Vous-méme à l'utilité publique. Pardonnez-moi, Monsieur, si je m'explique en ces termes, ce n'est que par sincerité d'affection, & nullement par depit ou malice. (Letter 23)

Grævius worked to reconcile printer and scholar, and by June 1685 he had persuaded Wetstein to print the Diogenes on terms agreeable to Ménage. In his letter of 29 June

(Letter 27) Ménage responded with a comment that recurs like a refrain in this context: 'C'est un étrange homme que ce Mr. Vestein, & dont j'ay bien sujet de me plaindre ...'. By 30 August all is (temporarily) well: 'Nous sommes daccord Mr. Westein & moy: & bons amis' (Letter 29). Although, three years later in 1688 and 1689, in another perfectly understandable crisis of impatience Ménage again asked Grævius to withdraw the Diogenes and find a printer who would actually print it, it turned out that the work was in progress and the fault lay with the breakdown in communications caused by the new war (Letters 41, 42, 43). Thereafter, despite a further contretemps over the frontispiece (Letters 57, 59, 62, 62A, 63, 64), Wetstein's letters are marked by increasing warmth and even affection for his idiosyncratic old correspondent. He ends his letter of 14 June 1691 (Letter 55): 'Je suis & serai toujours avec beaucoup d'afection Votre treshumble & tresobeïssant Serviteur', and on 9 August of the same year (Letter 58), looking forward to the eventual publication, concludes: 'J'espere que Dieu Vous conservera non seulement jusques là, mais encore au delà. Les honnetes gens ne vivent jamais trop. Adieu Monsieur je suis tout à Vous'.

Wetstein's letters convey a sense of his very attractive personality, with their unpredictable and sometimes surprisingly informal style. His use of French is equally distinctive, with occasional Germanic touches and frequent humorous colloquialisms and archaisms, and unexpected turns of phrase of all kinds: 'Baste, il faut tacher d'y remedier'; 'Je Vous asseure foi-de-galant-homme que Vous Vous trompez'; 'J'espere pourtant d'en sortir à la fin: s'il plaît à Dieu! & puis oncques n'y retourneray'; 'Kyrieeleison. Car je ne sai presque plus où j'en suis' (Letters 16, 37, 64, 65).

There is a tragi-comic running theme pervading his letters, of the interminable problems caused by the notoriously eccentric scholar Marcus Meibomius. Meibomius was engaged, for the considerable sum of a hundred *pistoles*, to oversee the order of the Diogenes edition, correct the proofs, and – a genuinely challenging task – review the Greek text, produce a new Latin translation, and add his own annotations (Letter 28). Grævius and Ménage had thoroughly approved of Meibomius's being involved in the new edition. There was no doubt about the depth of his learning or the very high quality of the work that he was capable of producing, as Wetstein fully acknowledges (e.g. Letters 62, 63). But he proved to be a maddeningly slow, unreliable, and egocentric collaborator, and impossibly difficult about everything. He insisted on having new Greek type cut, at great expense, and designed some of the letters himself (which Ménage detested);[26] he would disappear without trace, or become distracted by some bizarre new enthusiasm and abandon the Diogenes for weeks on end. Eventually almost every letter contains a new Meibomius anecdote, and Wetstein repeatedly vents his feelings about the 'tresdocte mais tresfascheux Mr. Meyboom' with picturesque exasperation: 'Si jamais Vous faites composer un nouveau Martyrologe, ayez soin de m'y faire inserer: car asseurement Mr. Meibomius est l'homme le plus capable d'exercer la patience d'un Job, & peut etre de la pousser à bout ... nous n'allons qu'à pas de tortue, & Mr. Meib. n'a guerre de soin de nous faire aller plus vite'; 'Il parle de mille pistolles comme d'une douzaine de champignons n'ayant avec cela pas un double de monnoye en son pouvoir. Enfin c'est une misere ...' (Letters 43, 44, 52). The deterioration of their relationship is charted through the letters to Ménage, until its climax in an appropriately bizarre row. Meibomius refused to write the preface to the Diogenes edition unless he was given the proceeds of Wetstein's well-turned dedicatory epistle to the Elector of Brandenburg; so Wetstein wrote the preface himself as well, to the fury of Meibomius ('Notre Heros'): '... il jetta feu & flamme, & voulut tout abismer: mais sans m'en inquieter le moins du monde, je fis imprimer fort tranquillement ma preface ... Enfin à cela prés me voila hors de ses griffes' (Letter 69).

Despite such entertaining vicissitudes, the greater part of Wetstein's letters to Ménage are concerned with the practical details of printing the two works that he undertook for him, the Diogenes edition and, previously, the *Poésies*. The correspondence is thus of exceptional value as a commentary on all the varied aspects of a complex major scholarly publication that have to be agreed and organized in the course of its printing; and especially as an illustration of how, almost without exception, these details could cause difficulties and delays. Wetstein and Ménage were both acutely aware of the importance of the new Diogenes and determined to make it a 'chef-d'œuvre d'édition', but their ideas on how this might best be achieved often differed radically. Nor was it simply a matter of disagreements between scholar and publisher: at times Wetstein's letters read almost like a case-study of all the possible things that can go wrong in a printer's workshop.

Before work could even start on the printing a legal challenge had to be dealt with. The English publisher and bookseller Robert Scott claimed to have purchased the rights to the Diogenes edition from the widow of Octavian Pulleyn, the publisher of the 1664 London edition. Despite Wetstein's forcibly-expressed doubts about his case, and about English commercial rapacity in general ('selon la bonne coutume des Anglois qui ne cherchent qu'à attrapper tout ce qu'ils peuvent d'un etranger'), Scott was one of his most important agents in the crucial English market, and had to be accommodated (Letter 16). Once Scott had been placated all the physical details of the new edition had to be agreed: the format, number of volumes, and disposition of the text and apparatus, the quality of paper, the types to be used, and the provision of illustrations, including a suitable frontispiece; in all of these there was fertile scope for disagreement. Then textual uncertainties had to be clarified, and sufficiently erudite and reliable collaborators found. And, of course, it all had to be paid for. Wetstein's letters are full of complaints about the rapidly-escalating expenses, with fascinating financial and other technical details: the relative costing of different type sizes; relative sales figures for folio and quarto editions; the difficulties of obtaining the right quality of paper from manufacturers' samples; the expense of a frontispiece; the payment that a Huguenot exile like Jean Le Clerc might receive for undertaking a major index; or the amount that is needed to bribe Imperial soldiers to allow a package of books across the Swiss border (Letters 23, 36, 37, 62, 63, 69).

The first questions to be settled were the related issues of format, number of volumes, and disposition. Ménage had set his heart on a folio publication like the 1664 London edition, which carried by far the highest prestige in the eyes of the scholarly community and would mark the work out as a definitive monument of erudition. Wetstein, on the other hand, envisaged an octavo edition in two or more volumes, on the model of the popular *variorum* editions of classical authors, of which he had himself recently published a number.[27] The smaller format was much cheaper to produce, more flexible, and would generate far higher sales. A vigorous disagreement ensued, with Ménage objecting – correctly – that the octavo *variorum* model, with notes at the foot of each page of text, was quite impractical for the vast apparatus of erudite commentary that he had assembled (Letter 34, to Grævius), and Wetstein responding with a decisive argument based on the hard facts of likely sales figures:

> Quant à ce que dites que je n'ai jamais voulu le faire in folio. Je Vous asseure foi-de-galant-homme que Vous Vous trompez. J'en ai plus d'envie que Vous. Mais l'utile l'emporte sur la beauté; ou plustot l'usage. On vendra 10. in 4° ou 8°. sans vendre 3. in folio. qu'y faire? le fort l'emporte. (Letter 37)

Eventually, after considering a variety of different options, an admirable compromise was reached which resulted in the eventual quarto publication in two volumes, whose details will be discussed below.

Wetstein proposed from the start that the edition should be illustrated with as many authentic portraits as possible of the philosophers but, like so many aspects of this work, the task proved to be far more problematic and time-consuming than anticipated. He mentioned the portraits in his first letter, of 25 October 1683 (Letter 14), and in his next, rather disappointed at Ménage's suggestions, specified that he expected to find over forty at least:

> Les portraits embelliront fort l'ouvrage, & nous en trouverons, je croy, bien plus que ceux dont Vous faites mention. Car s'il n'y en avoit que 20 de 86 cela ne vaudroit pas la peine, & rendroit l'ouvrage plus ridicule qu'il ne l'embelliroit. Il me semble qu'il nous faudroit pour le moins la moitié. (Letter 15)

However, seven years later the total had only risen to twenty-two (Wetstein lists them in Letter 57, of 26 July 1691). The only authentic representation of Speusippus, a headless bust, was rejected as absurd; but the number of illustrations was finally got up to twenty-five by the expedients of portraying Sextus Empiricus next to Epicurus, even though he is scarcely mentioned in the text; printing a symbolic picture of a riddle by Cleobulus personifying the divisions of the year; and including a highly dubious image of one Monimus who at least had the same name as the philosopher (Letter 64).

Things went no better with the frontispiece. Ménage had promised to send a design, and Wetstein had anticipated a rough sketch which could be worked up by the specialist engravers in Amsterdam. However what he received was a polished work of art by Charles Perrault, admirable in every way except for the fact that it was the wrong size and therefore useless. Perrault was understandably annoyed at having his work rejected, the more so because Wetstein refused to pay the agreed 25 livres for it, and he had to be placated by a typically polite-but-firm letter from the Amsterdam publisher (Letter 62A, dated 20 September 1691, and sent with a letter to Ménage). As so often with this work, though, the final outcome was delayed but successful. Wetstein managed to find an artist who, for a further pistole, adapted Perrault's picture to the right size to be engraved, although even then two engravers took more than two months to prepare the plate (see Letters 57, 58, 59, 63, 66); but when the Diogenes at last appeared it was indeed prefaced by Perrault's strikingly handsome design (Plate 5).

Even the paper caused problems and delays from the start. Wetstein was initially confident about the prospects, writing in 1684: 'nous n'avons pas ici du papier presentement qui soit propre pour cela; mais à cela il y auroit du remede, & on en peut faire faire' (Letter 16); but his optimism proved to be unfounded. Ménage was extremely fussy about the paper used for his works, but he was not able to choose from samples as he would have liked, supplies of high-quality paper were very limited, and production was seriously interrupted by a water-shortage in the hot dry summer of 1686, as Wetstein explained in detail in November of that year:

> Je ne disconviens pas de ce que Vous dites du papier pour le Diogene: Mais je Vous ai dit à quoi il tient que je n'en aye point d'autre. Celui pour lequel j'ai contracté est aussi beau que j'en aye jamais vû, & pour la forme & pour la couleur. Et je ne doute pas que Vous n'en demeuriez d'accord si Vous le voyiez. Mais comme je n'en ai qu'une seule feuille, & que je n'en puis avoir d'autre, & que c'est la feuille sur la quelle j'ai contracté, je n'oserois la mettre au hazard d'estre perdue en Vous l'envoyant. Avec tout cela il faudra en prendre d'autre, ou se resoudre d'attendre le mois de Mars, auquel temps les papetiers promettent l'autre. Mais ils me l'avoient aussi promis pour le mois d'octobre, & maintenant ils s'excusent sur le manque d'eau pendant l'été. Il faudra pourtant se resoudre d'une façon ou d'une autre. (Letter 36)

The difficulty persisted for years, made worse by the new war. Three years later Wetstein wrote: 'Je pousserois bien l'impression plus fortement, mais je n'ai que pour 36 à 38 feuilles de papier: le reste en est encore en France, & je ne sai comment le faire venir. Ainsi on marche petit à petit' (Letter 43); and again as late as 1691: 'Si j'eusse pû avoir le papier necessaire avant l'hiver, l'ouvrage seroit achevé à l'heure qu'il est. Presentement si Dieu nous préte vie nous le verrons avant la Toussaints . . .' (Letter 55).

It was not only hot summers which held up printing. Cold winters were worse, as in 1683-84, 1690-91, and 1691-92: the ink froze, engravers could not work, and all activity had to be suspended, sometimes for weeks on end; while to cap it all, in the autumn of 1691 Wetstein's workers fell ill with a mysterious fever (see for example Letters 15, 52, 65, 69).

The greatest problems of all, though, were the difficulties of communication, immensely exacerbated in time of war. At the best of times packages can go astray, be wrongly addressed, or remain forgotten and overlooked en route, and Wetstein's very first letter (Letter 14) gives an ominous foretaste of misadventures to come. In the war years of 1683-84 and the period after 1688 the problems became all but insuperable. Letters would usually reach their destination, and packages could generally be sent out of France (Letter 44); but any packages sent the other way would be routinely opened and confiscated. As early as 18 April 1689 Wetstein realised with a shock that his letters and proofs had not been reaching Paris, when Ménage concluded that he had abandoned the edition and wrote to him and to Grævius withdrawing from the project (Letter 42, of 25 February 1689). Wetstein's letter began:

> Il me sembloit que je venois du Royaume de Monomotapan, lors que je reçûs la Votre du XI. du courant. Je voi que Vous n'avez pas reçû mes lettres ni les feuilles que je Vous ai envoyées de la nouvelle impression de Laërce. Ce qui me fait juger qu'il est desormais inutile que je Vous en envoye, puis qu'elles non seulement ne Vous parviennent pas, mais même sont cause que mes lettres se perdent. (Letter 43)

Thereafter he deployed practised ingenuity in devising a series of different routes that might have a chance of success, and his letters in 1691-92 keep Ménage up to date with his latest plans. The risks of sending material by sea were too great for it to be contemplated (Letter 70), but he explored every possible overland route. He attempted to send a package via Lille, but it was confiscated (Letters 52, 53); he then tried sending packages via Frankfurt and Geneva, but they were held up by the indolent Genevan bookseller Tournes, who for over a year never troubled to forward them to Paris (Letters 55, 66, 69, 70). When he tried again via his brother, the distinguished scholar Johann-Rodolph Wetstein, in Basel, he hid the package in a 'ballot d'étoffes'; but it was still intercepted by Imperial troops on the Swiss frontier, and only redeemed by the efforts of Wetstein's brother-in-law and a bribe of three pistoles (Letters 55, 69). An incomplete portion of the edition sent via Strasbourg did get through (Letter 64); and to the end Wetstein was trying to arrange for a safe passage via Liège, through the good offices of Ménage's old friend Paul Pellisson (Letters 67, 70). Eventually, as we have seen, Ménage did receive two complete copies of the Diogenes, all that reached Paris before he died; but it was enough to enable him to enjoy the publishing triumph that the edition represented.

The Republic of Letters in Action

The two sequences of letters give a fascinating insight into the way the international network of contacts between scholars known as the Republic of Letters worked in practice. We can follow the often quite complex and indirect routes through which communications were transmitted, sometimes in relays. Because of the expense and uncertainty of communications, once a correspondence was established it was common to send a variety of pieces of information, messages, letters, or books for one's correspondent to pass on to other scholarly friends. However, given the great volume of correspondence that has survived from this period (itself, of course, only a small proportion of the vast amount that actually circulated), and the apparently inexhaustible complexity of the innumerable interlocking epistolary relationships across Europe, the systematic study of this vital aspect of European intellectual life can seem a hopeless enterprise. This is in part where the great value of the Ménage-Grævius and Wetstein-Ménage correspondences lies. Being clearly defined and limited, with a clear primary focus of interest, and with a precise beginning and end, the two correspondences give a revealing picture of how such international lines of communication actually operated in particularly unsettled times.

Ménage's first approach to Grævius on 19 May 1679 coincided with, and was no doubt partly prompted by, the conclusion of the Treaties of Nijmegen in February 1679. After a period of war it looked as though a more lasting peace was in prospect, which would greatly facilitate the ambitious programme of new editions of his principal works that Ménage intended to undertake. As it happened, the peace was fragile. It was soon interrupted by the War of the Reunions in 1683-84 and definitively ended by the General Coalition against France in September 1688; while in France the growing persecution of the Huguenot minority culminated in the Revocation of the Edict of Nantes on 18 October 1685.

It is no surprise to find these events reflected in Ménage's correspondence with Grævius and Wetstein. The effect of the wars on communications, especially on Wetstein's attempts to send anything more substantial than a letter, have already been discussed. The practical results of the growing religious intolerance in France are equally pervasive; they are seen in the letter of recommendation that Ménage wrote for Messieurs de Saumaise, sons of the great scholar, who were forced into exile because of their Protestantism in May 1686 (Letter 33), or in Wetstein's concern over the unjust imprisonment of his old friend André Morel (Letters 60, 62); and most strikingly in the number of learned Huguenot exiles in the Low Countries (and also in England and Switzerland) with whom Ménage remained on very friendly terms, and whose help was crucial in enabling the publication of his works when communications with France could be highly uncertain. The most prominent in this correspondence, among many, are Bayle, Rou, Jacques Basnage, Janiçon, and Jean Le Clerc, all of whom were able to give Ménage significant help. For through all the political and religious antagonisms, the networks of friendship of the Republic of Letters not only survived, but were more important than ever.

The very start of the Ménage-Grævius correspondence provides an excellent example of how they could work. Before he wrote his first letter to Grævius on 19 May 1679, Ménage was already on friendly terms with the scholar in Utrecht through the intermediary of Ménage's close friend Emery Bigot, who, as Ménage mentions, had regularly passed on Grævius's expressions of esteem and complimentary copies of his publications. With this first letter Ménage sent the material for the new edition of his *Juris civilis amœnitates*, for Grævius to forward to Friedrich-Benedikt Carpzov (Carpzovius) in Leipzig. However, the news of its safe arrival reached him by a different route: Carpzovius informed Heinsius in Holland, who forwarded the news to Bigot in France, and Bigot in turn told Ménage; the circle was completed on 6 October 1679 when Ménage wrote to Grævius to say that he had received the news, to thank him, and to ask him for further assistance.

Ménage later returned the favour for Carpzovius, acting as his intermediary with Huet over a German edition of one of Huet's works (see Letter 48, and note 2). He also frequently acted as an intermediary in this way for Grævius, passing on letters to and from his own wide range of scholarly friends. In the course of this correspondence he acts for Grævius in transmitting letters to and from Pierre Petit, Nicaise, Huet, Adrien de Valois, Spon, Thévenot, La Mare, Montausier, Félibien, and Baluze (Letters 9, 10, 11, 13, 19, 20, 21, 26, 27, 28, 34, 38, 39, 42). Similarly he enclosed messages for Grævius to pass on in Holland, the most important of which was a detailed letter to the printer Rudolf van Zyll (Letters 48, 48A).

Such avenues were essential for the circulation of new publications, and Ménage sent Grævius presentation copies of books from Petit, Spon, and Du Cange (Letters 9, 13, 31). Principally, of course, the two correspondents exchanged copies of their own works: in all, Ménage sent Grævius no fewer than eleven of his different works, and in return received at least six of Grævius's latest publications. Such a well-placed correspondent could be particularly useful in distributing presentation copies to others. When Grævius published his editions of Meursius's *Theseus* and Cicero's *Ad Atticum* in 1684 he used Ménage as a central distribution point in France, sending a packet of at least eleven copies of the works for Ménage to send out to named recipients all over France (Letters 18, 19, 25, 34); in the other direction we learn that Ménage has sent Heinsius six copies of the 1680 edition of his *Poésies* to distribute (including one for Grævius), and Jean Rou later acted on Ménage's instructions in distributing copies of *Anti-Baillet* in the Netherlands (Letters 5, 7, 8, 41, 42, 45, 46).

A particularly important aspect of these international networks in action was the provision of letters of recommendation for scholars travelling abroad, thus widening and renewing the scholarly community through the extension of personal contacts. Of course, such visits ceased almost entirely in time of war. Nevertheless there are no fewer than nine examples in the correspondence between Ménage and Grævius: three letters wholly or partly of personal recommendation from Ménage, on behalf of Hozou, Boylesve, and Messieurs de Saumaise (Letters 9, 12, 33), to which might be added his offer to help Daniel Elzevir's son if he can (Letter 5); and responses to six similar letters from Grævius, on behalf of Perstens, Goyer, Messieurs Gruter, Sisme, de Witt, and Bylandius (Letters 4, 11, 26, 29, 31, 40).

Ménage and Grævius themselves maintain a relationship of mutual help from the first letter onwards. Grævius is able to give invaluable assistance in finding printers for Ménage's works and negotiating with them on his behalf, and seeking out suitable proof-readers. He undertook this not only for the Diogenes edition, but also earlier for *Juris civilis amœnitates* and the final edition of the *Poésies*, and later for the *Discours sur l' Heautontimorumenos* and the *Historia mulierum philosopharum*. He keeps Ménage informed about mutual friends and scholarly developments in the Netherlands, and sends news of his own activities as well as the copies of his works.

In return, Ménage was exceptionally well-placed to help his friends abroad, for whom all his information about scholarly activity in France, and general social and political news, would have been of the greatest interest. Although increasingly infirm following an accident in 1684 he had an exceptionally wide range of useful connections and was as alert and well-informed as ever. He sends Grævius information for his prospective edition of Columella, and a collection of annotations, as well as a good deal of comment, for the edition of Lucian in which he had a hand (Letters 5, 11, 25, 27, 29, 30); similarly, he offers to help Carpzovius with his proposed new edition of Petau's Epiphanius (Letters 4, 7), and Jansson van Almeloveen with his lives of the Estiennes (Letter 18). His help was particularly important when Grævius was awarded his royal 'gratification' in 1685, and Ménage was able, through his friendship with the powerful duc de Montausier, to give a great deal of invaluable practical advice and assistance (Letters 26, 28, 29).

Although the correspondence between Wetstein and Ménage is, in contrast, inevitably primarily practical and commercial, it is nevertheless clearly situated within the same traditions of the Republic of Letters, and similarly engages with networks of friendship and mutual assistance. Wetstein received extremely generous help with the Diogenes text from 'Mr. Gale de Londres, un des plus honnetes gens du monde, &

obligeant au delà de tout ce qu'on en peut dire'; and when the incorrigible Meibomius purloined Gale's material and tried to pass it off as his own, Wetstein went to a great deal of trouble to restore full credit to Gale and celebrate his generosity ('M. M. en enrage ...': the full story is related in Letter 66). Wetstein frequently includes items of scholarly and personal information, passing on news about Bayle, at work on what was to become his *Dictionnaire historique et critique*, or a joke from Grævius (Letters 53, 64), acting as an intermediary between Ménage and his own friend the poet Petrus Francius (Letters 15, 16, 22, 32), asking about his old schoolmate André Morel in his undeserved difficulties in Paris (Letters 60, 62), telling Ménage about an interesting new publication (Letter 43), and sending some important information about a lost commentary by St Jerome for Ménage to pass on to the Benedictine editors of Jerome's works (Letter 55). In his turn, Ménage had earned Wetstein's gratitude early in their relationship by recommending him to Toinard as a printer (Letters 14A, 15).

All sustained correspondences develop a personality of their own, and a fascination that goes far beyond the sum of their separate parts. The reader gains a sense of familiarity with the correspondents and those they write about, following events as they unfold and the reactions that they provoke, always as seen through the eyes of an individual writer, and as described for an equally distinctive intended reader. The correspondences between Ménage and Grævius, and Wetstein and Ménage, are of exceptional value for their subject-matter itself and, especially, its broader context. This value is then immeasurably enhanced by the unusual way in which the two almost complete sequences of letters dovetail with one another, and by the strong interwoven narrative thread. Finally, often below the surface but never entirely absent is the human dimension to the correspondence, which adds so much to the interest and attraction of the epistolary relationship between these three remarkable men.

II

Diogenes Laertius: The 1664 and 1692 editions

Ménage's extraordinarily detailed commentary on Diogenes Laertius, his magnum opus of classical erudition, was the most sustained attempt that had ever been made to get to grips with this irreplaceable, but exceptionally problematic text. The *Lives of eminent philosophers* is an entertaining and digressive compilation, anecdotal and uncritical, most probably compiled between the middle of the second and the middle of the third centuries AD.[28] It has very obvious inadequacies; and yet to this day it forms by far our most important source of knowledge of the biography of ancient philosophers, containing an extensive corpus of quotations and extracts from works which have not survived elsewhere. It has been calculated that Diogenes includes 1,186 explicit references to 365 books by about 250 authors, as well as more than 350 anonymous references.[29] One can see why the challenge of Diogenes Laertius would have appealed so strongly to Ménage, with his own love of anecdote and digression, his vast reading and extraordinary ability to retain and recall what he had read, and his own highly accumulative scholarly methodology. One can also understand why, in the eyes of his contemporaries, his incomparably wide-ranging erudition made him uniquely well-qualified for the task of undertaking a thorough textual commentary. Ménage's achievement can be measured by the fact that Wetstein's edition of 1692 remained definitive until well into the nineteenth century, and even then Ménage's annotations, and those of other scholars that he had assembled, retained their prestige. When Huebner published the next major edition, in 1828-1831, it is significant that he followed it up with a new two-volume edition of Ménage's commentary, together with the notes of the Casaubons and Kühnius that Ménage had included in his second volume.[30] Indeed, despite subsequent partial critical editions, it was not until 1964 that the first modern critical edition of the complete text was published.[31]

The London edition of 1664 came out as a substantial folio volume. It is sometimes referred to as the 'Pearson' edition, because its publication was overseen by John Pearson, the learned Bishop of Chester; but the importance of Ménage's contribution was emphasised from the start. The volume opens with a dedicatory epistle from Pearson to Charles II, and then a second epistle, addressed to Ménage in terms of the warmest admiration. The text of Diogenes is printed in parallel columns, with the Greek on one side and the Latin translation of Aldobrandini on the other. It ends with three indices: a list of the names of philosophers mentioned, an Index Rerum, and an Index Authorum. The text is followed by the 'Epistola' from the *editio princeps*, the Froben Basel edition of 1533,[32] and then the principal scholarly commentaries to date, with their attendant dedicatory epistles and letters to the reader. They are designated as follows: Henrici Stephani epistolæ & annotationes; Is. Casauboni notæ; Th. Aldobrandini annotationes; Aeg. Menagii observationes et emendationes; Merici Casauboni notæ et emendationes. The volume ends with the short complementary text of the 'Vita Platonis ab Olympiodoro'. The overwhelming importance of Ménage's contribution is signalled in the title given to his commentary – 'observationes' indicating, quite correctly, something altogether more substantial than the 'annotationes' or 'notae' of the other scholars – as well as by its great length (283 double-column folio pages). Most significantly of all, this section alone is treated as though it were an original, distinct work of scholarship which has been included with the text and earlier commentators, which in effect is exactly what it was.[33] Ménage's *Observationes* open with a dedicatory epistle to Emery Bigot (sig. A2r – [A3]v) and letter to the reader (sig. [A4]r); the text is separately paginated (pp. 1-283), as are the following substantial 'Addenda & Mutanda' (pp. 1-18); while at the end the work has its own 'Errata emendata' (sig. [2Q4]r) and 'Index authorum'.

The London edition of Diogenes is a successful scholarly achievement, even though Ménage's dominant contribution is the only truly new element in it; despite, too, the considerable number of misprints in the text perpetrated by the printer Octavian Pulleyn, about which Ménage was to complain forcefully in his correspondence with Grævius. Nevertheless it was to be far overshadowed by the ambitions of the Amsterdam edition. The present correspondence demonstrates for the first time the central importance of Ménage in getting this edition under way, and the vital role then played

by Grævius as his irreplaceable representative in the Netherlands following the death of
Heinsius.[34] It was Grævius who chose Wetstein to print the new edition, a decision
which, despite Ménage's innumerable protests about 'Monsieur Vestein' over the
years, was completely justified by Wetstein's good sense, genuine learning and remarkable strength of character. Subsequently Marcus Meibomius was commissioned to
oversee the text and produce a new Latin translation, and Jean Le Clerc was commissioned to undertake the invaluable sequence of indices which complete the work;
while the obliging English scholar Thomas Gale provided new variant readings from
previously unused manuscripts in Canterbury and Arundel. Thus there was assembled a
formidable team of collaborators, including some of the most celebrated figures in
European scholarship, for an undertaking that soon took on the status of a definitive
monument of erudition.

Compared with the London 1664 edition, the contents of the 1692 edition are far
richer and the disposition of text and supplementary material far more complex.[35] The
protracted discussions in the correspondence between Wetstein and Ménage concerning the format and layout of the new work eventually resulted in a solution which,
with hindsight, seems ideal. The quarto format is impressive and substantial without
the unwieldiness of a folio, and greatly facilitates the constant cross-referencing needed
to make the most of the extensive critical apparatus. The division of the work into volumes is equally well handled. The first volume contains the text in Greek and Latin,
with the emendations and comments of the less voluminous annotators at the foot of
the page; while the second volume consists of Ménage's *Observationes* and *Historia mulierum philosopharum*, other more extensive secondary material (including the *Observationes* of the German scholar Joachim Kühnius), and the detailed indices. The complete
contents are as follows:

Volume I: Prefatory material: Wetstein's dedicatory epistle to the Elector of Brandenburg (sigs *3r – [*4]v) and his preface to the reader (sigs 2*1r – 2*2v); a list of all the
editions of Diogenes Laertius, from 1475 to the London edition, here dated as 1663
(sig. 2*3r-v); a catalogue of the names of philosophers mentioned by Diogenes (sig.
[2*4]r-v). The remainder of the volume (pp. 1-672) consists of the Latin and Greek
texts in parallel columns, with at the foot the annotations of Aldobrandini, Isaac and
Meric Casaubon, and Henricus Stephanus, which had been printed as separate items in
the 1664 edition. In Book 10 there have also been added the extensive and judicious
annotations of Marcus Meibomius, which concentrate on establishing the most satisfactory textual readings; Meibomius frequently refers to the suggestions that Gassendi
advanced in his celebrated commentary on Book 10, and also includes highly laudatory
references to Ménage's observations.[36]

Volume II: Prefatory material to Ménage's *Observationes*: Ménage's dedicatory epistle
to Bigot, his preface from the London edition, and the letter to him from John Pearson
(sigs *2r – [*4]v); the text of Ménage's *Observationes* (pp. 1-484); Ménage's *Historia
mulierum philosopharum* (pp. [485]-505) with its own index (sigs 3s1v – 3s2v); the *Observationes* of Joachim Kühnius (pp. [509]-556); variant readings from the Canterbury and

Arundel manuscripts, supplied by Thomas Gale (pp. 557-566, in three columns per page); the epistles and prefaces of all previous editions of Diogenes Laertius (pp. 567-581), an addition which is clearly intended to indicate that the present edition subsumes all previous ones; the *Vita Platonis* of Olympiodorus, in parallel columns of Greek and Latin, with annotations at the foot as for the text of Diogenes (pp. 582-588); and finally Meric Casaubon's dissertation on Diogenes (pp. 589-590). The volume, and the edition, concludes with Jean Le Clerc's extensive indices: 'Index I. Scriptorum et operum, quorum meminit Diogenes Laertius', which fills eight and a half pages in double columns (sigs [4e4]r − [4f4]r); 'Index II. Veterum & Recentiorum Scriptorum, in Ægidii Menagii Observationibus, Emendatorum, illustratorum, & notatorum.' (sigs [4f4]r − 4g1v), an impressive tribute to the range of Ménage's scholarship; 'Index III. Vocum Græcarum ab Interpretibus Diogenis expositarum.' (sigs 4g1v − 4h1v); and finally, unsurprisingly the most extensive of all, 'Index IV. Rerum & Verborum notatu dignorum quæ apud Diogenem, ejusque Interpretes occurrunt.' (sigs 4h2r − [4m3]r).

As well as in its large amount of new material, the 1692 edition differs from its predecessor of 1664 in two extremely important respects. The first, and most radical of these, is the provision of a different Latin translation of Diogenes's Greek text. There were two principal translations in currency, that of Ambrogio Traversari (1386-1439), sometimes called the 'Ambrosian' version, which was used in the great majority of editions up to 1594,[37] and the later translation of Tommaso Aldobrandini which was first printed in that year. The 1664 edition reproduces the Aldobrandini version; but as a measure of the ambition of Ménage and Wetstein's enterprise (and perhaps also Wetstein's acute commercial sense), it was decided to provide it with a new Latin translation.

The importance of the Latin translations that were commonly printed with Greek texts was twofold: they widened the readership, and filled a demand, by opening the text up to the much more extensive Latin-reading educated public; and, at least as importantly, they established the meaning of the Greek original by the act of translating it into Latin. The importance attached to these translations is seen in Ménage's repeated disparaging comments on Johannes Benedictus's 1619 edition of Lucian, and his disapproval of its being reproduced in the new edition that Grævius was associated with (see particularly Letters 27, 30, and 31). Ménage had clearly been aware that a possible weakness of the 1664 edition of Diogenes had been that it reproduced a sixteenth-century translation, even though a widely-admired one; he even mentioned in his preface that he had himself undertaken a new one (he refers to 'quam paratam habeo, Latinam Laërtii Interpretationem meam' (1664 preface, reprinted in 1692, Vol. II: sig. *3r)), which occasioned a surprised enquiry from Wetstein (see Wetstein's Letter 60). Ménage had never completed the daunting task; and so, as we have seen, the commission for a translation to accompany the new edition was entrusted to Marcus Meibomius.

Meibomius took as his starting-point the Traversari version, as is indicated on the title-page ('. . . *Latinam Ambrosii Versionem complevit & emendavit Marcus Meibomius*'), although he had clearly studied the Aldobrandini translation and drawn occasional readings from it. However, while Meibomius and Traversari often coincide, Meibomius has undertaken a thoroughgoing work of revision and clarification of his early fifteenth-century original. This was obviously essential: even in the *editio princeps* of the Greek text of 1533, Froben had commented on how Traversari did not measure up to his Greek original;[38] while many later readers would have been familiar with the criticism of Cardinal Pietro Aldobrandini, in his preface to the translation by his late uncle Tommaso, of the infelicities of his predecessor.[39]

In Meibomius's reworking of Traversari the fluency of reading of the Latin has been improved throughout, with a very large number of minor changes to the phraseology, reorganization of individual sentences, and minor explanatory additions; while in cases of real obscurity considerable passages have been re-translated from the Greek. His contribution on Book 10 in particular has already been noted, and was of the greatest importance: it was this book, entirely devoted to Epicurus, which formed by far the most valuable part of the work in the eyes of seventeenth-century readers. Meibomius's Latin version was widely praised as a masterpiece of accuracy and insight, complementing his editorial work on the Greek text, to which, as Wetstein had the generosity to admit, despite his impatience and exasperation with its author, 'M. Meib. fait des eclaircissemens extraordinaires' (Letter 63).

The second principal change to the materials already included in the 1664 edition concerns Ménage's *Observationes*. Ménage had undertaken a very thorough work of expansion and revision for the new edition, adding extensive new material and often reworking the Latin style of the original. Extensive as his commentary was in 1664, by the time he sent it to Wetstein in 1683 it had grown in size by almost a quarter.[40] Thus, right at the start, the introductory observations have been augmented by a passage of 49 lines (beginning 'Obiter hâc observamus . . .'), including a 28-line verse quotation (1664: pp. 1-2; 1692, Vol. II: pp. 1-3); while in the 'Procemium' to the first Book the third of Ménage's observations has grown from 2 lines to no fewer than 96 lines (1664: p. 2; 1692, Vol. II: pp. 3-4). Nor did the old scholar exhaust his energies on the early part of the work; similar augmentation has been carried out throughout, a high proportion of the observations have been added to or revised, and many new ones added.

At first glance Ménage's *Observationes* might seem little more than laborious pedantry, and it is not uncommon for many of his scholarly works to be dismissed in such terms. It is true that his annotations are in many ways very different from what one might expect from a modern critical edition, but it is impossible to maintain so rigorously pejorative a judgement after actually having read what he has written. The reader is often not given what he or she might have been looking for in a note, but rather has the pleasurable surprise of something quite unexpected as Ménage pursues parallels and reminiscences through his vast store of memory. The result is not dissimilar to what must have been the effect of listening to Ménage's conversation, as described in the *Mémoires pour servir à la vie de M. Ménage* in the *Ménagiana*:

Il parloit beaucoup, & aimoit à débiter ce qu'il savoit . . . Sa mémoire prodigieuse lui fournissoit toujours une infinité de belles choses sur tous les sujets dont on venoit à parler dans son assemblée . . . Une étude continuée pendant toute sa vie, & tant de correspondances qu'il avoit avec tous les savans & grands hommes de l'Europe, à qui il écrivoit, & dont il recevoit des lettres tous les jours, étoit un fond inépuisable pour les pensées d'érudition qu'il mêloit agréablement dans la conversation.[41]

It is this that explains the apparently genuine interest and appreciation with which works such as Ménage's biographical accounts of members of his own family were greeted by readers like Pierre Bayle to whom, one might have thought, the subjects were of little concern. In the *Vitæ Petri Ærodii et Guillelmi Menagii* (Paris, 1675) the 102 pages of text in Latin are followed by no less than a further 438 pages of 'Remarques', 'Additions', and 'Preuves' in French, which transform the effect of the whole work: one finds for example, among a huge amount of other material, such unexpected discoveries as one of the most detailed and precious first-hand accounts of the demonic possession at Loudun and the condemnation of Urbain Grandier (pp. 81-84, 339-46).

So, even when dealing with Book 10 where, Ménage assures us, he will be far briefer than elsewhere because of the excellence of Gassendi's commentary ('Eò brevior ero in hujus libri expositione'),[42] he still filled 25 pages in the 1664 folio, and expanded this by more than 14% to 40 quarto pages in 1692. Many of the additions are fairly minor, such as an incidental (and clearly late) reference to his very recently-written *Historia mulierum philosopharum* (1692, Vol. II: p. 447). Sometimes, though, he has appended considerable disquisitions, and often cannot resist incidental digressions, or lists of parallel examples or supplementary sources. Thus a typical new digression involves him in the listing of no fewer than twelve different sources (all of them almost certainly drawn effortlessly from memory) before he gives up: 'Est autem *Mithres*, nomen Persicum, quo *Sol* significatur. Ita explicant, Herodotus, Strabo, Plutarchus, Julianus ὁ παραβάτης, Hieronymus, Martianus Capella, Lutatius in Statium, Hesychius, Maximus in Dionysium Areopagitam, Suidas, Pachymeres, Nicetas ad Gregorium Nazianzenum, & quis non?' (1692, Vol. II: p. 447; the original note, without this addition, was 1664, pp. 259-60). This is not just a gratuitous parade of erudition. It is not without interest, and can be valuable, to know whether a detail in the text is a frequently-repeated commonplace or a touch not found elsewhere; and even if the former, it helps to build up a picture of the mental world of the author and his intended readers.

Despite Ménage's age, and some aspects of his accumulative erudition that seem to look backwards to an earlier time, the 1692 edition of Diogenes Laertius belongs firmly among the influential works of a new period of historical scholarship. The importance of Diogenes's work has long been acknowledged as a major source-text for the development of a certain type of erudite scepticism in the seventeenth century.[43] This importance derived largely from the long sections in Book 9 on Democritus and Pyrrho, and above all from Book 10, which is entirely devoted to Epicurus and his philosophy, with long extracts from Epicurus's own writings. Book 10 is a unique source: all of Epicurus's principal works are lost, and the only known remains of his writings until the late nineteenth century were the three letters and one collection of ethical aphorisms preserved by Diogenes.[44] It is for this reason that it became the focus of intense interest, whose most influential previous expression had been Gassendi's *Animadver-*

siones of 1649; and the work in general became intimately associated with an attitude of increasing scepticism towards the reliability of literary sources for accurate knowledge of the past. The definitive edition of the complete text of Diogenes in 1692 can therefore be seen both as the summation of an increasingly important current of seventeenth-century intellectual history, from which, it has been argued, emerged the foundations of modern historiography; and, in addition, as a significant contribution to the great progress of that current in the new century.

Thus Charles B. Schmitt cites Ménage's edition of Diogenes together with Bayle's *Dictionnaire historique et critique*, as two of the principal erudite compilations which enabled subsequent histories of philosophy to become increasingly comprehensive, and increasingly critical.[45] Implicit in Schmitt's comments is the intriguing possibility that Ménage's edition may even have had some influence on the evolution of Bayle's great work, as it developed far beyond his initial idea of a collection of the errors and false information in Moréri's *Dictionnaire*: it became in effect, as well as much else, a kind of modern 'lives of the philosophers'. The possibility is strengthened by the evidence in the present correspondence of the sustained friendly relations between the two scholars, and the keen interest that Bayle took in Ménage's works.

It is very striking to see how many people in the scholarly circles that feature in this correspondence are engaged in either meticulous textual scholarship or, even more interestingly, in turning away from literary and historical texts in their search for accurate information about the past, and looking instead to the evidence of objects and artefacts surviving from antiquity such as coins and medals, and inscriptions.[46] Ezechiel Spanheim and Jacob Spon, who figure prominently among the mutual friends of Ménage and Grævius, are the most important figures in this trend, and to them can be added many others, including Wetstein's old school-friend André Morel. Grævius himself was closely involved. He increasingly included reproductions of coins, medals, and other ancient images in his scholarly editions, and also incorporated them in the 1697 Callimachus that he published in the name of his late son: there are a particular number accompanying Spanheim's *Observationes* which were published with the Callimachus edition. The close relationship of the new Diogenes edition to this far-reaching evolution in scholarship is borne out by Wetstein's eagerness to illustrate the publication with as many authentic representations of the philosophers as possible. The importance of this search for representational authenticity forms one of the most frequently recurring themes of his letters, and underlies the concern expressed by all three of the correspondents about the accuracy of the depiction of Monimus, and Grævius's joke at its expense (Letter 64). In this context it is especially revealing to note that, as has been mentioned, Grævius devoted the greater part of the last decade of his life to his monumental series of publications of Latin inscriptions in twelve folio volumes, the *Thesaurus Antiquitatum Romanorum* (1694-99), followed by the even more ambitious *Thesaurus Antiquitatum et Historiarum Italiæ, Neapolis, Siciliæ . . . atque adiacentium terrarum insularumque* (45 folio volumes, 1704-25), which have exactly the same aim of making available the most complete and most accurate collection of non-literary primary materials for the advancement of scholarship, and of understanding of all kinds.

These letters show how, over a period of nearly ten years, and despite an exceptional sequence of complications and problems, the final success of the great edition of Diogenes Laertius was achieved. It is clear that, for all three correspondents, Diogenes was very far from being the only preoccupation in their lives during this period, or even, most often, the principal one: the fact is reflected in the innumerable points of valuable information on the wider scholarly scene, and in the considerable range of other subjects that are touched on incidentally in the letters. Nevertheless it is the creation of the edition that gives the correspondence, as a whole, its clear sense of structure. After so many years of uncertainty, Wetstein's final letter brings the entire sequence to an eminently satisfactory conclusion as he reports on public reactions to the publication of Diogenes Laertius: 'Ce livre ne trouve par deça que des approbations: & on estime le livre aussi parfait, en toutes manieres, que quelque autre qui ait esté imprimé depuis 50 ans. On Vous y donne toute la part que Vous meritez: & Vous meritez tout, ou peu s'en faut. ... Vive Monsr Menage!'

Notes to the Introduction

1 *Ménagiana ou les bons mots et remarques critiques, historiques, morales et d'érudition, de Monsieur Ménage, recueillies par ses Amis. Nouvelle édition*, revised and extended by Bernard de La Monnoye, 4 vols (Paris, 1729), I, 75-76. All future references are to this edition.

2 I am grateful to Dr Volker Schröder of Princeton University for bringing this letter to my notice.

3 The works are: *Vita Mathæi Menagii, primi canonici-theologi andegavensis, scriptore Ægidio Menagio* (Paris, 1674), and *Vitæ Petri Ærodii quæsitoris andegavensis, et Guillelmi Menagii advocati regii andegavensis* (Paris, 1675).

4 Madeleine de Scudéry, *Clélie, histoire romaine. Troisiesme Partie* (Paris, 1658), Livre III, pp. 1494-1500. Mme de La Fayette's reaction is expressed in her letter to Ménage of 13 March 1657, in Mme de La Fayette, *Correspondance*, ed. André Beaunier, 2 vols (Paris, 1942), I, 96. See Richard Maber, 'Scholars and friends: Gilles Ménage and his correspondents', *The Seventeenth Century*, 10 (1995), 255-76 (p. 257 and note 8).

5 *Ménagiana*, III, 23, and François Charpentier, *Carpentariana* (Paris, 1724), p. 56. See Maber, 'Scholars and friends', pp. 260-61.

6 Pierre Bayle, *Dictionnaire historique et critique*, 3rd edition, 4 vols (Rotterdam, 1720), III, 1970, note B.

7 See *Ménagiana*, I, 257.

8 *Correspondance*, ed. Beaunier, I, 120 (letter of 31 August 1657). Mme de La Fayette was engaged in a law suit at the time, and her comment refers to Ménage's potentially useful friendship with the wife of a senior legal officer.

9 'Avertissement' to *Ménagiana*, I, sig. [ã8]v.

10 Letter to Nicaise of 9/19 January 1693, in *Lettres de divers savants à l'abbé Claude Nicaise*, ed. E. Caillemer (Lyon, 1885), p. 28.

11 Letter of 11 February 1663, Biblioteca Medicea Laurenziana, Florence, MS Ashburnham 1866. 1245, fol. 1r, reprinted in G. Ménage, *Lettres inédites à Pierre-Daniel Huet (1659-1692), publiées d'après le dossier Ashburnham 1866 de la Bibliothèque Laurentienne de Florence*, ed. Lea Caminiti Pennarola (Naples, 1993), no. 99, p. 177 (hereafter 'Pennarola (ed.)').

12 See Maber, 'Scholars and friends', pp. 262-64.

13 *Ibid.*, pp. 264-65.

14 'Mémoires pour servir à la vie de Monsieur Ménage', in *Ménagiana*, I, sig. [e11]v.

15 Respectively: *Observations sur la langue françoise* (Paris, C. Barbin, 1672); *Observations . . . Segonde partie* (Paris, C. Barbin, 1676); *Vita Mathæi Menagii* (Paris, C. Journel, 1675); *Vitæ Petri Ærodii et Guillelmi Menagii* (Paris, C. Journel, 1675); *Histoire de Sablé. Première partie* (Paris, P. Le Petit, 1683 [=1686]) (the *Seconde Partie* remained in manuscript until 1844: *Seconde Partie de l'"Histoire de Sablé"*, ed. by M. B. Hauréau (Le Mans, Monnoyer, 1844)); his contribution to *Luciani Samosatensis opera . . . Cum notis . . . . A. Menagii . . .* (Amsterdam, P. & J. Blaeu, 1687); *Historia mulierum philos-*

opharum . . . Accedit eiusdem commentarius italicus in VII sonettum Francisci Petrarche, a re non alienus (Lyon, Anisson, J. Posnel & C. Rigaud, 1690); *Anti-Baillet ou critique du livre de Mr. Baillet, intitulé Jugemens des savans*, 2 vols (La Haye, E. Foulque & L. van Dole, 1688) (also L. & H. van Dole,1690); *Mescolanze d'Egidio Menagio* (Paris, L. Bilaine, 1678).

16 *Les Œuvres de Mr. Sarasin* (Paris, N. Le Gras, 1685); *Les Poésies de M. de Malherbe, avec les observations de M. Ménage* (Paris, C. Barbin, 1689); *Dictionaire etymologique ou Origines de la langue françoise* (Paris, J. Anisson, 1694).

17 *Juris civilis amœnitates, Tertia Editio, prioribus longè auctior et emendatior* (Frankfurt am Main and Leipzig, C. Günther for the heirs of F. Lanckisch, 1680); *Le origini della lingua italiana . . . Colla giunta de Modi di dire italiani, raccolti, dichiarati dal Medesimo* (Geneva, J. A. Choüet, 1685); *Poemata . . . Octava editio, prioribus longe auctior et emendatior, et quam solam ipse Menagius agnoscit* (Amsterdam, H. Wetstein, 1687); *Discours sur l'Heautontimorumenos de Térence* (Utrecht, R. van Zyll, 1690); *Mescolanze d'Egidio Menagio, secunda edizione, corretta, ed ampliata* (Rotterdam, R. Leers, 1692); *Diogenis Laertii de vitis, dogmatibus et apophthegmatibus clarorum philosophorum Libri X.*, 2 vols (Amsterdam, H. Wetstein, 1692).

18 The manuscript is entitled *Ruana ou Memoires et Opuscules du Sr Rou*, 2 vols, UB Leiden, MSS BPL 291 I-II; see for example I, fol. 206v, and II, fol. 87v. There is an incomplete edition by F. Waddington, as *Mémoires inédits et opuscules*, 2 vols (Paris, Société de l'Histoire du Protestantisme Français, 1857).

19 UB Leiden, MSS Burm. F.8.25, fol. 1r; reprinted in B. Bray, 'Les Lettres françaises de Ménage à Nicolas Heinsius', in *Mélanges historiques et littéraires sur le XVIIe siècle offerts à Georges Mongrédien* (Paris, 1974), p. 203.

20 Bray, 'Les Lettres françaises', p. 203, note 43.

21 UB Leiden, MSS Burm. F.8.26, fol. 2r; reprinted in Bray, 'Les lettres françaises', pp. 205-06.

22 The title-page notes that the edition incorporates earlier scholarship on Callimachus, but particularly draws attention to the very important new material that it contains: *Callimachi Hymni, epigrammata, et fragmenta ex recensione Theodori J. G. F. Graevii cum ejusdem animadversionibus. Accedunt N. Frischlini, H. Stephani, B. Vulcanii, P. Voetii, A. T. F. Daceriæ, R. Bentleii, Commentarius, et Annotationes viri illustrissimi, Ezechielis Spanhemii. Nec non Praeter Fragmenta, quae ante Vulcanius & Daceria publicarant, nova, quae Spanhemius & Bentleius collegerunt, & digesserunt. Hujus cura & studio quaedam quoque inedita Epigrammata Callimachi nunc primum in lucem prodeunt* (Utrecht, F. Halma & G. vande Water, 1697). The revolutionary nature of Bentley's contribution is indicated by the fact that while Spanheim's previously unpublished 'Fragmenta' occupy 26 pages (pp. 276-302), Bentley's take up no fewer than 124 pages (pp. 305-429). Spanheim also wrote a substantial commentary on Callimachus, which was published as a companion volume to the edition: *Ezechielis Spanhemii in Callimachi Hymnos observationes* (Utrecht, F. Halma & G. vande Water, 1697): here, his 'Observationes' fill 758 pages.

23 The importance of their correspondence is indicated by the care lavished on its publication in 1807, in a handsome quarto volume: *Richardi Bentleii et doctorum virorum epistolæ, partim mutuæ* (London, Bulmer, 1807). The work opens with 42 letters between Bentley and Grævius (pp. 1-141), from Bentley's of 4 July 1692 to Grævius's of 23 November 1702; it is illustrated with portraits of the two scholars and fine facsimiles of one letter by each (Grævius's facing p. 73, Bentley's facing p. 134). No other correspondent in the volume is so honoured.

24 Ménage first expressed his dismay in a letter to Huet of 3 August 1689: 'Notre Ami Mr. Graevius a publié depuis peu un Panégyrique pour le Prince d'Orange: ce que je souhaitterois qu'il n'ait point fait: car outre que la Piéce n'est que médiocre, vous savez les obligations qu'il a au Roy' (BML, Florence, MS Ashburnham 1866. 1277, reprinted Pennarola (ed.), no. 222, p. 258). Huet replied on 8 August, agreeing with Ménage but expressing sympathy for Grævius's difficult position: 'Je suis bien de votre avis, que notre amy Mr. Graevius, aprés les graces qu'il a receues du Roy ne devoit pas faire le Panégyrique du Prince d'Orange / mais peut estre y a t il esté obligé pour effacer l'opinion que ces graces mêmes avoient donnée de luy' (BN, Paris, n.a.f. 1341, fol. 288r).

25 *Œuvres diverses de Mr. Pierre Bayle*, 4 vols (La Haye, P. Husson et al., 1727-31), II, 735.

26 Letters 36 and 37. Ménage was used to the Renaissance style of Greek printing typified by the Garamond *grecs du roi* with extensive use of ligatures and contractions, and told Grævius how much he disliked the new type ('le Grec étoit si vilain qu'il offensoit les yeux', Letter 38); but in this case Meibomius was in the vanguard of changing taste and his modern type was widely applauded.

27 On the subject of *variorum* editions, see Bayle's comments in *Nouvelles de la République des Lettres*, Mai 1684, Article VII (*Œvres diverses*, I, 54). Bayle is critical of the quality of the majority of these publications, in the context of an extremely favourable review of Grævius's new edition of Cicero, *Epistolarum libri 16. ad T. Pomponium Atticum* (which was published by Blaeu and Wetstein). One can thus understand both Wetstein's enthusiasm for the format, and Ménage's dislike of it.

28 For a discussion of the theories about Diogenes's date see Jørgen Mejer, *Diogenes Laertius and his Hellenistic background* (Wiesbaden, 1978), pp. 55-58.

29 Richard Hope, *The Book of Diogenes Laertius* (New York, 1930), quoted in H. S. Long, 'Introduction' to Diogenes Laertius, *Lives of eminent philosophers*, trans. R. D. Hicks, Loeb Classical Library, 2 vols (Cambridge, Mass., and London, Harvard UP, new edition, 1972), I, xix.

30 *Diogenes Laertius de vitis . . .*, ed. by H. G. Huebnerus, 2 vols (Leipzig, Koehler, 1828-31), and *Comentarii in Diogenem Laertium*, 2 vols (Leipzig, Koehler, 1830-33). On the importance of the 1664 and 1692 editions, and Ménage's *Observationes* in particular, see the first two volumes of *Storia delle storie generali della filosofia*, general ed. G. Santinello, 5 vols (Brescia, La Scuola, 1981-): F. Bottin, L. Malusa, G. Micheli, G. Santinello, and I. Tolomio, *Dalle origini rinascimentali alla 'historia philosophica'*, pp. 161-62, and F. Bottin, M. Longo, and G. Piaia, *Dall'età cartesiana a Brucker*, pp. 81-83, 86-87. I am grateful to Dr Hans Blom of Erasmus University for referring me to this work. The full title-pages of the 1692 edition spell out the richness of its contents: *Diogenis Laertii de vitis, dogmatibus et apophthegmatibus clarorum philosophorum Libri X. Græce et latine. Cum subjunctis integris Annotationibus Is. Casauboni, Th. Aldobrandini & Mer. Casauboni, Latinam Ambrosii Versionem complevit & emendavit Marcus Meibomius. Seorsum excusas Æg. Menagii in Diogenem Observationes auctiores habet Volumen II. Ut & Ejusdem Syntagma de Mulieribus Philosophis; Et Joachimi Kühnii ad Diogenem Notas. Additæ denique sunt priorum editionum Præfationes, & Indices locupletissimi* (title-page of vol. I); and: *In Diogenem Laertium Ægidii Menagii observationes & emendationes, hac editione plurimum auctæ. Quibus subjungitur Historia Mulierum Philosopharum eodem Menagio scriptore. Accedunt Joachimi Kühnii in Diogenem Laertium observationes, Ut & variantes lectiones ex duobus codicibus* MSS. *Cantabrigiensi & Arundeliano, cum editione Aldobrandiniana collatis, quas nobiscum communicavit Vir Celeberr. Th. Gale. Epistolæ & Præfationes, variis Diogenis Laertii editionibus hactenus præfixæ Indices Auctorum, Rerum & Verborum locupletissimi* (title-page of vol. II).

31 *Diogenis Laertii Vitae Philosophorum*, ed. Herbert S. Long, 2 vols (Oxford, 1964); see also H. S. Long, 'Introduction' to Diogenes Laertius, *Lives of eminent philosophers*, trans. R. D. Hicks, Loeb Classical Library, I, xxv.

32 'Epistola Basileensi editioni Præfixa. Hieronymus Frobennius & Nicolaus Episcopius studiosis. S.P.D.', sig. B1r-v.

33 Ménage had had his *Observationes* printed separately in Paris in 1663, but only in a very small number of copies printed at his own expense, for private circulation. This was to facilitate the response of his scholarly friends before the definitive publication of the work the following year.

34 It also emphatically demonstrates the ambiguity of Meibomius's contribution to an edition for which he is sometimes given the chief credit. Thus when announcing the forthcoming publication in a letter to Minutoli of 18 February 1692, Bayle refers to 'Mr. Meibomius, qui a présidé à l'Edition' (*Œuvres diverses*, IV, 668). Wetstein's correspondence makes clear the extent to which such a statement needs to be qualified; but presumably Bayle was reflecting the version of events that Meibomius had put about.

35 Charles B. Schmitt comments of the definitive Amsterdam edition of 1692 that 'it is far more correct and has many more illustrative notes than any previous edition of the work' ('The development of the historiography of scepticism: from the Renaissance to Brucker', in Richard H. Popkin and Charles B. Schmitt (eds), *Scepticism from the Renaissance to the Enlightenment*, Wolfenbütteler Forschungen, 35 (Wiesbaden, 1987), pp. 185-200 (p. 199)).

36 Thus in note 30, Meibomius writes of a textual emendation: 'Hanc restitutionem debemus Isaaco Casaubono. Sed & ita in MSS. se invenisse testatur Gassendus. Adprobat quoque eruditiss. Ægid. Menagius. *M. Meibom.*' In note 38 similarly: 'Hanc Gassendi emendationem merito laudat diligentissimus Menagius'.

37 There were three other sixteenth-century translations, none of which gained anything like the circulation of the Traversari and Aldobrandini versions: one by Johannes Sambucus (Antwerp, Christophe Plantin, 1566); a collaborative effort by a group of scholars (Paris, Jérôme de Marnef, 1560); and an unattributed Latin edition published at the end of the century (Geneva, Jacques Choüet, 1595). See *Storia delle storie generali della filosofia*, I, 160.

38 After high praise of Traversari's learning, Froben continued: 'Et tamen qui Græca Diogenis cum Ambrosii Latinis conferre volet, facile videbit quantum intersit inter puros fontes, & lacunas, licèt non omnino turbidas' (quoted from the Wetstein 1692 edition, II, 569b). See *Storia delle storie generali della filosofia*, I, 158.

39 On the deficiencies of earlier editions and Latin translations, Pietro Aldobrandini wrote of the work 'quem innumeris antea mendis malè habitum, nec satis feliciter versum' (quoted from the Wetstein 1692 edition, II, 574b). See *Storia delle storie generali della filosofia*, I, 159.

40 There are 83 lines per page in the 1664 folio edition, and Ménage's *Observationes* fill 283 pages; while in the quarto of 1692 there are 60 lines per page, and the *Observationes* occupy 484 pages. The lines contain the same amount of material in each edition.

41 *Ménagiana*, I, sig. [e11]r-v.

42 Vol. II, p. 444. Ménage's expressions of admiration and friendship for Gassendi, and the importance of his own role in inspiring Gassendi's *Animadversiones in decimum librum Diogenis Laertii, qui est de vita, moribus, plascitisque Epicuri* of 1649 (confirmed also by Gassendi), are particularly interesting and worth quoting in full: 'Decimum hunc Laërtii librum; hoc est, Vitam Epicuri; mei caussâ Latinè vertit, & Notis accuratis & Commentariis luculentis illustravit, Petrus Gassendus, vir omnium Sectarum; Epicureæ imprimis; peritissimus. Eò brevior ero in hujus libri expositione. Quid enim de Epicuri Decretis quisquam proferre possit, quod Gassendus non viderit? post quem tacere modestissimum foret: nisi quædam in Textus Laërtiani enarratione vir mihi amicissimus non tam omisisset, quàm mihi reliquisset.' (cf. 1664, p. 258).

43 See for example Richard H. Popkin, *The history of scepticism from Erasmus to Spinoza* (Berkeley, Los Angeles, and London, 1979), especially Chapter 4, 'The influence of the New Pyrrhonism', pp. 66-86.

44 Apart from the texts in Diogenes there remain only a few papyrus fragments, a few quotes in ancient writers, and the eighty ethical aphorisms discovered in 1888 in a manuscript in the Vatican, the *Sententiae Vaticanae* (*Oxford Classical Dictionary*, article 'Epicurus').

45 'The development of the historiography of scepticism', p. 191 and n. 48.

46 See especially Arnaldo Momigliano, 'Ancient history and the antiquarian', *Journal of the Warburg and Courtauld Institutes*, 13 (1950), 285-315, reprinted in A. Momigliano, *Studies in historiography* (London, 1966), pp. 1-39; also the suggestive opening remarks in Brendan Dooley, 'Snatching victory from the jaws of defeat: history and imagination in baroque Italy', *The Seventeenth Century*, 15 (2000), 90-115 (p. 90).

THE MANUSCRIPTS

The letters from Ménage to Grævius

The forty surviving letters from Ménage to Grævius, and the letter that Ménage sent for Grævius to pass on to the printer Rudolph van Zyll, are preserved together in the Kongelige Bibliotek, Copenhagen, MS Thott 1263, 4°. The letters are unbound, and not numbered separately. Most consist of a single sheet folded in half to make two leaves; the exceptions are the letters of 23 March 1682 (Letter 8 in this edition), 4 November 1689 (Letter 45), and 10 September 1691 (Letter 61), where the folded sheet has been cut in half to make a single small sheet. Almost all the folded sheets are of a similar size, although sometimes unevenly cut or badly folded, each leaf being in the range 189-197mm x 131-138mm. Four letters are on smaller paper: the letters of 19 May 1679 and 16 June 1679 (Letters 1 and 2) are written on leaves measuring 185-6 x 123-4 mm, that of 6 September 1685 (Letter 30) measures 167 x 113 mm, and that of 22 May 1687 (Letter 39) measures 163 x 105 mm.

The letters are almost all written on fol. 1r of the folded sheets, extending where necessary to fol. 2r, and then occasionally being continued sideways on fol. 1v, as noted in the cases of individual letters. An exception is the double letter of 24 February 1690 (Letters 48, 48A), where the two letters follow consecutively on fols 1r-v and 2r. Where there is an address (as noted after the text) it is on fol. 2v. Twenty-three of the letters bear an address; sixteen of the addresses are written in Ménage's hand (Letters 1, 18, 24, 25, 28, 29, 31, 33, 34, 40, 41, 45, 46, 47, 48, 54), and seven are addressed by a secretary (Letters 6, 9, 13, 17, 20, 21, 68). All the letters are written in Ménage's hand except that of 2 June 1684 (Letter 17), which is written by a secretary, probably Simon de Valhébert, and signed by Ménage.

Twenty-one of the letters still bear all or most of their original red seals. These seals are of eight designs, which, so far as they can be deciphered, are as follows:

1   A figure drawing a bow at the stars, in an octagonal surround, with the legend: CEST MON PLAISIR (Letter 1).
2   The bust of a man wearing a laurel (?) wreath, looking to the right (Letter 6).
3   A variant form of the same design (Letters 17, 18, 20, 21, 25, 28, 29, 31, 34, 46, 47, 48, 54).
4   A third variant of the design of a male bust wearing a wreath (Letters 40, 41).
5   A classical figure standing in an oval surround (Letter 9).
6   A calligraphic design in an oval surround (Letter 13).
7   A full-length male figure facing to the left, with one leg advanced and one arm raised, surrounded by an illegible inscription (Letter 24).
8   A new calligraphic design in an oval surround (Letter 68).

Five of the letters have a modern pencil note of the date at the top of fol. 1r, in the form '1/8 1686' etc (Letters 34, 38, 40, 41, 47). There are early ink annotations, in

Grævius's hand, on fol. 2v of Letter 54, which are transcribed with the text; and the word 'menagii', also probably in Grævius's hand, is written on fol. 2v of Letter 30.

The letters from Wetstein to Ménage

The thirty surviving letters from Wetstein to Ménage, and the letter that Wetstein sent for Ménage to pass on to Charles Perrault, are preserved in the Universiteitsbibliotheek, Amsterdam, almost all in the sequence k 69/3109 Gm 8^a – Gm 8^{ae}: the references are written at the head of each letter. One of the letters in this sequence, Gm 8^n (letter of 28 December 1690, Letter 51 in this edition), is a twentieth-century copy: the original was purchased by the library in 1964, and is held separately (k 64/3207 Gl 87). All the letters in the main sequence have been numbered consecutively at the foot of fol. 1r, from 1 (Gm 8^a) to 31 (Gm 8^{ae}).

The majority of the letters (24 out of the 31) have been written on leaves of paper in the range 224-240 x 180-184mm; twelve of these consist of a single leaf, and twelve of a larger sheet folded to make two leaves of this size. Four letters (Letters 43, 44, 52, 62A in this edition) are on smaller leaves, in the range 182-187 x 124 mm; again, two are single leaves (Letters 44, 52) and two have been folded to form two leaves of this size (Letters 43, 62A, the latter being Wetstein's letter to Perrault enclosed with a letter to Ménage on the larger paper). Three letters are on paper of different sizes: that of 16 December 1684 (Letter 22) measures 210 x 164mm; that of 22 September 1686 (Letter 35) measures 232 x 168mm; and that of 28 December 1690 (Letter 51) measures 190 x 118mm, i.e. one of the larger sheets folded in half.

The letters are written on the recto of the single leaves, where necessary continuing on the verso; and on fol. 1r-v of the folded double leaves. Eighteen letters have the address (as noted after the text in the edition), written in Wetstein's hand, almost always on the verso of single leaves or on fol. 2v of double leaves; the exception is the letter of 18 April 1689 (Letter 43), which is written on fol. 1r, continues up the side of this leaf, then goes on to fol. 2v, with the address written on fol. 2r. The letter of 22 February 1691 (Letter 53) has had three-quarters of fol. 2 cut off at some point, which possibly held the address. In the letter of 9 August 1691 (Letter 58), Wetstein has pasted on to fol. 2r a printed list of the names of philosophers in two columns, with two manuscript additions. Almost all the letters with the address also bear more or less substantial traces of one or more red seals; the letter of 21 January 1692 (Letter 67) has a black seal.

Four of the letters have subsequent annotations. At the head of the letter of 16 December 1684 (Letter 22) the number '95' is written in an early hand; and on that of 22 September 1686 (Letter 35) is similarly written 'Wetstein' and '118'. At the top of fol. 1r of the letter of 6 March 1692 (Letter 69) has been written, in red ink, 'L'Ep. dedic. & la Preface sont de la façon de M. Wetstein. Il le mande à la 2e. page de cette Lre.'; and the relevant passage of the letter, on lines 4-5 of fol. 1v ('je fis & la dedicace & la Preface, dont les Connoisseurs disent plus de bien qu'elles ne meritent'), has been underlined in red ink. Finally, at the foot of fol. 1r of the letter of 28 December 1690 (Letter 51), which was acquired separately from the other letters, has been pasted an entry from an auction catalogue relative to this item.

EDITORIAL PRINCIPLES

The principle followed in establishing the text of this edition is that the printed text should aim to convey as closely as possible the meaning that the original writer was himself intending to convey in his letter. Conventional contractions which were familiar and stylistically neutral, and taken as such by both writer and reader of the letter, have been silently expanded when there is no equivalent in modern usage. This usually involves the common repertoire of single letters or other marks written in superscript to indicate that a word has been abbreviated; often, indeed, they were so familiar that they were simply indicated by a flourish for which there is no equivalent in type, and which could take a variety of forms which had no difference in their signification.

For example Wetstein frequently uses the conventional abbreviations for 'Votre' and '-mm-' ('V^{re}' and 'm' with a superscript line, flourish, or what can only be described as a squiggle), and also abbreviates the endings of words, with for example '-ment' being written '-m^t'. All such have been expanded, as have forms of place-names (such as 'Amsterdam' very often being contracted to 'Amstd^m' at the head of letters, or 'Angleterre' written 'Ang^{re}.' (Letter 16)) and months ('7bre', '8bre', '9bre', 'xbre/ Xbre'), all involving superscript marks, and all of which are unfamiliar to the modern reader. Similarly the contractions that Ménage uses when writing Greek, which are wholly unfamiliar today, have been expanded (Letters 20, 61). Where an abbreviation is still in common usage, it has of course been retained ('Nov.', 'Jan.', 'Mr.', 'St.'). Thus the ampersand has been retained, but similar abbreviations that Wetstein uses for 'pour' and 'par', which have no equivalent in modern usage or in type (approximately a 'p' with a superscript flourish and a subscript line, respectively), have been silently expanded.

Some abbreviations are of a different nature, and have been left unexpanded. These are cases where the abbreviation is an integral part of the meaning that the text conveys: it is used to produce a deliberate stylistic effect for the original reader, which would otherwise be lost. The most striking cases concern the various different ways in which Wetstein contracts the name of Meibomius, for humorous effect and to show his growing exasperation: as time goes by, the infuriating scholar's name is increasingly reduced to 'Mr. Meib.', 'Mr. M.', or even 'M. M.' (three times in Letter 62, also Letters 64, 66). Similarly Wetstein sometimes abbreviates the titles of Ménage's works, or constituent parts of the Diogenes edition. The impression of familiarity and immediacy, and also sometimes haste, would be lost if the titles were expanded: thus the 'Histoire des femmes philosophes' (properly 'Historia mulierum philosopharum') becomes 'l'histoire des femm: philos:', 'histoire des femmes phil:', then 'l'histoire des f. ph.', 'historia mul. phil.', and finally and neatly 'hist. mul. phil.'(Letters 64, 65, 66, 67).

Spelling and punctuation have been kept unchanged as in the originals. It is particularly important that Ménage's spelling and punctuation should not be changed, because he was extremely particular about these matters and insisted that his printers should follow his usage exactly. In the present correspondence, for example, he gave precise instructions to the printer Rudolph van Zyll on 24 February 1690: 'Ma Copie est tres correcte. Et vous direz s'il vous plaist à votre Compositeur qu'il la suive exactement, & pour l'orthographe & pour la ponctuation' (Letter 48A). The only exception is that the letters i/j and u/v have been regularized. As often in the seventeenth century, these are employed completely interchangeably by both Ménage and Wetstein. Ménage in particular is quite inconsistent in his usage, and clearly did not regard his use of these letters as part of his 'orthographe' that his printers had to respect; indeed, he often writes an intermediate form of both i/j and u/v, which could be read as either letter. In the case of diphthongs the printed text follows the authors' usage, even where it is not consistent. Capitalization is also kept as in the original, except in the case of those letters where the lower case was frequently used to stand for a capital in the seventeenth century, and is unambiguously intended to be read as such: thus 'Mr. francius' is printed as 'Mr. Francius'. Underlinings were the manuscript equivalent of italics, and were taken as such by printers when setting type; underlinings in the letters have accordingly been reproduced by italics in print. Wetstein sometimes punctuates the end of his sentences with an idiosyncratic mark like a small Greek ρ. To avoid confusion (as when it follows a passage of Greek, Letter 36) it has been signalled by / with an explanatory note.

All deletions and insertions have been noted. The text as printed is that of the final version, so the text of a letter is given as the author intended it to be read. However, all cases of deletions, insertions, and alterations are recorded in notes signalled by italic letters, and where still legible the deleted words are given, or the first version of altered words. Often, of course, an author is merely correcting slips; but sometimes there are conscious improvements in style or changes in meaning, and it can be revealing to see which passages of a letter occasioned second thoughts, and what the first thoughts were. Thus when Ménage did not like Wetstein's new Greek fonts, the printer originally began his response: 'Pour le grec de mon Diogene', before prudently changing it to the much more tactful 'Pour mon grec du Diogene' (Letter 37).

Each letter is followed by a short commentary, and explanatory annotations which are signalled by numbered notes. A small number of people mentioned in the letters have eluded clear identification, either because of a lack of any information or because a surname is relatively common; the problem is compounded by Ménage's very approximate versions of many Dutch and German proper names. Where plausible suggestions can be made this has been done, but it has not been possible for Perstens (Letter 4), Messrs Gruter (Letter 26), J.-B. Swaenen (Letter 37), or Bylandius (Letter 40).

TABLE OF THE LETTERS

THE CORRESPONDENCE

Ménage to Grævius. 19 May 1679

A Paris ce 19. May *1679*

Per veneranda mihi Musarum sacra, per omnes
Juro Deos, & non officiosus amo.[1]

C'estadire, Monsieur, que quoyque je ne me sois jamais donné l'honneur de vous écrire, j'ay pour vous toute la passion possible, & toute l'estime & toute la vénération que vous méritez. Je suis persuadé par tant de présents qu'il vous a plu me faire de vos ouvrages, que vous avez *a* aussi de l'amitié pour moi.[2] Et dans cette créance je prens, Monsieur, la liberté de vous adresser un Exemplaire de mes Aménitez de Droit, corrigé de ma main, & de vous supplier de le vouloir faire tenir surement à vostre ami de Lipsic, qui veut le faire imprimer à Lipsic.[3] J'y ay ajouté, pour la recommendation de l'ouvrage, les témoignages de ceux qui en ont parlé avantageusement. Mais comme je ne say point la qualité de Mr. Stauchius, je ne lui en ay point donné.[4] Si vous la savez, vous l'ajouterez s'il vous plaist à la teste de son témoignage. J'ay appris de Mr. Bigod[5] avecque bien de la joye, que vous estiez sur le point de faire imprimer Columelle: car c'est un Auteur que j'ayme fort.[6] Mr. Baluze a fait imprimer icy depuis peu le Traité de Lactance de *Morte persequutorum*, qui n'avoit jamais esté imprimé.[7] Ce Traité est fort curieux, estant rempli de plusieurs choses historiques. Il me reste, Monsieur, à vous demander la continuation de vostre amitié, & à vous assurer, que je suis toujours tout à vous avecque toute sorte d'estime & de respect, & avecque toute la reconnoissance dont je suis capable.

Ménage

[Address, fol. 2v: A Monsieur / Monsieur Grævius]

a. de *deleted*.

This is the inaugural letter of Ménage's correspondence with Grævius. He mentions having received a number of complimentary copies of Grævius's publications, which will have been sent through the intermediary of mutual friends, just as Ménage was later to act as an intermediary himself in distributing Grævius's works to French scholars. His motive in now responding favourably to these overtures is clearly his realization that Grævius can be useful to him through his friendship with the German scholar Friedrich-Benedikt Carpzov (Carpzovius; see note 3 below); Ménage is hoping to use his new correspondent as an intermediary in his dealings with the scholarly world in the Low Countries and Germany, specifically in arranging the publication of a new edition of his Juris civilis amœnitates *by Carpzovius in Leipzig. The letter follows a well-established format which, with variations, is found throughout Ménage's correspondence. It opens with expressions of admiration and praise for his correspondent, and a response to Grævius's presents of books. This is followed by the request for help, using the connection of their mutual friendship with Carpzovius; then an enthusiastic comment on Grævius's current scholarly activity, bringing in another mutual friend (Bigot), and news from Paris that would interest his correspondent. The letter concludes with conventional formulae of admiration and thanks. Ménage thus strikes a note of friendship, mutual respect, and mutual help, establishing what he hopes for from the correspondence – practical help with publishing his works outside France – and what he can offer in return: up-to-date scholarly news from Paris, and a very wide network of useful contacts.*

1 Martial, *Ep.* X. 58, 12-13. Ménage had used the same quotation in a letter to Huet of 12 September 1672, when sending him some Latin verses: Biblioteca Medicea Laurenziana, Florence, MS Ashburnham 1866. 1307, reprinted in G. Ménage, *Lettres inédites à Pierre-Daniel Huet (1659-1692), publiées d'après le dossier Ashburnham 1866 de la Bibliothèque Laurentienne de Florence*, ed. Lea Caminiti Pennarola (Naples, 1993), no. 166, p. 225 (hereafter 'Pennarola (ed.)'). Pennarola misreads the opening phrase of the quotation as 'Per memoranda mihi …'.

2 Although this is Ménage's first letter directly to Grævius, the two scholars were already on friendly terms, passing on greetings through mutual friends. Just previously, on 3 May 1679, Ménage had ended a letter to Heinsius: 'Quand vous écrirez à Mr. Grevius, je vous conjure de le bien assurer de mon service et de mon estime' (UB Leiden, MSS Burm. F.8.23, fol. 2r; reprinted in B. Bray, 'Les Lettres françaises de Ménage à Nicolas Heinsius', in *Mélanges historiques et littéraires sur le XVIIe siècle offerts à Georges Mongrédien* (Paris, 1974), pp. 191-206 (p. 201)). It is clear from Ménage's fourth letter to Grævius, of 12 August 1680, that the latter usually sent copies of his works through the intermediary of Emery Bigot.

3 The 'Aménitez de Droit' is Ménage's *Juris civilis amœnitates* (Paris, G. de Luyne, 1664; second edition Paris, G. Martin, 1677). He has now prepared a revised edition of the work to be published in Leipzig. 'Vostre ami de Lipsic' is Carpzovius (Friedrich-Benedikt Carpzov, 1649-1699), one of an extensive family of highly distinguished scholars and lawyers. The progress of this new edition can be followed in Ménage's subsequent letters to Grævius and his surviving correspondence with Carpzovius.

4 'Mr. Stauchius' is the legal scholar Johann Strauch (1612-1679). Grævius had studied under him at the university of Leipzig, where Strauch was professor of history and Latin literature. He had written *Amœnitatum juris canonici semestre* (Jena, S. A. Müller, 1674) on canon law, in direct emulation of Ménage's work on civil law; his encomium of the work of 'Ægidii Menagii, Jurisconsulti præstantissimi' in his epistle, 'Johannes Strauchius Lectoribus' (pp. [1-3]) is given pride of place at the head of the 'Elogia' prefacing the new edition of Ménage's book (sig. b2v). Ménage's uncertainty about Strauch's title is unsurprising: Strauch was appointed to chairs at several German universities, and fulfilled a variety of official positions in different German states. At the time of his death he was professor of law and vice-chancellor of the university of Giessen. In the event, Grævius settled for calling him 'Joh. Strauchius Jurisconsultus'.

5 Emery Bigot (1626-1689), a deeply learned scholar and one of Ménage's oldest and closest friends. He lived in Rouen, but generally spent several months every year staying with Ménage in Paris; when apart they corresponded constantly. It was to Bigot that Ménage dedicated his edition of Diogenes Laertius: *Laertii Diogenis de vitis, dogmatis et apophthegmatis eorum qui in philosophia claverunt libri X* (London, Pulleyn, 1664). The depth of this friendship is movingly shown later in this correspondence, when Ménage

reports to Grævius the news of Bigot's death, in his letters of 9 January 1690 (Letter 47) and 24 February 1690 (Letter 48). Bigot travelled extensively, in the Low Countries and Germany, and also in England and Italy, to visit libraries and meet scholars. It is uncertain whether he met Grævius (see Leonard E. Doucette, *Emery Bigot: seventeenth-century French humanist* (Toronto, 1970), p. 135, who thinks not), but it is clear, despite the survival of relatively few letters, that they maintained a regular correspondence from as early as 1662 (see for example KB Copenhagen, MS Thott 1258, 1268).

6 Ménage repeats this phrase and expands on it in his letter of 14 November 1680 (Letter 5). Columella was a first-century agricultural writer whose principal work, *De re rustica*, contains both prose and verse. Huet had hoped that Grævius would contribute an edition to his great series of texts *Ad usum Delphini*, but, like others among Grævius's many projects, the work was never completed.

7 Etienne Baluze (1630-1718), the historian, scholar, and collector of manuscripts and books, was at this time librarian of Colbert's library. The work *De mortibus persecutorum* is concerned with the Diocletian persecution, although its attribution to 'the Christian Cicero' Lactantius (?250-?317) is doubtful.

LETTER 2

Ménage to Grævius. 16 June 1679

A Paris ce 16. Juin *1679*

Monsieur

Je me donnay l'honneur de vous écrire, il y a aujourdhuy trois semaines, pour vous donner avis que je vous avois envoyé par un Gentilhomme de Mr. vostre Ambassadeur de Hollande un exemplaire de mes Aménitez de Droit, reveu, corrigé, & augmenté;[1] & pour vous supplier de le faire tenir à vostre ami de Lipsic, qui veut faire faire en Allemagne une nouvelle édition de ce livre. Voicy encore quelques corrections & quelques additions, que je vous prie de mettre en leur lieu.[2] Je serois bien aise aureste que ce livre fust imprimé en bon papier; & pour cela je donnerois volontiers à l'Imprimeur ce que vostre ami de Lipsic jugeroit apropos que je lui donnasse.[3] Mr. Bigot qui est icy présent, vous baise tres-humblement les mains. Je suis toujours, comme je dois, avecque toute sorte d'estime,

Monsieur,
Vostre tres humble & tres
obeissant serviteur
Menage

[No address]

A letter following up Ménage's first, recording what he had written in May in case it had gone astray, adding some further material for the edition, and a specification for its appearance:

Ménage is particularly concerned that his work should be printed on good paper, for which he is prepared to pay. The letter ends with greetings from their mutual friend Bigot, with the personal touch that Bigot is 'icy présent' as Ménage writes.

1 It was in fact exactly four weeks, not three, since Ménage's first letter. He had sent the book separately, using a personal intermediary for the irreplaceable corrected copy rather than entrust it to the regular postal service. He was so concerned about his new correspondence with Grævius that only three days later, on 19 June 1679, he ended a letter to Heinsius: 'Je suis en peine de savoir si Mr. Grevius a receu deux lettres que je lui ay écrites depuis un mois; ces lettres estant de conséquence; & quand vous lui écrirez, je vous supplie de le lui demander, & de me faire savoir ensuite ce qu'il vous aura répondu là dessus' (UB Leiden, MSS Burm. F.8.24, fol. 2r; reprinted Bray, 'Les Lettres françaises ...', p. 203 and n. 42). Heinsius did as he was asked, and in two letters, of 27 June and 29 June, Grævius confirmed that he had replied to Ménage's letters. Ménage must have received the first reply shortly afterwards; in his next letter to Heinsius, of 27 June, he writes: 'Quand vous verrez Mr. Grævius, ou quand vous lui écrirez, je vous prie de le bien assurer de mon service, de mon estime, & de ma reconnoissance' (UB Leiden, MSS Burm. F.8.25, fol. 2r; reprinted Bray, 'Les Lettres françaises ...', p. 204), and he begins his next letter to Grævius on 6 October: 'J'ay reçu les deux lettres qu'il vous a plu m'écrire'.

2 The corrections and additions have not survived with the letter, and were no doubt sent on to Carpzovius.

3 Ménage was deeply suspicious about the quality of German paper, and damns it in his letter of 12 August 1680 (Letter 4). In the event, though, he was to be pleasantly surprised by that used for his book (see Letter 5, 14 November 1680).

LETTER 3

Ménage to Grævius. 6 October 1679

A Paris ce 6. Oct. *1679*

Monsieur

J'ay reçu les deux lettres qu'il vous a plu m'écrire. Je vous suis bien obligé de toutes ces marques que vous m'avez données de vostre amitié: & je vous en fais icy un million de tres humbles remercimens. J'ay appris par une lettre de Mr. Heinsius à Mr. Bigot,[1] que Mr. Capsovius avoit reçu l'Exemplaire de mes Aménitez de Droit que vous lui avez envoyé, dont j'ay bien de la joye: mais j'ay aussi appris par la mesme lettre que l'Imprimeur qui devoit rimprimer ce livre, estoit mort, dont je suis tres mortifié; prévoyant qu'il sera difficile d'en trouver un autre qui entreprenne cette edition.[2] Au cas qu'il ne s'en trouvast point, je vous supplie, Monsieur, de retirer cet Exemplaire de Mr. Capso-

vius, & de me le renvoyer par la premiére occasion que vous en aurez: car je n'ay point [fol. 2r] retenu de copie des additions que j'y ay mises. Que s'il se présentoit quelque Imprimeur pour l'imprimer, non seulement je ne lui demande point d'exemplaires, mais je vous donne ma parole d'en acheter un grand nombre, au cas que le livre soit imprimé correctement, & en beau papier. Mr. Elzevir part dans deux jours pour s'en retourner en Hollande.[3] Il vous dira comme nous avons fait icy commémoration de vous & de Mr. Heinsius le verre à la main, Mr. Hüet, Mr. Bigot, Mr. Bouïlliau, Mr. Fromentin, Mr. Justel, & moi.[4] Je vous demande toujours la continuation de vostre amitié, & suis toujours, comme je dois, de toute ma passion, & avecque toute l'estime possible,
Monsieur,

Vostre tres humble &
tres obéissant serviteur
Ménage

[No address]

In the three and a half months since his previous letter Ménage has received two letters from Grævius, and the correspondence is now established. This letter provides an interesting example of how the international network of scholars who made up the Republic of Letters worked in practice (see Introduction): Ménage sent his book to Carpzovius via Grævius in Utrecht; the news of its fortunes in Leipzig was transmitted back to him via Heinsius and Bigot, and he in turn informs Grævius. There are problems in Leipzig caused by the death of the printer. Ménage sends detailed instructions about finding a new printer, including the financial inducement that he will buy a large number of copies of his work himself. He sends news of mutual friends, and once again the letter ends with an attractive personal touch in the 'commémoration' of the Dutch scholars, 'le verre à la main', by a distinguished gathering at Ménage's house. The concluding formulae are now noticeably more friendly (for the first time Ménage expresses his 'passion').

1 Nicolaas Heinsius (1620-1681) and Ménage had been on very friendly terms for many years and had corresponded since 1644. Ménage is quoted in the *Ménagiana* as saying 'N. Heinsius ... étoit un bon homme, doux, et d'une grande moderation. Je l'ai reçu chez moi, et lui ai donné à dîner plusieurs fois' (I, 81); but, familiar as he was with Ménage's unreliability as a correspondent, it is not surprising that Heinsius should have chosen to pass on information to him via Bigot. However in this case he later wrote directly to Ménage, on 24 October 1679, with the same news (UB Amsterdam, MS G.k.64)
2 The intended printer was Friedrich Lanckisch, but despite his death Carpzov was able to get the work published with little delay: see Ménage's next letter, of 12 August 1680. Lanckisch's heirs ensured that the work was completed, as is signalled on the title-page: *Ægidii Menagii Juris civilis amoenitates Ad Ludovicum Nublæum, Advocatum Parisiensem. Tertia Editio, prioribus longè auctior et emendatior* (Francofurti & Lipsiæ, Impensis Hered. Friderici Lanckisii, Typis Christophori Güntheri, 1680).
3 Daniel Elzevir (1617-1680), son of Bonaventure Elzevir, was the last of the extensive family to be a printer of major importance. He was based in Amsterdam, and often vis-

ited Paris. From his childhood onwards he was completely at home in the scholarly world: Daniel Heinsius was his godfather, and his godmother was the wife of Meursius. 4 The participants in this agreeable scholarly celebration, all close friends and correspondents of Ménage, were also mutual friends of Grævius and Heinsius. With the possible exception of Fromentin they all corresponded with Grævius: see for example KB Copenhagen, MSS Thott 1250 (D. Elzevir), 1259 (Bouilliau), 1262 (Justel, Huet), 1263 (Huet, Ménage), 1258, 1268 (Bigot).

Pierre-Daniel Huet (1630-1721) was at this time *précepteur* of the Dauphin. He had only taken Holy Orders in 1676, but was appointed Bishop of Soissons in 1686, which he later exchanged for the see of Avranches: see Ménage's letter of 4 November 1689 (Letter 45). His correspondence was vast and is now widely scattered; but the Ashburnham collection in the Biblioteca Medicea Laurenziana, Florence, contains over 3,000 letters addressed to him, and there are further large holdings in the BN, Paris (notably fonds fr. 15189, n.a.f. 1341, 4564, and Rothschild A. XVII).

Ismaël Boulliau (or Bouillaud, etc) (1605-1694) was an astronomer, mathematician, and scholar. He travelled extensively in Europe and the Middle East, and kept up a very extensive correspondence: see H.J.M. Nellen, *Ismaël Boulliau (1605-1694). Nieuws-jager en Correspondent* (Nijmegen, 1980). Much of his correspondence is preserved in the BN, Paris, fonds fr. 13024-13041.

Raymond Fromentin (or Formentin) (died 1703), physician and hellenist.

Henri Justel (1620-1693) was a Protestant scholar whose extensive international contacts included Locke and Leibniz. In the atmosphere of increasing French religious intolerance of the 1680s he emigrated to England, where the king appointed him librarian of the Royal Library at St James's.

LETTER 4

Ménage to Grævius. 12 August 1680

A Paris ce 12. Aoust *1680.*

Monsieur

J'ay fait en vostre considération toutes sortes de caresses à Mr. Perstens: & je lui rendray icy en vostre considération tous les services dont je suis capable. Il m'a paru un tres honneste homme, & tres digne de vostre amitié. Je n'ay point encore reçu les exemplaires de mes Aménitez de Droit, que Mr. Carpsovius m'a envoyez.[1] Quand je les auray reçus, je vous diray ce qu'il me semble du caractére des Imprimeurs de Lipsic. Il ne peut pas estre comparable en beauté à celui des Imprimeurs de Hollande. Et le papier d'Allemagne est dailleurs tres mauvais. Cestpourquoy, Monsieur, j'aimerois beaucoup mieux que mon Diogéne Laërce fust rimprimé en Hollande qu'en Allemagne. Et si vous pouviez obliger quelqu'un de vos Imprimeurs à le rimprimer, vous m'obligeriez tres sensiblement. Non seulement je n'en demande point d'exemplaires: mais j'offre de donner 20. pistoles au Correcteur. J'apprens que Mr. Carpsovius fait rimprimer à Lipsic l'Epiphane du Pére Petau.[2] Le Pére Petau a fait sur cet auteur des Additions, des Corrections, & des Changemens tres considérables, qui sont entre les mains des Jésuites de Paris; & qui les donneroient volontiers à Mr. Carpsovius, sans qu'ils en ont traité avecque Mr. Mabre Cramoisi, leur Imprimeur.[3] Mais comme Mr. Mabre Cramoisi ne se [fol. 2r] dispose point à imprimer ce livre; & que je suis comme assuré qu'il ne l'imprimera point, je suis d'avis que Mr. Carpsovius le desinteresse, en lui donnant un nombre d'exemplaires de l'Epiphane de l'édition de Lipsic: car en ce cas, les Jésuites de Paris donneroient à l'Imprimeur de Lipsic, les Additions, les Corrections, & les Changemens, dont je viens de vous parler. Je vous suis, Monsieur, infiniment obligé, & à Mr. Heinsius, de la commémoration que vous avez faite de moi dans vostre savante débauche:[4] & je vous en fais icy, & à l'un & à l'autre, un million de tres humbles remercimens. Mr. Bigot est encore en Normandie: & ainsi, Monsieur, je n'ay point encore receu l'exemplaire de vostre Florus que vous m'avez destiné, & que vous lui avez adressé.[5] Je ne laisse pas de vous en remercier par avance. Mille tres humbles baisemains à Mr. Heinsius. Je suis toujours, à l'ordinaire, avecque toute sorte d'estime, & avecque toute la passion imaginable,

Monsieur,

                         Vostre tres humble & tres
                               obéissant serviteur
                                    Ménage

[No address]

After a gap of ten months, Ménage is prompted to write again by a letter of recommendation from Grævius borne by a M. Perstens. Ménage reports on the progress of his Juris civilis amœnitates (he has not yet received any copies of the completed edition), and for the first time discusses his plans for a new edition of one of his most important scholarly works, his edition of Diogenes Laertius, which will come to dominate this correspondence for the next twelve years. He asks Grævius to act as his intermediary for this, as indeed he did. The letter continues with important scholarly news to be passed on to help Carpzovius, in return for his help over the Juris civilis amœnitates. As usual, the concluding section involves mutual friends (Heinsius and Bigot), with another attractive personal detail: the response of Heinsius and Grævius to the celebratory toast from the Parisian scholars was their own 'commémoration' of Ménage in a 'sçavante débauche'.

1 Ménage's favourable verdict on the edition, when he finally received a copy, is expressed in his next letter.
2 The learned Jesuit Denis Petau (1583-1652) had published his edition of the works of St Epiphanius in two folio volumes in 1622: *Epiphanii ... opera omnia in duos tomos distributa. Dionysius Petavius ... recensuit, Latine vertit, & ... illustravit* (Paris, M. Sonnius, C. Morellus and S. Cramoisy, 1622).
3 The Cramoisy dynasty were the most powerful printing establishment in seventeenth-century Paris, and were the royal printers as well as being the official printers of the Jesuits. Sébastien Mabre-Cramoisy took over the family presses from his grandfa-

ther Sébastien Cramoisy in 1660. (See H.-J. Martin, *Le Livre français sous l'Ancien Régime* (Paris, 1987), Chapter 2, 'Un grand éditeur parisien au XVIIe siècle, Sébastien Cramoisy', pp. 55-64.)

4 At this time Heinsius was living in the small town of Vianen near Utrecht, where his friend Grævius frequently visited him.

5 L. A. *Florus, Epitome rerum romanarum, recensitus et illustratus a J. G. Grævio* (Utrecht, 1680). 'C'est une des meilleures productions de Grævius. La préface est particulièrement remarquable. Il y traite avec goût du style et de la latinité de Florus' (Boissonade in Michaud, *Biographie universelle*).

LETTER 5

Ménage to Grævius. 14 November 1680

A Paris ce 14. Nov. *1680.*

Monsieur

J'ay reçu, il y a déja quelque tans, vostre Florus qu'il vous a plu m'envoyer. Et comme il est rempli d'un nombre infini de choses doctes & curieuses, je l'ay lu avecque beaucoup de profit & avecque beaucoup de plaisir. Je vous suis[a] bien obligé, Monsieur, de la grace que vous m'avez faite de me faire un si beau présent: & je vous en rens mille tres humbles actions de graces. Je n'ay point reçu les exemplaires de mes Aménitez de Droit dont vous me parlez: mais j'en ay reçu un, qui m'a esté rendu de la part de Mr. Carpsovius par un de ses amis. L'édition ne m'en déplaist pas: le caractére estant assez beau, & le papier n'estant pas mauvais. Et si j'estois bien persuadé que les Imprimeurs de Lipsic imprimassent aussi bien mon Laërce, je me resoudrois volontiers à le leur donner. Mais j'aymerois beaucoup mieux qu'il fust imprimé en Hollande. Et vous m'obligerez tres-sensiblement, si vous obligez Messieurs Boom à l'imprimer.[1] Mais je souhaitterois qu'il fust imprimé correctement. Et pour cela, j'offre de donner à un habile Correcteur tout ce que vous jugerez apropos que je lui donne. Quand mes Origines de la Langue Italienne seront rimprimées, je ne manqueray pas de vous en faire [fol. 2r] part.[2] Et cependant, Monsieur, si vous en desirez un exemplaire de la premiére édition, je vous l'envoieray par la premiére occasion qui se présentera. Le livre n'est pas fort excellent: mais il est fort rare: car on n'en a tiré qu'un tres petit nombre d'exemplaires. J'ay bien la vanité de croire qu'il ne sera pas mauvais de la segonde édition. *Est bene, non potuit dicere, dixit, erit.*[3] Je suis bien fasché de l'indisposition de Mr. Heinsius:[4] Et je vous prie de le lui bien témoigner. Je me donneray l'honneur de lui écrire dans peu: en lui envoyant une demidouzaine d'exemplaires d'une nouvelle édition qu'on a faite icy de mes Poësies; qui est un chédeuvre d'édition.[5] Un de ces exemplaires vous est destiné. Je vous prie, Monsieur, de l'avoir agréable, & de le recevoir comme un témoignage de la vénération que j'ay pour vostre mérite. J'apprens avecque bien de la

joye, que vous vous disposez à nous donner Columelle:[6] car c'est un Auteur que j'aime fort: & sur lequel j'ay u autrefois dessein: mais sur lequel je n'ay pourtant jamais rien écrit. Si j'y puis faire quelques remarques dignes de vous estre communiquées, je vous les communiqueray volontiers. Je vous diray cependant, qu'il y a beaucoup d'apparance que l'Orateur de Quintilien a esté fait à l'imitation du pére de famille de Columelle: Quintilien ayant donné le mesme titre à son ouvrage que Columelle au sien; & l'ayant divisé, comme lui, en douze livres; & ayant visé à beaucoup [fol. 1v, sideways] d'endroits du livre de Columelle ./. La nouvelle de la mort de Mr. Elzevir m'a fort affligé:[7] car outre qu'il estoit[b] honneste homme, il estoit fort de mes amis. Je voudrois pouvoir estre de quelque usage à Monsieur son fils. Nous avons aussi en cette ville, & aux environs de cette ville, beaucoup de maladies. Et la Maison Royale n'en[c] a pas esté exante.[8] Conservez vous bien, Monsieur, pour la satisfaction de vos amis, & pour la gloire de nostre siécle. Je salue Monsieur Heinsius de toute mon affection: & suis toujours à l'ordinaire, avecque toute l'estime & toute la tendresse possible,
Monsieur,

Vostre tres humble & tres
obéissant serviteur
Ménage

[No address]

^a. suis *inserted*.
^b. un ami fort *deleted*.
^c. n' *deleted*.

Ménage sends thanks for the edition of Florus, *now received via Bigot, and responds with news of four of his own works. Each of these is on a completely different subject-area – law, Greek scholarship, Italian philology, and poetry – and they give an excellent illustration of the extraordinary range of his achievements. He approves of the Leipzig* Juris civilis amœnitates, *gives details of his plans for Diogenes Laertius (including the perennial problem of finding an 'habile correcteur' for an edition which cannot be overseen personally), and promises to send copies of his* Origines de la langue italienne *and the new Paris edition of his* Poésies, *the latter via Heinsius. Grævius immediately set about finding a printer for Diogenes: see note 4 below. As regards Grævius's interest in Columella, Ménage provides a possibly useful suggestion and promises further help. He responds to bad news from the Netherlands – Heinsius's illness, Daniel Elzevir's death – and sends similar news from Paris. The concluding formulae, expressing 'tendresse', again show an increase in the note of intimacy.*

1 Hendrick and Dirk Boom ran one of the most active Amsterdam publishing houses in the later seventeenth century. However, no more is heard of their possible involvement with the Diogenes Laertius edition.
2 Ménage's work was first published eleven years earlier: *Le Origini della lingua Italiana compilate dal Signore Egidio Menagio* (Paris, Sebastien Mabre-Cramoisi, 1669). The new edition, published in Geneva, did not finally appear until 1685; Ménage's early optimism in this letter was soon replaced by complaints, as in his letter to Huet of 24 June 1681: 'On imprime à Geneve mes Origines de la Langue Italienne, mais je suis tres mal

satisfait de l'édition', BML, Florence, MS Ashburnham 1866. 1385, reprinted Pennarola (ed.), no. 179, pp. 230-31.

3 An anonymous maxim quoted in Suetonius, *Domitian*, 23. 2.

4 Heinsius's health was giving his friends cause for concern. In a letter to Huet the following year Ménage reported that Heinsius had recovered from his illness: 'Mr. Heinsius ... a esté tres long tans et tres périlleusement malade. J'ay reçu depuis cinq ou six jours une de ses lettres, par laquelle j'ay appris avec bien de la joye, qu'il estoit présentement en bonne santé' (letter of 9 September 1681, BML, Florence, MS Ashburnham 1866. 1260; reprinted Pennarola (ed.), no 180, p. 231); but he died the following month (see next letter). Ménage's letter to Heinsius of November 1680 has been lost: none survive between 27 June 1680 and 10 March 1681 (UB Leiden, sig. Burm. F.8). However a letter does survive in which Grævius immediately passed on Ménage's greetings to Heinsius, along with other information from Ménage, and which shows his eagerness to help with the new edition of Diogenes: 'A *Menagio* heri litteras accepi, quibus significat, se tua valetudino summopere conciari, et proxime ad te scripturum, missurumque aliquot exemplaria suorum poëmatum denuo editorum. Genevae recuditur quoque Etymologicum ejus Italicum. Optat, ut nostris bibliopolis possit persuaderi, ut novam etiam commentarii ejus in Diogenem Laërtium editionem velint adornare. Scribam hoc nomine ad Amsterodamenses et Leidenses bibliopolas.' (Burman, *Sylloges epistolarum a viris illustribus scriptarum*, 5 vols (Leiden, Samuel Luchtmans, 1727), IV, 689: Letter DCXLVII from Grævius to Heinsius, wrongly dated 11 November 1680 (for 19 November?)).

5 *Ægidii Menagii poemata; septima editio, prioribus longe emendatior* (Paris, Le Petit, 1680).

6 It is absolutely typical of Ménage's epistolary style that he should here repeat, almost word for word, his comment in his first letter to Grævius eighteen months previously; but also typical that he should now expand his remark with further information and offers of help.

7 Daniel Elzevir died on 13 September 1680. See also Letter 3, note 3. His only surviving son was Louis (1662-1688), at this time scarcely 19 years old and barely completing his studies at Oxford. Daniel's untimely death effectively signalled the end of the Elzevirs as a major publishing house: see A. Willems, *Les Elzevier: histoire et annales typographiques* (Brussels, 1880), pp. ccxli–ccxlvi.

8 An allusion to remarkable events at Versailles. The Dauphin and Dauphine had been seriously ill with a prevalent fever, but had been cured, to the fury of the court doctors, by an English physician named Talbot (or Tabor or Talbor) with a miraculous secret remedy. He was very richly rewarded by the King, who bought the remedy and made it public: the secret ingredient was quinine, mixed with wine. See Mme de Sévigné's letters to Mme de Grignan of 6 November and 8 November 1680 (*Correspondance*, ed. R. Duchêne, 3 vols (Paris, 1977-78), III, 55-56, and II, 1415, note 3 to letter 683), and the letter to Bussy-Rabutin from Mme de Scudéry (Georges de Scudéry's widow) of 14 November 1680: 'Toute la maison royale est guérie par le médecin anglois; les autres médecins sont enragés contre lui: il a eu du roi deux mille francs de pension et deux mille pistoles une fois payées. Il s'appelle Talbot ...' (*Correspondance de Roger de Rabutin, Comte de Bussy*, ed. L. Lalanne, 6 vols (Paris, 1858-58), V, 182).

Ménage to Grævius. 17 December 1681

A Paris ce 17. Dec. *1681.*

Monsieur

J'ay reçu les deux lettres qu'il vous a plu m'écrire sur la mort de nostre excellent ami, Mr. Heinsius.[1] Mais je n'ay reçu la première que depuis deux jours: parceque vous l'aviez adressée à Mr. Bigot, qui a passé toute cette autonne à la campagne. Quoyque la nouvelle de cette mort soit la plus fascheuse de toutes celles que vous pouviez jamais me mander, je ne laisse pas, Monsieur, de vous estre infiniment obligé du soin que vous avez pris de me la mander: & je vous en rens, Monsieur, un million de tres humbles graces. Vous me priez de mon inclination, en me priant de célébrer sa mémoire par mes vers. Mais pour cela, je vous demande quelque delay: Vous savez que les vers demandent un esprit tranquille. *Carmina lætum Sunt opus: & pacem mentis habere volunt:*[2] Et je suis présentement accablé d'affaires. Je fais imprimer des Remarques sur l'Histoire de la province d'Anjou; qui est le lieu de ma [fol. 2r] naissance: & je les compose dans le cours de l'impression.[3] Et avec cela, je viens de perdre un frère unique que j'avois,[4] qui a laissé douze enfans, de la conduite desquels je suis chargé. Je persévére toujours dans le dessein[a] de faire imprimer mon Diogéne Laërce en Hollande. Et je vous l'envoieray par la première commodité qui se présentera pour vous l'envoyer. Je suis toujours, comme je dois, avec toute la passion imaginable, & avec toute l'estime & toute la vénération que vous méritez,

Monsieur,
Vostre tres humble & tres
obéissant serviteur
Ménage

[Address, fol. 2v: A Monsieur / Monsieur Grævius / A Utreict]

[a]. dans le dessein *inserted.*

There has been a gap of thirteen months since Ménage's last surviving letter to Grævius, which might seem strange in view of his protestations of affection; but it is clear from the end of his next letter (18 January 1682) that at least one intervening communication has not survived. He has now received two letters almost at once, the first delayed by being sent via the absent Bigot. This letter is concerned with the death of Heinsius, and Grævius's invitation to write a poem on the subject. Ménage has himself suffered a bereavement in the death of his brother. Nevertheless he is persevering with his project for a new edition of Diogenes Laertius, and sends news of a new work on yet another completely different field of scholarship, his historical study of Anjou (subsequently entitled Histoire de Sablé*).*

1 Heinsius died on 7 October 1681, in Grævius's arms (according to Marron, in Michaud, *Biographie universelle*, XIX, 586).
2 Ovid, *Tristia*, V. 12, 3-4. Ménage had quoted the same lines twenty years earlier in a letter to Huet of 18 February 1662, in the context of verses on the death of Mambrun

(BML, Florence, MS Ashburnham 1866. 1228, reprinted Pennarola (ed.), no. 64, pp. 139-40), and again in his *Mescolanze* (Paris, 1678), p. 382: see Pennarola (ed.), p. 336. It is interesting that in the *Ménagiana* Ménage is quoted as attributing similar sentiments to Heinsius himself: 'Il faut avoir l'esprit libre pour faire des vers. Je me souviens d'avoir vû une lettre de M. Heinsius (Nicolas) qui s'excusoit de n'avoir pas fait des vers sur la mort de M. du Puy (Pierre) qui mourut en 1651, dans le temps qu'Heinsius étoit à Rome, parce, disoit-il, qu'il avoit l'esprit entierement occupé aux extraits qu'il faisoit alors dans la bibliotheque du Vatican, & qu'il craignoit même d'en devenir malade. Il travailloit sur Ovide dans ce tems-là ...' (*Ménagiana*, II, 282-83). For Huet's rather similar response, see Letter 11, 2 August 1682, note 1 below.

3 Ménage entitled this work *Histoire de Sablé*. The first part was published as: *Histoire de Sablé. Première partie qui comprend les généalogies de Sablé et de Craon, avec des remarques et des preuves* (Paris, Pierre Le Petit, 1683). The printing history of the work was protracted, no doubt because of Ménage's method of writing which he describes in this letter; and despite the date on the title-page the first part was not completed until 1686. The *privilège* is dated 26 August 1680, and the *achevé d'imprimer* is 17 August 1686. See Ménage's letter to Grævius of 1 August 1686 below, when, with the book imminently forthcoming at last, he promises to send a copy. He had mentioned his new project in a letter to Huet of 24 June 1681 (BML, Florence, MS Ashburnham 1866. 1385; reprinted Pennarola (ed.), no. 179, p. 230). The second part remained in manuscript until 1844: *Seconde Partie de l' "Histoire de Sablé"*, ed. M. B. Hauréau (Le Mans, Monnoyer, 1844).

4 Ménage expressed his grief over the death of his brother Guillaume in a letter to Magliabecchi of 24 December 1681: 'Je viens de perdre un frère que j'avois, qui estoit un très honneste homme et un très grand personnage, que j'aimais uniquement et qui m'aimoit de mesme' (Bibl. Naz. Cent., Florence, MS Magi. viii. 362, fols 34-35; reprinted in L.-G. Pélissier (ed.), *Lettres de Ménage à Magliabecchi et à Carlo Dati* (Montpellier, 1891), p. 28). In 1650 Ménage published a Latin letter to his brother, 'Ægidius Menagius Guillelmo Menagio Proprætori Andecavensi Fratri Carissimo S.D.', whose end expresses this family affection: 'Vale mi carissime & suavissime Frater, & me, ut facis, ama amore illo tuo singulari'. (First published in Jean de Launoy, *Dissertatio duplex ... Accedit Ægidii Menagii ad Guillelmum fratrem epistola* (Paris, E. Martin, 1650); and reprinted in Ménage's *Miscellanea* (Paris, A. Courbé, 1652), separately paginated section, pp. 9-18.)

Ménage to Grævius. 18 January 1682

Monsieur

J'ay reçu les trois lettres qu'il vous a plu m'écrire. Je ne pus faire réponse à la première dans le tans qu'elle me fut rendue, estant accablé de douleur & d'affaires au sujet de la mort de mon frère. Mais j'y fis réponse quelque tans aprês, en répondant à la segonde: & j'adressay ma lettre à Mr. Bigot, pour vous la faire tenir. Comme je ne doute point que vous ne l'ayiez reçue, je ne vous répeteray point icy ce que je vous disois par cette lettre. Je vous envoye, Monsieur, les vers que vous m'avez demandez sur la mort de nostre ami.[1] Si vous y trouvez quelque chose adire, je vous supplie de les corriger. *Tibi in me, meáque, æterna auctoritas esto.*[2] J'approuve fort que vous fassiez imprimer les lettres de nostre ami: estant persuadé que rien ne peut contribuer davantage à sa gloire que cet ouvrage. Vous me mandez que vous faites son Oraison Funébre. Mais avec cela, il faut que vous écriviez sa Vie.[3] Les Oraisons Funébres sont suspectes de flaterie: & les Vies ont un caractère de vérité. Les Jésuites ne veulent point donner à Mr. Carpsovius les Additions du Père [fol. 2r] Petau. Mr. Bigot vous aura pu témoigner comme lui & moy nous les avons sollicitez de les lui donner. Le Père Garnier, qui est celui qui les avoit, est mort à Boulogne en Italie.[4] Ils doivent estre présantement entre les mains du Père Hardouin;[5] qui est un des compatriotes & un des amis de Mr. Bigot. Et je vais présantement écrire à Mr. Bigot, pour le prier de faire une derniére tentative auprês de ce Père Hardouin: car il y en a déja écrit. Pour mon Diogéne Laërce; aussitost que je seray sorti de mon Histoire de Sablé: cest ainsi que j'ay intitulé ce que je fais des Genéalogies de la province d'Anjou: & j'espere que cette Histoire*a* sera achevée d'imprimer dans deux mois: je ne manqueray pas de le relire soigneusement, affin de vous l'envoyer.[6] Je suis en peine de savoir si vous avez reçu un exemplaire de la nouvelle édition de mes Poësies que je vous envoiay, il y a cinq ou six mois, par le Professeur de Philosophie de Leyden.[7] Il me reste, Monsieur, à vous demander la continuation de vostre amitié; & à vous assurer que j'ay toujours pour vous toute l'estime & toute la vénération que vous méritez; & que je suis toujours de toute ma passion,

Monsieur,
Vostre tres humble & tres
obéissant serviteur
Ménage

[No address]

a. que cette Histoire *inserted, replacing* qu'elle *deleted.*

A month later: Grævius has written again, but had not yet received Ménage's last letter, which had been sent via Bigot. In the aftermath of Heinsius's death Ménage now sends his poem, applauds Grævius's plan to edit Heinsius's letters, and urges him to write a life of their friend. Ménage gives details of his efforts to help Carpzovius over Petau's edition of St Epiphanius, a typical example of how he could mobilize his extensive network of friends and contacts, and sends the latest news of his own works.

1 Ménage repeatedly sent corrections and improvements to these verses in subsequent letters. He had already sent them for comments to Huet, who was in Paris, with an accompanying note: 'Je vous envoye les vers que j'ay faits sur la mort de Mr. Heinsius. Je vous conjure de les lire soigneusement, et de me les corriger le plus exactement que vous pourrez. Hoc mihi gratius facere nihil potes. Je suis obligé de les envoyer dimanche à Mr. Grævius: c'est pourquoi vous me les renvoierez s'il vous plaist demain au soir, ou samedi matin, sur les huit heures.' (BML, Florence, MS Ashburnham 1866. 1314; reprinted Pennarola (ed.), no. 181, p. 232. Pennarola dates the note simply as '[1682]', but it must be c15 January 1682).

2 This phrase was a favourite of Ménage's. He used it again in his letter to Grævius of 27 April 1685 (Letter 25).

3 Grævius never did complete his edition of Heinsius's letters and life of Heinsius. They were left in manuscript at his death in 1703, and at his request taken in hand by Pieter Burman. Burman published the letters in the third and fourth volumes of his *Sylloges epistolarum a viris illustribus scriptarum*; but, in his turn, he was never able to complete the rest of the task. The life of Heinsius and the collection of 'Eloges' were finally published in 1742 by Burman's son, Pieter Burman the younger, in his: *Nicolai Heinsii Dan. Fil. Adversariorum Libri IV. Numquam antea editi. In quibus plurima veterum Auctorum, Poëtarum praesertim, loca emendantur & illustrantur. Subjiciuntur ejusdem Notae ad Catullum et Propertium nunc primum productae, curante Petro Burmanno, juniore ... Qui Praefationem & Commentarium de Vita Nicolai Heinsii adjecit* (Harlingen, Folkert vander Plaats, 1742). The life of Heinsius occupies pp. 1-56: 'Petri Burmanni junioris historiarum et eloq. in Academia Franequerana professoris ordinarii. De vita viri inlustris, Nicolai Heinsii Dan. Fil. commentarius', with an account of the vicissitudes of the biography on pages 2-3. The poems follow: 'Manes Heinsiani sive Epicedia in obitum Viri Illustris Nicolai Heinsii Dan. Fil.', sigs [†1], †2r − [3†4]v, with Latin verses by Janus Broukhusius, Petrus Francius, Aegidius Menagius ('In mortem Nicolai Heinsii, ad Johannem Georgius Graevium', sigs [2†4]v − 3†1v), Johannes Commirus (also addressed to Grævius), and Fridericus Benedictus Carpzovius.

4 The learned Jesuit Jean Garnier (1612-1681) devoted a great deal of energy to seeking out old manuscripts for the Jesuits' library. He had died in Bologna, on his way to Rome, on 16 October 1681. The Jesuits were notorious for their reluctance to permit their manuscripts to be used by others. Bigot had encountered similar problems in 1659 when attempting to help Heinsius by collating an Ovid manuscript owned by the Jesuits: see Doucette, *Emery Bigot*, p. 123.

5 Jean Hardouin (1646-1729) was born in Quimper, Brittany, so was not really a 'compatriote' of the Norman Bigot. He had been Garnier's assistant as librarian of the Collège Louis-le-Grand, and succeeded him in 1683; he became famous for his brilliant but highly eccentric erudition.

6 Grævius was delighted by Ménage's plan for a new edition of his Diogenes Laertius, and glad to help in having it published in Holland. He wrote to Nicaise on 30 March

1682: 'Gaudeo quoque te celeberrimum Menagium inflammare ad novam Diogenis Laertii editionem adornandam, eamque committendam nostris hominibus' (E. Caillemer (ed.), *Lettres de divers savants à l'abbé Claude Nicaise* (Lyon, 1885), p. 138): on Nicaise see below, letter of 5 July 1682 (Letter 10), note 1.
7 This copy of the *Poésies* must have been sent in July/August 1681.

LETTER 8

Ménage to Grævius. 23 March 1682

A Paris ce 23. Mars *1682*

Monsieur

Je vous demande des nouvelles de vostre santé: dont je suis en peine; y aïant tres long temps que je n'ay reçu de vos lettres. Quand vous m'aurez satisfait là dessus; ce qui est le plus pressé; vous me direz aussi s'il vous plaist, Monsieur, à vostre loisir, en quel estat est[a] vostre Recueuil[b] des Eloges de feu Mr. Heinsius.[1] Et cependant je vous envoye mon Elégie de la derniére révision. Je ne say point toujours si vous avez reçu l'exemplaire de mes Poësies que je vous ay envoyé, il y a si long-temps. Si vous ne l'avez pas reçu, je vous en envoyeray un autre. Mr. Petit attent avec la derniére des impatiences des nouvelles de la publication de son livre.[2] Et j'attans icy demesme[c] apres Pasque nostre ami Mr. Bigot. Je suis toujours, comme je dois, de toute ma passion, & avec toute sorte d'estime & de respect,

Monsieur,
Vostre tres humble & tres
obéissant serviteur
Ménage

[No address]

[a]. est *inserted*.
[b]. Recueuil *sic*.   [c]. demesme *inserted*.

After two more months Ménage has still not had a reply to his two previous letters, and writes with a conventional formula (asking after Grævius's health) to prompt a response. Although short, this note includes many of the elements of Ménage's more developed letters: enquiring after his correspondent's work in progress and sending some of his own, acting as an intermediary for a scholarly friend, and sending news of another.

1 See Letter 7, note 3 above: Grævius's planned 'Recueil des Eloges de Heinsius' was not finally published until 1742, by Pieter Burman the younger.
2 The physician and scholar Pierre Petit (1617?-1687) was impatient because he had been trying to publish his book of philological observations in the Netherlands since

1679. Its history provides a typical example of scholarly co-operation: Petit asked Bigot for help, Bigot wrote to Heinsius about it, Heinsius arranged for the publication, Daniel Elzevir brought most of the work with him when he returned from Paris in October 1679 (see Doucette, *Emery Bigot*, p. 112), and Grævius oversaw the printing. The work was printed in Utrecht: *Petri Petiti, philosophi & doctoris medici, Miscellanearum observationum libri quatuor, nunquam antehac editi* (Utrecht, Rudolph a Zyll, 1682). Petit had been friendly with Ménage since the 1660s, and was a distinguished Latin poet. He rejected the Cartesian philosophy, but, bizarrely, shared the same name as one of its most prominent defenders, the mathematician and 'géographe du roi' Pierre Petit (1594-1677). The latter was appalled by the confusions that arose, and affected an exaggerated contempt for the poet.

LETTER 9

Ménage to Grævius. 7 June 1682

A Paris ce 7. Juin *1682*.

Monsieur

J'ay reçu les deux derniéres lettres, qu'il vous a plu me faire l'honneur de m'écrire: pour lesquelles je vous fais mille tres humbles remercimens. Je suis bien aise que vous vous soyiez enfin déterminé à écrire la Vie de Mr. Heinsius, plustost que son Oraison Funébre. Ses parents vous informeront des particularitez de sa jeunesse. Je lui ay oui dire autrefois, que lorsqu'il commança à composer en Latin, son pere lui défendit la lecture de tous les Auteurs Latins modernes, à la reserve de Muret.[1] Il est arrivé un grand malheur à nostre ami Monsieur Bigot. Il a perdu son frére.[2] Et il a esté obligé ensuite de prendre la tutelle des enfans de son frére[a]: ce qui renverse tout le plan de ses études: & ce qui l'a empesché de venir cette année à Paris. Je lui feray savoir que vous vous estes souvenu de lui. Mr. de Montausier,[3] dont vous me demandez des nouvelles, se porte parfaitement bien. La derniére fois que je le vis, il me dist [fol. 2r] qu'il s'étonnoit que vous ne lui ussiez point écrit sur la mort de Mr. Heinsius. Je vous envoye une lettre de Mr. Petit. Il vous est bien obligé du soin que vous avez pris de l'édition de son livre: & comme il est fort de mes amis, je prans part à l'obligation qu'il vous a. Mr. Hozou[4] partira d'icy dans cinq ou six jours, pour aller en Hollande. Il m'a prié de vous écrire en sa faveur: ce que je ferois tres volontiers; car c'est aussi un de mes amis intimes; s'il avoit besoin de ma recommandation auprês de vous. Mais il n'en a pas[b] besoin: estant tres[c] recommandable par son [p]ropre mérite: & son mérite estant [con]nu[d] de tout le monde. Si l'Elégie que je vous ay adressée sur la mort de Mr. Heinsius, n'est point encore imprimée, aulieu de *Qualia voluebat pulchra Corinna manu*, vous y mettrez, s'il vous plaist, *Qualia versabat*, &c. On imprime enfin à Genêve mes Origines de la Langue Italienne. Aussitost qu'elles seront achevées d'imprimer, je donneray ordre qu'on vous en envoye un exemplaire. Je suis toujours, comme je dois, avec toute l'estime & toute la passion possible,

Monsieur,
Vostre tres humble & tres
obeissant serviteur
Ménage

[Address, fol. 2v: A Monsieur / Monsieur Grævius / A Utrecht]

ª. frére *inserted, replacing* neveu *deleted.*
ᵇ. de *deleted..*
ᶜ. tres *inserted.*
ᵈ. *small hole in page affecting text of* [p]ropre *and* [con]nu.

Ménage has now had two letters from Grævius. This reply provides another varied example of the practical working of the epistolary Republic of Letters. Ménage sends help, in the form of an anecdote about Heinsius; and news, of Bigot's bereavement and subsequent difficulties. He acts as an intermediary for Grævius with Montausier (in which role he can render very important service), with Bigot, and with Petit, whom Grævius in his turn has helped. He writes to recommend a friend who will be visiting the Low Countries; and sends a late revision to his elegy on Heinsius, and news of his own works.

1 Heinsius's father was of course Daniel Heinsius (1580-1665), one of the greatest and most influential scholars of his age. The humanist Marc-Antoine Muret (1526-1585) wrote in a Ciceronian rhetorical style which, like his poetry, was widely admired.
2 After the death of Bigot's brother Nicolas in 1682 he was troubled for the rest of his life by the legal complications that ensued. There is a passage on the subject in the *Ménagiana*: 'M. Bigot étoit Normand, fort honnête homme, & grand ennemi de la chicane & des procès. Après la mort de son frere en 1682, il me dit qu'il lui étoit arrivé le plus grand malheur qui pouvoit jamais lui arriver. C'est, me dit-il, que je suis chargé d'une tutelle très-longue & très-onereuse, qui renverse entierement l'ordre de ma vie. Une autre fois il m'écrivit: *N'y a t-il aucun Auteur qui ait fait quelque livre* de infelicitate Tutorum? *Non,* ajoûtoit-il, *pour en bien écrire, il faudroit être tuteur; & quand on l'est, on n'a pas le loisir de composer. Je pense,*me disoit-il dans une autre lettre, *que si je ne suis bientôt déchargé de ce fardeau, je deviendrai fou, & que j'aurai moi-même besoin de tuteur*' (II, 308-09). See Doucette, *Emery Bigot*, p. 44, with no date for the death (suggestion of 1680); it can definitely be ascribed to 1682.
3 Charles de Sainte-Maure Précigny, duc de Montausier (1610-1690) is a good example of the range of Ménage's influential friends, on whom he could draw so usefully for the benefit of his correspondents. Ménage had been on very friendly terms with Montausier since at least 1640, when both men frequented the salon of the Marquise de Rambouillet; Ménage contributed prominently to the famous poetic *Guirlande de Julie* that Montausier elaborated for the Marquise's daughter, Julie d'Angennes (whom he married in 1645). Despite his somewhat rebarbative temperament Montausier was celebrated for his absolute integrity; he was generally believed to be a model for Molière's Misanthrope. He had a genuine respect for men of learning, and remained on excellent

terms with Ménage as his power and authority increased: Gouverneur de Normandie from 1663, created Duc et Pair in 1664, Gouverneur du Dauphin in 1665.

4 As is clear from subsequent letters, Hozou in fact went to England first instead. Hozou, or Ozou, was admired for his learning although he seems to have left no publications. The formidable Abbé de Longuerue named him, with characteristic hyperbole, as one of three outstanding scholars who had not been rewarded as they deserved – all three, curiously, being particular friends of Ménage: 'Pendant que le Roi faisoit des libéralités aux Sçavans des pays étrangers, nous avons vu à la honte du Roi, de M. Colbert, et de son Abbé Gallois, trois Sçavans du premier ordre mourir de faim. Bouillaud très-sçavant en toutes les parties des Mathématiques et Belles-Lettres: Ozou, et le malheureux le Févre de Saumur, qui vivoit de quelques douzaines de pistoles que lui envoyoit secrétement tantôt l'un, tantôt l'autre' (*Longueruana, ou recueil de pensées, de discours et de conversations, de feu M. Louis du Four de Longuerue*, 2 vols (Berlin, 1754), II, 95-96).

LETTER 10

Ménage to Grævius. 5 July 1682

A Paris ce 5. Juillet *1682*

Monsieur

Voicy deux lettres que je vous envoie: l'une, de Mr. Nicaise,[1] par laquelle il vous offre les nouvelles Observations de Mr. de Saumaise sur Pline:[2] & l'autre de Mr. Petit, par laquelle il vous remercie du soin que vous avez pris de l'édition de son livre. Mr. Hosou est allé directement en Angleterre. Il passera de là en Hollande, où il ne manquera pas d'avoir l'honneur de vous voir. Mr. Bigot est toujours à Rouen, où il n'a pas peu d'affaires au sujet de la curatelle de son neveu. Je suis toujours à l'ordinaire, cesta-dire avec toute la passion imaginable,

Monsieur,
Vostre tres humble &
tres obeissant serviteur
Ménage

[No address]

A short covering note enclosing two letters, from Nicaise and Petit, with a brief update of news about Hozou and Bigot.

1 Claude Nicaise (1623-1701) lived in Dijon, where he had been a canon of the Sainte-Chapelle. He industriously maintained an extremely extensive correspondence. Ménage was on very friendly terms with him, and often helped by passing on books and letters to and from his correspondents abroad. Ménage mentioned Nicaise's letter

for Grævius in a letter to Nicaise of 15 June 1682: 'Je ne manqueray pas de faire tenir vostre lettre à Mr. Grævius. Je ne doute point qu'il n'accepte avec joye le parti que vous lui proposez touchant cet ouvrage de Mr. de Saumaise' (Universitätsbibliothek Basel, Autograph-Sammlung, Geigy-Hagenbach Nr. 1374; printed in full by Gilles Banderier, 'Une lettre inédite de Gilles Ménage', *French Studies Bulletin*, no. 87 (Summer 2003), 11-13; see also Richard Maber, 'Ménage, Nicaise, and Madame de La Fayette: the evidence of a newly-discovered letter', *French Studies Bulletin*, no. 91 (Summer 2004), 15-17). Nicaise was in Paris from 1685 to 1692; hence while Ménage several times acts as an intermediary between him and Grævius up to and including his letter of 22 June 1685 (Letter 26), in a later letter (9 January 1690, Letter 47) he is able to show Nicaise Grævius's latest letter personally.

2 Claude de Saumaise (1588-1653) first published his great work on Pliny, *Plinianæ exercitationes in Caii Julii Solini Polyhistora*, in 1629 (Paris, C. Morell), in two folio volumes.

Ménage to Grævius. 2 August 1682

A Paris ce 2. Aoust *1682*

Monsieur

J'ay fait tenir vostre lettre à Mr. Huet: Et je vous envoye sa réponse.[1] Je pense vous avoir mandé, que Mr. Hozou, qui devoit aller en Hollande, & de là en Angleterre, est allé premiérement en Angleterre. Je prendray, comme je vous l'ay déja dit, toute sorte de part dans toutes les obligations qu'il vous aura. Monsieur Goyer m'a visité de vostre part. S'il avoit besoin de recommendation auprês de moy, il ne pourroit en avoir de meilleure que la vostre: mais il n'en a pas[a] besoin; estant tres recommendable par lui mesme. Je lui ay[b] fait offre de tout ce qui dépendoit de moy: Et je croy qu'il est satisfait de moy. Il m'a dit que vous travalliez toujours à vostre Columelle: ce qui me fait souvenir de vous faire part de cette épigramme de Théodore de Béze sur Columelle:

Orphea mirata est Rhodope, sua fata canentem,
    Si modò Virgilii carmina pondus habent.
[fol. 2r]   Tu verò, JUNI, silvestria rura canendo,
    Post te, ipsas urbes in tua rura trahis.
Ô Superi! quales habuit tunc Roma Quirites,
    Cùm tam facundum cerneret agricolam?[2]

Cette epigramme peut estre employée dans vostre Préface. Mr. Bigot est toujours à Rouan; où il plaide contre sa belle-soeur, en qualité de Tuteur des enfans de cette belle-soeur. Aimez moi toujours, je vous en conjure: Et ne doutez point que je ne sois toujours comme je^c dois, avec toute l'estime & toute la vénération possible,

Monsieur,
Vostre tres humble &
tres obéissant serviteur
Ménage

Monsieur Petit vous fait mille
tres-humbles baisemains.

[No address]

^{a}. de *deleted*.　^{b}. témoigné *deleted*.　^{c}. je *inserted*.

Ménage is now acting as intermediary between Grævius and Huet, passing on letters each way. This letter also features reciprocal recommendations: Ménage renews his commendation of Hozou, and reports on the visit of M. Goyer, whom Grævius had recommended to him. He also sends scholarly help, in an epigram by de Bèze that might be useful for Grævius's edition of Columella; and news of Bigot's family problems.

1 Ménage had forwarded Grævius's letter to Huet on 12 July. He wrote: 'Je vous envoye une lettre de Mr. Grævius. Par la derniére qu'il m'a écrite, il me mande qu'il fait imprimer le Catalogue des livres de Mr. Heinsius. On a imprimé en Hollande les Miscellanea de Monsieur Petit: et on les débite présentement à Paris' (BML, Florence, MS Ashburnham 1866. 1261; reprinted Pennarola (ed.), no. 182, p. 233). Huet replied on 17 July, incidentally explaining why he had not written verses on Heinsius's death: 'Je vous supplie de faire tenir ma response à M. Grævius / Je me suis excusé par une lettre précédente de ce que je n'ay point fait des vers sur la mort de M. Heinsius / Il n'eut jamais de poëte plus bizarre que moy / Je ne fais pas des vers quand je veux et j'en fais quelque fois sans le vouloir. / Cela dépend de la verve / Ainsi je ne fais point de vers de recommande ...' (BN, Paris, n.a.f. 1341, fols 232-33).
2 Ménage had already commented on Grævius's projected edition of Columella in his first letter (19 May 1679) and that of 14 November 1680 (Letter 5). Bèze's epigram is 'In L. Iunii Columellae libros De re rustica, elegantissimè scriptos'; it is sometimes found with the variant penultimate line 'Vah, quales, quantosque habuit tunc Roma Quirites' (e.g. *Theodori Bezae Vezelii poemata varia. Sylvæ. Elegiæ. Epitaphia. Epigrammata. Icones. Emblemata. Cato Censorius. Omnia ab ipso auctore in unum nunc Corpus collecta & recognita* (Hanover, Guilielmus Antonius, 1598, p. 163)).

Ménage to Grævius. 14 August 1682

A Paris ce 14. Aoust *1682.*

Monsieur

C'est pour vous recommander Monsieur Boylesve,[1] qui vous rendra cette lettre de ma part; & pour vous le recommander de toute ma passion: estant une personne pour qui j'aime*[a]* beaucoup d'estime & d'amitié. Il me reste à vous demander pour moy la continuation de vostre bienveillance, & à vous assurer que je seray toute ma vie avec toute la reconnoissance possible, & avec toute l'admiration & toute la vénération que vous méritez,

Monsieur,
Vostre tres humble &
tres obéissant serviteur
Ménage

[No address]

[a]. j'aime *sic, for* j'ai.

Only twelve days after the previous letter; Ménage sends a short note of recommendation for M. Boylesve, a typical example of the introductions to useful contacts with which travelling scholars would equip themselves.

1 Presumably a member of the distinguished Angers family of lawyers and theologians of that name, whose earlier generations had included Charles Boylesve, bishop of Avranches (1595-1667), his brother Claude (born Angers 1611), the sixteenth-century lawyer François Boylesve, and his son Marin (died 1669), Lieutenant-Général en Anjou, a famous jurist and also a poet. In the *Ménagiana*, I, 286, there is a reference to 'M. de Boiléve' as a benefactor of Polycarpe Sengebere, Ménage's mentor in law, in Angers.

Ménage to Grævius. 31 May 1683

A Paris ce lundi 31. May *1683.*

Monsieur

Vous m'avez tres sensiblement obligé d'obliger Mr. Vestein[1] a*[a]* imprimer mon Diogéne: & il m'obligera demesme s'il l'imprime correctement. Sur l'assurance qu'il m'en a donnée, je le lui envoieray sans faute à la quinzaine. Mes Origines de la Langue Ita-

62

lienne sont achevées d'imprimer. Mais j'y ay*b* ajouté l'explication de plusieurs façons de parler proverbiales, qui n'est pas achevée d'imprimer.² Quand le livre sera en estat de paroistre, je ne manqueray pas de vous en faire part. Pour mon Histoire de Sablé, elle n'est pas encore en estat de paroistre. Les Remarques du Père Vavasseur sur la Langue Latine, sont publiques, il y a déja quelques mois.³ Mr. Petit vous a envoyé une demie-douzaine d'exemplaires de ses Poësies.⁴ Mr. Bigot est encore à Rouen: mais je l'attans icy au premier jour. [fol. 2r] J'apprans avec bien de la joye qu'on imprime à Leyden le Catulle de Mr. Vossius.⁵ Et j'attans avec la plus grande impatience du monde vostre Vie de Mr. Heinsius. Mr. Petit a reçu l'exemplaire des Poësies de Mr. Francius que vous lui avez envoyé.⁶ Mais vous, Monsieur, n'avez vous pas reçu les Inscriptions de Mr. Spon,⁷ que je mis, il y a cinq ou six mois, entre les mains d'un de vos Compatriotes, pour vous les faire tenir?⁸ Voicy un billet que m'a écrit Mr. Nublé,⁹ Avocat au Parlement de Paris, touchant un passage des Offices de Cicéron: dont vous me direz, s'il vous plaist vostre avis, à vostre loisir.

A faute d'avoir quelque chose de plus nouveau & de plus important à m'entretenir avec vous, je vous diray, Monsieur, qu'en fesant réflexion sur l'endroit du 3. livre des Offices de Cicéron, où il traite le plus chretiennement du monde du coup d'ami: cestadire, de ce que la consciance d'un Juge lui permet,*c* de faire en cette qualité en faveur de son ami; je m'estois imaginé qu'il n'estoit pas bien correct: *Et ut orandæ liti, quod per leges liceat, accommodet:* & qu'il valoit mieux lire, *Et ut ordinandæ liti,* &c. Car on dit en Latin *orare causam. Orabunt causas meliùs.*¹⁰ [fol. 1v, sideways] *Orare litem,* aucontraire, m'estoit, & m'est encore fort suspect. Mais ce qui m'aide beaucoup à me confirmer dans ma conjecture; c'est ce passage du 2. livre de Cicéron de Oratore, *Ea mihi videntur, aut in lite ordinanda, aut in consilio dando esse posita.*ᵈ

Quand vous écrirez à Mr. Francius, vous m'obligerez de le bien assurer de mon service & de mon estime. J'ay ses Poësies*e* avec admiration. Je suis toujours, comme je dois, avec toute la vénération possible,

Monsieur,
Vostre tres humble & tres
obéissant serviteur
Ménage

[Address, fol. 2v: A Monsieur / Monsieur Grævius / A Utrect]

a. a *sic, for* à.   *b*. ay *inserted.*   *c*. en *deleted.*
d. *The extract from Nublé's letter is not indented in the original, but separated from the rest of Ménage's letter by spaces before and after the quoted text.*
e. J'ay ses Poësies *sic,* lu *omitted.*

This letter marks the beginning of Ménage's relations with the printer Henrik Wetstein and the innumerable vicissitudes that ensued before the eventual publication of his edition of Diogenes Laertius in 1692. In return for Grævius's help in finding a printer, Ménage sends a great many items of scholarly information about his own and others' works, including an extract from a letter from Nublé proposing a textual emendation to Cicero.

1 On Wetstein see Introduction. Ménage had considered several possible printers for his work: in his letter of 14 November 1680 (Letter 5) he mentions the Boom brothers, while Wetstein's first letter, of 25 October 1683 (Letter 14), suggests that Blaeu and Elzevir had also been approached.

2 It was in fact to be another two years before the Geneva edition of the *Le Origini della lingua italiana* was finally published.

3 *Observationes de vi et usu quorumdam verborum cum simplicium tum conjunctorum,* by the Jesuit François Vavasseur (1605-1681), were published posthumously with his *Poemata* by his colleague Père Lucas (Paris, Veuve C. Thiboust and P. Esclassan, 1683).

4 *Petri Petiti philosophi et doctoris medici, selectorum poematum libri duo: accessit dissertatio de furore poetico* (Paris, Jean Cusson, 1683).

5 This news seems not to have come from Grævius, but from England. In December 1682 Ménage was visited by an English scholar ('Mr. Arnod'), bearing a letter of recommendation from Vossius, who lived in London. He wrote to Vossius on 24 December 1682: 'J'ay appris de luy avec bien de la joye, qu'on imprimoit en Hollande vostre Catulle. C'est un livre que j'attens avec bien de l'impatience estant persuadé que je le liray avec un extreme plaisir' (UB Leiden, MSS Burm. F.11.II, fol. 293v). Ménage passed the news on to Huet: 'Mr. Grævius m'a envoié un exemplaire du Catalogue de la Bibliothéque de Mr. Heinsius. On imprime en Hollande in 4 le Catulle de Mr. Vossius' (BML, Florence, MS Ashburnham 1866. 1312; reprinted Pennarola (ed.), no. 185, p. 235. Pennarola dates this letter '[1682-83]'; it can thus be more precisely dated December 1682-January 1683). The edition of Catullus by Isaac Vossius (1618-1689) was started in Leiden, but eventually issued in England with a new title-page: *Caius Valerius Catullus et in eum Isaaci Vossii observationes* (Leiden, D. à Gaesbeeck, 1684 / London, Isaac Littlebury, 1684). It was enthusiastically received; see for example Bayle's review in the *Nouvelles de la République des Lettres,* June 1684 (reprinted in Bayle, *Œuvres diverses,* 4 vols (La Haye, P. Husson *et al.,* 1727), I, 67-69). According to Bayle, Vossius had prepared this edition more than thirty years before finally printing it, which explains Ménage's impatience and delight. The review also lays emphasis on the diversity of fascinating information contained in the annotations, which again might account for Ménage's anticipation of reading it. One might also mention that, again according to Bayle, the publishing of the work was moved to England because of a controversy in Holland about 'beaucoup de choses impures' that it was (erroneously) believed to contain.

6 Petrus Francius (1645-1704) was one of the most celebrated Latin poets of the later seventeenth century. On an earlier visit to France he had been made Doctor of Law at Angers. The 'estime' and 'admiration' that Ménage expresses at the end of this letter were no doubt reinforced by the fact that Francius had written a poem in his praise. In an undated letter to Huet, Ménage wrote: 'Je ne pus hier faire réponse à vostre billet dans le tans qu'il me fut rendu, estant occupé à écrire à un Mr. Francius, Professeur d'Amstredam, qui m'avoit envoyé une belle Elegie Latine qu'il a faite à ma louange' (BML, Florence, MS Ashburnham 1866. 1386; reprinted Pennarola (ed.), no. 186, p. 236, provisionally dated '[1682-83]'). In return, the following year Ménage wrote a Greek 'Idylle' dedicated to Francius. Francius and Wetstein were friends, and Wetstein

often passes on messages and greetings from the poet. See also Wetstein's letter of 27 January 1684 (Letter 15), note 4.

7 The Lyonnais doctor and antiquarian Jacob Spon (1647-1685) had travelled extensively in the Levant collecting ancient inscriptions. He used these as the basis for two important works, *Recherches curieuses d'antiquité contenues en plusieurs dissertations sur des médailles, bas-reliefs, statues, mosaïques & inscriptions antiques* (Lyon, Thomas Amaulry, 1683); and *Miscellanea eruditae antiquitatis* (Lyon, frères Huguetan, 1685).

8 It appears from this comment as though at least one communication from Ménage to Grævius has been lost, dating from December 1682/January 1683; although it is possible that his present of Spon's work was not accompanied by a letter.

9 The lawyer Louis Nublé was one of Ménage's small circle of most intimate and long-standing friends: it was to Nublé that he dedicated his *Juris civilis amœnitates* in 1664. As early as the 1640s, when Nublé spent long periods in Grenoble and later Amboise, Ménage wrote to him at least once a week (see the collection in the Österreichische Nationalbibliothek, Vienna, MS 7049). There are numerous anecdotes involving Nublé in the *Ménagiana*, characteristically praising his learning (II, 348), critical acuity (II, 198-99), honesty and generosity (II, 198-99, helping Scarron), and integrity (II, 326-7: 'M. Godeau, le P. Sirmond, M. Nublé & M. Bigot étoient des hommes de l'ancienne vertu. J'estimois encore plus leur probité que leur science, quelque vaste qu'elle fût').

10 Virgil, *Aeneid*, VI, 849.

LETTER 14

Wetstein to Ménage. 25 October 1683

d'Amsterdam ce 25e. d'Octobre *1683*.

Monsieur

Pendant que je fus en Allemagne travailler à ma santé, mes gens Vous ont donné advis de la reception de Votre Diogene Laerce, des feüilles qui y manquent à Vos observations, & de la cause pourquoi je ne l'ai pas receu plustot. Car non seulement que le ballot de Mr. Horthemels[1] n'est pas venu à son maitre, mais aussi le pacquet du Diogene ne portoit aucune adresse, autrement je l'aurois eu aussi-tot que le ballot a esté au païs. Mais tout est bien, puis qu'il n'y a rien de perdu. Je suis de retour depuis quatre jours, & la premiere chose que je fis à mon arrivée ce fut de voir votre livre, que j'espere de faire bien plus beau & en meilleur ordre qu'il n'est presentement, & ne crains pas de dire que Vous trouverez n'avoir rien perdu en ce qu'il n'aura pas été imprimé par Mrs Blau ou Elsevier.[2]

Mon premier soin c'est de trouver un homme capable & de loisir pour revoir le texte & les notes des autres, car pour les Votres elles sont en fort bon ordre & bien corrigées. J'ai la pensée de mettre toutes les notes ensemble au bas du texte, comme nous faisons en nos Variorums; ce qui à mon advis aura bien plus de grace que tous ces renvois. Je croi qu'en*[a]* cela Vous serez de mon goust, car sans Votre approbation je n'y veux rien changer. De plus s'il y avoit des portraits veritables et antiques de ces philosophes dont Laërce décrit les vies, je les y joindrois en taille-douce, ce qui embelliroit encore l'ouvrage.

Je serai bien aise d'avoir le plus-tot que je pourrai le reste de Votre copie,[3] & si Vous savez moyen de la faire tenir seurement à Bruxelles entre les mains de Mr. Foppens[4] je suis seur de l'avoir sans faute. J'attendrai sur tout cela un mot de reponse s'il Vous plait. Vous priant cependant de me conserver l'honneur de Vos bonnes graces, & demeurant

Monsieur
Votre tres humble & tres obeissant serviteur
H Wetstein

[No address]

[a]. small illegible deletion following qu'en.

Henrik Wetstein's first surviving letter to Ménage. According to his previous letter to Grævius, Ménage must have sent the text of his Diogenes Laërtius in early June, at least four months earlier. This letter already establishes most of the main themes of the Wetstein-Ménage correspondence over the next eight and a half years, which is dominated by the projected edition. These are: Wetstein's apologies and concern about delays, which have extremely varied causes; difficulties of communication between Paris and Amsterdam, particularly in sending packages; the problem of finding a local scholar to correct the text and apparatus; the arrangement and appearance of the edition; and the planned series of illustrations of portraits of philosophers.

1 Gillis Horthemels was a printer in Middelburg; this refers either to Gillis I (active 1666-1689) or Gillis II (active 1682-1692). The connection with Paris is presumably through the Parisian printer Daniel Horthemels (who was to print Huet's *Censura philosophiæ cartesianæ* in 1689). There is a joke involving the Horthemels' 'enseigne' of a bust of Virgil in the *Ménagiana*, II, 339.

2 Negotiations had clearly gone some way with other printers before Grævius approached Wetstein. In his letter to Huet of 9 September 1681, Ménage mentions that '[Heinsius] me mande que les Imprimeurs d'Amstredam se sont enfin resolus d'imprimer mon Diogéne Laërce: mais en trois volumes in 8°' (BML, Florence, MS Ashburnham 1866. 1260; reprinted Pennarola (ed.), no. 180, p. 231). As is clear from the later correspondence with Wetstein, Ménage was extremely unwilling to have his work printed in this smaller format. In naming 'Mrs Blau ou Elsevier' as the two printers whom he aims to surpass, Wetstein is singling out the two outstanding publishers of classical texts in the 17th-century Netherlands. The Blaeu (or Blaeuw) publishing dynasty had been continued after the death of the great cartographer Dr Joan Blaeu (1598-1673) by his three sons, Willem, Pieter, and Joan II. Until a catastrophic fire in 1672 it was 'the largest printing house in Europe, and effectively the largest in the World' (John Goss, Introduction to J. Goss (ed.), *Blaeu's The Grand Atlas of the 17th Century World* (London, Royal Geographical Society, 1990), p. 12.

3 With printing now apparently about to get started, Ménage devoted his energies to
this work. When Nublé wrote to Ménage from Amboise on 28 December 1683, he
began the letter: 'Tandis que j'ai vu, Monsieur, que vous estiés occupé a votre Diogene
Laërce, j'aurois fait grand scrupule de vous interrompre …' (BN, Paris, n.a.f. 17270, fol.
73). It is ironic, and all the more galling for the French scholar, that in his next letter at
the end of January (as in so many subsequent ones) Wetstein reported no progress
whatever with the printing.
4 The Brussels printer Foppens was habitually used by Wetstein as an intermediary
between France and the Low Countries.

LETTER 14A

Ménage to Toinard. 11 December 1683

A Paris ce xi. Dec. *1683*

Monsieur

Wetstein, Libraire d'Amstredam, qui rimprime mon Diogéne Laërce, vient de m'écrire
au sujet de vostre Harmonie des quatre Evangélistes,[1] les paroles suivantes: *Il y a passé*
deux ans, que j'eus une lettre de M. Toinard, que vous connoissez sans doute. Je lui avois écrit*
au sujet de la belle Harmonie Grecque qu'il a faite des quatre Evangélistes: ce qui, à mon avis, est
un ouvrage incomparable. J'en ay quelques cahiers. J'en suis si charmé, que je donnerois dix pis-
toles pour un exemplaire complet: & cela, pour mon seul usage. Je lui ay parlé de le faire imprimer
icy: & il ne restoit qu'à la satisfaction qu'il auroit pour les frais, & pour un voyage qu'il devoit
faire pour cela en ces quartiers. Je l'ay prié de me spécifier une somme, & que je lui répondrois
promptement & positivement ce que je pourrois faire: & mesme je croy que j'aurois trouvé un
expédiant [fol. 2r] *dont il auroit esté satisfait: mais il ne m'a jamais répondu là dessus: ce que*
pourtant j'aurois bien souhaitté qu'il ust fait: car j'ay grande inclination pour cet ouvrage: &
j'emploirois toute chose pour en venir à bout. Vous me ferez grand plaisir, Monsieur, si vous vou-
lez bien avoir la bonté de m'aider en cette affaire. Je vous supplie, Monsieur, de me faire
savoir là dessus vostre volonté. Et je vous diray cependant, que ce Libraire est un tres
honneste homme & tres intelligent dans son mestier. Je vous demande toujours la continuation de vostre amitié: en vous assurant que de mon costé je seray toute ma vie de
toute ma passion, & avec toute sorte d'estime & de respect,

Monsieur,
Vostre tres humble &
tres obéïssant serviteur
Ménage

[No address]

Following his letter of 25 October, Wetstein must have written again around the end of November or beginning of December 1683. The letter from Wetstein has been lost, but Ménage transcribed a substantial portion of it in this letter to Nicolas Toinard of 11 December, now in Princeton University Library, John Wild Autograph Collection, V, 142. Wetstein asks Ménage to act as intermediary in procuring Toinard's current major work in progress for him to publish. Ménage's approach was successful in stimulating a response from the dilatory scholar, as is clear from Wetstein's next letter.

1 The scholar and numismatist Nicolas Toinard (or Thoynard) (1629-1706) had numerous projects for publication, many of which never reached fruition. He is best known for this work, his posthumously-published *Evangeliorum harmonia Graeco-Latina* (Paris, Cramoisy, 1707), which he was already working on in the early 1680s. Wetstein found him exasperatingly slow and elusive to deal with (see his letter of 18 April 1689 (Letter 43), and especially his last letter to Ménage, 8 May 1692), and he was not alone. Toinard held on for years to precious books that Bigot had lent him without publishing or returning them, even when directly asked to so that Du Cange could publish the work concerned, the *Chronicon Paschale* (see Doucette, *Emery Bigot*, pp. 110-11 and pp. 171-73, reprinting letters from Bigot to Du Cange, 28 April 1684, and Toinard to Du Cange, 16 May 1684).

LETTER 15

Wetstein to Ménage. 27 January 1684

d'Amsterdam ce 27e. de Janvier 1684.

Monsieur

Le froid est si excessiv en ces quartiers, qu'on ne songe qu'à se chauffer, sans faire aucunes affaires, tout estant glacé, & l'ancre autant que le reste. C'est ce qui a retardé la reponse que je devois à Vos lettres du 5e & 17. du passé. D'ailleurs je voulois Vous envoyer une epreuve du Diogene, pour Vous faire voir qu'il estoit fort aisé de mettre toutes les notes au dessous du texte sans en interrompre aucunement la suitte. Mais ce froid empeche tout & on ne sauroit rien faire aux imprimeries. Quand nous serons un peu mieux, & que j'aurai le reste de la copie j'examinerai le tout avec soin, & Vous en parlerai alors plus precisement. Car il est incontestable que si l'affaire estoit faisable cela seroit beaucoup mieux. Nous verrons.

Il y en a d'autres qui me rompent la téte d'imprimer le livre in 8°. comme sont faits tous nos Variorums, & de mettre le texte dans un volume & les notes dans un autre; mais je n'ai pas grande inclination[a] pour cela; bien que peut etre j'y trouverois mieux mon compte.

Les portraits embelliront fort l'ouvrage, & nous en trouverons, je croy, bien plus que ceux dont Vous faites mention. Car s'il n'y en avoit que 20 de 86 cela ne vaudroit pas la peine, & rendroit l'ouvrage plus ridicule qu'il ne l'embelliroit. Il me semble qu'il nous faudroit pour le moins la moitié.[1]

Je ne sai s'il sera expedient de hazarder Votre copie par les chemins, à present que les trouppes de France font tant de desordres aux païs-bas; & je doute fort si on epargneroit le voiturier de Bruxelles, en cas qu'il fut rencontré, soit des françois, soit des espagnols.[2]

Je Vous suis infiniment obligé de m'avoir procuré une lettre de Mr. Toinard, car sur ce que lui avez mandé de moi, il m'a écrit & parlé de son livre.[3]

J'ai oublié de Vous dire, qu'on sçaura bien à Paris si le voiturier de Brusselles pourra passer seurement ou non? En tout cas j'en ai ecrit à Mr. Foppens, qui aura soin pour tout ce qui lui sera adressé pour moi, & me l'enverra fidellement.

Tous mes soins sont pour un bon correcteur: si j'y pouvois vaquer je n'en serois pas fort en peine;[4] mais je suis assez accablé d'affaires d'autre part. Je finis en me recommandant à l'honneur de Vos bonnes graces & demeurant

Monsieur

Votre tres humble & tres obeissant serviteur

H Wetstein

Monsr. Francius Vous baise tres humblement les mains.
Il m'a dit qu'il Vous ecriroit au premier jour.

[No address]

^a. s *deleted at the end of* inclination.

Ménage has written twice to Wetstein in December, and the printer gives a new excuse for his delay in sending a sample proof: it is too cold, and the ink is frozen. Wetstein's concerns are, again, the arrangement and format of the text, the illustrations, difficulties of communication (greatly exacerbated by the state of war between their two countries), and problems of finding a 'bon correcteur'. However at the same time, in the tradition of the Republic of Letters, Wetstein and Ménage engage in mutual assistance through their respective contacts, as they are to do throughout their correspondence. Here, Wetstein thanks Ménage for his help with Toinard, and hinself transmits greetings to Ménage from the poet Petrus Francius.

1 The question of finding portraits of philosophers became increasingly urgent as the work neared completion. When it finally appeared, the edition was illustrated with 25 portraits: see Wetstein's letter of 26 July 1691 (Letter 57), note 4.
2 During the War of the Reunions (1683-84) the French and Spanish armies along the borders of the Spanish Netherlands engaged in increasingly violent acts of escalating reprisals. By February 1684, under direct orders from Louis and Louvois, the French army had embarked on a campaign of destruction that was seen as excessively brutal even for the time.
3 The satisfactory result of Ménage's letter to Toinard of 11 December, printed above.

4 Wetstein undoubtedly had the scholarly ability, if not the time, to correct the text himself. He was eventually to write both the dedicatory epistle and the preface for the completed work; see his letter of 6 March 1692 (Letter 69). Wetstein's comments gave Ménage the idea of asking Francius to take on the task. In a note to Huet of 25 February 1684, in which he asked his friend to look over the Greek 'Idylle' that he had written for Francius, Ménage explained his ulterior motives: 'Il y a un Professeur à Amstredam qui s'appelle Mr. Francius, qui est sans contestation le premier Poëte de toute la Hollande. Ce Mr. Francius m'envoya il y a quelque tans le Recueil de ses Poësies, avec une belle & grande Elégie Latine qu'il avoit faite à ma louange, Je me suis trouvé obligé par reconnoissance de faire aussi des vers pour lui. Et d'un autre costé, j'ay interest de lui plaire; aïant dessein de le prier de corriger les épreuves de mon Diogéne Laërce qu'on rimprime à Amstredam. Et comme il se pique d'Eglogue & de vers Grecs, je luy ay adressé un Idylle Grec. Je vous envoye cet Idylle. Je vous prie de le lire soigneusement, & de me le corriger le plus exactement que vous pourrez, & de m'envoyer vos corrections aussitost que vous les aurez faites' (BML, Florence, MS Ashburnham 1866. 1264; reprinted Pennarola (ed.), no. 187, p. 236).

LETTER 16

Wetstein to Ménage. 19 May 1684

d'Amsterdam ce ce^a 19e. de May *1684.*

Monsieur

Je Vous asseure que j'ai appris avec un extreme regret la nouvelle de Votre indisposition. Se demettre la cuisse à l'age de soixante ans ou environ, ne peut etre que douloureux, & d'assez longue haleine pour etre gueri.[1] En verité j'en suis fort faché, & voudrois de bon cœur pouvoir contribuer quelque chose à Votre retablissement, que je prie le bon Dieu de vous donner bien-tot.

Je ne suis pas encore assez heureux pour Vous pouvoir donner des nouvelles de notre Diogene, qui fussent à Votre satisfaction, & à la^b mienne. Je cherche un bon correcteur, & m'en trouve assez en peine; m'etant impossible (accablé que je suis d'affaires:) de m'en mesler; & quand je pourrai lire la derniere épreuve, ce sera aller au bout de la terre. Outre cela nous n'avons pas ici du papier presentement qui soit propre pour cela; mais à cela il y auroit du remede, & on en peut faire faire. Il y a bien une autre affaire qui me touche de plus prés: c'est que m'ayant conseillé de bonne foi avec Mr. Scott Libraire de Londres[2] pour cette edition du Diogene, je viens de recevoir sa reponse qui me fait un peu rever. C'est qu'il dit que feu Mr. Pulleyn ayant imprimé ledit livre,[3] qui se trouvoit privilegié & enregistré sur le Livre de leur Communeauté de Londres, & luy (Scott) ayant acheté de depuis de la veuve dudit Pulleyn le droit dudit livre, il m'en empecheroit le debit en Angleterre & comme au reste il ne s'explique pas fort avantageusement, cela me fait soupçonner que (: selon la bonne coutume des Anglois qui ne cherchent qu'à attraper tout ce qu'ils peuvent d'un etranger) comme j'ai beaucoup d'effets en Angleterre & que mon principal negoce y est, il ne tache de se prevaloir la dessus, du pretendu tort que je lui ferois. Ainsi il sera necessaire de m'accommoder avec lui, ou au moins de tacher de faire en sorte qu'il ne me puisse faire du mal. Veritablement si j'eusse sçû qu'il y eut quelqu'un au monde qui auroit à pretendre sur cette copie, ou qui s'en [fol. 1v] attribuast le droit, je n'y aurois pas voulu m'y engager; car je ne veux point de dispute avec qui que ce soit; mais comme je croyois Pulleyn & tous les siens mort & ensevely je ne me figurois aucunement, que quelqu'autre se resusciteroit pour [y]^c pretendre. Baste, il faut tacher d'y remedier; mais aussi s'il fait monter ses pretensions plus haut qu'à la discretion, il faudra voir comment faire alors.

A tout hazard je m'en vai^d travailler à une epreuve, & je tacherai d'accommoder [les]^e remarques en telle sorte que Vous en soyez satisfait. A mon advis il faudra ou tout sous le texte ou rien. Voici la lettre que Monsr. Francius vient d'apporter chez moi, & qu'il me charge de fermer, ainsi je mets la mienne dans son pacquet, & Vous asseure que je suis avec beaucoup de respect

Monsieur
Votre tres humble & tres
obeissant serviteur
H Wetstein

[No address]

^{a}. ce ce *sic.*
^{b}. *small deletion following* la.
^{c}. *[y] lost at the end of the line.*
^{d}. s *deleted at the end of* vai.
^{e}. *[les] lost at the end of the line [?].*

After nearly four months Wetstein is still finding excuses for not having started on the Diogenes. He has still not found a 'bon correcteur'; but he has also run out of suitable paper, and faces a legal challenge from London over the rights to print the work. In the course of the letter Wetstein attacks English commercial rapaciousness, but also notes that England provides his principal market as a Dutch printer. However he begins and ends on a personal note, commiserating with Ménage on his recent accident, and sending another letter from Francius.

1 Wetstein has considerably underestimated Ménage's age; he was in fact nearly 71. This letter and the following one enable Ménage's accident to be dated precisely to Good Friday, April 1684; hitherto its year has been uncertain. The *Ménagiana* says simply: 'M. Ménage étant à genoux à Notre-Dame un Vendredi saint à Ténebres, se démit la cuisse en voulant se relever' (I, 161). Pennarola (ed., pp. 30, 427 n. 1) dates it to 1685, with 1684 as a possibility; although on 20 July 1684 Ménage wrote to Huet that he was in good health, 'à la reserve de ma cuisse blessée, où je souffre toujours beaucoup de douleur, et où je n'ay toujours point de mouvement.' (BML, Florence, MS Ashburnham 1866. 1265; reprinted Pennarola (ed.), no 192, p. 238). The confirmation of

the date means that Madame de La Fayette's letter expressing her concern can also be dated to the period following April 1684: 'Je vous conjure de m'aprendre en quel estat vous estes, si vous souffres toujours des douleurs, et si vous estes sans [esperance] de marcher' (BN, Paris, n.a.f. 18248. 1, fol. 1r-v, dated '[en 1685]' in a different hand; printed in *Lettres de Madame de La Fayette et de Gilles Ménage*, ed. H. Ashton (London, 1924), pp. 137-8 (dated '[1685?]'), Mme de La Fayette, *Correspondance*, ed. A. Beaunier, 2 vols (Paris, 1942), II, 119-20 (dated '[juin ou juillet 1684]'), and *Œuvres complètes*, ed. R. Duchêne (Paris, 1990), p. 642 (dated '[début 1684]'; see also n.1, p. 710, 'peut-être le vendredi saint').

2 Robert Scott (c1633-1706?) was one of the leading English publishers and booksellers of the second half of the century. On his career see Leona Rostenberg, *Literary, Political, Scientific, Religious and Legal Publishing, Printing and Bookselling in England, 1551-1700: Twelve Studies*, 2 vols (New York, 1965), II, 281-313: 'The Liberal Arts: Robert Scott, importer and university agent'. Scott dealt extensively with the Continent, including with Wetstein (p. 308). Against Wetstein's complaints may be set Rostenberg's comment: 'Scott was regarded by his contemporaries as "the greatest librarian in Europe, an expert bookseller and a conscientious good man, the only person of his time for his extraordinary knowledge in books"' (p. 282; quotation not attributed).

3 Octavian Pulleyn the elder and the younger, London booksellers and publishers, were active 1636-1667, and had published the first edition of Ménage's Diogenes Laertius in 1664. Octavian Pulleyn the younger had been a client of Robert Scott (see Rostenberg, II, 318).

LETTER 17

Ménage to Grævius. 2 June 1684

A Paris ce vendredi 2. Juin. *1684.*

Monsieur

J'ay grand sujet de me plaindre de vostre Monsieur Wetstein. Depuis que je luy ay envoyé mon Diogene Laërce à vostre prière, il devroit estre achevé d'imprimer. Et nonseulement il ne la*[a]* pas commencé, mais il ne se dispose pas à le commencer. Il me mande par sa derniere lettre, qu'il n'a point de papier pour l'imprimer, qu'il n'a point de Correcteur pour en corriger les épreuves, & que quand il l'aura imprimé, les héritiers de Pullein qui l'a imprimé en Angleterre, lui en empescheront*[b]* le débit en Angleterre où il fait son principal trafic. Cestadire, Monsieur, qu'il a changé de dessein, & qu'il ne*[c]* veut plus imprimer mon livre*[d]*: c'est pourquoy je lui mande aujourdhuy de le remettre entre vos mains auplustost:*[1]* & je vous supplie de lui écrire aussi de vostre costé de vous l'envoyer*[e]* auplustost. Quand vous l'aurez, s'il se presente quelque Libraire en Hollande qui le veille*[f]* imprimer, vous pourrez le luy donner. Et si il*[g]* ne s'en présente [fol. 2r] point, vous l'envoyerez s'il vous plaist à Lipsic à Mr. Carpzou; qui, comme vous savez, me l'avoit demandé avec beaucoup d'empressement, aussibien que Messieurs Meyer de Francfort.[2] Je ne say si vous avez su le fascheux accident qui m'est arivé depuis deux mois. J'ay u la cuisse droite demise. Le mal sera long: et il est douloureux.[3] Je suis toujours de toute ma passion, & avec toute l'estime & toute l'admiration que vous méritez

Monsieur
Vostre tres humble & tres
obeissant serviteur
Ménage

[Address, fol. 2v: A Monsieur / Monsieur Grævius Professeur / A Utrecht]

[This letter is not in Ménage's hand, except for the signature. It is written in the same neat hand as the addresses of many of the letters, presumably by Ménage's secretary.]

^a. la *sic, for* l'a.   ^b. *originally* empescheroient; ie *deleted.*
^c. le *deleted.*   ^d. mon livre *inserted.*
^e. auplu *deleted at end of line.*   ^f. veille *sic.*   ^g. si il *sic.*

Ménage is still severely incapacitated by the effects of his fall, and apart from his signature this letter is written in a neat scribal hand. Exasperated by Wetstein's delays and excuses, he asks Grævius to withdraw the Diogenes and explore the possibility of other printers in the Low Countries or Germany. The opening phrase, 'J'ay grand sujet de me plaindre de vostre Monsieur Wetstein', runs like a leitmotiv through much of the rest of the correspondence.

1 There appears to be a lost letter from Ménage to Wetstein written on the same day, withdrawing the Diogenes; but subsequent letters to Grævius suggest that Ménage changed his mind, before once again losing patience six months later (letter of 8 December 1684, Letter 21)
2 Carpsovius, in Leipzig, had of course overseen the printing of the new edition of *Juris civilis amœnitates* in 1680.
3 See note 1 to Wetstein's letter of 19 May (Letter 16).

LETTER 18

Ménage to Grævius. 13 October 1684

A Paris ce 13. Oct. *1684*

Monsieur
Je reçus enfin vos livres avanthier,[1] Et des le mesme jour j'envoyay au Père Hardouin,

& à Mrs. Thevenot,[2] Baluze, Du Cange,[3] Bouïlliaud, Petit, & Morel,[4] ceux qui leur estoient destinez. Et j'ay envoyé aujourdhuy à Lyon à Mr. Spon, & à Nismes à Me. Dacier,[5] ceux qui estoient inscrits de leurs noms. Pour Mr. Spanheim[6] & Mr. Mowe,[7] ils sont à Fonteine-Bleau; & j'attendray leur retour, pour leur donner ceux que j'ay reçus pour eux[a]. Il me reste à vous rendre mille tres humbles actions de graces des deux[b] exemplaires que vous m'avez fait l'honneur de me donner, & à vous dire que je les ay reçus avec toute la joye & toute la reconnoissance imaginable.[c] Je suis bien aise que vous ayiez approuvé la correction de Mr. Gassendi au sujet de cette épitre de Cice-ron à Atticus:[8] car je l'ay aussi approuvée dans mes Observations sur Laërce, en la Vie d'Epicure. Mais apropos de mes Observations sur Laërce, je [fol. 2r] vous prie, quand vous écrivez à Mr. Wetstein, de l'obliger à en commancer l'édition, & de lui remontrer qu'il y a deux ans qu'il les a. J'ay lu depuis peu les Vies des Estiennes qui vous sont adressées;[9] & je les ay leues avec beaucoup de plaisir. Si l'Auteur les fesoit rimprimer, je pourrois lui fournir quelques Mémoires qui pourroient les illustrer. Nous attendons icy vostre Vie de Mr. Heinsius avec impatience. Je suis toujours avec admiration

Monsieur,

Vostre tres humble

& tres obéissant serviteur

Ménage

[Address, fol. 2v (in Ménage's hand): A Monsieur / Monsieur Grævius / A Utrecht]

[a]. ceux que j'ay reçus pour eux *inserted, replacing* les leurs *deleted*.
[b]. des deux *inserted, relacing* pour les *deleted*.
[c]. imaginable *sic*.

There has been a gap of more than four months since Ménage's last surviving letter, although at least one in between must have been lost. Ménage is helping his correspondent by distributing complimentary copies of Grævius's latest book; and he exchanges scholarly news and opinions. He is now still hoping that Wetstein will finally start on the Diogenes, and asking Grævius to apply some pressure on the recalcitrant printer.

1 It is clear from the following two letters that Grævius sent copies of two works to be distributed, his editions of Meursius's *Theseus, sive de eius vita rebusque gestis liber pos-tumus* (Utrecht, F. Halma, 1684) and of Cicero's *Epistolarum libri XVI ad T. Pomponium Atticum* (Amsterdam, Blaeu brothers and H. Wetstein, 1684). Ménage was used to helping his scholarly friends in this way. Earlier the same year he had similarly distrib-uted copies of Gisbert Cuper's latest work, and wrote to Cuper on 4 January 1684: 'Je viens d'envoyer à Mr. Spanheim & à Mr. Huet les exemplaires que vous m'avez envoyez pour eux. Mr. Spon est à Lyon, & Mr. Bigot à Rouan. Je ne manqueray pas de leur faire tenir ceux que vous leur avez destinez' (KB Den Haag, MS 72.C.46, fols 7-8); and in a subsequent letter, of 4 February 1684, he sent on to Cuper letters of thanks from Huet and Spon (*ibid*, fols 9-10).
2 Melchisédech Thévenot (1620-1692) was a scholar and orientalist who compiled extensive series of *récits de voyage*. He was appointed Bibliothécaire du Roi later in 1684, a post which he held until just before his death (see Ménage's letter of 8 Decem-

ber 1684, Letter 21). He had already provided scholarly help for both Heinsius and
Grævius – on Cicero in the latter case, which made it particularly appropriate for
Grævius to send his edition of *Ad Atticum* now. Ménage had written to Heinsius on 27
June 1680: 'Mr. Thevenot m'a prié de vous faire savoir qu'il vous préparoit quelque
chose de considérable, & qu'il avoit quelques remarques d'Estienne sur Cicéron pour
Mr. Grævius (UB Leiden, MS Burm. F.8.25, fol. 2; reprinted in Bray, 'Les Lettres
françaises ...', p. 204).

3 Charles du Fresne, sieur Du Cange (1610-1688), a close friend of Ménage, was one
of the most dedicated, and most productive, scholars of the century. He was celebrated
as a historian and editor, but above all for his monumental glossaries of late Latin and
Greek: *Glossarium ad scriptores mediæ et infimæ latinitatis*, 3 vols, fol. (Paris, E. Martin and
L. Billaine, 1678), and *Glossarium ad scriptores mediæ et infimæ græcitatis*, 2 vols, fol.
(Lyon, Ancillon, 1688). Bigot assisted with the latter work, and in turn specifically
requested the help of Heinsius and Grævius (see Bigot's letter to Heinsius of 8 January
1680, UB Leiden, BPL 1923. II. 140, quoted in Doucette, *Emery Bigot*, p. 108).

4 The numismatist André Morel (1646-1703), a native of Berne, was assistant keeper
of Louis XIV's *cabinet de médailles*. Because of his Protestantism he encountered severe
difficulties after the Revocation of the Edict of Nantes, and ultimately had to leave
France. He was an old friend of Wetstein's, whom Ménage kept informed about
Morel's problems: see Wetstein's letters of 4 September 1691 (Letter 60) and 20 September 1691 (Letter 62).

5 Anne Dacier, née Le Febvre (1651-1720), an outstanding classical scholar and pas-
sionate defender of the Anciens in the 'Querelle des Anciens et des Modernes', was the
daughter of the distinguished Protestant scholar Tanneguy Le Febvre (1615-1672).
Ménage had been a friend and correspondent of her father (for Tanneguy Le Febvre's
letters to him see BN Paris, n.a.f. 1344), and later dedicated to her his *Historia mulierum
philosopharum* (dedicated 'Ad Annam Fabram Daceriam').

6 Ezechiel Spanheim (1629-1710) was a deeply learned numismatist and diplomat. He
was born in Geneva, and travelled widely in Europe on diplomatic and scholarly mis-
sions for the Elector Palatine and, later, the Elector of Brandenburg. From 1678 to
1687 he was the latter's 'envoyé extraordinaire' in Paris. He died as ambassador in London, and is buried in Westminster Abbey.

7 It has not proved possible to identify with certainty 'Mr. Mowe', presumably the
same person as 'Mr. Mowen' of Ménage's letter of 24 November 1684 below (Letter
20): possibly the German jurist Friedrich Movius (1641-1696)?

8 Although principally celebrated as a Christian Epicurean philosopher and opponent
of Descartes, Pierre Gassendi (1592-1655) had extremely wide interests and published
and corresponded on a remarkable range of subjects. Among his works on Epicurus is
his *De vita, moribus et placitis Epicuri, seu animadversiones in lib. X Diogenis Laertii* (Lyon,
G. Barbier, 1649), which is often cited in the apparatus to Ménage's edition.

9 *De vitis Stephanorum, celebrium Typographorum, Dissertatio epistolica ad virum Cl. Joh.
Georgium Grævium* (Amsterdam, Jansson and Waesberge, 1683). The work was written
by the doctor and scholar Theodore Jansson van Almeloveen (1657-1712), a former
student of Grævius's at the University of Utrecht and an occasional correspondent of

Ménage's. Bayle described the contents in a letter to Minutoli of 15 July 1683: 'Un Médecin d'Amsterdam, nommé Janssonius, petit-fils de ce grand faiseur d'*Atlas*, vient de publier en Latin *la Vie des Etiennes*, ces fameux Imprimeurs, & y a joint plusieurs Particularitez concernant leur Imprimerie, & un Catalogue de tous les Livres qu'ils ont mis au jour; même il y a quelques Opuscules d'Henri Etienne à ce sujet' (*Œuvres diverses*, IV, 606). See also Ménage's letters of 8 December 1684 and 27 April 1685 below (Letters 21 and 25), where Jansson is possibly taking up Ménage's offer of 'quelques Mémoires' made in this letter.

LETTER 19

Ménage to Grævius. 9 November 1684

A Paris ce 9. Nov. *1684*

Monsieur

J'ay envoyé à Mr. de Valois[1] l'endroit de la lettre que vous m'avez écrite qui le regarde. Il n'y avoit point pour lui d'exemplaires de vos livres parmy les exemplaires que j'ay reçus. Ces exemplaires estoient paquetez, & inscrits du nom de ceux auquels ils estoient adressez. Et il y avoit un exemplaire du Thesée sur lequel il n'y avoit point d'inscription. Vous me ferez savoir s'il vous plaist ce que vous desirez que j'en fasse. Comme il y en avoit un dans le pacquet à Mr.[a] Spon, je croiois que cet exemplaire sans inscription estoit pour Mr. Bouïlliau: & je le lui eusse envoyé, sans que le Memoire de Mr. Bigot portoit qu'il n'y en avoit point pour lui. J'ay reçu une lettre de Mr. Wetstein, par laquelle il me mande qu'il ne peut toujours commancer l'édition de mon Diogéne Laërce acause de la difficulté que lui font les Anglois, pour laquelle il doit passer en Angleterre.[2] Cestadire, que je ne verray jamais cette édition achevée. Mr. Meibomius[3] nous propose de nous servir de sa Version: à quoy j'ay consenti: quoyqu'il y ait plusieurs choses dans mes Observations qui sont relatives a la Version d'Aldobrandin.[4] Puisque vostre Vie de Mr. Heinsius n'est point encore imprimée, je vous prie de mettre dans mon Elégie, *Parte sui vivet nobiliore dies*, aulieu de *Parte sui vivet iam meliore*. Mais apropos de vers, ne savez vous point [fol. 2r] qui est ce Poëte dont parle Cujas dans cet endroit du chapitre XVI. du livre XII. de ses Observations:[5] *Nam quoties impares sententiæ sunt, necesse est minoris numeri voces, etiam si eæ sunt forsitan honore vel æquitate majores, cedere numero majoribus*, parvaque, *ut quidam Poëta ait*, silescere parte. Si vous le savez, vous m'obligerez de me l'apprendre. J'oubliois à vous dire, que Mr. Nicaise est à Dijon. Je vous baise tres humblement les mains, & suis toujours de toute ma passion,

Monsieur,
Vostre tres humble
& tres obéissant serviteur
Ménage

[No address]

a. de *deleted*.

Ménage is again acting in his role of scholarly intermediary, sorting out a series of problems over the distribution of Grævius's complimentary copies. Once again he despairs of Wetstein; but for the first time mentions Meibomius as a potential participant in the edition, a collaboration that was to prove rich in unpredictable complications. He ends the letter by sending a late revision to his elegy on Heinsius, and a scholarly query apropos of Cujas.

1 Adrien de Valois (1607-1692), named 'Historiographe du Roi' in 1660 conjointly with his elder brother Henri (1603-1676). The two were regarded as among the most outstanding latinists of their generation.

2 This must be a lost letter rather than Wetstein's letter of 19 May 1684 (Letter 16), since there is no mention in that of Wetstein travelling to England. Wetstein himself refers to this letter when writing on 16 December 1684 (Letter 22).

3 Marcus Meibomius (c1630-1711), a member of a distinguished family of German scholars, was born in Tonningen (Schleswig); after a career that had taken him to Sweden, Denmark, England, and France, he was now settled in the Netherlands. He combined great learning with considerable eccentricity. Meibomius is to figure frequently throughout the rest of this correspondence, especially in the increasingly exasperated and amusing portrayal of him in Wetstein's letters. His 'Version' was a new Latin translation of the Greek text of Diogenes Laertius that he undertook. It was eventually used in Wetstein's edition, and was generally regarded as a masterpiece.

4 The scholar Tomaso Aldobrandini was a brother of Pope Clement VIII. His annotated Latin translation of Diogenes Laertius was published posthumously (Rome, 1594), and was highly regarded. This is the Latin translation used by Ménage in his 1664 edition of Diogenes.

5 Jacques Cujas (1522-1590) was one of the outstanding legal scholars of the sixteenth century. A complete edition of his works had been published by Charles Annibal Fabrot in ten folio volumes in 1658: *Iacobi Cuiacii … opera omnia in decem tomos distributa … Editio nova emendatior et auctior … cura Caroli Annibalis Fabroti* (Paris, S. & G. Cramoisy *et al.*, 1658). Ménage was particularly interested in Cujas at this time and planned to write his life: a *Cujacii Vita* is listed among the 'Ouvrages manuscrits, et promis' at the start of the *Ménagiana* (I, sig. oiv). He had already collected some details which he published in his life of Pierre Ayrault (*Vitæ Petri Ærodii et Guillelmi Menagii* (Paris, 1675); see Ménage's next letter, note 7), and was actively seeking more: two letters from his lawyer friend Louis Nublé, of 2 November 1684 and 24 February 1685, contain a considerable amount of information about Cujas (BN, Paris, n.a.f. 17270, fols 80-81, 82-83). Similarly there are many further details and anecdotes in the *Ménagiana*.

Ménage to Grævius. 24 November 1684

A Paris ce 24. Nov. *1684*

Monsieur

Je ne manqueray pas d'envoyer aujourdhuy vostre lettre à Lyon à Mr. Spon. Dans le pacquet de livres que je lui ay envoyé de vostre part, il y avoit quatre exemplaires des Epitres de Ciceron à Atticus, & un Meursius. Je ne manqueray pas aussi de donner à Mr. de Valois le Meursius qui me reste. Mademoiselle le Feuvre n'est plus Mademoiselle le Feuvre: Elle est présantement Madame Dacier. Et elle est avec Mr. Dacier, son mari, à Castres.[1] Mais elle n'y est que pour quelques mois: & elle reviendra icy bientost. Mr. de Médon est plein de vie.[2] ἐστί, καὶ ἐίη.[3] Ne prenez point s'il vous plaist la peine de chercher dans Stace cet hémistiche, *parvæque silescere parte*: car il n'est pas de Stace.[4] Vous m'obligerez tres-sensiblement si vous pouvez obliger Mr. Vestein à commancer bientost l'édition de mon Laërce: Je suis fort de vostre avis, qu'il doit s'accommoder avec Mr. Meibomius pour la correction des épreuves.[5] Je vous envoye par la voye de Mr. Mowen[6] un exemplaire de quelques Vies de mes parents.[7] Le livre n'est pas fort excellent: mais il est fort rare: car on n'en a imprimé qu'une centaine. Tel qu'il est, je vous prie de l'avoir agréable, & de le recevoir comme une marque de mon amitié, & comme un tribut que je vous dois.

Ménage

[Address, fol. 2v: A Monsieur / Monsieur Grævius / A Utrecht]

Ménage is still engaged in the complicated process of distributing Grævius's books. He includes news of scholarly friends, again asks Grævius to try to stimulate Wetstein to some action, and ends with a present of one of his own works that he is sending.

1 André Dacier (1651-1722) was a favourite student of Tanneguy Le Febvre, and studied alongside his daughter Anne Le Febvre (see letter of 13 October above (Letter 18), note 5). They were married in 1683. They both converted to Roman Catholicism, and retired for a period to André Dacier's native Castres to avoid both unwelcome publicity and the (incorrect) suspicion that they might have been motivated by concerns of worldly advancement.

2 Presumably Bernard de Médon (Bernardus Medonius) of Toulouse, a friend and correspondent of Heinsius who had helped him with his edition of Ovid. Fifty-six letters between Heinsius and Médon, extending from 1648 to 1668, are included in Burman's *Sylloges epistolarum a viris illustrium scriptarum*, V, 607-75. See also F. F. Blok, *Nicolaas Heinsius in dienst van Christina van Zweden* (Delft, 1949), pp. 82, 124-5,

3 'He is, and may he be'.

4 The phrase is indeed not to be found in Statius, but has proved impossible to locate – perhaps not surprisingly, considering that it escaped even Ménage's vast reading and prodigious memory, and apparently Grævius as well.

5 This is the first mention of Meibomius as a possible proof-corrector for the Diogenes

edition (apparently at Grævius's suggestion), in which role, as over his *version*, he was to exasperate Wetstein in subsequent years.

6 See Ménage's letter of 13 October 1684 above (Letter 18), note 7.

7 *Vitae Petri Ærodii quaesitoris andegavensis, et Guillelmi Menagii advocati regii andegavensis. Scriptore Ægidio Menagio* (Paris, C. Journel, 1675). Grævius subsequently lent the work to Bayle, who expressed his appreciation in a letter to Ménage of 13 March 1692: 'Mr Gravius m'a preté l'Ouvrage que vous avez fait sur les vies Petri Ærodi et Guillhelmi Menagii; ces vies sont ecrites avec une extreme politesse de stile, et un choix exquis de choses, et les notes sont un thresor inestimable de faits curieux' (Bibl. de la Sorbonne, Bibl. Victor Cousin, Collection d'autographes, v, no. 7, fols 1-2). Bayle is right: in his usual accumulatory way, and despite the rather limited ostensible subject-matter, Ménage has incorporated a great deal of diverse and interesting material into the notes.

LETTER 21

Ménage to Grævius. 8 December 1684

A Paris ce 8. Dec. *1684*

Monsieur

J'écris à Mr. Vestein qu'il vous remette mon Diogéne Laërce entre les mains. Quand vous l'aurez, si vous pouvez trouver quelqu'autre Imprimeur en Hollande*ᵃ* qui le vueille imprimer, vous le lui donnerez. Si vous n'en trouvez point, vous me le renvoyerez s'il vous plaist. Il faut avouer que j'ay grand sujet de me plaindre de ce Mr. Vestein. J'ay fait rendre en main propre à Mr. Thévenot la lettre que vous m'avez adressée pour lui. Vous saurez s'il vous plaist qu'il est présantement Garde de la Bibliothéque du Roi.¹ J'ay aussi envoyé à Mrs. de la Mare,² Nicaise, & Spon, les lettres que vous leur avez écrites. Mr. Spon ne m'a point encore écrit qu'il ust reçu vostre pacquet de livres: dont je suis toutafait étonné. Mr. Huet est en cette ville. Je lui ay fait voir les endroits des deux lettres où vous me parlez de lui. Je feray réponse à Mr. Janson:³ mais ce ne sera pas sitost: car pour cela j'ay besoin de livres: & mes livres sont tous en confusion. Mr. Bigot est toujours en Normandie à sa [fol. 2r] Terre. Il me fait espérer qu'il retournera icy au mois de Fêvrier. Mr. Mowen vous envoiera par la première occasion le livre que je lui ay donné pour vous.⁴ Adieu, Monsieur. Aimez moy toujours: & ne doutez point que je ne sois toute ma vie de toute ma passion,

Monsieur,
Vostre tres humble &
tres obéissant serviteur
Ménage

[Address, fol. 2v: A Monsieur / Monsieur Grævius / A Utrecht]

ᵃ. vous le lui donnerez *deleted*.

Six months after his letter of 2 June Ménage has once again lost patience with Wetstein, and asks Grævius to withdraw the edition of Diogenes. He must have written directly to the printer at the same time, as is shown by Wetstein's response of 16 December. The remainder of this letter is filled with scholarly news, and an account of the variety of ways in which Ménage has been helping Grævius in acting for him in Paris.

1 On Thévenot see letter of 13 October 1684 (Letter 18), note 2. Ménage had himself been offered the post of 'Garde de la Bibliothéque du Roi' in 1662, but rejected it after negotiations with Colbert partly because the financial arrangements were unsatisfactory, and partly for another reason; as he wrote to Huet in May 1662: 'Et puis, pour vous en parler franchement, il y a quelque pudeur à un homme qui a quelque reputation parmi les gens de Lettres, *nam pervenisse me ad aliquam ingenii & doctrinæ famam existimo*, d'acheter de semblables emplois' (dated 'ce sabmedi' [May 1662]; BML, Florence, MS Ashburnham 1866. 1290, fol. 2; reprinted Pennarola (ed.), no 75, p. 148).

2 The learned Philibert de La Mare (1615-1687) had been a friend of Saumaise and corresponded with Heinsius; some of this correspondence is included in Burman's *Sylloges epistolarum a viris illustribus scriptarum*. He lived in Dijon, which is why Grævius has asked Ménage to send on his letter.

3 'Mr. Janson' is Theodore Jansson van Almeloveen (see letter of 13 October 1684 (Letter 18), note 9; the nature of the help requested from Ménage is unclear. A draft of a rather later scholarly letter from him to Ménage survives (UB Utrecht, MS 6 k 12.30a: undated, but late 1686 – early 1687), and a letter-book of Almeloveen's contains a copy of a lengthy letter of thanks, dated 18 March 1687, for a copy of Ménage's *Poésies* sent directly by Wetstein (UB Utrecht, MS 995, II (5 k 9), fols 29r-30r).

4 This is the *Vitae Petri Ærodii et Guillelmi Menagii* referred to in the previous letter. It is unclear when the work was eventually sent: in his letter of 30 August 1685 (Letter 29), Ménage refers to what was evidently an effusive letter of thanks from Grævius.

Plate 1:   Gilles Ménage, 1613-1692, in old age.   From Charles Perrault, *Les hommes illustres qui ont paru en France pendant ce siècle; avec leurs portraits au naturel*, Paris, Antoine Dezallier, 1696-1700.
Reproduced by permission of Durham University Library.

Plate 2: Johann-Georg Grævius, 1632-1703. From *Grævius, Thesaurus antiquitatum et historiarum Italiæ*, Leiden, Petrus Vander Aa, 1704. Reproduced by permission of Durham University Library.

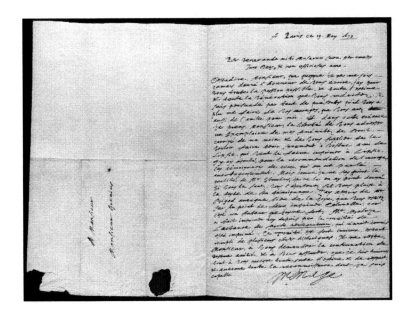

Plate 3: Ménage's first letter to Grævius, 19 May 1679.
Kongelige Bibliotek, Copenhagen, MS Thott 1263, 4°. Reproduced by
permission of the library.

Plate 5: Frontispiece to the Wetstein edition of Diogenes Laertius, 1692, designed by Charles Perrault.
Reproduced by permission of Durham University Library.

Plate 6: Engraving of 'Monimus' from the Wetstein edition of Diogenes Laertius, 1692.
Reproduced by permission of Durham University Library.

LETTER 22

Wetstein to Ménage. 16 December 1684

d'Amsterdam adj 16e. Decembre *1684.*

Monsieur

Je croi qu'aurez receu ma precedente avec la lettre de M. Meybom.[1] C'estoit lui qui m'avoit empeché à Vous repondre plustot*a* à Votre precedente. J'envoye ce soir, sui-vant Votre ordre, Votre Diogéne à Mr. Grævius; j'y ai joint toutes Vos lettres où Vous me parliez de quelque chose qui concernoit l'impression, ou où il y avoit quelques additions. Ainsi que celui qui l'imprimera se pourra regler là dessus.

De l'air que me donnez ledit ordre, je crois inutile de discuter ici la question, si j'ai abandonné le dessein d'imprimer ce livre, ou non? & je voi bien qu'il sera envoyé en Allemagne. Aussi je suis trespersuadé que Vous serez le premier à Vous en repentir, & bien plus-tot que moi. Bien que je ne nie pas, que je serai tres-fasché si cet excellent ouvrage ne se doit pas faire comme il faut.

Monsieur Francius Vous salue, & promet de Vous envoyer une autre de ses elegies. S'il me l'auroit envoyée je l'aurois jointe ceans. Je demeure toujours

Monsieur
Votre tres humble & tres obeïssant serviteur
H Wetstein

[No address]

a. *comma deleted after* plustot.

Wetstein's first response to Ménage's withdrawing the edition of Diogenes: his protest is vigor-ous, and not in the least overawed by the French scholar's eminence. As in much of the corre-spondence he occupies an ambiguous position, between printer-tradesman responding to a client's instructions, and learned fellow-member of the scholarly community: thus he ends this letter in his scholarly role, acting as an intermediary between Francius and Ménage.

1 At least one intervening letter from Wetstein has not survived; this is presumably the one referred to by Ménage on 9 November 1684 (Letter 19).

Wetstein to Ménage. 25 December 1684

d'Amsterdam ce 25ᵉ. de Decembre. *1684.*

Monsieur

Votre Diogene est entre les mains de Mr. Grævius. Je n'ai pû & ne puis encore le commencer faute de Correcteur, sur lequel je me pusse fier. Ce que je Vous proteste estre veritable. Et je Vous demande excuse si je ne*ᵃ* me puis empecher de Vous dire ici, que je suis tout etonné de Vous trouver à Votre age un feu de jeune-homme de 20. ans, & qu'à 72. ans*ᵇ* Vous*ᶜ* ayez encore tant de passion pour une poignée de fumée, preferant une petite satisfaction de Vous-méme à l'utilité publique. Pardonnez-moi, Monsieur, si je*ᵈ* m'explique en ces termes, ce n'est que par sincerité d'affection, & nullement par depit ou malice.

Je n'ai jamais pensé à mettre Vos poesies in 8°. mais bien in 12°. pour obvier à tous mal-entendus j'en ai fait faire une epreuve, comme verrez ci-joint. Vous choisirez des deux characteres celui que Vous voudrez. Du petit Vous payerez vint & cinq sols, & du grand 30. sols par piece; & je commencerai quand Vous voudrez à l'imprimer.

Mr. Meybom est à la Haye. Il eust asseurement eté tres-propre à revoir le Diogene; je lui ai offert pour cela tout ce qu'il me demanderoit. Mais il semble qu'il a d'autres desseins en téte. Je suis de tout mon cœur

Monsieur

Ces epreuves sont faits fort à la haste,
le papier n'ayant pas eu le temps d'etre
bien trempé, ni la matiere corrigée.

Votre tres humble & tres obeissant serviteur
H Wetstein

[No address]

ᵃ. ne *inserted.*   *ᵇ*. ans *inserted.*
ᶜ. *small deletion following* Vous.   *ᵈ*. je *inserted.*

Wetstein's forthright follow-up to the previous letter, reproving Ménage in even blunter terms for withdrawing the Diogenes edition – although with the subtle flattery that its publication would be so valuable for 'l'utilité publique'. The printer's excuse for his delay is now that he does not have a reliable 'correcteur', Meibomius apparently not being available. Meanwhile he is persevering with his edition of Ménage's Poésies, *sending proof sheets in sample types, and pricing them.*

82

LETTER 24

Ménage to Grævius. 16 February 1685

A Paris ce 16. Fevr. *1685.*

Monsieur

Je n'ay point reçu de lettres de Mr. Westein touchant la proposition qu'il vous a faite d'imprimer mon Diogéne Laërce in 8°.*ª* Pour response à cette proposition, il faut la rejeter absolument, si Mr. Westein ne veut imprimer que mes Observations avec le texte de Laërce, sans les Remarques d'Aldobrandin, de Henri Estienne, & des deux Casaubons.¹ Que s'il veut imprimer le tout, comme je croy que c'est sa pensée, je vous supplie, Monsieur, de lui remontrer, que l'ouvrage ne peut estre imprimé qu'en trois volumes: ce qui seroit tres incommode pour les Lecteurs. Et s'il ne défére point à vos remontrances, & que vous ne trouviez point en Hollande d'autre Imprimeur qui le vueille imprimer in folio, vous le lui renvoierez s'il vous plaist, pour l'imprimer in 8°.*ᵇ* Quand il me le demanda, non seulement il vouloit l'imprimer in folio, mais il vouloit l'imprimer avec les portraits des Philosophes, & en faire un chef doeuvre d'impression*ᶜ*. Je [fol. 2r] lui écrivis il y a quelque tans pour lui demand[er]*ᵈ* ce qu'il me demandoit pour imprimer mes Poësies. Il me fit réponse qu'il ne me demandoit rien;² pourveu que j'en prisse deux cents exemplaires à vint-cinq sous.*ᵉ* Je lui écris ce voyage, que je veux bien lui païer les exemplaires a 25. sous:*ᶠ* mais que je n'en prendray que cent: mais que je lui païeray ces cent par avance: & que je donneray outre cela 25. livres à son Correcteur: pourveu*ᵍ* que mon livre soit imprimé correctement. En cas qu'il le vueille imprimer à ces conditions; & je croy qu'il le doit vouloir; vous le lui donnerez s'il vous plaist: car je vous l'envoieray par la première occasion. Sil ne le veut pas imprimer à ces conditions, vous le donnerez à un autre Imprimeur. Le plus petit caractère me sera le meilleu[r]*ʰ* pourveu qu'il soit net. J'ay fort augmanté & fort corrigé mes Poësies: & de tous mes livres, c'est présentement celui¹ que j'estime le plus.³ Mr. de la Marre a achevé la Vie de Mr. de Saumaise.⁴ Je lui ay conseillé de la faire imprimer en Hollande: & je croy qu'il suivra mon conseil: & si quelqu'un de vos Imprimeurs la veut imprimer, je vous l'envoieray pour la lui donner. Mes Origines de la Langue [fol. 1v, sideways] Italienne sont enfin achevées d'imprimer.⁵ Je vous en envoieray un exemplaire, aussitost que j'auray reçu ceux que l'Imprimeur me doit donner. Mr. Bigot est toujours en Normandie: où je ne manqueray pas de lui faire savoir ce que vous me dites de lui. Il retournera à Paris vers le commancement de ce caresme. Je vous baise tres humblement les mains: & suis toujours de toute ma passion, & avec toute la reconnoissance que je dois,

Monsieur,
Vostre tres humble & tres
obéissant serviteur
Ménage

[Address, fol. 2v (in Ménage's hand): A Monsieur / Monsieur Grævius / A Utrecht]
ª. 8°. *altered from* 4°.   *ᵇ*. 8°. *altered from* 4°.

^c *. deletion between* d' *and* impression *[edi ?]*
^d *. last two letters of* demander *lost in tear at top corner.*
^e *. piéces. deleted.*
^f *. piéces: deleted.*
^g *. pourveu inserted, replacing* en cas *deleted.*
^h *. last letter of* meilleur *lost in tear at edge of page.* J'ay fort augmanté & corrigé mes Poësies *deleted.*
ⁱ *. celui inserted, replacing* le livre *deleted.*

Despite, or perhaps because of, Wetstein's plain speaking, Ménage is continuing to negotiate with him, both directly and through the intermediary of Grævius, who is holding the text of the Diogenes edition and Ménage's Poésies. *Discussions about the Diogenes edition now regard the format and arrangement, and Ménage even reluctantly envisages having to agree to an octavo edition; while negotiations over the* Poésies *centre on the financial arrangements, which are discussed in detail. The letter ends, as usual, with an assortment of scholarly news from Paris.*

1 The annotations to Diogenes Laertius by Aldobrandini, Henri Estienne, and the two Casaubons were indeed included in the edition when it finally appeared.

2 This letter from Wetstein concerning the financial details of printing Ménage's *Poésies* has not survived.

3 Ménage frequently expresses his particular affection for his poetry, in his correspondence and in the *Ménagiana*.

4 La Mare had not rushed to complete his life of Saumaise. He had embarked on the work more than twenty-two years earlier: in a letter to Huet of 24 February 1663 Ménage had commented 'je pense que vous aurez seu que Mr. de la Mare, Con[seill]er au Parlement de Dijon fait la Vie de Mr. de Saumaise. Ce Mr. de la Mare escrit tres bien en Latin, et comme il a eu de bons memoires, il est à croire que son ouvrage sera curieux' (BML, Florence, MS Ashburnham 1866. 1247, reprinted Pennarola (ed.), no. 101, p. 179). Four months after the present letter La Mare had still not decided what to do: see Ménage's letter of 29 June 1685 (Letter 27) below, with its revealing repeated 'enfin': 'Je croy que Mr. de la Mâre prendra enfin le parti de vous envoyer sa Vie de Mr. de Saumaise: qui est enfin achevée'.

5 *Le origini della lingua italiana compilate dal Sre. Egidio Menagio, Gentiluomo Francese. Colla giunta de Modi di dire italiani, raccolti, dichiarati dal Medesimo* (Geneva, J. A. Choüet, 1685).

LETTER 25

Ménage to Grævius. 27 April 1685

A Paris ce 27. Avril 1685.

Monsieur

Vous estes toujours l'homme du monde le plus obligeant: mais je vous prie de croire
que de mon costé je suis toujours aussi l'homme du monde le plus reconnoissant. Je
vous abandonne mon Laërce pour en faire ce qu'il vous plaira. Tibi in me, meaque,
æterna auctoritas esto.[1] Si on l'imprime in 8°. il faudra l'imprimer en 3. volumes: & il
faudra que le premier comprenne le Texte de Laërce: le segond, les Remarques de
Henri Estienne; de Casaubon le pere; de Thomas Aldobrandin; & de Casaubon le fis; &
le troisiéme, les miennes. Si on l'imprime in 4°. il faudra mettre les Remarques de
Casaubon le fis aprês les miennes. J'y ay fait quelques nouvelles Additions: que je vous
envoieray quand vous aurez trouvé un Imprimeur. J'en avois envoyé à Mr. Westein: &
je l'avois prié & conjuré de les mettre en leur lieu: ce qu'il n'a pas fait. Je vous supplie,
Monsieur, tres humblement & tres instamment d'obliger quelqu'un de vos Ecolliers à
prendre ce soin. J'ay mis mes Poësies entre les mains de Mr. Mowe: qui m'a promis de
vous les envoyer par la premiere occasion. Ce livre, en l'estat qu'il est présantement, est
mon ouvrage favori: ce qui fait que je ne veux rien épargner pour le faire imprimer élé-
gamment & correctement. Le plus petit caractère, pourvu qu'il soit net, me sera le plus
agréable: ce qui soit dit, tant à l'égard du Grec que du Latin. Si on ne trouve point de
petit [fol. 2r] caractère net, il en faudra*a* prendre un plus gros; & faire le volume en petit
8°. En ce cas,*b* le caractère dont le Virgile de Mr. Heinsius est imprimé, me plairoit
fort.[2] J'en prendray cent volumes de l'édition dont on conviendra: & je les payeray par
avance. Et si le livre est imprimé correctement, je feray, outre cela, un honneste présant
au Correcteur. Mr. de la Marre & Mr. Nicaise n'ont point encore reçu les exemplaires
de vos Epitres ad Atticum:*c* & cestpourquoy ils ne vous ont point encore écrit pour
vous remercier. Je ne say de quoy s'est avisé celui qui a fait vos paquets d'adresser à Mr.
Spon, qui demeure à Lyon, des livres pour faire tenir à ces Messieurs qui demeurent à
Dijon; & à Mr. de Court,[3] qui est toujours à Versailles. Madame Dacier est encore*d* à
Castres: &*e* j'ay toujurs icy*f* l'exemplaire de vos Epitres, & celui du Thésée de Meursius,
que vous lui*g* avez destinez. Je feray savoir à Mr. de la Marre ce que vous m'écrivez de
sa Vie de Mr. de Saumaise. Je ne doute point qu'il n'accepte vos offres. Mr. Bigot n'est
point encore icy: mais je l'y attans dans peu de jours. Mr. Westein ne m'a point écrit.
C'est un homme dont j'ay bien sujet de me plaindre. Je vous envoieray par le prochain
ordinaire*h* quelques Remarques sur Lucien.[4] Vous avertirez s'il vous celui*i* qui travaille
sur cet auteur, qu'il y a icy, dans la Bibliothéque du Roi, trois ou quatre manuscrits de
cet Auteur. Je vous envoieray aussi dans [fol. 1v, sideways] quelque tans ce que je vous
ay promis pour Mr. Janson. Vous ne me parlez point de vostre Vie de Mr. Heinsius,
que vous nous aviez fait*j* espérer avec les premières hirondelles. Aimez moi toujours,
Monsieur, je vous en conjure: & soyez bien persuadé que j'ay toujours pour vous toute
l'estime & toute l'admiration que vous méritez,

Ménage

Je serois bien aise de savoir le nom de celui qui veut faire imprimer Lucien: & vous m'obligerez de me le faire savoir.

[Address, fol. 2v (in Ménage's hand): A Monsieur / Monsieur Grævius / A Utrecht]

^a. *final letter of* faudra *inserted, replacing* oit *deleted.*
^b. cas, *inserted above deletion.*
^c. Je ne *deleted.*
^d. encore *inserted, replacing* toujours *deleted.*
^e. ainsi *deleted.*
^f. les exemplaires *deleted.*
^g. aviez dest *deleted.*
^h. *final letter of* ordinaire *inserted, replacing* es *deleted.*
ⁱ. s'il vous celui *sic* (plaist *omitted).*
^j. fait *inserted.*

The first half of this letter is again taken up with instructions concerning the Diogenes edition and the Poésies. The second half largely relates to Ménage's activities on behalf of Grævius: distributing complimentary copies of his works, acting as an intermediary in Paris, and passing on news and information.

1 The opening of this letter is a fine example of Ménage's self-repetition in his correspondence. He had already used this quotation in his letter to Grævius of 18 January 1682 (Letter 7); and he used the opening sentence again in practically identical form at the start of a letter to Magliabecchi of c1687-88: 'Monsieur, Vous étes toujours l'homme du monde le plus obligeant. Mais je vous prie de croire, Monsieur, que de mon coté je suis aussi toujours l'homme du monde le plus reconnoissant …' (in *Anti-Baillet*, 2 vols (La Haye, Estienne Foulque and Louïs van Dole, 1688), II, 357; reprinted in *Mescolanze d'Egidio Menagio. Secunda edizione, corretta, ed ampliata* (Rotterdam, R. Leers, 1692), p. 330, an addition to the first edition of the *Mescolanze* (Paris, L. Bilaine, 1678)).

2 This is the 12° edition of 1676 of Heinsius's Virgil. After the end of hostilities between France and the United Provinces there was a second printing in March 1679 of 48 copies on large paper, dedicated to Louis XIV, so that they could be distributed in Paris (see A. Willems, *Les Elzevier*, no. 1523, pp. 389-91). Heinsius sent one of these copies to Ménage, who warmly thanked him in a letter of 19 June 1679 (UB Leiden, Burm. F.8.24, fol. 1r; reprinted in Bray (ed.), 'Les Lettres françaises …', pp. 202-03).

3 Charles Caton de Court (1654-1694) was a great-nephew of Saumaise. In a letter of recommendation to Redi of 23 December 1678, Ménage wrote of him: 'Je vous le recommande, Monsieur, de toute ma passion, & comme petit-neveu de Mr. de Saumaise, dont la mémoire m'est en vénération; & comme un des plus savans hommes de l'Europe; & comme un de mes plus chers & un de mes plus intimes amis' (BML Florence, Cod. Laur. Rediano, 224, No. 44); and again, to Magliabecchi on 3 February 1679: 'C'est l'homme de l'Europe le plus savant pour son âge. Il sait toutes les sciences & toutes les langues, mais il est encore plus considérable par sa vertu que par son savoir' (BNC Florence, Magi. VIII. 362, fols 28r-29r; reprinted in Pélissier (ed.) *Lettres de Ménage à Magliabecchi et à Carlo Dati*, p. 25).

4 There are frequent references in Ménage's subsequent letters to this proposed new edition of Lucian, the 'Remarques' and other information that Ménage sends to help the editor, and his intense curiosity to know who this editor might be. Grævius himself was, of course, heavily involved, and wrote the preface, although Jean Le Clerc seems also to have played an important role. The edition, including Ménage's 'Remarques', was eventually published as *Luciani Samosatensis opera … ex versione J. Benedicti. Cum notis … J. Bourdelotti, J. Palmerii a Grentemesnil, T. Fabri, A. Menagii, F. Guieti, J.G. Grævii, J. Gronovii, L. Barlæi, J. Tollii, et selectis aliorum* (Amsterdam, P. and J. Blaeu, 1687).

LETTER 26

Ménage to Grævius. 22 June 1685

A Paris ce 22. Juin *1685*.

Monsieur

J'ay reçu la lettre que vous m'avez écrite en faveur de Messieurs Gruter. Ces Messieurs n'ont point besoin de recommendation, estant recommendables par leur propre mérite; Mais s'il*ᵃ* en avoient besoin, ils ne pourroient pas en avoir une meilleure auprès de moy que la vostre: Et je vous prie de croire, Monsieur, que je leur rendray en vostre consi-dération tout le service dont je seray capable. J'ay envoyé vostre livre & vostre lettre à nostre ami Mr. l'Abbé Nicaise: & je vous envoye aussi de sa part un livre & une lettre. Il y a déja quelque tans que je vous envoiay mes Poësies de la derniere revision. Je suis en peine de savoir si vous les avez receues: *sunt enim archetypæ nugæ.*[1] Et je vous écrivis en mesme tans que vous pouviez disposer de mon Diogéne Laërce de la façon que vous le jugeriez apropos. Mais j'oubliay de vous mander [fol. 2r] qu'en l'imprimant in 4°. ou in octavo, il faudra*ᵇ* changer tous les chiffres des pages sur lesquelles il y a des Notes: ce qui ne sera pas une petite peine. Je croy que Mr. de la Mare prendra enfin le parti de vous envoyer sa Vie de Mr. de Saumaise. Le Pline du Père Hardouin est*ᶜ* public.[2] Je ne doute point qu'il ne vous en donne un exemplaire. Ce livre est icy fort estimé. J'ay u une fluxion sur les yeux, qui m'a empesché de travailler au Lucien. J'ay appris avec une extréme joye que le Roi vous avoit donné deux mille écus:[3] car je vous souhaitte toute sorte de félicitez: & si vous aviez tout ce que je vous souhaitte, vous auriez apeuprès tout ce que vous méritez. Je suis toujours, à l'ordinaire, de toute ma passion,

Monsieur,
Vostre tres humble &
tres obéissant serviteur
Ménage

[fol. 1v, sideways]

Dans ma Fable Esopienne,^{d} qui commance par *Annosa vulpes*, aulieu de *Latas, non abtas, tergore plagas geris: Mi pariorem quæ potarent sanguinem*,^{e} vous y mettrez, s'il vous plaist, *Latas, non abtas, scilicet plagas geris: Quæ mi qui superest perpotarent sanguinem.*

[No address]

^{a}. s'il *sic*.
^{b}. *last letter of* faudra *inserted, replacing* oit *deleted*.
^{c}. enfin *deleted*. ^{d}. auli *deleted*. ^{e}. je *deleted*.

Ménage responds to a letter of recommendation from Grævius in favour of visiting Dutch schol-
ars, and reports on his other helpful activities and more general scholarly news. For his part, he
returns again to the Poésies *and his latest thoughts on the Diogenes edition. The letter ends with*
Ménage's delight that the king has rewarded Grævius with a substantial 'gratification'.

1 Not a direct quotation, but an allusion to Martial, VII. 11, 4. Ménage used exactly the same phrase in a different context in a letter to Huet, who was at Versailles at the time: 'Je suis obligé necessairement d'envoier lundi prochain à mon imprimeur les papiers que je vous ay envoiez ... Et si vous les avez laissés à Paris, je vous prie d'y envoier un de vos laquais, avec ordre de me les apporter surement en mon logis: sunt enim archetypæ nugae. Je pers beaucoup de ce que vous n'avez pas eu le temps de les examiner' (BML, Florence, MS Ashburnham 1866. 1400, reprinted Pennarola (ed.), no. 189, p. 237). Pennarola prints 'archetypa nugae', and wrongly dates this letter '[25 Avril 1684]'; the manuscript is dated 'ce jeudi 25 Avril', which cannot be 1684, quite apart from the fact of Ménage's accident in that month which would make such a letter unlikely (see above, Wetstein's letter of 19 May 1684 (Letter 16), note 1). It could, however, be 1686.

2 Hardouin's edition of Pliny was greeted with universal acclaim: *Caii Plinii Secundi naturalis historiæ libri XXXVII interpretatione et notis illustravit J. Harduinus ... in usum ... Delphini*, 5 vols (Paris, F. Muguet, 1685), 4°. Ménage originally wrote 'enfin' because this work had been forthcoming for some years. As early as 7 August 1682, Ménage wrote to Magliabecchi: 'Le P. Hardouin, bibliothécaire des jésuites de cette ville, fait imprimer son Pline en 4 volumes in-quarto' (BNC, Florence, Magl. VIII. 362, fols 36-37; reprinted in L.-G. Pélissier (ed.), *Lettres de Ménage à Magliabecchi et à Carlo Dati* (Montpellier, 1891), p. 29).

3 Grævius's financial reward from the king is a striking testament to his international status as a scholar. The system of royal 'gratifications' for scholars and writers had been instituted by Colbert in 1662-63 and continued sporadically since. The largesse was extended to foreign scholars: Nicolaas Heinsius, Gronovius, and Huyghens were among those who had already been rewarded. The aims were utilitarian: to establish the King of France as the greatest patron of letters in Europe, and to ensure expressions of gratitude and praise from famous figures in many countries. It was made quite clear that some appropriate celebration of Louis's glory was expected in return, perhaps in the form of a substantial Latin poem, or the dedication of a prestigious work of scholar-

ship. Ménage himself had received one of the largest 'pensions' in the first round in 1663 (an annual 2,000 livres), but he was deeply sensitive about his personal independence, refused to make any public demonstration of flattery and humble gratitude, and provocatively dedicated his next two major works not to the king but to his two oldest friends, Bigot and Nublé. His 'pension' was withdrawn after 1665. Although pleased to have made his point on a personal level, Ménage was very active – as in this episode with Grævius – in helping his friends to obtain royal 'gratifications', and advising them on how to respond appropriately. See Richard Maber, 'Colbert and the scholars: Ménage, Huet, and the royal pensions of 1663', *Seventeenth-Century French Studies*, 7 (1985), 106-14.

LETTER 27

Ménage to Grævius. 29 June 1685

A Paris ce 29. Juin 1685.

Monsieur

Je me donnay l'honneur de vous écrire, il y a aujourdhuy huit jours: & le mesme jour, quelques heures après que je vous us écrit, je reçus vostre dernière lettre, par laquelle vous me mandez que vous avez donné mes Poësies à imprimer à Mr. Vestein, & que vous lui avez proposé d'imprimer mon Diogéne Laërce in 8°. ce qu'il a accepté. C'est un étrange homme que ce Mr. Vestein, & dont j'ay bien sujet de me plaindre. Il ne m'a point écrit: ce qu'il[a] me fait croire, ou qu'il n'imprimera point mes livres, ou qu'il ne les imprimera de long tans. Je vous envoye quelques unes de mes Remarques sur Lucien. Si vous croyez qu'elles puissent estre de quelque usage à celui qui fait imprimer le Lucien, je vous envoieray d'autres. Toutes les remarques que j'ay sur cet auteur sont peu de chose[b]: & elles ne méritent pas d'estre imprimées a part.[c] Elles ne méritent pas mesme d'estre imprimées: mais celui qui travaille au Lucien, [fol. 2r] pourra s'en servir pour corriger la version. Mr. Bigot est toujours à Rouen: où il est retenu par des procès qu'il y a pour son pupille. Je vous envoye une lettre de Mr. de la Mâre, & une autre de Mr. Petit. Je croy que Mr. de la Mâre prendra enfin le parti de vous envoyer sa Vie de Mr. de Saumaise: qui est enfin achevée.[1] Je vous prie encore une fois de faire insérer dans leur lieu par quelqu'un de vos Ecoliers mes Additions à mon Diogéne. Je suis toujours à l'ordinaire de toute ma passion, & avec toute la reconnoissance possible,

Monsieur,
Vostre tres humble &
tres obéissant serviteur
Ménage

[No address]

ᵃ. qu'il *sic, for* qui.
ᵇ. *final letter of* chose *inserted, replacing* es *deleted*.
ᶜ. et *deleted*.

A sequel to the previous letter, written a week later. Grævius has given Wetstein Ménage's Poésies, *and the* Diogenes *is to be printed in an octavo edition. In return, Ménage now sends some of his 'Remarques' on Lucian (with a good deal of self-disparagement on their account), and passes on news of Bigot and two letters, from La Mare and Petit.*

1 See note 4 to Ménage's letter of 16 February 1685 (Letter 24).

LETTER 28

Ménage to Grævius. 27 July 1685

A Paris ce 27. Juillet 1685

Monsieur

Je pense vous avoir mandé autrefois que rien ne me succédoit, & que*ᵃ* j'avois pris pour devise, *Nil agere semper infelici, est optimum*.[1] Mr. Westein a commancé l'édition de mes Poësies, & il m'en a envoyé les deux premieres feuilles. Mais le caractère & le papier m'ont tellement déplu, que je lui ay écrit de ne pas continuer; lui offrant de lui payer ces deux feuilles, & le port des lettres que je lui ay écrites. Je lui ay proposé ensuite*ᵇ* d'imprimer mes Poësies du caractère & avec le papier du Virgile de Mr. Heinsius. Et en cas qu'il voulust les imprimer de la sorte, je lui ay promis cinquante écus sans lui demander aucun exemplaire: & de les lui payer par avance: Et je lui ay promis, outre cela, d'en*ᶜ* acheter pour cinquante francs. Et comme je ne croy pas qu'il prenne ce parti-là, je me suis relasché à consentir qu'il*ᵈ* les imprimast du caractère dont il a commancé à les imprimer; quoyque tres mauvais; pourveu qu'il me donnast de meilleur papier. Je ne croy pas pas*ᵉ* nomplus qu'il accepte cette proposition-là. En ce cas,*ᶠ* je vous prie, Monsieur,*ᵍ* de me chercher un [fol. 2r] autre Imprimeur, qui ait des caractères plus nets, & de meilleur papier. Le plus petit caractère me plairoit le plus, pourveu qu'il fust bien net. Mais comme le papier est l'ame de l'édition, je souhaitte sur tout*ʰ* que le papier soit bon.[2] Je viens au Laërce. Mr. Westein a enfin traité avec Mr. Meibomius à cent pistoles:[3] pour lesquelles Mr. Meibomius*ⁱ* s'oblige à corriger les épreuves, à mettre le livre en ordre, à en faire une nouvelle version, & à l'enrichir de ses Remarques. Si on imprime mes Observations en un volume a part, & que Mr. Meibomius vueïlle bien prendre la peine d'en faire la Table, je lui donneray pour cela ce que vous jugerez apropos que je lui donne. J'ay reçu vostre lettre pour Mr. Petit: & je la lui ay rendue en main propre. Je lui dis hyer,*ʲ* que vous m'aviez écrit, qu'on rimprimoit au lieu où vous estes son Poëme du Thé:[4] dont il est bien glorieux. Je suis toutafait étonné de ce que vous m'écrivez que vous n'avez point u de nouvelles de Mr. de Montausier touchant la gratification que le Roi vous a faite. Je vais présantement en écrire à Mr. de Montausier: Et je vous feray savoir par le prochain ordinaire ce qu'il m'en aura écrit.[5] Vostre obligé en mille articles,

Ménage

[Address on fol. 2v (in Ménage's hand): A Monsieur / Monsieur Grævius / A Utrecht]

a. pour cela *deleted.*
b. ensuite *inserted.*
c. prendre *deleted.*
d. imprim *deleted.*
e. pas pas *sic.*
f. Monsieur, *deleted.*
g. Monsieur, *inserted.*
h. sur tout *inserted.*
i. deletion (illegible) after *Meibomius.*
j. ce *deleted.*

The letter is largely taken up with Ménage's dissatisfaction with Wetstein over his Poésies, *concerning the type and, particularly, the paper. Meibomius has agreed to help with the Diogenes edition, for a fee: he is to provide a Latin 'version' and his 'remarques', organize the work as a whole, correct proofs, and possibly draw up a table for Ménage's 'Observations'. Ménage has passed on a letter and news from Grævius to Petit; he is now actively concerned over complications regarding Grævius's royal 'gratification', and will intercede with Montausier on his behalf.*

1 Publilius Syrus, *Sent.*, N. 1. A passage of the *Ménagiana* deals with the *devises* adopted by various scholars, and Ménage includes his own: 'La mienne est: *Rien ne me réussit. Nihil agere semper infelici est optimum*' (*Ménagiana*, II, 44). It was a useful phrase, which Ménage used again in early 1689 to console his nephew, Pierre Ménage de Pigneroche, for two recent disappointments (he had failed to be appointed *capitaine de milice*, and an advantageous marriage project had fallen through): 'Je vois bien que vous n'êtes pas plus heureux que moy. Rien ne me succéde: et j'ai pris pour devise: *Nil agere semper infelici, est optimum*' (Baron de Villebois-Mareuil, 'Correspondance de Gilles Ménage', *La Revue Angevine*, 3 (1896), 242).
2 Ménage's particular concern about the paper used for his works was already evident in his comments about the German edition of his *Juris civilis amœnitates* six years earlier.
3 'Cent pistoles' is 1,100 livres, a substantial reward for Meibomius's help.
4 Ménage's reference is an interesting indication of the type of news that Grævius was passing on from the Low Countries, keeping his Parisian correspondent up to date with publications in progress there. Petit's poem was actually republished in Leipzig, edited by F. B. Carpzov: *P. Petiti ... Thea sive de Sinensi herba Thee carmen, ... cui adjectae F. N. Pechlini de eadem herba epigraphae* (Leipzig, 1685).
5 On Montausier's appreciation of scholarship, and his longstanding friendship with Ménage, see above, Letter 9, n. 3.

Ménage to Grævius. 30 August 1685

A Paris ce 30. Aoust *1685*

Monsieur

J'écrivis à Mr. le Duc de Montausier dans le tans que je vous manday que je lui écrirois. Et quelques jours après il me fit l'honneur de me venir voir, pour me dire que le Roy avoit ordonné qu'on vous donnast deux mille écus, & une chaisne d'or: & que cette chaisne seroit apparamment de quinze cents livres. Je connois particuliérement Mr. le Peletier Controleur Général des Finances;[1] & je lui aurois écrit pour lui recommander vostre affaire, sans qu'il en faut laisser la gloire toute entière à Mr. le Duc de Montausier. Mes Origines de la Langue Italienne sont enfin arrivées à Paris. Je vous en envoye un exemplaire; que je vous prie d'avoir agréable. Mon livre des Vies de Pierre Ayrault & de Guillaume Ménage, ne mérite pas le remerciment que vous m'en faites. Je vous envoieray à mon premier loisir le reste de mes Remarques sur Lucien: mais je ne desire pas qu'elles soient imprimées sous [fol. 2r] mon nom, ny séparément. Celui qui fait imprimer le Lucien, en fera ce qu'il lui plaira. Je les lui donne. Je vous envoyeray en mesme tans des Remarques de Mr. Guyet sur la Comédie de Lucien.[2] Mr. Bigot ne viendra point cette année à Paris, acause de quelques procês qu'il a à Rouen, comme Tuteur de son neveu. Je lui feray savoir la manière obligeante avec laquelle vous vous souvenez de lui. Nous sommes daccord Mr. Westein & moy: & bons amis. Je rendray à Mr. Sisme en vostre considération tout le service dont je seray capable.[3] Tout à vous: & sans reserve: & de tout mon coeur: & avec toute l'estime & toute l'admirati[on][a] que vous méritez.

Ménage

[Address on fol. 2v, in Ménage's hand: A Monsieur / Monsieur Grævius / A Utrecht]

a. *last two letters of* admiration *lost in tear at edge of page.*

Ménage has kept his promise at the end of the previous letter, and now writes to tell Grævius of the true, and very satisfactory, situation regarding his 'gratification': Ménage's powerful friends include not only Montausier but also Claude Le Peletier, the Contrôleur-Général des Finances. As usual, he also sends news of his works and mutual friends (including Bigot, still embroiled in family difficulties in Rouen), and general scholarly help. He responds to a letter of recommendation from Grævius; and there is a rare note of harmony in his relations with Wetstein, despite the hint of irony detectable in Ménage's comment.

1 Claude Le Peletier (1631-1711) was a scholarly lawyer of great probity and distinction, who in 1683 was appointed by Louis XIV to succeed Colbert as Contrôleur-Général des Finances.
2 This offer refers to an important source of information that Ménage would make available for fellow-scholars. After the death of the learned François Guyet (1575-1655), Ménage bought his library. Guyet had covered his books with marginal annotations which were extremely highly regarded by scholars working on new editions of

Latin and Greek texts. See B. Bray, 'Les Lettres françaises ...', p. 196, n. 9, which includes an account of the lengths that Gronovius went to in order to borrow Guyet's copy of Seneca's tragedies from Ménage for his own edition (1662). Ménage sent Guyet's notes on Lucian with his next letter. Nearly three years later, he refers to Guyet's notes on Terence in his letter of 21 March 1688. Grævius did incorporate Guyet's 'remarques' into his edition of Lucian, and he is mentioned on the title-page – as also is Ménage, despite his modest disclaimers in this letter (see letter of 27 April 1685 (Letter 25), note 4).

3 Sisme was an acquaintance of Bayle, and apparently lived in Rotterdam; on 8 July 1686 Bayle wrote to Minutoli: 'J'ai cherché Mr. Sismus, mais sans le trouver. Il n'est pas en Ville apparemment' (Œuvres diverses, IV, 625).

LETTER 30

Ménage to Grævius. 6 September 1685

A Paris ce 6. Sept. *1685*

Je vous envoie la suite de mes Remarques sur Lucien: & les Notes de Mr. Guyet sur l'Ocypus & sur la Tragopodagre.[1] Les Remarques sur les Notes de Mr. Guyet sont d'un jeune garçon de 20. ans, fort savant, qui s'appelle Mr. Boyvin.[2] Je seray bien aise de savoir comment s'appelle celui qui travaille sur Lucien: Et je vous prie de me le faire savoir. S'il se sert des anciennes versions, je croy qu'il sera apropos qu'il nomme les auteurs de ces Versions.[3] / . Madame Dacier est toujours à Nismes. Je lui feray demander si elle a quelque chose, ou d'elle, ou de son père, sur Lucien.[4] / . Le vostre tout vostre.

Ménage

[No address]

A short note a week later, accompanying the varied material that Ménage has promised to send to help with the new edition of Lucian: a good example of how Ménage can draw on his network of scholarly contacts, just as he was able to draw on his Court and administrative contacts to help Grævius over his 'gratification'.

1 'Tragopodagre': 'Gout – a tragedy', and its pseudo-Lucianic pendant 'Ocypus', 'Swift-of-Foot', two burlesque dramas.
2 Jean Boivin de Villeneuve (1663-1726) distinguished himself as a Latin and Greek scholar at an early age, and maintained that promise through his life; he also cultivated a taste for modern literature, particularly poetry. He was appointed Professor of Greek at the Collège Royal in 1705, and elected to the Académie in 1721 as successor to Huet.

3 Ménage's concern about naming the authors of earlier 'Versions' of Lucian is explained in his next letter: their names had been omitted in the Saumur edition.

4 She must have sent some notes by her father, Tanneguy Le Febvre, beacuse his name is mentioned in the title of the finished work ('T. Fabri').

Ménage to Grævius. 17 January 1686

A Paris ce 17. Jan. *1686.*

Monsieur

Je n'ay reçu que depuis quatre jours la lettre qu'il vous a plu m'écrire du 7. du mois d'Octobre: Et ainsi, Monsieur, je n'ay pu vous y faire réponse plustost qu'aujourdhuy. Monsieur de Wit m'a fait l'honneur de me visiter. Pour achever son éloge en un mot: c'est un fis digne de son pere.[1] Il ne m'a point encore rendu l'exemplaire de la Thémis de Meursius que vous lui avez donné*ᵃ* pour moy.[2] Je ne laisse pas de vous en remercier par avance. Il y a déja quelque tans que Mr. Du Cange me donna sa Dissertation de l'Hebdome de Constantinople contre Mr. de Valois, le jeune,[3] pour vous la faire tenir. Je l'ay mise entre les mains de Mr. de Mowe: qui vous l'aura sans doute envoyée avec mes Origines de la Langue Italienne. Mr. Wetstein n'a point encore commancé l'édition de mes Poësies: dont je suis étonné: m'aïant écrit il y a plus de six mois qu'il fesoit fondre des charactères pour cette édition.[4] De la façon que vous me parlez du Lucien qu'on imprime en Hollande, ce sera peu de chose. Il y falloit une nouvelle version. Benoist, qui a publié celui de Saumur,[5] a oublié de marquer [fol. 2r] le nom de ceux qui avoient fait les versions. Je viens de recevoir une lettre de Mr. Bigot, par laquelle il me mande qu'il vous écrira au premier jour. Mr. de Wit m'a dit que vous estiez sur le point de faire imprimer vostre Vie de Mr. Heinsius: dont j'ai bien de la joye.[6] Je vous souhaitte une bonne année, suivie de plusieurs autres semblables: & suis toujours à l'ordinaire,

Monsieur,
Vostre tres humble
& tres obéissant serviteur
Ménage

[Address on fol. 2v, in Ménage's hand: A Monsieur / Monsieur Grævius / A Utrecht]

ᵃ. final letter e deleted from donné.

Problems of communication (a letter has taken more that three months to reach Ménage), a visitor bearing a letter of recommendation, and reciprocal exchanges of books. The current themes of the correspondence are maintained: Ménage complains of Wetstein's slowness, comments further on the proposed edition of Lucian, and passes on news of Bigot.

1 Johan de Witt (1662-1701), son of the Grand Pensionary, and Town Clerk of Dordrecht, corresponded with Bayle and Nicaise (see E. Labrousse, *Inventaire critique de la correspondance de Pierre Bayle* (Paris, 1961), pp. 151, 242).

2 . J. *Meursii Themis Attica, sive de legibus Atticis libri II* (Utrecht, J. Van de Water,1685), edited by Grævius.

3 'Mr. de Valois, le jeune' is Adrien de Valois (see above, letter of 9 November 1684 (Letter 19), note 1). His 'dissertation sur l'Hebdome' was published at the end of the second edition of his brother's *Ammiani Marcellini Rerum Gestarum qui de XXXI supersunt Libri XVIII ...* (Paris, A. Dezallier, 1681), and extracts were included in the *Journal des Savants* of 2 February 1688. Adrien de Valois also noted highly critical 'Remarques' on the first volume of Du Cange's *Glossarium ad scriptores mediæ et infimæ latinitatis*, which were published in the *Valesiana* (Paris, F. and P. Delaulne, 1694), pp. 208-34.

4 The letter from Wetstein, of *c.* early July 1685, has been lost. In Wetstein's next letter (28 February 1686) he refers to casting new type for the Diogenes edition rather than the *Poésies*.

5 The Saumur edition of Lucian was published in 1619 in two volumes by the German scholar Johannes Benedictus ('Jean Benoist'): *Luciani Samosatensis opera omnia in duos tomos divisa Iohannes Benedictus Medicinæ Doctor, & in Salmuriensi Academia Regia linguæ Græcæ Professor* (Saumur, Petrus Piededius, 1619); the Latin translation had already been criticised by Tanneguy Le Febvre and Lucian's French translator Nicolas Perrot d'Ablancourt. D'Ablancourt's version was first published in 1654 (*Lucien, de la traduction de N. Perrot, Sr. d'Ablancourt*, 2 vols (Paris, A. Courbé, 1654)), and frequently reprinted; he even appended to it a section of 'Remarques critiques de quelques endroits mal traduits dans la Version Latine de Lucien, reveuë par Monsieur Benoist, et imprimé à Saumur l'an 1619'.

6 On Grævius's long-planned life of Heinsius, see Ménage's letter of 18 January 1682 (Letter 7), note 3; it was to be another fifty-six years before the work was finally published.

LETTER 32

Wetstein to Ménage. 28 February 1686

d'Amsterdam ce 28e. de Février[a] *1686.*

Monsieur

Si Monsieur Francius ne nous auroit pas amusé, Vous auriez eu cette epreuve par la derniere poste. Cependant comme il ne l'a pas encore leûe et ne le pourra faire de quelques jours (: à cause de sa harangue inaugurale[b] de la Profession grecque,[1] qu'il doit faire dans peu de jours) j'ai crû plus expedient de Vous l'envoyer cependant sans qu'elle soit corrigée, pour gaigner ce temps, & d'avancer toujours[c] d'autant en besogne.

Nous avions deja corrigé toutes les fautes de la premiere feuille, que Vous avez marquées dans Votre derniere lettre, sans qu'il y eut aucune, qui nous eut echapée. Fab: 1a. pag. 18. l. 14. Mr. Francius a corrigé *transferam* au lieu d'*auferam*, à cause que 8. lign. devant il y avoit *transferat*; & qu'il croyoit qu'il valoit mieux de mettre le méme mot, qui auroit meilleure grace. Plus pag. 21. l. 14. il a oté *ut*, croyant que cela faisoit l'elocution meilleure. Notez Monsieur, que Monsr Francius ne veut aucunement entreprendre de corriger des choses de cette nature à Votre insçû, mais il ecrit seulement à la marge que cela lui paroissoit mieux de telle ou telle façon. / .*ᵈ* Mais comme Vous m'avez marqué que Vous seriez bien aise quand il feroit de tels changemens, je ne fais aucun scrupule, de corriger suivant sa penséeᵉ. Vous me direz si je fais bien ou mal.

Le Diogene s'accroche sur une seule lettre grecque qui est l'H, que j'ai deja fait graver deux ou 3. fois sans qu'elle ait reüssi; ainsi on est aprés à la faire de nouveau. Dieu veuille qu'elle succede. Au reste tout est prest, characteres latins & grecs tous nouveaux, le papier, etc: tout. Ce m'est une grande perte que ce retardement. Mais Monsr. Meybomius ne veut point d'η, comme il ne vouloit point de γ, qu'il a falu faire Γ, & qui a bien reussi. J'èspere que nous serons en etat de commencer dans peu. Je suis

Monsieur
Votre treshumble & tresobeissant serviteur
H Wetstein

[no address]

ᵃ. Février *inserted, replacing* Mars *deleted.*
ᵇ. *final letter* s *deleted from* inaugurale.
ᶜ. tou *altered from* toj *in* toujours.
ᵈ. *the text contains at this point a mark like a small italic ρ that Wetstein sometimes uses in punctuation.*
ᵉ. sa pensée *originally written as one word, then separated by /:* sa/pensée.

This letter is dated fourteen months after the previous surviving communication from Wetstein (25 December 1694), although in his previous letter to Grævius Ménage alludes to one of early July 1685 that has been lost, and correspondence has clearly been continuing about the Poésies *and the Diogenes edition. Wetstein now sends a proof of the* Poésies, *and refers to Ménage's corrections to an earlier proof, and Francius's suggestions for occasional improvements to the Latin verses (which Wetstein takes care to allude to tactfully). Wetstein has a new excuse for delays over the Diogenes: problems in designing new Greek characters, which have been insisted on by the difficult and particular Meibomius.*

1 Francius had held the chair of eloquence and history at Amsterdam since 1674, and in 1686 was also appointed professor of Greek.

LETTER 33

Ménage to Grævius. 10 May 1686

Monsieur

J'ay esté prié de vous recommander Messieurs de Saumaise,[1] qui se sont retirez en Hollande acause de leur religion: Et je vous les recommande, Monsieur, de toute ma force: feu Monsieur de Saumaise, leur pere, estant une personne a qui j'avois beaucoup d'obligation, & pour qui j'avois toute sorte d'estime & de respect.[2] Je suis toujours à l'ordinaire,

Monsieur,
Vostre tres humble
& tres obéissant serviteur
Ménage

A Paris ce 10. May
   1686.
[Address on fol. 2v, in Ménage's hand: A Monsieur / Monsieur Grævius / A Utrecht]

A short note of recommendation on behalf of Messieurs de Saumaise: two sons of the great scholar, Huguenots like him, who were leaving France for the Low Countries following the Revocation of the Edict of Nantes.

1 Louis, sieur de St-Loup, and Louis-Charles were the only two of Saumaise's five sons still alive in 1686. They both settled in the Netherlands, where Louis edited his father's posthumous *Exercitationes de homonymis hyles iatricæ* (Leiden, 1688).
2 Ménage's surviving correspondence with the great French protestant scholar Claude de Saumaise (1588-1653) is preserved in the Universiteitsbibliothek Leiden (sig. PAP. 7 (1-11)). After Ménage published his *Antibaillet*, one of the sons wrote to Nicaise on 16 December 1688: 'Je doibs un fort grand compliment à l'illustre M. Menage, pour avoir si bien deffendu la memoire de feu mon Pere son bon ami, contre l'injuste attaque du sieur Baillet; chargés vous en, je vous prie, lors que vous le verrés' (Caillemer (ed.), *Lettres à Nicaise*, p. 100).

LETTER 34

Ménage to Grævius. 1 August 1686

Monsieur

Je reçus avanthier la Thémis Attique de Meursius qu'il vous a plu m'envoyer:[1] pour laquelle je*ᵃ* vous fais mille tres humbles remercimens. De mon costé, j'ay aussi à vous faire un présant: qui est mon Histoire de Sablé. Je vous prie de me mander par quelle voye je puis vous la faire tenir. Mr. le Duc de Montausier me fit hier l'honneur de me venir voir. Je lui donnay en main propre la lettre que vous m'avez envoyée pour lui; avec vostre Discours sur l'Université d'Utrech.[2] Il reçut ces marques de vostre souvenir avec bien de la joye: & il m'assura bien qu'il ne manqueroit pas de vous en remercier. Je feray savoir à Mr. Gallé; qui est celui qui m'a apporté cet exemplaire de la Thémis de Meursius de vostre part;[3] que celui qui est adressé à Mr. Petit, est destiné pour Mr. Baluze: affin qu'il me l'envoie, & qu'il ne le porte pas à Mr. Petit, comme il en avoit dessein. [fol. 2r] L'édition de mes Poësies procéde: mais pour celle de mon Diogéne Laërce, elle n'est point encore commancée. Mr. Wetstein m'écrivoit par sa derniere lettre, qu'il l'alloit commancer par mes Observations.[4] Je lui ay mandé que je ne comprenois pas son dessein;[b] que mes Observations devoient estre rélatives aux pages du Texte; & qu'ainsi il falloit commancer par le Texte. Mr. Westein a cru[c] épargner en imprimant le livre in 8°. Et il se trouvera qu'il lui coustera davantage que s'il l'ust imprimé in folio. Je viens d'apprandre par une lettre de Mr. Justel, que Mr. Vossius alloit faire imprimer en Angleterre les Lettres de son pere, & celles qu'on avoit écrites à son pere.[5] L'ouvrage sera curieux. J'oubliois à vous dire, que Mr. Gallé ne m'a point donné[d] d'autres exemplaires de la *Themis Attica*, que celui qui m'estoit destiné. Je vous baise tres humblement les mains: Et suis toujours à l'ordinaire: cestadire, de toute ma passion, & avec toute sorte d'estime & de respect

Monsieur,
Vostre tres humble & tres
obéissant serviteur
Ménage

A Paris ce 1.
Aoust 1686.

[Address on fol. 2v, in Ménage's hand: A Monsieur / Monsieur Grævius / A Uthrech]
a. fais *deleted*. *b*. & *deleted*. *c*. cru *inserted, replacing* voulu *deleted*. *d*. donné *inserted, replacing* remis *deleted*.

The first part of the letter is taken up with an exchange of publications between the two scholars, Ménage's activities in distributing complimentary copies for Grævius, and, notably, his invaluable help in maintaining the links between Grævius and Montausier. Ménage complains yet again about Wetstein's delays and obtuse planning of the Diogenes edition, and ends with the news of a proposed edition of Vossius's correspondence.

1 See Ménage's letter of 17 January 1686 above (Letter 31), note 2.
2 *Joannis Georgii Grævii Oratio in natalem quinquagesimum Academiæ Trajectinæ habita ... a.d. XVII. Kal. Apriles 1686* (Utrecht, F. Halma, 1686). Grævius's speeches and addresses were collected after his death as *Johannis Georgii Grævii Orationes quas Ultrajecti habuit* (Leiden, J. de Vivié, 1717).
3 The scholar Servat Gallé (or Gallæus, Gael, Gal), who died in 1709, is mentioned several times as the intermediary Grævius used for transmitting letters and packets to

France, for example when Ménage sent Grævius his *Histoire de Sablé* on 6 February
1687 (Letter 38). His relative importance is indicated in a letter from Grævius to Nicaise of 1689: 'Quinque minimum ad te his tribus quatuorve mensibus ad te [*sic*] misi
epistolas. Tres per Gallæum, cum vobiscum ageret, unam per Illustrem Spanhemium,
quintam curavi ad Menagium' (Caillemer (ed.), *Lettres à Nicaise*, p. 162).
4 The letter from Wetstein that Ménage refers to has been lost.
5 Isaac Vossius asked the Huguenot refugee scholar Paul Colomies to edit his father's
correspondence. The work came out four years later: *Gerardi Joannis Vosii et clarorum
virorum ad eum Epistolae, collectore Paulo Colomesio* (London, R. R. and M. C. for Adiel
Mills, 1690). Grævius mentioned that the work had finally been published in a letter to
Ménage of March 1690 (draft in letter-book of J.G. Grævius, UB Utrecht, Hs.7.c30, p.
58).

LETTER 35
Wetstein to Ménage. 22 September 1686

                        d'Amsterdam ce 22e. de Septembre *1686*.
Monsieur,
Vous m'aviez demandé la page 88. à ce que me semble, & je Vous l'ai envoyée. Voici
les 5. vers restans que demandez

    Lectis scilicet his, beatiores,
    Vitam vivere quos priùs juvabat,
    Projecere animas, diem perosi.
    Sic vitæ mala Suasor ille mortis;
    Sic mortis bona Phædo disserebat.
    Si non incitat, etc.

Voici la 1re. feuille, avec la table: à laquelle manquent beaucoup de chiffres; d'autres
sont fausses, & mémes plusieurs. Ainsi il Vous plaira de les faire conferer. Il me semble
qu'aurez plustot fait à me renvoyer cette feuille corrigée que d'en transcrire les errata.
Vous aviez mis aux errata BUSSIADEN: cependant cela est dans l'imprimé comme
Vous le corrigez, & ainsi non-necessaire d'étre mis[a] aux errata. De meme la correction
de la page 166 ne change rien de l'imprimé. Je Vous enverrai encore une epreuve de la
feuille grecque avant que de la tirer. Cependant je demeure

                         Monsieur
            Votre treshumble & tresobeïssant
                      serviteur
                      H Wetstein

[No address]
[a]. mis *inserted*.

A practical letter, concerned entirely with the proofs of Ménage's Poésies *and his corrections to them. The sense here is of the difficulty of working at such a distance, and of the printer coping with a rather erratic author.*

Wetstein to Ménage. 25 November 1686

d'Amsterdam ce 25e. de Novembre *1686.*

Monsieur

Je Vous ai ecrit par le dernier ordinaire, dans la pensée, que ma precedente du 31e. du passé ne Vous eut pas été rendue. De depuis je reçois la votre du 9e. du courant, que je devois avoir reçu le 13e. ensuite, & qui à mon grand etonnement ne m'est rendue que le 22e.[1]

Pour le *Doctis Grajugenum* je n'en trouve rien à la page 88. Mais voici mot à mot ce qui y est:

In Sulpitium, qui libellum de morte cordi suo dicavit. Ad Poly-
carpum Sengeberum Antecessorem Andegavensem. XVI.[2]

Quem de Morte mihi, venuste noster,	Misti Sulpitij tui libellum,
Legi sedulò, sedulò relegi.	De quo judicium meum hoc habero,
Quando judicium meum requiris.	Quos de Morte Süasor ille mortis,
Quos dîus Plato scripserant, libellis	Haud multùm inferior mihi videtur.
Lectis scilicet his, beatiores,	Vitam vivere quos priùs juvabat,
Projecere animas, diem perosi.	Sic vitæ mala Suasor ille mortis;
Sic mortis bona Phædo disserebat.	Si non incitat ad necem legentes etc.

Voila tout ce qui concerne la question. Pour la nouvelle Epigramme de Bajuletus, je ne sai pas asseurement où la placer, puis qu'aprés la table il n'y a point de place pour 3 lignes; Elle se pourroit mettre sur un feuillet ou page separée, pour etre inserée aprés la page 160. & faire le sixiéme carton. Mais où placer en ce[a] cas les 2.[b] Epigrammes de M[r]. Sladus que je Vous ai envoyé par ma dernière.

Revoyant Vos epreuves, je trouve qu'avez effacé les 2. vers suivans de la XVI. Epigr: *Doctis Grajugenum (quis hoc negabit?) Libris cedere vix Sophûm videtur.* Ainsi il n'y a point de miracle que je ne l'y aye pas trouvés.

Je ne disconviens pas de ce que Vous dites du papier pour le Diogene: Mais je Vous ai dit à quoi il tient que je n'en aye point d'autre. Celui pour lequel j'ai contracté est aussi beau que j'en aye jamais vû, & pour la forme & pour la couleur. Et je ne doute pas que Vous n'en demeuriez d'accord si Vous le voyiez. Mais comme je n'en ai qu'une seule feuille, & que je n'en puis avoir d'autre, & que c'est la feuille sur la quelle j'ai contracté, je n'oserois la mettre au hazard d'estre perdue en Vous l'envoyant. Avec tout cela il faudra en prendre d'autre, ou se resoudre d'attendre le mois de Mars, [fol. 1v] auquel temps les papetiers promettent l'autre. Mais ils me l'avoient aussi promis pour le mois d'octobre, & maintenant ils s'excusent sur le manque d'eau pendant l'été. Il faudra pourtant se resoudre d'une façon ou d'une autre.

Voici une epreuve in 4°. on est maintenant aprés d'en faire une avec les notes au dessous. (Notez que mon papier accordé est d'un doit plus long sur chaque page^c que l'epreuve ci-jointe) Je commence d'y trouver tant de goût, que je suis presque entierement resolu pour l'in 4°. il ne me manque que votre sentiment.

Les Γ & H sont de l'invention de M^r. Meibomius, qui m'a forcé de les faire faire; (ce qui m'a couté une 20e. d'ecus & plus^d) pretendant de m'avoir decouvert un secret de la derniere importance, pour lequel il devroit estre recompensé par le public. Il n'y en aura point dans les Notes.

Lec^e grec du garamond estoit asseurement plus beau que celui-ci qui est de Cicero.^{3} Mais qu'y faire? il n'y a aucun grec de Cicero au monde qui soit beau. Au moins n'en ai-je jamais vû.

Les chiffres de la marge sont des sections, par lesquelles Mr. Meybom subdivise le texte pour la commodité du lecteur, & sur lesquelles il pretend faire sa table plustot que sur les chiffres des pages.

Ni l'ypsilon jota n'est pas lié, ni méme l'omicron-ypsilon. par le principe de M^r. Meybom, qui veut oter toutes les ligatures. ઠ - ου: ᘯ - σθ: ς - στ.^{f}

[No formal ending or signature, no address]

^{a}. s *deleted at the end of* ce. ^{b}. les 2. *inserted, replacing* l' *deleted*. ^{c}. sur chaque page *inserted*.
^{d}. & plus *inserted*. ^{e}. Lec *sic*. ^{f}. *the Greek is followed by Wetstein's* ρ *mark*.

The first part of this letter deals with the progress of the Poésies, *and the second part with the lack of progress of the Diogenes edition. There are problems over the paper, about which Ménage was so particular, and a new excuse for the delays: the paper-makers ran short of water in summer, and will not deliver the paper ordered until March in the following year. It is perhaps not surprising that Ménage found Wetstein's excuses – which include his further claim that he only had a single sheet of the proposed paper for the edition – less than wholly convincing. Wetstein now favours a quarto format for the work. The Greek type is still a contentious subject, with Wetstein's complaints about Meibomius an ominous foretaste of problems to come.*

1 Interesting evidence concerning the time-scale of correspondence between Paris and Amsterdam, and how it could be disrupted. Two letters from Wetstein have not survived (31 October and mid-November), and the first was possibly lost in transit. Post from Paris normally took four days, but Ménage's last letter took thirteen days.
2 This poem, like many others, underwent repeated revisions in successive editions. In the fourth edition (Amsterdam, Elzevir, 1663) it is dedicated 'Ad Joannem Allemannum' (pp. 58-59).
3 The Greek founts cut by Claude Garamond (died 1561) at the order of François I – the 'grecs du roi' – were first used in the early 1540s. They were often praised for their beauty, but a more critical evaluation by a modern historian of printing tends to sup-

port Meibomius's dislike of Garamond's basic principles: 'Typographically ... the *grecs du roi* constitute a huge advance over Aldus's types, but ... Garamond, too, used as his model a contemporary Greek hand which, if anything, contained even more contractions and ligatures than the one that served the Venetian cutter' (S.H. Steinberg, *Five Hundred Years of Printing* (2nd edition, Harmondsworth, 1961), pp. 113-14).

LETTER 37

Wetstein to Ménage. 12 December 1686

d'Amsterdam ce 12ᵉ. de Decembre. *1686.*

Je reçu Monsieur toutes Vos corrections & toutes Vos lettres. On alloit imprimer la feuille du titre lors que Votre derniere arriva. cependant rien n'etoit fait encore, & on a oté les mots *post JULIUM II Pont. Max.* Ainsi que tout est venu à point. Demain on fera le reste. Aprés quoi je ferai relier incontinent les exemplaires pour ces Messieurs que m'avez indiquez.[1] Mais comment Vous faire tenir les autres? Par Rouen ou par Bruxelles?[2] J'en suivrai Votre ordre.

J'ai donné aujourdhuy un billet de 83 ¹/₃ ecus ou 250 livres à un certain Monsr. Jean Batte. Swaenen, que je Vous prie d'avoir la bonté de payer quand il Vous sera presenté de sa part.

Pour monᵃ grec duᵇ Diogene,[3] Monsr Meiboom s'etonne pour le moins autant que Vous le trouviez laid, que Vous Vous etonnez que lui le trouve beau. A son advis il n'y a rien qui soit plus exact, ni qui ressente mieux la netteté de l'antiquité grecque: tout y est fabriqué à dessein. Pour les ligatures qu'il retranche toutes, il en trouve des approbateurs par tout, & tous nos doctes du païs & de l'Allemagne sont pour lui. De distinguer en sections les livres est presentement la grande mode, & une table & des renvois faits sur les sections, servent pour toutes sortes d'editions de quelque forme ou charactere qu'on les veuille faire, sans qu'on ait besoin d'y changer quoi que ce soit.

Pour ce qui est de mettre les notes au dessous du texte, je croi que cela se peut sans difficulté; & que chaque note se trouvera fort juste au dessous & dans la méme page où se trouve le texte; si cela ne se peut pas, il n'y faut pas songer asseurement; mais si cela se peut comme je le croi, je suis d'avis de n'y pas balancer. & j'examinerai cela exactement pour demain, ensuite dequoi on en fera une epreuve.

Quant à ce que dites que je n'ai jamais voulu le faire in folio. Je Vous assure foi-de-galant-homme que Vous Vous trompez. J'en ai plus d'envie que Vous. Mais l'utile l'emporte sur la beauté; ou plustot l'usage. On vendra 10. in 4° ou 8°. sans vendre 3. in folio. qu'y faire? le fort l'emporte.[4] Je suis Monsieur de tout mon cœur

Votre tres humble & tres obeïssant serviteur

H Wetstein

[No address]

^a. mon *inserted, replacing* le *deleted*.
^b. du *altered from* de, mon *deleted*.

The final stages of the printing of the Poésies: *last-minute corrections from Ménage, and details from Wetstein about his bill and problems of communication. On the Diogenes edition, Ménage has clearly objected strongly to all the proposals in Wetstein's last letter, and is still complaining in his next letter to Grævius nearly two months later. Wetstein has to defend Meibomius's Greek type, the plan to sub-divide the work into sections, the arrangement of the notes beneath the text, and the format. He ends with interesting details of the comparative sales of different formats.*

1 Wetstein distributed copies of the work on Ménage's behalf to his Dutch and German friends. In his effusive letter of thanks of 18 March 1687, Theodore Jansson van Almeloveen mentions that he was sent the book directly by Wetstein (copy in his letter-book: 'Theod. Janssonius ab Almeloveen. Epistolae ad eruditos', UB Utrecht, Hs. 5. K9, fols 29r-30r), as also did Gisbert Cuper in his equally effusive letter dated 'Mars 1687': 'Mr. Wetsteyn m'a rendu vos poësies .. .' (KB Den Haag, MS 72. C. 46, fol. 14r-v).
2 That is to say, by sea or overland.
3 Wetstein had originally written 'le grec de mon Diogene', but tactfully changed it to 'mon grec du Diogene'.
4 The 1664 London edition had been in folio; however, the greater prestige of this format is countered by the commercial practicalities of likely sales figures.

LETTER 38

Ménage to Grævius. 6 February 1687

Monsieur

J'appréhendois que vous ne fussiez malade, ne recevant point de vos lettres. J'apprens par vostre dernière avec bien de la joye que vous vous estes toujours bien porté, & que vous n'avez cessé de m'écrire qu'acause du voyage que vous avez fait en Allemagne. Je ne manqueray pas de mettre au premier jour entre les mains de Mr. Gallé l'exemplaire de mon Histoire de Sablé que je vous ay destiné. Mr. Wetstein n'aura pas manqué de son costé à vous donner^d mes Poësies. Je verray volontiers les livres de Meursius que vous me promettez. Je n'ay point de nouvelles qu'on ayt encore commancé l'édition de mon Laërce. Il y a déja quelques mois que Mr. [fol. 1v] Westein m'en envoya une page: dont le Grec étoit si vilain qu'il offensoit les yeux. Avec cela, il veut mettre toutes les Notes avec le Texte. Je lui ay mandé que cela seroit tres mal: & que comme il y a de tres grandes Notes, & de plusieurs Ecrivains, un article du Texte seroit si éloigné d'un autre, qu'on ne pourroit lire commodément le Texte: qui est la chose principale pour laquelle on achetera son livre. Cependant je voy par la réponse qu'il m'a faite qu'il persévére dans son dessein. Quand il m'écrivit pour me demander mon Laërce, il me dît qu'il en vouloit faire un chédoeuvre d'édition. Et son édition sera la plus vilaine chose du monde. Et si avec cela, elle n'est pas correcte, il en sera mauvais marchand. Je vous envoye un Mémoire de la part de Mr. Failibien, sur lequel on vous demande un mot de réponse à vostre loisir. Ce Mr. Failibien est un homme de mérite dans les Lettres: & qui est fis de Mr. Failibien qui a écrit les Vies des Peintres.[1] A l'heure que je vous écris, Mr. Baluze est chez [fol. 2r] moy, où il est venu me prier de vous faire tenir la lettre que vous trouverez dans ce pacquet. J'ay fait vos baisemains à ceux à qui vous m'avez ordonné de les faire. Monsieur Bigot me fait espérer qu'il sera icy dans peu de jours. Je suis toujours de tout mon coeur, & avec toute sorte d'estime, de respect, & de vénération,

Monsieur,
Vostre tres humble
& tres obéissant serviteur
Ménage

A Paris ce 6.
Fevr. *1687.*
Le Cardinal Bona a écrit dans son Indice sur son livre des Liturgies,[2] que Suidas étoit un Moine de Bysance. Ne savez vous point où il a pris cette particularité?
[No address]

a. un exemplaire de *deleted.*

Ménage has just heard from Grævius after a six-month gap caused by Grævius's voyage to Germany, and can at last send his Histoire de Sablé. *The* Poésies *are now printed, and a complimentary copy sent from Wetstein. As usual, Ménage complains at length about Wetstein's handling of the Diogenes edition. The conclusion is taken up with a variety of ways in which Ménage is acting as an intermediary for Grævius in Paris, enclosing two letters from scholars, and passing on greetings on behalf of his correspondent.*

1 The architectural historian Jean-François Félibien (1658-1733) was the son of the distinguished polygraph André Félibien (1619-1695), whose most celebrated work remains his *Entretiens sur les vies et sur les ouvrages des plus excellens peintres, anciens et modernes,* first published in 1666.
2 The erudite Cardinal Giovanni Bona (1609-1674) published his work in 1671: *Rerum liturgicarum libri duo* (Rome, N. A. Tinassius, 1671); it was reprinted in Paris the following year (Paris, L. Billaine, 1672). Ménage's surprise at Bona's claim is understandable: 'Suidas' is not an author, but the title of a lexicon compiled around the end of the tenth century AD (the word is taken from Latin and means 'fortress' or 'stronghold').

LETTER 39

Ménage to Grævius. 22 May 1687

Monsieur

Je suis bien aise que mes Poësies ne vous ayent pas déplu. Vous devez présantement avoir reçu mon Histoire de Sablé. Je vous prie d'y corriger ces trois fautes. Page 197. ligne 8. du Chapitre 3. *frere de Jan.* Il faut, *pere de Jan.* Page 269. ligne 8. à conter par la fin de la page: *dans la paroisse S. Remi de la Varenne, dite en Latin* Chiriacum. Effacez cela. Page 358. *Fondation du Prieuré de Montguyon, par Juhel, Seigneur de Maïenne & de Dinan, en 1098.* Il faut, *en 1198.* Page 360. à la fin de la Fondation de ce Prieuré, aulieu de, *anno Domini ab Incarnatione millesimo nonagesimo octavo,* il faut, *millesimo centesimo nonagesimo octavo.* /. Je n'entens point de nouvelles de mon Laërce. Il faut avouer que [fol. 2r] Mr. Westein est un étrange homme. Il y a six ans que je lui envoiay ce livre à vostre prière. Je vous envoie une lettre de Mr. Bigot: lequel sera icy dans deux jours. Mr. Félibien vous rent mille tres humbles graces. On m'a fait voir depuis peu ce qu'a dit de moy Mr. Henninius dans son livre de la Langue Grecque.[1] Je vous supplie, Monsieur, de lui dire que je lui en suis tres obligé, & de lui en faire de grands remercimens de ma part. Aimez moy toujours: & croyez que je seray toute ma vie de toute ma passion,

Monsieur,

Vostre tres humble

& tres obéissant serviteur

Ménage

A Paris ce
22. May 1687.
[No address]

Ménage sends corrections to errata in his Histoire de Sablé, *complains about Wetstein, and sends messages from and to mutual scholarly friends.*

1 The scholar-physician Heinrich Christian de Hennin (c1655-1703) lived in Utrecht, which is why Ménage asks Grævius to pass on his thanks personally. The work concerned is Hennin's treatise expounding his theories of Greek pronunciation: *Henrici Christiani Henninii Hellenismos orthoidos. Seu, Græcam linguam non esse pronunciandam secundum accentus; dissertatio paradoxa* (Utrecht, Rudolf van Zyll, 1684). He praises Ménage in his 'Praefatio': ' ... uti nec magnum illud Galliæ suæ decus MENAGIUM certo fiebam certior' (sig. *4r).

Ménage to Grævius. 21 March 1688

Monsieur

Je reçus, il y a deja quelque tans, l'Helladius de Meursius,[1] qu'il vous[a] a plu m'envoyer: pour lequel je vous rens mille & mille tres humbles actions de graces. Je n'ay point encore reçu vos Offices de Cicéron:[2] mais je les recevray au premier jour: car Mr. Vroesen me dit avant hier qu'elles étoient enfin arrivées en France. Mr. Gallé me rendit le mesme jour la lettre que vous m'avez écrite en faveur de Mr. Bylandius:[3] lequel s'en est retourné en Hollande, sans que j'aye u le bien de le voir. Ce que vous me dites par cette lettre, que Mr. Westein n'a pas encore commancé l'édition de mon Diogéne Laërce, m'a extrémement surpris & extrémement affligé. Je[b] croyois ce livre[c] prest d'être publié: Mr. Westein m'aïant écrit, il y a plus d'un an, qu'il l'avoit commancé: & m'en aïant mesme envoyé la premiere facille. Il faut avouer que j'ay grand sujet de me plaindre de ce Mr. Westein. Il y a plus de six ans qu'il me demanda & que je lui envoyay mon Laërce. Et en ce tans-là, il m'assuroit qu'il seroit imprimé en moins d'un an. D'un autre coté, il m'a imprimé mes Poësies en de mauvais papier, & en mauvais caracteres: & peu correctement. [fol. 2r] Il est vray que je suis sur le point de faire rimprimer ma Dissertation sur l'Heautontimorumenos de Térence.[4] J'y soutiens qu'il faut lire dans la premiere Scene, *Fodere, aut arare, aut aliquid ferre*[d] *denique. Nullum remittis* tempus, &c. & non pas, *Fodere, aut arare, aut aliquid ferre: denique Nullum remittis*, &c. Outre que c'est la leçon de plusieurs[e] Manuscrits de Térence,[f] & celle de la pluspart des éditions, & entr'autres de celle de Mr. le Fêvre, Professeur de Saumur, qui est tres correcte,[5] Ciceron, au livre I. *de Finibus*, cite ce premier vers de la sorte que je soutiens qu'il doit être lu. Voicy les paroles de Cicéron: *Terentianus Chremes non inhumanus, qui novum vicinum non vult*

Fodere, aut arare, aut aliquid ferre denique.

Non enim illum ab industria, sed ab illiberali labore deterret. Il est vray que quelques exemplaires des livres de Finibus de Cicéron n'ont point le *denique*, comme l'a remarqué Lambin.[6] Mais outre qu'il se trouve dans tous les manuscrits & dans un nombre infini d'éditions, il ne peut être révoqué en doute que Térence n'ayt fini son vers par *denique*; Donat,[7] sur ces paroles du Phormion, QUID FIT DENIQUE, qui sont de la Scene 2. de l'Acte I. aïant remarqué que Térence a mis *denique* dans cet endroit-là à la fin du sens, comme dans celui-cy de l'Héautontimoruménos,[g] *Fodere, aut arare, aut aliquid ferre denique.* Voicy les paroles de Donat: *More suo posuit Terentius denique in fine sensus. Et est adverbium ordinis. Sic in Heautont. Fodere, aut arare, aut aliquid facere denique.* Après avoir soutenu cette ponctuation, je soutiens ensuite que la leçon de *facere* de Donat doit être préférée à celle [fol. 1v, sideways] *ferre*,[h] qui est celle de toutes les éditions de Térence, & de la pluspart de ses Manuscrits. Outre l'autorité de Donat, j'ay encore celle d'Eugraphius:[8] car Eugraphius cite aussi cet endroit avec *facere*. Dailleurs, quelques Manuscrits de Térence, selon le témoignage de Mr. Guyet,[i] ont *facere*:[9] Et quelques

Manuscrits de Cicéron, selon le témoignage de Rivius dans ses Castigations[j] sur Térence,[10] ont la mesme leçon. Mr. Guyet dit que *facere* ne marque rien de différant d'avec *fodere* & *arare*: *bécher* & *labourer* étant faire quelque chose. Et moi je soutiens que, *aut aliquid facere denique* n'est pas le mesme que *fodere* & *arare*: & que le mot de *denique* importe *aliquid aliud facere*: Et qu'on dit fort bien, *Je ne sors jamais si matin, & je ne reviens jamais si tard, que je ne vous[k] voye dans votre champ, ou bécher, ou labourer, ou enfin faire quelque chose*: Et qu'on ne dit pas si bien, *Je ne sors jamais si matin, & je ne reviens jamais si tard, que je ne vous voye en votre champ, ou bécher, ou labourer, ou enfin porter quelque chose[l]*. Aprês *fodere* & *arare*, il faut un mot plus général que *ferre*: tel qu'est celui de *facere*. Je vous supplie, Monsieur, de me dire à votre loisir ce que vous pensez de ces deux remarques. Mr. Bigot vous fait mille baisemains. Je suis toujours de tout mon coeur, & avec toute l'admiration que vous méritez,

Monsieur,
Votre tres humble & tres obeissant
serviteur
Ménage

A Paris ce 21.
Mars *1688*.

[Address on fol. 2v, in Ménage's hand: A Monsieur / Monsieur Grævius / A Utrecht]

[a]. vous *inserted*.
[b]. le *deleted*.
[c]. ce livre *inserted*.
[d]. small deletion following *ferre*.
[e]. plusieurs *inserted, replacing* quelques *deleted*.
[f]. selon le témoignage de Mr. Guyet *deleted*.
[g]. de *deleted*.
[h]. celle ferre, *sic*, de *omitted*.
[i]. ont facere *deleted*.
[j]. de *deleted*.
[k]. vous *deleted*.
[l]. chose *inserted, replacing small illegible deletion*.

A ten-month gap since Ménage's previous surviving letter; there is no evidence of any intervening letters that have been lost, although, unusually, Ménage does not excuse or explain the delay in the correspondence. He begins with some catching-up of news, then complains about Wetstein, who has still *not begun to print the Diogenes edition; furthermore, Ménage is dissatisfied with the paper and printing of his* Poésies. *He confirms that he is preparing a new edition of one of his earliest works, his* Discours sur l'Heautontimorumenos de Térence, *and then in the greater part of the letter expounds at length some of his arguments about the text of that play.*

1 *J. Meursii de Regno Laconico libri II, de Piraeo liber I, et in Helladii Chrestomathiam animadversiones* (Utrecht, G. Van de Water, 1687), edited by Grævius.
2 *M. Tullii Ciceronis de officiis libri tres ... Ex recensione Ioannis Georgii Grævii* (Amsterdam, P. and J. Blaeu, 1688).

3 It has not been possible to identify Vroessen or Bylandius (unless the former name represents Gerard de Vries, Professor of Philosophy at Utrecht, and author of the anti-Cartesian *Exercitationes rationales de Deo, divinisque perfectionibus* (Utrecht, van de Water, Ribbius, and Halma, 1685)).

4 This early work was first published as *Responce au discours sur la comedie de Terence, intitulée Heautontimorumenos, ou par occasion sont traittées plusieurs questions touchant le Poëme dramatique* (Paris, Veuve Jean Camusat, 1640).

5 *Publius Terentius Afer. Diligenter recensuit et notulas addidit T. Faber* (Saumur, R. Péan, 1671).

6 The scholar Denis Lambin (c1516-1572), Professor of Eloquence and Greek at the Collège Royal; he published an edition of Cicero in four folio volumes in 1566.

7 Ælius Donatus, the fourth-century grammarian; his commentaries on Terence were particularly highly valued.

8 Eugraphius (early sixth century) was the author of a commentary on Terence.

9 On Guyet's notes see above, letter of 30 August 1685, note 2.

10 Joannes Rivius of Attendorn (1500-1553), *Castigationes plurimorum ex Terentio locorum, et in his obiter quidam explicati, per Jo. Rivium* (Cologne, J. Gymnicus, 1532). The work was reprinted several times in the sixteenth and early seventeenth centuries.

LETTER 41

Ménage to Grævius. 2 August 1688

Monsieur

La difficulté qu'il y a icy d'avoir des Priviléges pour l'impression des livres,[1] m'a fait prendre la résolution de faire imprimer en Hollande mon Discours sur l'Héautontimo-rumenos de Térence. Je l'ay envoié à la Haye à Mr. Foulque, avec ordre de vous l'envoier incessamment.[2] Quand vous l'aurez reçu; & vous le recevrez sans doute au premier jour; je vous supplie, Monsieur, de le parcourir. Et quand vous l'aurez parcouru, si vous le jugez digne d'estre imprimé, & que vous trouviez quelque Libraire qui s'en vueille charger, je vous supplie aussi, Monsieur, de me le faire imprimer. Mais ce n'est pas assez de trouver un Libraire qui l'imprime, il faut trouver un Correcteur qui en corrige les épreuves. Je donneray à ce Correcteur s'il fait bien son devoir, ce qu'il me demandera. Je souhaitte que le volume soit in seize. J'ay écrit depuis peu*a* en Latin l'Histoire des Femmes Philosophes. [fol. 1v] J'ay aussi dessein de faire imprimer ce livre en Hollande: & je vous l'envoieray par la première occasion qui se présentera de vous le faire tenir surement.[3] L'ouvrage est curieux: & il ne contient que six feuilles: & ainsi vous n'aurez pas peine à trouver un Imprimeur qui l'imprime. Je pense que vous savez qu'on imprime à la Haye mon Antibaillet.[4] Je n'entens plus parler de Mr. Vestein: ce qui me fait croire qu'il ne songe plus à imprimer le Diogéne Laërce. En ce cas, vous m'obligerez de retirer de lui mon exemplaire. Je me plains fort de ce Mr. Vestein: & vous savez que j'en ay[b] tous les sujets du monde. Mr. Bigot vous fait mille[c] baisemains. Je suis toujours à l'ordinaire de tout mon coeur,

Monsieur,

Votre tres humble &

tres obéissant serviteur

Ménage

A Paris ce 2. Aoust
1688.

[Address on fol. 2v, in Ménage's hand: A Monsieur / Monsieur Grævius, / A Utrecht]

ᵃ. en deleted; originally written en en, at the end and beginning of consecutive lines.
ᵇ. que j'en ay inserted.   ᶜ. s deleted at end of mille.

This letter is entirely concerned with Ménage's works in progress. He follows up his previous letter on his Discours sur l'Heautontimoroumenos de Térence *by asking for Grævius's help in having it printed in Holland, and also a short new Latin account of women philosophers (*Historia mulierum philosopharum*); and gives news of a new work of controversy in French,* Antibaillet. *He is again convinced that Wetstein has abandoned the Diogenes edition, and once more, as four years earlier, asks Grævius to withdraw the book.*

1 Two years earlier Bayle had commented 'L'Inquisition est devenuë effroiable en France contre les bons Livres', when describing how Malebranche could not get his books printed in Paris (letter to Lenfant, 11 June 1686, *Œuvres diverses*, IV, 624).
2 The printer Étienne Foulque was active in The Hague c.1688-1711. It was he who printed Ménage's *Antibaillet* (note 4 to this letter), which led to a severe deterioration in their relations: see Ménage's letters of 4 November and 2 December 1689 below (Letters 45 and 46).
3 The work was in fact published in Lyon: see Ménage's letters of 9 January 1690 (Letter 47), note 6, and 24 February 1690 (Letter 48). A revised version was included in the second volume of Wetstein's edition of Diogenes Laertius in 1692 (pp. 487-505, with index pp. [506-8]), and often discussed in Wetstein's letters below.
4 *Anti-Baillet ou Critique du livre de Mr. Baillet, intitulé Jugemens des savans*, 2 vols (La Haye, Estienne Foulque and Louïs van Dole, 1688).

Ménage to Grævius. 25 February 1689

Monsieur

J'ay reçu la lettre qu'il vous a plu m'écrire au sujet de ma Dissertation sur l'Héautonti-
morumenos de Térence. Je vous suis bien obligé du soin que vous avez pris de me
trouver un Imprimeur pour imprimer ce petit ouvrage: & je vous en fais icy, Monsieur,
un million de tres humbles remercimens. Je vous supplie, Monsieur, de me faire savoir
le nom & la demeure de cet Imprimeur, affin que je puisse lier commerce de lettres
avec lui.[1] Et je vous supplie cependant de lui faire dire de m'envoyer par la poste la
première feuille devant que de la tirer: & si d'avanture elle estoit tirée quand cette lettre
vous sera rendue, qu'il ne laisse pas de me l'envoyer. En mettant sur les paquets qu'il
m'adressera, [fol. 2r] *A Mr. l'Abbé Ménage au Cloistre Notre Dame A Paris*, ils me seront
rendus surement. Vous lui ferez dire aussi s'il vous plaist, Monsieur, de chercher un
bon Correcteur, qui suive fidellement & mon orthographe & ma ponctuation. Je donneray à ce Correcteur tout ce qu'il me demandera. Il me reste à vous parler de mon
Diogéne Laërce. Si Mr. Vestein a commancé de l'imprimer, à la bonne heure. S'il n'a[a]
pas commancé, il y a apparance qu'il ne l'imprimera point. Et en ce cas, je vous prie,
Monsieur, de retirer de lui mon exemplaire, qu'il a depuis sept ans. Mr. Rou vous
envoyera de ma part mon Antibaillet.[2] Je ne vous prie point de le lire; car il est si plein
de fautes d'impression, qu'il n'est pas lisible. On a icy rimprimé mon Malherbe.[3] Je
vous en ay destiné un exemplaire: mais je ne say comment vous l'envoyer. On com-
mancera [fol. 1v, sideways] au premier jour l'édition de mon Histoire des femmes Philosophes.[4] Mr. Bigot est icy depuis deux mois. Il vous écrit: & je vous envoye sa lettre.
Je vous demande un compliment auprês de Mr. Goyer & auprês de Mr. Héninius, qui
leur témoigne bien l'estime que j'ay pour eux. Mais je vous demande sur tout, Monsieur, la continuation de votre bienveillance. Je croy, Monsieur, n'en estre pas indigne,
si c'est la mériter que d'avoir pour vous toute sorte d'estime, de respect, de vénération,
& d'admiration.

Ménage

A Paris ce 25.
Fevr. 1689.

[No address]

a. *n'a inserted, replacing ne l'a deleted.*

*Following on from the previous letter, this is concerned with the progress of no fewer than five of
Ménage's works. Grævius has found a printer for the* Discours sur l'Heautontimoroumenos; *Wetstein's progress with the Diogenes edition, if any, is unknown;* Antibaillet *is printed, but
badly; Ménage's edition of Malherbe has been reprinted in Paris; and the* Historia mulierum
philosopharum *will soon be started. The letter ends, as usual, with the transmission of news
and greetings from and to mutual scholarly friends.*

1 The printer was Rudolph van Zyll, active in Utrecht 1674-1691. See Ménage's letter of 4 November 1689 (Letter 45) and that of 24 February 1690, which includes a letter addressed to 'Monsieur Van Syll' (Letters 48 and 48A).

2 Jean Rou (1638-1711) was a Parisian lawyer before, as a Protestant, leaving France for the Netherlands in 1681 where he became 'secretaire-interprète' of the States General. He saw Ménage's *Antibaillet* through the press and corrected the proofs, although, as subsequent letters graphically show, he was badly served by the printer. He left manuscript memoirs which make clear how much he admired Ménage and was proud to have helped him (*Ruana ou Memoires et Opuscules du Sr Rou*, 2 vols, UB Leiden, MSS BPL 291 I-II; there is an incomplete edition by F. Waddington, as *Mémoires inédits et opuscules*, 2 vols (Paris, 1857)). Rou copied a letter from Ménage of 25 February 1689 sending his instructions: 'Quand mon Antibaillet sera en état d'estre publié, je vous prie d'en donner de ma part à mes amis de Hollande, parmi lesquels M^r. Cuper ne sera pas oublié' (MS BPL 291 I, fol. 206v; see also II, fol. 87v); and indeed a letter of thanks from Cuper survives, dated 2 June 1689, with effusive praise of the work (KB Den Haag, MS 72.C.46, fol. 15r-v).

3 *Les Poésies de M. de Malherbe, avec les observations de M. Ménage* (Paris, C. Barbin, 1689). The first edition had been published in 1666 (Paris, T. Jolli).

4 See note 3 to the previous letter.

LETTER 43

Wetstein to Ménage. 18 April 1689

d'Amsterdam ce 18e. d'Avril *1689*.

Il me sembloit que je venois du Royaume de Monomotapan,[1] lors que je reçûs la Votre du XI. du courant. Je^a voi que Vous n'avez pas reçû mes lettres ni les feuilles que je Vous ai envoyées de la nouvelle impression de Laërce. Ce qui me fait juger qu'il est desormais inutile que je Vous en envoye, puis qu'elles non seulement ne Vous parviennent pas, mais méme sont cause que mes lettres se perdent.[2]

Je Vous avois marqué dans une de mes precedentes les depenses excessives que j'avois faites pour ledit Laerce, qui se montoient à peu prés de mille écus blancs,[3] pour lesquels je n'avois autre chose, qu'un peu de caracteres & quelques 3. ou 4 rames de maculature. Outre un nombre infini de chagrins & de fascheries qu'il faut souffrir tous les jours du tresdocte mais tresfascheux Mr. Meyboom. /^{b}

Enfin l'ouvrage est commencé dés le temps que les glaces nous ont quittées. On a commencé aujourdhui à composer le second livre, qui est à la dixiéme feuille la 6e. page. On range toutes les notes sous le texte excepté les Votres qu'on imprimera separement. Je pousserois bien l'impression plus fortement, mais je n'ai que pour 36 à 38 feuilles de papier: le reste en^c est encore en France, & je ne sai comment le faire venir.

Ainsi on marche petit à petit. Si je ne me trompe ce sera quelque chose de beau. Aussi
je n'y laisse rien [sideways in left margin of fol. 1r] manquer. Je le fais faire par un autre
Imprimeur que celui qui m'a gaté Vos poësies, & encore un autre livre de plus grande
importance, dont je me chagrine fort autant de fois que j'y pense. Mais c'en est fait; &
il faut tascher de se garantir de ces acci-[fol. 2v, sideways]dents pour l'avenir.

Monsr. Leers m'a rendu les feuilles d'addition envoyées par lui. Comme je ne suis
pas encore à Votre Commentaire je ne les ai pas voulu rendre à Mr. Meyboom, de
peur qu'elles ne s'egarent chez lui. Comme il a toute Votre Copie je ne les puis inserer
moi-méme, mais j'aurai soin que cela soit fait ponctuellement.

Si Vous me pourriez fournir quelque moyen de Vous faire tenir les feuilles qui sont
faites je Vous les enverrois de bon coeur, ne doutant nullement qu'en auriez de la satisfaction. Je viens d'achever les œuvres latines[d] de Sannazarius[4] avec des notes de Mr.
Brœkhusius,[5] bien que son nom n'y paroisse pas; j'y ai ajouté les poesies des trois freres
Amalthées.[6] /[e] Monsieur Toinard est-il encore en vie,[7] & où demeure-t-il? Je suis toujours & de tout mon coeur Monsieur Votre treshumble & tresobeïssant serviteur

H Wetstein

[No address]

a. small deletion following Je.   *b*. Wetstein's ρ mark.
c. en inserted.   *d*. latines inserted.   *e*. Wetstein's ρ mark.

*Wetstein's first surviving letter for sixteen months, and the mystery of his silence is explained:
his letters, and the proof sheets that he has sent with them, have all been lost in transit. The Diogenes edition is indeed underway at long last. Wetstein reports on its current state and its slow
progress, caused by a shortage of paper and Meibomius making a fussy nuisance of himself. He
ends on a more general scholarly note, reporting on his latest publication and asking for Ménage's
help in contacting the elusive Toinard.*

1 Monomotapan (or Monomotapa, etc) appears on seventeenth-century maps as a
large empire occupying the southernmost part of the continent of Africa. The name
was used to designate an immensely distant and possibly mythical land, as in La Fon-
taine's fable 'Les Deux Amis' (VIII, 11): 'Deux vrais amis vivaient au Monomotapa ...'
2 The War of the League of Augsburg had begun with Louis XIV's declaration of war
on the Habsburg Emperor on 24 September 1688, and its effects are felt throughout
the remainder of this correspondence. Again and again, Wetstein's letters return to
problems of communication While the transmission of letters was relatively unaffected
it was extremely difficult to send packages into France from the Netherlands, whether
of printed books or, as here, simply proof sheets; and similarly, Wetstein notes in this
letter that he has been unable to receive from France the paper that he had ordered for
the Diogenes edition.
3 The *écu blanc* was a silver coin worth three *livres* or *francs*.
4 Wetstein's edition of the pastoral poet Jacopo Sannazaro (1457-1530) appeared as:
*Actii Synceri Sannazarii ... Opera latina omnia, & integra. Accedunt notae ad eclogas, elegias &
epigrammata. Item 3 fratrum Amaltheorum, Hieronymi, J. Baptistæ, Cornelii Carmina*
(Amsterdam, H. Wetstein, 1689).

5 Janus Broukhusius, or Jan van Broekhuizen (1649-1707), had been a pharmacist and adventurous soldier as well as a distinguished poet and scholar. He was a close friend of Petrus Francius and also of Grævius. Grævius once saved his life by interceding for Broekhuizen after he had been condemned to death under military law for acting as second in a duel.

6 Grævius had published an edition of the poetry of the three Amalteo brothers – Girolamo (1506-1574), Giovanni Battista (1525-1573), and Cornelio (1530-1603) – with Wetstein in 1684, and this was reprinted, with his preface, in later editions of Sannazaro.

7 Toinard was indeed alive, although not showing many signs of activity. See Wetstein's letters of 20 September 1691 (Letter 62) and 8 May 1692 (Letter 70).

LETTER 44

Wetstein to Ménage. 9 August 1689

d'Amsterdam ce 9e. d'Aoust *1689*.

Monsieur

Si jamais Vous faites composer un nouveau Martyrologe, ayez soin de m'y faire inserer: car asseurement Mr. Meibomius est l'homme le plus capable d'exercer la patience d'un Job, & peut etre de la pousser à bout. Les chagrins qu'il me fait souffrir sont insupportables, & il ne tient pas à lui de me ruiner. Il me coute deja plus de mille ecus sans que je sois plus riche d'un sols. Ainsi soit par charité soit par reconnoissance je ne saurois manquer de trouver quelque place en Votre testament parmi Vos legataires, puis que tout cela ne m'arrive qu'au sujet du Diogene, lequel (si j'etois moins stoicien) je devrois souhaiter n'avoir jamais vû. Et outre cela j'ai le chagrin de ne Vous en pouvoir rien faire voir, puis que les feuilles que je Vous en ai envoyées par la poste ont esté perdues. Je m'asseure que si Vous en voyiez quelque chose, que cela Vous agreeroit. Mais nous n'allons qu'à pas de tortue, & Mr. Meib. n'a guerre de soin de nous faire aller plus vite. Nous en sommes à la 19e. feuille.

Pour les 6. feuilles de Vos Vies des femmes philosophes,[1] Vous pourrez bien me les envoyer en un seul pacquet. Nous n'avons pas par deça les mémes difficultez à la poste, aux quelles on est sujet en France; et des gros pacquets le port en est moins. les 6. feuilles en un pacquet ne me couteront guerres plus que la moitié de ce qu'elles couteroient en 3.

Adieu Monsieur je demeure tout & entierement à Vous

H Wetstein

[No address]

The letter consists mainly of Wetstein's picturesque exasperation with Meibomius's awkwardness and extreme slowness. He has agreed to print the Historia mulierum philosopharum, *and the letter ends with an interesting note that in the war situation between France and the Netherlands there are no problems with packages coming from France, but only in the reverse direction. The problem of sending packages to France is to become increasingly important and complicated through the rest of this correspondence.*

1 On the *Historia mulierum philosopharum* see note 3 to Ménage's letter to Grævius of 2 August 1688 above (Letter 41).

LETTER 45

Ménage to Grævius. 4 November 1689

A Paris ce 4. Nov. *1689.*

Monsieur

Je vous demande des nouvelles de votre santé, dont je suis en peine, y aïant tres longtans que nous n'avons reçu icy de vos lettres. Quand vous m'aurez satisfait là dessus, vous me direz aussi s'il vous plaist, Monsieur, si Mr. Ven Syll[1] veut imprimer ma Dissertation sur l'Heautontimorumenos de Térence. Et pour cela je vous prie de le voir, conjointement avec Monsieur Goyer. Il y a plus d'un an que le tans que Mr. Ven Syll vous avoit demandé pour commancer l'impression de ce livre, est passé. Je croy que Mr. Rou vous aura donné un exemplaire de mon Antibaillet. Celui qui l'a imprimé[2] m'a fait un[a] insigne friponnerie: dont je ne puis m'empescher de vous parler. Il a supprimé un Errata fort ample & fort exact qu'avoit fait de ce livre Mr. Rou, & en a mis un autre en sa place, où les principales fautes ne sont point marquées. Mr. Huet a permuté son Evesché de Soissons avec celui d'Avranche:[3] Et il s'appelle présantement Mr. l'Evesque d'Avranche. Il a fait depuis peu un livre intitulé *Concordia Rationis & Fidei.*[4] Mr. Bigot est retourné en Normandie: mais il reviendra icy dans six semaines. Tout à vous à l'ordinaire. Si vous savez quelques nouvelles de mon Laërce, je vous prie de me les apprendre.

Ménage

[No address]

[a]. un *sic, for* une.

Ménage has not heard from Grævius since his last letter eight and a half months previously, and is anxious for news of his Discours sur l'Heautontimoroumenos. *He begins with the conventional formula of asking after Grævius's health (as in his letter of 23 March 1682), which is not simply an empty phrase: as is illustrated in the following two letters, such silences might well have more serious implications. Ménage is outraged by an 'insigne friponnerie' of the printer of*

Antibaillet; *and passes on news of Huet (now Bishop of Avranches) and Bigot. The last note is a plaintive afterthought about the Diogenes.*

1 See Ménage's letter of 25 February 1689 (Letter 42), note 1.

2 Étienne Foulque: see Ménage's letters of 2 August 1688 above (Letter 41), and especially 2 December 1689 below (Letter 46), where he gives further details of the affair of the suppressed errata.

3 Huet was appointed bishop of Soissons in 1685, but the appointment had not yet been formally confirmed when in 1689 the newly-appointed bishop of Avranches, Brûlart de Sillery, proposed that they should exchange dioceses. Huet was delighted to agree: although considerably more remote from Paris than Soissons, Avranches was much more attractive to him, being in Normandy and close to his native Caen.

4 On this work see also Ménage's letters of 2 December 1689 and 24 February 1690 (Letters 46 and 48). It was published as: *Alnetanæ quæstiones de concordia rationis et fidei* (Paris, Thomas Moette, 1690).

LETTER 46

Ménage to Grævius. 2 December 1689

Monsieur

J'écrivis il y a trois mois à Mr. Goyer, pour le prier de me dire des nouvelles de ma Dissertation sur Térence. N'aïant point reçu de lui de réponse, j'ay cru que ma lettre ne lui avoit pas été rendue: Et dans cette créance, je lui écrivis une segonde fois il y a un mois, pour lui faire la mesme priere. Je n'ay point nomplus reçu de réponse de lui à cette segonde lettre: ce qui me fait croire qu'il n'est plus en Hollande. Et c'est, Monsieur, ce qui me fait prendre la liberté de vous écrire, pour vous demander des nouvelles de cette Dissertation, & pour vous supplier tres instamment d'obliger Mr. Van Syll de vous tenir la parole qu'il vous a donnée de l'imprimer. Mr. Bigot est en Normandie: mais je l'attans icy dans un mois. Mr. Huet, qu'on [fol. 2r] appelle présantement Monsieur l'Evesque d'Avranche, aïant permuté son Evesché de Soissons avec celui d'Avranche, fait icy imprimer un livre, intitulé *Concordia Rationis & Fidei*. Mr. Dacier y^a vient de faire imprimer les dernieres Tomes de sa Traduction d'Horace.[1] Et Me. Dacier, sa femme, y^b va faire imprimer, la^c Traduction qu'elle a faite^d de Marc Auréle.[2] Mr. Faure, célebre Docteur en Théologie de la Faculté de Paris, mourut^e avanthier.[3] Il avoit une grande Bibliothèque. Je ne puis finir cette lettre sans vous parler d'une friponnerie que m'a faite Mr. Foulque, Libraire de la Haye. Je l'avois prié par plusieurs lettres de ne point tirer l'Errata de mon Antibaille[t]^f que je ne l'usse vu: ce qu'il m'avo[it] promis. Et en effet, il m'envoya cet Er[rata] imprimé: qui étoit fort exact, & qui avoi[t] été fait par Mr. Rou. Je le lui renvoiay corrigé: & il le tira. Mais après l'avoir tiré, il l'a supprimé: & il en a mis un autre en sa place, qui n'est que de dix ou [fol. 1v, sideways] douze lignes, & qui ne contient que de tres légeres fautes.[4] Je laisse ce facheux discours; car cette friponnerie de ce Libraire me fache extrémement; pour vous demander la continuation de votre amitié, & pour vous assurer que je suis toujours tres cordialement, avec toute sorte d'estime & d'admiration,

Monsieur,

Votre tres humble & tres

obéissant serviteur

Ménage

A Paris ce 2.

Dec. *1689*.

[Address, fol. 2v, in Ménage's hand: A Monsieur / Monsieur Grævius, / Professeur / A Utrecht]

[a]. y *inserted*.

[b]. y *inserted*.

[c]. la *altered from* sa.

[d]. qu'elle a faite *inserted*.

[e]. icy *deleted*.

[f]. *the final letters of several subsequent words are missing because of a piece torn from the edge of the leaf.*

The mysterious silence of Goyer. Apart from this initial enquiry, and a few extra items of scholarly news, the letter repeats and expands the topics of the previous one a month earlier; Ménage is, in particular, still infuriated with Foulque, the printer of Antibaillet.

1 André Dacier published his edition and translation of Horace, *Remarques critiques sur les Œuvres d'Horace, avec une nouvelle traduction* (Paris, D. Thierry and C. Barbin), in ten volumes from 1681 to 1689.

2 Anne and André Dacier in fact worked in collaboration on their translation of Marcus Aurelius: *Reflexions morales de l'Empereur Marc Antonin avec des remarques*, 2 vols (Paris, C. Barbin, 1690).

3 This news would have been of great interest to Grævius. Faure had played a leading role in a scandalous episode of ecclesiastical censorship in 1680, of which Bigot was the victim. Bigot had discovered, in the library of the Convento di San Marco in Florence, the lost Greek text of St John Chrysostom's letter to Caesarius; but when he attempted to publish it with another major discovery, the full Greek text of Palladius's life of Chrysostom, the Sorbonne censors led by Faure banned publication of the letter because of fears that it undermined the doctrine of transsubstantiation. The attempted suppression inevitably backfired: great interest was aroused, the letter was published by Protestant scholars abroad, and finally in France by Bigot's friend Jean Hardouin in 1689, the year of Faure's death. Ménage is strongly critical of Faure's conduct in *Ménagiana*, III, 357-58. See Bigot, *Palladii episcopi Helenopolitani de vita S. Johannis Chrysostomi dialogus...* (Paris, Veuve E. Martin, 1680), with severely disrupted pagination and signatures between sigs 2G2 and 2H3 amounting to a total of three leaves (six pages) omitted; and Hardouin, *Sancti Joannis Chrysostomi epistola ad Caesarium monachum* (Paris, Muguet, 1689). See also Doucette, *Emery Bigot*, pp. 60-74; Doucette quotes (p. 71)

from a letter of 19 January 1680 from Henri Justel to Grævius keeping him up to date
with the scandal (KB Copenhagen, MS Thott 1262, 13).

4 Foulque's conduct over the errata seems extraordinary, and it is difficult to work out
exactly what occurred. Ménage must have seen one or more copies of *Antibaillet* where
the errata had been suppressed as he describes, and such copies can be found of this edition and of the re-issue of 1690, which does not bear Foulque's name but differs only
in the title-page (*Anti-Baillet* ... (La Haye, Louïs and Henry van Dole, 1690)); for
example the BN, Paris, copy shelfmarked 16.Z.9846. However, some copies at least of
the 1688 edition of *Antibaillet* do certainly contain an extensive section of errata at the
end of both volumes I and II. In the BN copy shelfmarked Z.54974 the first volume
ends with an 'Avertissement' followed by five and a half pages of errata, sigs T1r –
[T4]r; the second volume similarly ends with five and a quarter pages of 'Errata de la
Segonde Partie', followed by a further page of instructions for the systematic correction
of the spelling which set out Ménage's principles of French orthography (sigs T1r –
[T4]r). Ménage took the latter very seriously, and his comments in the 'Avertissement'
in vol. I explain his apparently excessive indignation when he believed that both substantial sections had been suppressed by the printer: 'Et comme ce livre a été imprimé
en païs étranger, il s'y est, nonobstant des inspections assez soigneuses, glissé quelques
fautes d'impression, dont les Lecteurs sont priez de vouloir corriger les plus considérables conformément à cet Errata: par le moyen duquel, pour le dire en passant, bien loin
qu'il doive donner du chagrin, les Etrangers auront une instruction assez commode tant
pour l'exactitude de l'orthographe Françoise que pour la justesse de la prononciation.'

LETTER 47

Ménage to Grævius. 9 January 1690

Monsieur
Les afflictions ne viennent jamais seules. Il y ut vendredi quinze jours que j'appris par
votre lettre la mort de Mr. Goyer: Et le jour d'auparavant j'avois appris par une lettre
d'un de mes amis de Rouen celle de Mr. Bigot, arrivée à Rouen le 18. du mois passé.[1]
J'ay eté tres affligé de la mort de Mr. Goyer. C'étoit un tres honneste homme & tres
obligeant, qui avoit beaucoup de mérite dans les lettres; qui m'aimoit tendrement, &
pour qui j'avois toute sorte d'estime & de considération. Mais je suis accablé d'affliction
de la mort de Mr. Bigot: Et je ne vous prie point, Monsieur, de m'en consoler: car j'en
suis inconsolable. Il y a trente cinq ans que nous logions ensemble, & que nous estions
amis à n'estre qu'une mesme chose. Vous perdez en lui un ami tres fidelle & [fol. 2r]
tres sincere, & un tres passioné admirateur. Je laisse ce facheux discours, pour vous
remercier de toutes les peines que vous avez prises au sujet de ma Dissertation sur
l'Heautontimorumenos de Térence. Mr. Janisson, Ministre d'Utrecht,[2] a écrit icy à

Monsieur son frere³ que vous lui aviez dit qu'on avoit commancé a imprimer cette Dissertation: ce qui m'a été une nouvelle tres agréable. Mandez moy, je vous prie, qui est celui qui en corrige les épreuves, affin que je l'en remercie: & envoyez moy par la poste la premiere feuille imprimée. J'ay fait voir à Mr. l'Evesque d'Avranche & à Mr. l'Abbé Nicaise votre derniere lettre. Mr. Anisson, Libraire célebre de Lyon,⁴ imprime me[s]ᵃ Origines de la Langue Françoise & mon Histoire des Femmes Philosophe[s].⁵ Les trois derniers volumes de l'Horace de Mr. Dacier paroissent icy depuis quinze jours. Le tout votre à l'ordinaire

Ménage

A Paris ce 9
Jan. 1690.
[Address, fol. 2v, in Ménage's hand:
A Monsieur / Monsieur Grævius / Professeur d'Utrecht / A Utrecht]

ᵃ. *the final letters of two words are missing because of a piece torn from the edge of the leaf.*

Goyer has died, and Ménage responds appropriately. However the heart of the letter is the devastating news of the death of Bigot, one of Ménage's oldest and closest friends. The remainder concerns the progress of Ménage's works – with a typical example of the networks of communication along which information could be passed – and the more general maintaining of contacts through personal relations and scholarly news.

1 Emery Bigot died, as Ménage says, on 18 December 1689, of an apoplectic stroke.
2 Michel Janiçon or Janisson had been a Protestant minister at Blois before the Revocation, and then settled in Utrecht.
3 François Janiçon, sieur de Marsin (1634-1705), was a scholarly Protestant lawyer. After the Revocation he feigned conversion to Catholicism, but his family maintained their Protestantism in private and were able to give great help to fellow-Huguenots. He kept up active friendships with Catholic scholars in Paris, including Ménage, while his regular correspondents abroad included Bayle (see Labrousse, *Inventaire*, pp. 363-65). It is interesting to note the workings of the Republic of Letters in the way that Ménage heard about his book: Grævius told Janiçon in Utrecht, Janiçon wrote to his brother in Paris, and he in his turn told Ménage.
4 The famous printing dynasty was founded by Laurent Anisson and continued by his sons Jean (who later was appointed to direct the Imprimerie Royale in Paris) and Jacques. Jean Anisson often acted as an intermediary for Ménage in sending his works to his Italian correspondents, and passing on their letters to him (see for example Ménage's letter to Magliabecchi of 23 April 1679, in which he writes that he is sending his *Juris civilis amœnitates* and *Mescolanze italiane* via Anisson: Pélissier (ed.), *Lettres à Magliabecchi et à Carlo Dati*, p. 26; also pp. 27 (24 December 1681), 28-29, etc).
5 *Historia mulierum philosopharum. Scriptore Ægidio Menagio. Accedit eiusdem Commentarius Italicus in VII. Sonettum Francisci Petrarchæ, à re non alienus* (Lyon, Anisson, J. Posnel and C. Rigaud, 1690).

LETTER 48

Ménage to Grævius. 24 February 1690

A Paris ce vendredi 24. Fevr. 1690

Mr Janisson, Ministre François de votre ville, a écrit icy à Mr. son frere, que Mr. Van Syll avoit enfin commancé à imprimer ma Dissertation sur l'Heautontimorumenos de Térence, & qu'il en avoit vu la premiere feuille: que cette feuille étoit d'assez beaux caracteres, mais qu'il y avoit beaucoup de fautes d'impression. C'est, Monsieur, ce qui me fait prendre la liberté de vous écrire, pour vous supplier tres humblement & tres instamment, de vous souvenir de la promesse que vous m'avez faite de me trouver un habille Correcteur. De mon coté, je vous ay promis de lui donner tout ce qu'il me demanderoit. Il faudra s'il vous plaist lui dire qu'il suive mon orthographe & ma ponctuation. Ma copie est fort correcte. J'écris à Mr. Van Syll de m'envoyer par la poste ce qu'il aura imprimé de feuilles quand ma lettre lui sera rendue, & de ne point tirer la feuille suivante qu'il n'ait reçu de mes nouvelles. /. Anisson, célebre Libraire de Lyon, imprime mes Origines de la Langue Françoise, & mon Histoire des Femmes Philosophes. Cette Histoire est écrite en Latin. Et je l'avois faite pour estre imprimée à la fin de mes Observations [fol. 1v] sur Laërce. Le livre de Mr. Huet de la Concorde de la Raison & de la Foy sera bientost publié. Je ne puis me consoler de la mort de notre ami Mr. Bigot. Ses parents se disposent à faire imprimer toutes les Lettres qui lui ont été écrites par les personnes savantes avec lesquelles il avoit commerce.[1] Vous pouvez bien croire que celles que vous lui avez écrites, étant des plus considérables, ne seront pas oubliées dans ce Recueil . /. Mr. Meybomius d'Allemagne a fait rimprimer en Allemagne le livre de Mr. Huet contre les Cartésiens.[2] Et Mr. Carpsovius, à qui cette segonde édition est dédiée, m'en a envoyé la Préface. Je suis toujours tout à vous, & de tout mon coeur, & avec toute l'admiration que vous méritez,

Ménage

The letter falls into two distinct parts, dealing first with Ménage's own publications and then with more general scholarly news. The first section is primarily concerned with practical details of printing the Discours sur l'Heautontimoroumenos, *and Ménage encloses a letter for Grævius to pass on to the printer Van Zyll. He also now claims that he had written his* Historia mulierum philopharum *(currently being printed separately in Lyon) to be included as a pendant to his edition of Diogenes, which is not borne out by the earlier correspondence (see in particular Letters 41 and 42 above). The more general information introduces a new running theme: a planned edition of Bigot's learned correspondence, in which both Ménage and Grævius would necessarily be heavily involved.*

1 On the projected edition of Bigot's correspondence see Doucette, *Emery Bigot*, pp. 77-80.

2 Heinrich Meibom (1638-1700), anatomist and polymath, was Professor of Medicine, History, and Eloquence at the University of Helmstadt. As Ménage says, he wrote a

preface to this second edition of Huet's work, and dedicated it to Carpzovius: *Petri Danielis Huettii ... Censura philosophiae cartesianae, cum H. Meibomii praefatione* (Helmstadt, G. W. Hammius, 1690). Ménage's role as intermediary is shown by an interesting exchange of correspondence preserved in the Biblioteca Medicea Laurenziana, Florence; it includes the letter from Carpzovius to which Ménage is referring here, and which must have only very recently reached him. The exchange begins with a letter from Henricus Meibomius to Carpzovius of 21 December 1689, dedicating the edition to him (MS Ashburnham 1866.1185); then a lengthy letter from Carpzovius to Ménage of 12 February 1690, enclosing the one he had received from Meibomius (MS Ashburnham 1866.208a); and an undated note from Ménage to Huet enclosing the previous two, and asking for a letter of thanks to the two German scholars which Ménage will send back to Carpzovius (MS Ashburnham 1866.208b).

LETTER 48A
Ménage to Van Zyll. 24 February 1690

Pour Monsieur Van Syll.

Monsieur

J'ay appris avec bien de la joye par une lettre de Mr. Janisson, Ministre de votre ville, à Mr. son frere, que vous aviez enfin [fol. 2r] commancé à imprimer ma Dissertation sur l'Heautontimorumenos de Térence. Mais cette joye a été troublée par ce que Mr. Janisson dit ensuite à Mr. son frere, qu'il y a beaucoup de fautes d'impression dans la premiere feuille qu'il en a veue. C'est, Monsieur, ce qui m'oblige à vous écrire pour vous supplier de vous joindre à Mr. Grævius pour me trouver un Correcteur habile. Je lui donneray tout ce qu'il me demandera. Aussitost que cette lettre vous sera rendue, envoyez moy par la poste tout ce qu'il y aura de feuilles imprimées. Et ne tirez point la feuille suivante que vous n'ayiez reçu de mes nouvelles. En mettant sur les lettres que vous m'écrirez *A Mr. l'Abbé Ménage au Cloistre Notre Dame à Paris*, elles me seront rendues surement. Ma Copie est tres correcte. Et vous direz s'il vous plaist à votre Compositeur qu'il la suive exactement, & pour l'orthographe & pour la ponctuation. Je vous [bai]se[a] tres humblement les mains, & suis de toute mon affection,

Monsieur
Votre tres humble &
tres obéissant serviteur
Ménage

[Address, fol. 2v, in Ménage's hand: A Monsieur / Monsieur Grævius / A Utrecht]

[a]. *letters lost because of a hole in the page made by the seal.*

Ménage repeats for the printer the points made in his letter to Grævius, insisting particularly on the importance of textual correctness. As always when attempting to oversee works printed at a distance, he lays great stress on the need to find a 'Correcteur habile', and the necessity of following his spelling and punctuation exactly.

LETTER 49

Wetstein to Ménage. 9 October 1690

d'Amsterdam ce 9e. d'Octobre *1690*.

Je Vous ai ecrit Monsieur, trois ou quatre fois, depuis 18. mois, & Vous ai envoyé des feuilles du Diogene, sans savoir ce qu'ils sont devenus, puis que jamais je n'ai eu de reponse. Enfin le Diogene s'avance tout doucement, graces à Mr. Meiboom qui est l'homme du monde le plus lanternier: cependant je n'ai osé discontinuer de faire faire le texte, de peur que Mr. Meiboom étant vieux & ayant prés de 70. ans ne vint à mourir avant que le livre fut achevé,[1] ce qui nous auroit beaucoup trouble[a] puis qu'il nous fait une nouvelle version latine, & qu'on ne lui en arrache la copie que par morceaux, ne travaillant jamais d'avance, mais toûjours quand il ne s'en peut defendre d'en donner pour une page ou deux. Enfin c'est l'homme le plus propre du monde à exercer la patience d'un ange. Les faux-frais qu'il m'a fait faire pour le seul Diogene, me mangeront aussi-bien cinqmille francs que cinq sols. Mais qu'y faire; j'y suis, il faut finir par force.

Nous sommes donc à la fin du 7e. livre de Diogene; & pour tascher d'avancer autant que nous pourrons la besoigne, j'ai resolu de commencer aussi Votre Commentaire ou Vos notes, qui feront le second volume: dont je Vous ai voulu avertir afin que si Vous avez encore quelque chose à ajouter, Vous le puissiez faire en temps: tout ce que m'avez communiqué par ci-devant a été inseré en son lieu. En attendant Votre reponse je ferai composer une feuille; puis que je ne me figure pas que Vous[b] aurez quelque chose à changer dans la premiere feuille. J'espere avoir fait en huit mois, s'il plait à Dieu; & si Mr. Meiboom ne nous en empesche. Je suis fasché qu'il ne se trouve aucune occasion à Vous envoyer les feuilles qui sont faites: je m'asseure que Vous Vous trouveriez consolé du retardement par la beauté de l'ouvrage. J'atendrai de Vos nouvelles au plustot, s'il Vous plait. Cependant je demeurerai toujours Votre treshumble & tresobeïssant serviteur

H Wetstein

[No address]

[a]. trouble *sic*.
[b]. y *deleted*.

Wetstein's first surviving letter for fourteen months, in which he claims not to have heard from Ménage for eighteen months. Curiously the difficulties in communication, which include the loss of proof sheets, do not seem to have affected Ménage's other publications in the Low Countries during this period. Wetstein develops his familiar complaints about Meibomius's eccentricity and slowness, and the resulting expense of the Diogenes edition. He adds a new worry: that the apparently aged scholar will die before completing his part of the work. However, as in his previous letter he is now increasingly confident about the quality of the edition and its ultimate typographical success. It is definitely being printed in two volumes, although the exact arrangement is still not decided; and Wetstein suggests a new time-scheme for publication, which is now (God and Meibomius willing) set for June 1691.

1 Meibomius was born c1630, so would only have been about sixty years of age at this time, a great deal younger than Ménage. Wetstein refers again to Meibomius's 'grand age' in his letter of 28 December 1690 (Letter 51).

Wetstein to Ménage. 26 October 1690

d'Amsterdam ce 26e. d'Octobre *1690*

Suivant Votre ordre, Monsieur, je Vous acuse la reception de la Votre du 16. de ce mois, & qui devroit avoir été ici le 20e. cependant je ne l'ai que du 24e.[1] Je plains le malheur de mes lettres qui ne Vous sont pas parvenues: & pour remedier à celui des feuilles du Diogene qui se sont perdues & que n'avez jamais veües, j'ai trouvé ces jours passéz une occasion de Vous envoyer un exemplaire cousu des 48 premieres feuilles, que j'espere qu'il Vous sera rendu seurement en son temps: & de plus, qu'il Vous consolera de l'ennui de Votre longue attente.

[*space left in MS*]

On a commencé à composer Vos Observations; mais comme je ne savois pas si Vous auriez quelques additions à y faire au commencement je n'ai pas osé en pousser la composition: mais je m'en fai faire achever la 1re. feuille, que je commence par la matiere, laissant le titre & les prefaces jusques à ce que tout le reste de la matiere soit fait: quand elle sera faite je Vous l'enverrai par la poste, encore que je craigne fort qu'elle ne courre le risque des precedentes.

Pour le defaut que Vous remarquez à l'edition d'Angleterre (touchant le renvoy des pages en menüe lettre /[a]) nous y avons remedié: Mr. Meiboom par tout le texte de Laërce a[b] fait des sections de 15 en 15 lignes, qui sont marquées à la marge 1. 2. 3. etc. jusques à la fin de chaque livre. Ainsi nous mettrons en marge de Vos Observations les mémes chiffres 1. 2. 3. etc qui correspondront aux chiffres des sections qui sont à la marge du texte. Ainsi que cela sera[c] fort distinct, & fort aisé à trouver.

Le papier ordinaire du Diogene ne fera qu'un volume d'environ 160. feuilles d'un assex grand in 4°. Ainsi je ne crois pas qu'il sera trop gros. Mais pour le grand papier, dont est l'exemple que je Vous ai envoyé, il en faudra faire, 2. volumes qui ne seront que mediocres[d] en grosseur.

Je travaille aux portraits: mais je ne puis trouver celui d'Anacharsis, ni l'Iconografie de Caninius. Voici la liste de ceux que j'ai:[2] & j'aimerois fort que Vous m'en pûssiez indiquer d'autres

Æschines	Democritus	Plato.	Xenocrates
Antisthenes	Diogenes	Pythagoras.	Zeno.
Archytas	Epicurus	Socrates	Sextus Empyricus.
Aristippus	Heraclitus	Solon	
Aristoteles.	Herillus	Speusippus	
Carneades[e]	Pittacus	Theophrastus	

Je marquerai à Mr. Grævius par la premiere lettre que je lui ferai, ce que Vous me mandez pour lui.[3] Je Vous enverrai la 1re. feuille aussi-tot qu'elle sera faite. Cependant je demeure toujours Votre treshumble & tres-obeïssant serviteur

H Wetstein

[No address]

[a]. Wetstein's ρ mark.   [b]. a originally written as à; ` deleted above the letter.
[c]. sera inserted.   [d]. full stop deleted after mediocres.   [e]. n altered from d within word.

After the long gap before the previous letter, and whatever the reason for it, regular correspondence has now resumed between printer and scholar, much of it concerned with the practical details of the edition and problems of communication. It is interesting to note that it normally takes four days for a letter to reach Amsterdam from Paris, and a time of eight days is commented on as exceptional. Ménage replied quickly to Wetstein's last letter, and Wetstein has despatched a sewn copy of the first 48 leaves: the fate of this package is to feature in a number of subsequent letters. Wetstein now also gives details of the sequence of engraved portraits planned to illustrate the text, another theme which will figure prominently in the correspondence.

1 An interesting indication of the normal delivery time of post between Paris and Amsterdam.

2 By the time of his letter of 26 July 1691, Wetstein had added four new portraits (Anacharsis, Chrysippus, Euclides, Thales) and abandoned two (Herillus and Speusippus).

3 It is no surprise to find that Wetstein and Grævius are in regular contact by letter, as one would presume, and it was not unusual to minimise the dangers of disruption in the postal system (particularly in time of war) by enclosing letters to be forwarded in the country of destination; thus Wetstein enclosed a letter from Grævius with his own letter to Ménage on 14 June 1691 (Letter 55; see Wetstein's next letter of 21 June, Letter 56). It is rather more surprising to find Wetstein here passing on a message from Ménage, rather than Ménage sending a complete letter to be forwarded to his friend in Utrecht – perhaps another example of the French scholar's economy of effort as a letter-writer.

Wetstein to Ménage. 28 December 1690

Ce 28e. Decembre *1690*

Je suis tres-aise Monsieur, d'aprendre qu'à la fin Vous aiez reçû les 2 feuilles de notre[a] ouvrage, & que par là Vous en aiez vû un echantillon, aprés tant de voïes que j'ai tentées pour Vous en faire avoir. J'espere qu'à la fin cet exemplaire que je Vous ai envoyé en octobre dernier Vous parviendra aussi. Je le croi encore à Gand, ou tout au plus à Lisle.[1] Je serai tres-aise d'avoir les deux medailles d'Anacharsis & de Chrysippe le plustot que cela se pourra.[2] J'attends aussi en belle devotion Votre traitté des femmes philosophes, que je joindrai à Vos notes. Je n'en ai encore fait que 2. feuilles, parce que je souhaitte sur toutes choses d'achever le texte, à cause du grand age de Mr. Meibomius, & du chagrin qu'il me fait eternellement, je ne voudrois plus depandre de son caprice. Nous n'avons plus à mon compte que 14. ou 15. feuilles à faire, aprés quoi vos notes suivront sans cesse. Si Dieu Vous donne vie & santé jusques à mi-été ou environ, j'espere de Vous le faire voir entier & achevé. Mais faites moi le plaisir de ne me parler jamais plus de M. Meib. dans vos lettres: il n'en sera ni plus ni moins: & Vous m'epargnerez beaucoup de chagrin. Adieu Monsieur, je suis de tout mon cœur Votre treshumble & tresobeïssant serviteur

H Wetstein

[Address, f. 2v: A Monsieur / Monsieur l'Abbé Menage au / Cloitre N. D. à / Paris.]

[This letter is not with the rest of Wetstein's letters to Ménage. In its place is a copy of it, not completely accurate but nearly so, Gm 8[n].]

[a]. notre: *written* nre; *the reading is unambiguous, but the copy transcribes it as* Vre.

A progress report on the printing, concerned mainly with practical details: problems of communication (the sewn sample is held up in Ghent or Lille); illustrations; the addition of Ménage's Historia mulierum philosopharum; *complaints about Meibomius. Wetstein still hopes to have the work finished around mid-summer 1691.*

1 The packet was held up at Lille: see Wetstein's next letter.
2 Ménage sent the two illustrations, which Wetstein refers to having received in his following two letters; and they figure in his list of the illustrations that he has, in his letter of 26 July 1691 (Letter 57).

LETTER 52

Wetstein to Ménage. 5 February 1691

d'Amsterdam ce 5e. de Fevrier 1691.

J'ai bien reçu le crayon d'Anacharsis avec la feuille d'aditions pour l'histoire des femmes philosophes, que m'avez envoyés avec la Votre du 29e du passé. Mais je n'ai aucunes nouvelles ni de Mr. Gal, ni de l'exemplaire des femmes philosophes qu'il me devoit porter. Si Vous pouvez me donner quelque adresse où je puisse m'informer de lui, Vous me ferez plaisir. J'attendrai en méme temps le crayon de Chrysippe. Par l'extréme froid qu'il a fait pendant un mois ou six semaines, nous n'avons pû avancer avec le Diogene, & nous ne sommes qu'au commencement du 9e. livre. Je suis plus fasché que Vous d'avoir été contraint de discontinuer vos Observ: & ce sont les belles boutades de Mr. Meibomius qui en sont la cause; Mais il y a cette consolation, que le texte une fois fini, on avancera d'autant plus à Votre ouvrage. Outre qu'alors j'aurai l'esprit plus libre, n'etant plus dans l'aprehension où je suis presentement que Mr M. ne quitte l'ouvrage en refusant d'achever la traduction du texte. C'est l'homme le plus capable du monde à ruiner un libraire, qui le*ª* voudroit croire, comme j'ai fait quelque temps à ma grande perte. Il parle de mille pistolles comme d'une douzaine de champignons n'ayant avec cela pas un double de monnoye en son pouvoir. Enfin c'est une misere; mais il n'y a plus de remede, & il*ᵇ* faut finir avec lui. Aprés cela, bien fin, s'il me ratrappe. Adieu Monsieur. Je suis tout à Vous & de tout mon cœur

H Wetstein

P.S. J'avois donné à un ami un pacquet marqué M. M. qui me promit de le faire tenir en France. Il y avoit les 46 premieres feuilles du Diogene cousues, couvertes d'un car-ton & du papier marbré en bleu. C'etoit [fol. 1v] pour Vous. On me dit que Monsr l'Intendant de Lisle s'est saisi du ballot,¹ & qu'il l'a ouvert. Je ne sai s'il sera confisqué, ou non. Quand je le saurai, je Vous le manderai. Si alors Vous auriez quelque ami qui pût Vous faire rendre cet exemplaire imparfait, lequel aussi bien ne peut servir à per-sonne, j'en serois fort aise. Mais s'il est rendu sans cela, il ne faut pas s'en mettre en peine.

[No address]

ª. le *altered from* lui.
ᵇ. il *altered from* ils.

More problems of communication: the Historia mulierum philosopharum *has not yet reached Wetstein, while the missing partial copy of Diogenes has been intercepted at Lille. Wetstein claims that printing has been held up for weeks by the exceptionally cold weather (as in January 1684), and as usual complains eloquently about Meibomius with a new fear − that he might abandon his Latin translation of Diogenes altogether, and never complete it.*

1 The 'Intendant de Lille' was Dreux-Louis du Gué-Bagnols (1645-1709), named in Wetstein's next letter: see Letter 53, note 2.

Wetstein to Ménage. 22 February 1691

d'Amsterdam ce 22e. Fevrier *1691*

J'accuse Monsieur la recepte de la Votre du 16e. du courant avec le portrait de Chrysippe. En méme temps on me rendit une autre lettre de Paris*ᵃ* où il y en avoit une enclose pour Mr. Bayle à Rotterdam,¹ à laquelle je fis une enveloppe où je lui marquai ce que Vous me mandez de Mr. Gael, le priant de s'en informer, de lui demander le pacquet que lui aviez confié pour moi, & de me l'envoyer par la poste, ou au moins de me faire response, pour savoir où j'en suis. Je Vous manderai aussitot ce qu'il m'en ecrira.

Quand Mr. Meib. ne voudroit pas corriger Vos notes, cela ne Vous doit pas faire de peine, puis que cela ne m'en fait point. Car je trouverois en ce cas des gens capables à les corriger, quand je ne le pourrois pas faire moiméme. Mais ce sont ses caprices qui me font presser d'achever promtement le texte duquel il fait une nouvelle version latine, qu'un autre n'acheveroit pas de méme peut-etre comme il a commencé. Et pourvû que j'aie cela, je me soucie peu du reste, où il n'y a qu'à suivre ce qui est fait deja.

On me dit que Mr. de Bagnols Intendant de Lille confisque le ballot auquel je Vous avois envoyé les 46. feuilles du Diog. Si Vous y aviez quelque ami qui pût Vous faire obtenir cet exemplaire, j'en serois fort aise.² Aussi bien il ne peut servir à qui*ᵇ* que ce soit, étant une piece imparfaite & detaschée. Si non; il faut s'en consoler. Je suis entierement à Vous

H Wetstein

Ce 26e de Fevrier. Je ne sai par quelle fatalité mes gens n'ont point porté à la poste du dernier ordinaire cette lettre. Ce matin j'en reçois une de Mr. Bayle,³ qui aprés diverses peines a enfin trouvé & retiré Votre livre, qu'il me promet de me l'envoyer aussitot qu'il l'aura lû; n'y ayant point d'aparence, dit-il de renvoyer un tel livre sans savoir ce qu'il contient. Je croi que c'est pour en faire des extraits pour les nouvelles augmentations du Dictionnaire de Moreri auxquelles il travaille.⁴

[No address]

ᵃ. lettre de Paris *inserted.*   *ᵇ*. qui *altered from* quoi.

Wetstein has used Pierre Bayle in Rotterdam as an intermediary to retrieve the copy of the Historia mulierum philosopharum *(and in his postscript refers to Bayle's omnivorous reading for his great work in progress, the* Dictionnaire historique et critique*); and in his turn asks Ménage to use his influence to retrieve the confiscated package from the Intendant de Lille. The printer sends practical details about correcting the printed text of Ménage's notes, and further complaints about Meibomius's 'caprices'.*

1 Bayle and Ménage had been on friendly terms since the younger scholar first attended one of Menage's celebrated *Mercuriales*, or Wednesday gatherings, on a visit to

Paris in 1675; twenty surviving letters from Bayle to Ménage are recorded in Labrousse's *Inventaire*, all dating from the period 1685-1692. Wetstein's letter gives another example of the practical working of the scholarly network. The letter to Bayle, and Wetstein's insert, is not noted by Labrousse, and the author is unknown.

2 Ménage would certainly have had friends who could act as intermediaries with M. de Bagnols. He and his wife, Anne du Gué-Bagnols, were friends of Mme de Sévigné and figure frequently in her correspondence.

3 No letters from Bayle to Wetstein are recorded in Labrousse's *Inventaire*.

4 The *Dictionnaire* of Louis Moréri (1643-1680) was first published in one folio volume in 1673, and repeatedly reprinted and augmented until the final edition, in ten folio volumes, in 1759. The early editions were notorious for the mistakes thay they contained, and Ménage himself is quoted as saying: 'Je ne voudrois point lire le Dictionnaire de Moréri: ce n'est pas que je ne l'estime fort bon, mais c'est qu'il y a beaucoup de fautes; & que si je m'en étois mis quelqu'une dans la tête, j'aurois de la peine à m'en corriger' (*Ménagiana*, I, 84-85). Wetstein's description of Bayle's work reflects Bayle's original intention, which was a compilation listing and correcting Moréri's mistakes. He published an 'essai' of his project in 1693. By the time Bayle's *Dictionnaire historique et critique* was finally published in 1697 it had of course far exceeded its modest starting-point. The *Ménagiana* quotes a perceptive and prescient remark of Ménage's on the subject: 'Il paroît que M. Bayle a dessein de faire un ouvrage touchant les fautes que les Biographes ont fait en parlant de la mort & de la naissance des Savans; mais c'est une matiere qui est bien seche: cependant comme il a de l'esprit, elle peut devenir riche entre ses mains. Je meurs d'envie de voir l'essai de son Dictionaire critique qu'il nous a promis' (I, 293).

LETTER 54

Ménage to Grævius. 18 May 1691

Monsieur

Il y a un siécle que je ne me suis donné l'honneur de vous écrire.[1] Mais, Monsieur, je vous supplie de croire, que quoyque j'aye cessé de vous écrire, je n'ay point cessé de vous honnorer, de vous estimer, de vous admirer, & de vous louer. Je rons aujourdhuy ce long silence, pour vous demander de vos nouvelles, & pour vous prier de la part de Mr. Bigot, Conseiller au Parlement de Paris, de lui faire copier les lettres que feu Mr. Bigot vous a écrites, & à Mr. Heinsius.[2] Mr. Basnage, le Ministre de Roterdam,[3] a ordre de vous envoyer l'argent qu'il faudra pour le Copiste. J'ay fait imprimer une feuille d'Additions à mon Histoire des Femmes Philosophes. Et parmy ces Additions, vous y trouverez la Vie de Cærelia, Maitresse de Ciceron.[4] Je vous envoyeray cette feuille par la premiere occasion qui se présentera pour vous l'envoyer. Mr. Vestein ajoutera cette Histoire des Femmes [fol. 1v] Philosophes à mes Commentaires sur Laërce. Mais je desespere toujours de voir ces Commentaires achevez d'imprimer. L'impression de mes Origines de la Langue Françoise procéde. On en est à l'H. Le volume sera un tres gros in folio. J'y ay inséré au mot *Gabelle* la remarque que vous m'avez envoyée sur ce mot.[5] Les Oeuvres[a] Diverses du Pere Sirmond, de l'édition du Louvre, en 2. volumes in folio, sont sur le point de paroistre.[6] Dom Mabillon a fait imprimer une Dissertation de l'Etude des Moines, qui paroistra aussi au premier jour. Le livre est écrit en François: & il est écrit contre Mr. l'Abbé de la Trape.[7] Le volume est in 4°. Les Bénédictins de St. Germain font aussi imprimer plusieurs ouvrages de St. Athanase, non encore imprimez.[8] Vous aurez su qu'on a trouvé à Bellegrade le Pétrone entier. Mais vous ne savez peutestre pas encore que nous l'avons icy.[9] Honnorez moy toujours de votre bienveillance; Et songez quelquefois en moy, qui songe en vous continuellement.

Ménage

A Paris ce
18. May *1691.*

[Address, fol. 2v, in Ménage's hand: A Monsieur / Monsieur Grævius / Professeur / A Utrecht]
[Miscellaneous notes on this outer side with the address, in Grævius's hand].
   at top: contextus usque ad H. h. h.
folia 616, in Epicuri vita.
stetne 15 folia
   at bottom: Tuis[10]

[a]. Oeuvres *sic.*

Ménage's first surviving letter to Grævius for about fifteen months, with no evidence of any lost ones during this period. The purpose of the letter is to pass on a request for help from Emery Bigot's cousin, who is compiling the collection of Bigot's correspondence that Ménage had already mentioned. To compensate for Ménage's 'long silence', this letter opens with unusually extended formulae of admiration and esteem; the request for help is followed by news of Ménage's own publications, with personal touches for his correspondent; and it concludes with a section of varied scholarly news from Paris.

1 Ménage's last letter to Grævius was dated 24 February 1690. His opening formula to excuse his non-communication was one that he had used before; a letter to Francisco Redi of 4 February 1686 begins with the same words: 'Monsieur, Il y a un siécle, que je ne me suis donné l'honneur de vous écrire; dont je vous fais un million d'excuses' (printed in *Mescolanze d'Egidio Menagio. Secunda edizione, corretta, ed ampliata* (Rotterdam, R. Leers, 1692), pp. 327-28; this letter was among the additions to the first edition of the *Mescolanze* (Paris, L. Bilaine,1678)).
2 See Ménage's letter of 24 February 1690 (Letter 48). Bigot's cousin Robert Bigot de Monville died in 1692, and the project was never brought to completion.
3 Jacques Basnage (1653-1723) had been a celebrated preacher and scholarly pastor in

Rouen before having to leave France at the Revocation; he settled in Rotterdam before later moving to The Hague. He was distinguished for his natural inclination towards toleration and conciliation in the sometimes turbulent world of the French émigré divines. With his brother Henri Basnage de Beauval (1656-1710), the editor of the journal *Histoire des Ouvrages des savants* (1687-1709), he maintained a friendly if respectful correspondence with Ménage: the French scholar sent regular news from Paris, while Basnage, like so many of Ménage's émigré friends, helped with organising the printing of Ménage's works in the Netherlands.

4 Ménage is quoted in the *Ménagiana* as giving credit to his friend Antoine Galland (1646-1715), the learned orientalist, numismatist and traveller, for the addition of Cærellia: 'M. Galland m'a donné Cærellia maîtresse de Ciceron que j'avois oubliée' (*Ménagiana*, I, 295). The passage on Cærellia is on p. 496 of the second volume of the Diogenes edition.

5 This work did not finally appear until after Ménage's death: *Dictionaire etymologique ou Origines de la langue françoise* (Paris, Jean Anisson, 1694).

6 It was in fact another five years before the collected edition of Sirmond's works was completed, in no fewer than five folio volumes: *Opera varia*, 5 vols (Paris, e Typogr. Regia, 1696).

7 A reference to a crucial development in a famous contemporary controversy. The outstanding Benedictine scholar Jean Mabillon published in 1691 his *Traité des études monastiques*, insisting on the necessity of intellectual activity among the more scholarly monastic orders. This was in direct reply to a powerful but deeply provocative work by Armand-Jean de Rancé (1626-1700), the great reforming abbot of La Trappe, entitled *La sainteté et les devoirs de la vie monastique* (1683), in which all such activity was totally condemned.

8 The great work appeared as: *Sancti patris nostri Athanasii archiepiscopi Alexandrini opera omnia quae extant vel quae eius nomine circumferuntur, ad mss. codices Gallicanos, Vaticanos, &c. necnon ad Commelinianas lectiones castigata, multis aucta: nove interpretatione, praefationibus, notis, variis lectionibus illustrata: nova sancti doctoris vita, onomastico, & copiosissimis indicibus locupletata. Opera & studio Monachorum Ordinis S. Benedicti e Congregatione Sancti Mauri*, 2 vols in 3 (Paris, J. Anisson, 1698).

9 Petronius is an author who figures prominently in the seventeenth century, being widely admired (perhaps most outspokenly by Saint-Évremond) despite his often scandalous subject-matter. Intense interest and controversy was aroused by the discovery in 1663, at Trau in Dalmatia, of the previously unknown fragment of the *Cena Trimalchionis*; despite the scepticism and hostility of a large number of the most distinguished scholars, Ménage was prominent in, correctly, declaring it to be authentic. Then in 1688 a French officer claimed to have found a new fragment, in Belgrade. Like the earlier discovery this was also brought to Paris, although at the time of writing this letter Ménage had almost certainly not seen it (as is shown by his description of it as 'le Pétrone entier'). The new fragment was not published until 1694, but was not well received and is generally accepted not to be authentic.

10 Grævius's note refers to the first volume of the Diogenes edition: p. 616 is the last page of gathering Hhhh (not Hhh), in the middle of the life of Epicurus. This must

show how much of the volume he had seen so far, which agrees with Wetstein's progress report in his next letter to Ménage (14 June). When completed the volume contained 672 pages.

Wetstein to Ménage. 14 June 1691

Ce 14. de Juin *1691*.

Quand je n'aurois pas eu l'enclose à Vous faire tenir, je n'aurois pas laissé, Monsieur, de vous ecrire ces peu de mots, pour Vous avertir, que puis que les feuilles du Diogene n'ont pû passer à Lille, j'ai voulu essayer si je ne pouvois Vous en faire tenir par une autre voye. Ainsi ayant eu à Francfort un exemplaire cousu, depuis A jusques à Mm, qui contient les 4. premiers livres & une partie du 5e. je l'y ai fait rendre à Mr. de Tournes Libraire de Geneve, à pasques dernieres;[1] & il s'est chargé de Vous le faire tenir. Ainsi il se pourroit que Vous l'auriez deja reçu. Si non, Vous aurez la bonté de lui en demander des nouvelles.

Cependant ayant trouvé la semaine passée une autre commodité, j'ai fait coudre ensemble les feuilles Nn jusques à Hhhh, (ou le reste du 5e., avec les 6e. 7e. 8e. & une partie du 9me livres) & de Vos Observationes[a] a jusques p. qui font les 2 premiers livres à peu prés[b] que j'ai mis dans un pacquet, & adressé à mon frere à Basle en Suisse, qui est le Sr. Wetstein Doctr. & Prof en Theol. audit Basle;[2] Et je lui ai mandé depuis de Vous l'envoyer en diligence dés qu'il l'auroit reçû. Mais il n'y a aucune apparence qu'il le puisse avoir avant la fin du mois de Juillet, ou au commencement d'Aoust.

Je souhaiterois que Vous eussiez deja ces deux pacquets, car je ne doute pas que Vous n'en ayez de la satisfaction en les voyant.

Si j'eusse pû avoir le papier necessaire avant l'hiver, l'ouvrage seroit achevé à l'heure qu'il est.[3] Presentement si Dieu nous prête vie nous le verrons avant la Toussaints, si quelque force majeure ne nous en empesche: ce que je n'espere pas: puis que nous n'avons plus que 6 ou 7. feuilles du texte, & environ 36. de Vos Observations à faire. Des portraits, la moitié en est prête, & on travaille incessament au reste. Mais je souhaiterois fort que quelcun me pût & voulût communiquer quelque beau dessein pour une planche du titre: & si je pourrois l'avoir de Vous, je Vous en aurois beaucoup d'obligation.[4]

Je ne sai si ma memoire me trompe, ou si Vous m'avez par ci-devant parlé de faire faire un indice ou table sur le Diogene ou sur Vos observations. Si cela etoit, il seroit temps d'y songer. Mr. Meibomius ne le croit pas necessaire: Mais je ne m'arreterois pas fort à ses avis: tout le monde ne sachant pas le Diogene par cœur comme lui.

A propos de Mr. Meibomius. On m'a dit que les Moines Benedictins de Paris se preparoient à donner un nouveau St. Hierome. le Sr. Meibom m'a parcidevant fait voir

un tres-beau Manuscrit ancien, sur du parchemin, m'assûrant que c'estoit le Commentaire de St. Jerome sur Job, qui est perdu & qu'on ne trouve nulle part:[5] & il asseure
d'en pou-[fol. 1v]voir donner des bonnes preuves, par des passages de ces commentaires, cités par Ruffin[6] & d'autres /[c] Voyez si cet avis peut servir à quelqu'un par delà, à
qui Vous le communiquiez.

Je suis & serai toujours avec beaucoup d'afection Votre treshumble & tresobeïssant
Serviteur

H Wetstein

[Address sideways in the middle of fol. 1v (which had been folded so that the text of
the letter was inside): A Monsieur / Monsieur l'Abbé Menage au / Cloître Notre
Dame à / Paris.]
[In the middle of this address, 16 has been written in an old (17c?) hand]

[a]. Observationes sic.   [b]. à peu prés inserted.   [c]. Wetstein's ρ mark.

*After the interception of his package at Lille, Wetstein has tried a more elaborate route to send a
partial copy of Diogenes to Ménage, via Frankfurt and Geneva; and he is now attempting a
third route, by way of his brother in Basel. The estimated completion date has been put back to
the beginning of November (the blame falling this time on a paper shortage). Wetstein raises two
new matters in the need for a picture for the engraved title-page, and for indices, with an incidental comment at Meibomius's expense. He ends on a quite different scholarly note, concerning a
lost commentary on Job by St Jerome which Meibomius claims to have found. With this letter
Wetstein enclosed a (lost) letter to Ménage from Grævius, a reply to Ménage's of 18 May (see
Wetstein's next letter of 21 June).*

1 The de Tournes family, one of the great European printing dynasties, were leading
printers in Lyon and Geneva from the sixteenth to the late eighteenth century. Wetstein would have met the Genevan printer at the Easter Frankfurt book fair, to which
he no doubt took the Diogenes proofs as a sample of a forthcoming work. The Frankfurt fair was held twice a year, the Fastenmesse (starting on the second Sunday before
Easter, and lasting for eight days), and the Herbstmesse in September; although in
decline at this stage, it still was much more international in character than its rival, the
Leipzig fair. See A.H. Laeven, 'The Frankfurt and Leipzig book fairs and the history
of the Dutch book trade in the seventeenth and eighteenth centuries', in C.
Berkvens-Stevelinck, H. Bots, P.G. Hoftijzer, and O.S. Lankhorst (eds), *Le Magasin de
l'univers: the Dutch Republic as the centre of the European book trade* (Leiden, 1992), pp.
185-97.
2 Wetstein's brother, the distinguished scholar Johann-Rodolph Wetstein (1647-
1711), was appointed to the chair of Greek at Basel in 1684, and on the death of his
father (also Johann-Rodolph, 1614-1684) in the same year succeeded him as Professor
of New Testament Theology.
It is interesting to note Wetstein's estimate of a time of 6-7 weeks for his package to
reach Basel from Amsterdam.
3 Once again Wetstein mentions the problems caused by a shortage of good-quality

paper, a recurring subject in this correspondence: see for example his letters of 19 May 1684 (Letter 16) and 18 April 1689 (Letter 43). Ménage was, of course, very particular about the quality of the paper for his works.

4 Ménage did send a design for the frontispiece, which in turn caused endless further difficulties: see below, Letters 57, 59 (and note 1), 60, 62, 62A, 63, 64.

5 Jerome's commentary on Job was highly praised by St Augustine, but long believed to have been lost. Meibomius did apparently offer his precious manuscript to the Benedictine editors in Paris, but asked such an immense sum for it that they were constrained to decline. The manuscript was lost from view on the dispersal of Meibomius's library at his death in 1711; however there is a curious note on the subject in Michaud, *Biographie universelle*, XXVIII (1821), 142, n. 1, article 'Meibomius': 'Ce manuscrit était, en 1765, entre les mains de M. Gressier, de Vévai, héritier de la fille de Meibom. Il l'offrait pour 1,200 fr. à D. Berthod, qui le proposa au P. Paciaudi, bibliothécaire du duc de Parme; mais celui-ci n'en voulait donner que 450 fr. On ignore si le marché a été conclu à ce prix. (*Correspondance de D. Berthod*, à la Bibliothèque publique de Besançon.)'.

6 Tyrannius Rufinus (c340-410), a contemporary of St Jerome.

LETTER 56

Wetstein to Ménage. 21 June 1691

d'Amsterdam ce 21. de Juin *1691*

Si Vous ne m'ordonniez pas si precisement de Vous accuser la recepte de la Votre du XI. du courant, je ne le ferois point; Vous ayant ecrit aujourdhui huit jours avec une lettre de Monsr. Grævius.

J'ai reçu il y a long temps Votre histoire des femmes philosophes, & j'y ai inseré les additions que m'aviez envoyé*a* par la poste: je la joindrai à la fin de Vos notes, ou au commencement comme Vous voudrez.

pour Vos aditions aux notes de Diogene je les ai aussi inserées toutes, horsmis celle pour la page 83. qui etoit deja imprimée, & encore 2 ou 3 feuilles de plus.

Il est vrai que Monsr. l'Intendant à Lille n'a pas fait confisquer mon ballot, mais il l'a fait rendre à condition qu'il seroit renvoyé. L'ami qui l'a reçû pour le renvoyer m'a mandé que c'etoit une afaire faite. Cependant mon ami de Gand ne l'a pas encore reçû depuis 4. mois: ainsi je le crois perdu.

Vous aurez vû par ma precedente que je Vous ai envoyé les feuilles du Diogene, cousues, en 2 differens pacquets par la Suisse. Cependant si Vous pouviez me donner une adresse d'authorité à Lille, qui le pourroit faire passer, je Vous en enverrois encore un exemplaire par cette voye là. Cependant je demeure toujours Tout à Vous

H Wetstein

[No address]   ª. envoyé *sic.*

*A short message to confirm the safe receipt of a letter from Ménage sent on 11 June, which must
have arrived just after Wetstein sent his previous one. Wetstein briefly updates the current state of
the Diogenes edition. The Lille package seems irreversibly lost; however the printer proposes,
with Ménage's help, to try again to send a copy by this route.*

LETTER 57

Wetstein to Ménage. 26 July 1691

d'Amsterdam ce 26. Juillet *1691.*

J'attens en belle devotion le dessein pour le frontispice qu'il Vous a plû me promettre
par la Votre du 29. du passé,¹ & je souhaiterois de le recevoir au plustot afin de le faire
faire incessament pour ne point retarder*ᵈ* la publication de notre livre, que j'espere
d'achever en trois mois, & il nous faut bien ce temps pour faire bien graver une taille
douce de cette importance. Nous allons finir le VIe. livre de Vos Observations: mais il
n'y a pas moyen de faire finir le texte à Mr. Meibom: il nous lanterne de ses Observations qu'il veut joindre à ce qui reste à faire du 10e. livre, & au bout du compte je
crains fort qu'il n'y fasse rien. Pour les tables que souhaitez pour Vous Observations,
j'en ai parlé à un habile homme,² qui m'a promis d'en faire un essai pour la huitaine &
de declarer en méme temps, ce qu'il lui faudroit pour sa peine. Aussitot que je le saurai
je Vous le manderai.

Pour toutes les prefaces, lettres des precedentes editions de Laërce*ᵇ* etc. je croi que
nous en ferons un recueil que nous mettrons à la fin de Votre Ouvrage. Et cela à cause
que nous ne pouvons les joindre au 1r. volume qui en seroit trop gros, puis que sans cela
il s'en va à 90 ou 100 feuilles. Ainsi le 2d volume commencera par Votre Ouvrage,
qui avec les tables*ᶜ* ne fera en tout que 60 à 64 feuilles: On y fera suivre les Observations
de Mr. Kuhnius³ de Strasb. sur Diog. qui ne feront que 4. ou 5. f.: puis les paralipo-
mena pour le Diog: sçavoir les prefaces, tables: etc. pour faire monter tout cela à 75. ou
80. feuilles: & rendre par la le 2d volume d'autant plus egal en grosseur au premier.

Hier me fut rendu ici*ᵈ* mon ballot qui avoit été à Lisle; je tascherai de trouver
moyen de Vous faire passer un exemplaire quand il sera achevé. Cependant je demeure
tout & entierement à Vous

H Wetstein

[fol. 1v]
J'ai vingtdeux portraits des Philosophes dont parle Diogéne: n'y a-t-il pas moyen
d'en avoir d'avantage parmi les Curieux de Vos quartiers. Celui de Sextus Empyricus

feroit le 23e. mais je ne sai si je dois l'y mettre, puis que Diog. n'en parle qu'en passant.[4] Voici ceux que j'ai: & qui sont prets:

Æschynes	Chrysippus	Plato
Anarchasis	Democritus	Pythagoras
Antisthenes	Diogenes	Socrates
Archytas	Epicurus	Solon
Aristippus	Euclides	Thales
Aristoteles	Heraclitus	Theophrastus
Carneades	Pittacus	Xenocrates
		Zeno

De Speusippus je ne trouve par tout que le buste sans téte: & il me semble ridicule de le
faire graver.

[No address]

[a]. l'impress *deleted*.   [b]. des precedentes editions de Laërce *inserted*.   [c]. avec les tables *inserted*.
[d]. ici *inserted*.

*Wetstein is still hoping to publish the Diogenes by the end of October, and this letter deals with
a variety of practical details: the frontispiece design that Ménage has promised, the progress of
Meibomius's Latin version (excruciatingly slow), the indices for Ménage's Observations (well in
hand), the disposition of secondary material, and the state of the portrait illustrations. The lost
Lille package has at last been returned to Amsterdam.*

1 Ménage's letter of 29 June, which has not survived, would have been a reply to Wetstein's two previous letters.
2 The 'habile homme' was no less than the French Protestant émigré man of letters
Jean Le Clerc (see Wetstein's next letter).
3 Joachim Kühn (1647-1693), professor of history and Greek at Strasbourg. Kühnius's
'Observationes' are printed on pp. 557-66 of Volume II.
4 Wetstein was only able finally to add two further illustrations to this list: a symbolic
representation of a riddle by Cleobulus personifying the divisions of the year, and a
dubious image of Monimus discussed in subsequent letters. The final total came to 25
illustrations. Sextus Empiricus was included, next to Epicurus at the start of Book X
(on Epicurus); and the headless Speusippus was omitted.

LETTER 58

Wetstein to Ménage. 9 August 1691

d'Amsterdam ce 9e. d'Aoust *1691*
J'espere Monsieur qu'aurez reçû celle que je me donnois l'honneur de Vous ecrire il y

a huit ou dix jours, & qu'en suitte d'icelle les desseins du frontispice seront en chemin. Je Vous asseure que je les attends avec grande impatience parce que les beaux jours s'en vont, & l'ouvrage tire vers la fin. Nous avançons fort dans le VIIe. livre de Vos Observ. dont il y a, à peu prés, un tiers de fait. J'espere de finir sans faute Votre Ouvrage dans le mois prochain à la reserve des tables.

A propos des tables. j'en ai parlé à Mr. Le Clerc /: l'Autheur de la Bibliotheque universelle[1] :/ il en a fait un essai, pour convenir du prix. Il m'a dit que ce qui lui donneroit le plus de peine ce seroit le Catalogue des Auteurs. Et que si Vous entendiez qu'il y mît tous les endroits où Vous en citez, il ne pourroit faire ces deux tables (: des Autheurs & des choses) à moins de 18 pistoles. Mais que si Vous vouliez qu'il n'y mit que les endroits où Vous corrigez ou expliquez quelque Autheur, qu'il les feroit pour douze pistoles.[a] Il dit qu'il y a beaucoup plus de peine à faire ces tables qu'on ne penseroit, parce qu'il y a furieusement de la matiere dans Vostre ouvrage & grande diversité.

Voici un billet des portraits qui me manquent encore. Vous m'obligerez de m'envoyer incessamment celui de Monymus, & tous ceux que pourrez rencontrer. Car le temps presse.

J'ai effacé dans Votre histoire des femmes philos. ce que Vous me marquez.[2]

Monsr Meibomius nous a promis de reprendre le texte de Laërce, pour le faire achever entierement: mais cela ne retardera pas[b] la continuation de Votre Ouvrage qui s'avancera en méme temps. Car j'ai une extreme envie de Vous faire voir cet Ouvrage entier & achevé, & de Vous procurer cette satisfaction à l'âge où Vous étes: ayant un extreme regret de ne l'avoir pû faire plutot. J'espere que Dieu Vous conservera non seulement jusques là, mais encore au delà. Les honnetes gens ne vivent jamais trop. Adieu Monsieur je suis tout à Vous.

H Wetstein

[On fol. 2r there is pasted a printed list of 58 philosophers, in two columns, with random punctuation of occasional full stops. There are two MS additions to the names of Menedemus *Coloti Disci*pulus and Menedemus *Phædonis* Disc.]

[fol. 2r]		
	Alcmæon	Lycon.
	Anaxagoras	Melissus
	Anaxarchus	Menedemus
	Anaximander	*Coloti Disci*pulus[c]
	Arcesilaus	Menedemus
	Archelaus	*Phædonis* Disc.[d]
	Bias	Menippus
	Bion	Metrocles
	Cebes	Metrodorus
	Chilon	Monimus
	Cleanthes	Myson
	Cleobulus	Onesicritus
	Clitomachus	Parmenides
	Crates Thriasius	Periander

Crates Thebanus	Phædon
Crantor	Pherecydes
Criton	Philolaus
Demetrius	Polemon
Diogenes Apolloniates	Protagoras
Empedocles	Pyrrhon.
Epicharmus	Speusippus.
Epimenides	Simon
Eudoxus.	Symmias
Glaucon	Stilpon
Heraclides	Sphærus
Herillus	Strato
Hipparchia	Timon
Hippasus.	Xenophon
Lacydes	Xenophanes
Leucippus	Zeno Eleates

[No address]

^a. douze pistoles *originally written as one word, then separated by* /: douze/pistoles.
^b. que *deleted.*
^c. Coloti Disci *added in* MS *to printed list.*
^d. Phædonis *added in* MS *to printed list.*

Wetstein follows up his current preoccupations over the Diogenes edition: the frontispiece, the indices, the portraits – including one of Monimus which will figure again in later letters – last-minute changes to the Historia mulierum philosopharum, *and getting Meibomius to finish his Latin translation. A new and prescient theme is introduced at the end: a concern, in view of Ménage's great age, that the Diogenes should be completed in time for him to see it. With this letter Wetstein included a printed list of all the philosophers featured in the work, as a check-list for Ménage to seek out portraits.*

1 The *Bibliothèque universelle* was a learned journal published by Le Clerc in Amsterdam in monthly parts from 1686 to 1693; it was particularly notable for its coverage of foreign works, especially English ones. Le Clerc followed it with his *Bibliothèque choisie* (1703-13), then *Bibliothèque ancienne et moderne* (1714-27).
2 The principal detail deleted from the first edition of 1690 was in Chapter 3, where Cicero's daughter was wrongly named as Terentiola; in 1692 (p. 496) Ménage removed the name (she was in fact named Tullia, and Cicero's wife was Terentia: see Zedler (ed.), *The History of Women Philosophers*, p. 75, note 5).

LETTER 59

Wetstein to Ménage. 30 August 1691

d'Amsterdam ce 30e. d'Aoust *1691*

J'ai reçû Monsieur les deux Votres du 17 & 24. du courant, & avec la derniere le frontispice. C'est quelque chose de beau; mais qui me devient inutile par deux raisons,
l'une qu'il est trop grand d'un quart; l'autre, qu'il n'y a aucune place pour mettre convenablement deux mots d'ecriture, bien loin d'y pouvoir mettre le titre du Diogene
Laërce. C'est pourquoi il faudra que j'en fasse faire ici un autre dessein: & pourcela*a* le
moindre crayon m'auroit eté aussi utile que cette belle peinture.[1]
    Je n'ai pas encore eu de reponse de Mr. Grævius sur la medaille de Monimus.[2] J'ai
communiqué Votre lettre à Mr. LeClerc, qui se reglera là dessus touchant les tables sur*b*
Vos Observations: mais il n'est pas d'avis, non plus que moi, de les faire suivre à l'histoire des femmes phil. à moins que de mesler la table de cette histoire parmi celles des
Observations. autrement ce seroit une incongruité. Les notes de Meric Casaubon[3] sont
meslées avec celles qu'on a joint*c* au texte, à la reserve du Discours préliminaire, qui est
au commencement, & celui qu'il a fait sur le 10e. livre. On fera une table de matieres
au texte de Laërce, & une autre des auteurs qu'il cite. Mr. LeClerc dit ne pas compren-
dre ce que veut dire ce qu'avez mis à la fin de Votre P.S. Comme cette table a été faite
par Mr. Kings, qui est encore en vie, il faudra ajouter à la table de Mr. LeClerc *ce que ce*
Mr. Kings a ajouté à la sienne. Que signifie cet *ajouté*?[4] Nous allons finir cette semaine le
7e. livre de Vos Observ. qui est le plus long, à ce que je croi. Mr. Meib. lanterne toujours miserablement, & me fait perdre un temps qui m'est si precieux: je ne saurois lui
extorquer le 10e. livre de Laërce, qui demeure là depuis 3 mois. C'est un homme à
faire devenir foû le plus patient homme de la terre, & tout ce qu'on lui peut dire ne sert
de rien. Si le texte etoit fini, on feroit les tables, prefaces, etc. qui n'interromperoient
nullement la continuation de Vos Observ. Enfin cela fait pitié, & s'il ne change pas, il
Vous fera dire vrai que nous n'aurons fait que pour la fin de l'année. Bien que tresfaci-
lement nous aurions pû avoir fait à la Toussaint, & méme plustot. Je suis tout à Vous &
de tout mon cœur

H Wetstein

[No address]

a. pourcela *sic.*
b. sur *inserted, replacing* de *deleted.*
c. joint *sic.*

Ménage has sent a picture for the frontispiece which has caused more problems: it is too large, and
not easy to adapt to include the necessary wording. Wetstein is asking Grævius's advice about
the picture of Monimus, at Ménage's suggestion. Much of the letter deals with details of Le
Clerc's indices; it ends with the familiar laments over Meibomius's dilatory obtuseness, with the
likely date for completion now being provisionally deferred to the end of the year (as Ménage had
apparently predicted).

1 The frontispiece design, which is not signed in the engraved version, was by Charles Perrault. Ménage had intended to use a different design, by the artist and writer Roger de Piles; but Wetstein's repeatedly-expressed impatience to have the frontispiece caused him to send Perrault's drawing instead – which ultimately caused even longer delays for the unhappy printer. The details are recorded in the *Ménagiana*: 'Il [M. de Piles] avoit fait un dessein pour mettre Laërce au commencement de mon Diogéne; mais comme il fut achevé trop tard, & que les lettres de Hollande me pressoient, j'envoiai celui de M. Pérault qui se trouva plûtôt en état d'être envoié' (*Ménagiana*, II, 173). Perrault took umbrage at Wetstein's criticism, and Wetstein subsequently wrote to him in explanation of his remarks (letter 62A, 20 September 1691).

2 Wetstein is here acting as intermediary between Ménage and Grævius, and Ménage and Le Clerc. On Monimus, see Ménage's letter to Grævius of 10 September 1691 (Letter 61) and Wetstein's to Ménage of 18 October (Letter 64).

3 Meric Casaubon's notes were indeed placed at the foot of the text in Volume I, along with those by Henri Estienne, Aldobrandini, Isaac Casaubon, and Meibomius.

4 Ménage was presumably referring to the note in the 1664 edition appended, not to the sequence of indices at the end of the text of Diogenes, sigs (*)r-[(b2)]v, but to the index at the end of Ménage's 'Observationes', sigs *‡*r-[*‡*6]r, 'Index Authorum Qui in Doctissimis Observationibus Ægidii Menagii laudantur, notantur, illustrantur, emendantur'. This note is headed 'Gul. Kings Lectori S.', and Ménage might have been anxious to retain it partly because of its high praise for himself and his annotations: 'Cum ingenuus Vir Dom. Octavianus Pulleyn à doctis bene meritus mihi mentem Reverendissimi amplissimique authoris Ægidii Menagii communicavit de indice authorum faciendo, qui in ejus doctissimis Observationibus & emendationibus citantur, laudantur, notantur, vel emendantur; Quò tanto viro summis impedito negotiis inservirem, & desiderio Domini Pulleyn satisfacerem, præcendentem Indicem contexui; Cujus ope non Laertianas solum, sed plurimorum doctiss. Authorum etiam emendationes habes. Quo nomine si aliquid doctissimo authori gratum, aut lectori benigno utile præstiterim, gaudeo. Vale.' (sig. [*‡*6]r).

LETTER 60

Wetstein to Ménage. 4 September 1691

Ce 4e. de Septembre 1691 d'Amsterdam.

Pendant que Mr. Meib. exerce ma patience à me faire atendre qu'il lui plaise de nous faire finir le texte du Diogene, j'ai voulu voir à gagner quelques jours, en faisant imprimer quelques autres feuilles, qui n'interromproient pas la continuation de Vos Observations. Il n'y avoit rien qui*a* fut si*b* pret, ou au moins qui me le parut, que Votre Dedic: à Mr. Bigot, la preface, & la lettre de Mr. Pearson;[1] mais avant que de les donner à l'Imprimeur, je voulûs les relire, pour en savoir au moins le contenu: & pour voir s'il n'y avoit rien à changer à cause de la difference de mon edition à la precedente. La dedicace est fort bien comme elle est. Mais la preface me paroit avoir besoin de changement. Car *lin. 11.* Vous parlez des *Addenda & Mutanda quæ ad calcem horum Commentt: edita sunt*

lin. 16. latinam Laërtij interprett:, quam paratam habeo (: futuræ nimirum editioni) addere cogito. Si j'eusse*ᶜ* sû cela plustot, Mr. Meib. ne m'auroit pas tenu si long temps entre ces serres, comme il a fait jusques ici. Mais pourquoi ne m'en avez vous jamais parlé?²

lin. ult. Errata enim sive potius portenta typographica, non est meum excusare. Cela ne quadre point à mon edition.

En tout cas Monsieur, ne Vous paroit-il pas necessaire ou de changer celle-ci*ᵈ* de faire une autre preface, soit pour l'ajouter à celle-ci, soit pour l'y inserer.³ Ne faudroit il pas avertir Votre lecteur de Vos augmentations ou changemens: & pourquoi Vous n'avez pas donné Votre version latine, qu'aviez promis?

Comme depuis deux ans Vous ne me parlez plus des *Doctor. Viror. Testimonia*, je ne sai si Vous voulez qu'on les ajoute ou non: et en quel lieu?⁴

Si Vous avez ocasion de voir Mr. Morel,⁵ Vous m'obligerez fort à lui faire mes salutations. Nous avons été compagnons d'ecole il y a 30 ans. Vous me feriez beaucoup de plaisir, de me faire savoir en quel etat il se trouve. Je demeure cependant tout & entierement à Vous

H Wetstein

[No address]

ᵃ. qui *altered from* que.
ᵇ. si *inserted.*
ᶜ. u *deleted at the end of* eusse.
ᵈ. ou de changer celle-ci *inserted.*

This letter is mainly concerned with the preliminary material in the first edition of Diogenes, and how far it now needs to be revised. Wetstein ends on a more personal note, with an enquiry after an old friend currently in difficulties.

1 John Pearson (1613-1686), Master of Trinity College, Cambridge, 1662-73, then Bishop of Chester from 1673, was one of the most outstanding English scholars of the seventeenth century; his greatest achievement, his *Vindiciæ Epistolarum S. Ignatii* (1672), has effectively never been surpassed. His commendatory letter printed with the 1664 edition of Diogenes (sigs [A3]r-[A4]r) speaks of Ménage in terms of the warmest admiration, and was a particularly valuable statement of the importance and scholarly prestige of Ménage's edition.
2 Ménage's promised Latin version never appeared, and it is most likely that his claim 'quam paratam habeo' owed more to intention than to achievement.
3 Ménage did not write a new preface, but insisted that his first preface be reprinted unchanged (see Wetstein's next letter, 20 September). It was indeed reprinted without alteration (II, sig. *3r-v). However, Wetstein wished emphatically to dissociate himself

from the comments it contained on errata, which he quotes here. He put this into his own preface to the complete work, explaining that Ménage's references to printing errors do not apply to *his* extremely careful edition (I, sig. 2*1v); and even added a note to the reprint of Ménage's 1664 preface, repeating the same point (II, sig. *3v).

4 Ménage must never have finished compiling the 'Doctorum Virorum Testimonia'.

5 The Swiss numismatist André Morel (1646-1703) became joint conservator of the 'cabinet royal des médailles' in 1683 and undertook great works of classification. However, his position became difficult after the Revocation of the Edict of Nantes. He made the mistake of complaining when his years of effort failed to receive the official reward that he had been promised, and Louvois had him put in the Bastille in 1688 and again in 1690. He was released in November 1691 and returned hastily to his native Bern.

LETTER 61

Ménage to Grævius. 10 September 1691

A Paris ce 10. Sept. 1691.

Monsieur

N'aïant pu rien obtenir de Mr. Colleville touchant les écrits postumes de Mr. Bochart,[1] je me suis adressé à Mr. l'Evesque d'Avranches, qui m'a écrit là dessus la lettre que vous trouverés en ce pacquet. Mr. Bigot, Conseiller au Parlement de Paris, m'a promis de faire voir parmy les lettres que Mr. Bochart a écrites à son parant & à notre ami Mr. Bigot, s'il n'y en aura point qui méritent d'être données au public. Je vous ay mandé qu'il lui*a* en avoit autrefois écrite une περὶ τῶν ἅπαξ ἐιρημενων.[2] L'édition de mes Observations sur Laërce procéde: Et à l'heure que je vous écris, on en est au huitiéme livre. Cestadire, qu'elle*b* seront achevées d'imprimer dans un mois: Et l'ouvrage sera en état d'être publié au commancement de l'année. J'ay écrit à Mr. Vestein de vous demander votre avis touchant une Médaille de Monimus. Je ne say ce que c'est que ce Monimus.*c* Il n'y a point d'apparance que ce soit le Monimus, disciple de Diogéne le Cynique. Je salue Monsieur votre fis:[3] Et je l'embrasse de tout mon coeur: Et je l'assure icy de la continuation de mon service & de mon estime. Tout à vous à l'ordinaire avec toute sorte d'estime, de respect, & de vénération.

Ménage.

[No address]

a. lui *inserted, replacing* y *deleted.*
b. qu'elle *sic.*
c. Et *deleted.*

Ménage writes in reply to a letter from Grævius, and encloses a letter that he has received from Huet relating to Grævius's enquiry. This leads Ménage to news of Bigot's correspondence, then to the progress of the Diogenes edition. He estimates the likely date of publication as the New Year, and follows up his earlier enquiry, sent via Wetstein, about the problematic image of Monimus. For the first time Ménage sends his greetings to Grævius's son, no doubt in response to news in Grævius's letter of the young man's recent academic appointment.

1 Mr Colleville is presumably a member of the distinguished Norman family of that name. The biblical scholar Samuel Bochart (1599-1667), a Protestant minister in Caen, was a close friend of Bigot. The search for any posthumous works by Bochart does not seem to have resulted in any new publications.

2 'Concerning things that are said once only.'

3 Grævius had 18 children, but only one son and four daughters were still alive in 1691. His son, Theodor Georg, newly appointed *lector* in eloquence and history at the university of Utrecht, was preparing an edition of Callimachus. See Ménage's letter of 8 February 1692 below (Letter 68).

LETTER 62

Wetstein to Ménage. 20 September 1691

d'Amsterdam ce 20e. Septembre *1691*

Ci-joint je repons au billet de Monsr Perraut,[1] & je croi qu'il me fera la grace de trouver ma reponse juste. Mais à Vous dire le vrai Monsieur, il faut que je Vous avoüe que j'ai un autre chagrin dont je ne lui parle pas: & ce chagrin est d'autant plus grand que j'ai de la peine à m'en expliquer avec Vous. Il faut pourtant franchir le pas, & Vous dire que je serois un peu chagrin de payer 25 livres d'une chose qui ne me peut*[d]* servir. D'ailleurs j'avoüe qu'il m'est un peu dur à Vous proposer d'en prendre la perte sur Vous, qui n'avez travaillé que par amitié & à bonne intention, bien que l'affaire n'y ait pas reüssi: comme de l'autre coté il n'y a pas de ma faute non plus. Ainsi je laisse la chose indecise, & m'en raporte à ce que Vous voudrez. Car je dois Vous dire que Monsr Le Clerc m'a dit qu'il donneroit son billet sur Vous des 120 livres entierement. Neantmoins si Vous n'en voulez payer que 95 livres ou autant de plus que jugerez à propos, on ne laissera pas de les recevoir, & d'en donner la quittance au dos. De façon Monsieur que Vous etes le maitre de l'afaire, & Vous en ferez ce qui Vous plaira. Je passe à d'autres choses.

Il est certain que le 10e. livre donne beaucoup de peine à M. M. mais ce n'est ni cela, ni la difficulté de le traduire, qui nous ait empesché de continuer. M. M. a une autre affaire en tete. C'est qu'il pretend que la poësie est le langage de Dieu méme; ce qu'il pretend prouver par ce que toute la Sainte Ecriture est écrite en vers en Ebreu.[2] Et pour prouver cette derniere proposition[b] il a fait un Systeme, dont je suis aprés d'imprimer un Specimen, qui a deja prés de 50. feuilles. Cette besogne l'embarrassoit furieusement, & il vouloit l'achever avant que d'entreprendre le X. livre de Laerce. Ainsi nous laissames là ce dernier, sans qu'on avançat pourtant gueres[c] à l'autre, puis que dans 5 mois nous n'en avons pas fait plus de 3 feuilles, & il en reste encore trois pour finir entierement. Cependant voyant que de cette façon nous ne faisons que perdre temps, j'ai declaré à M. M. que plustot je ferois le Diog. comme il etoit imprimé auparavant, que d'en discontinuer plus long temps l'impression. Ce qui l'a fait resoudre à nous fournir de la copie, & nous continuons tout doucement, n'ayants[d] plus que cinq feuilles à faire. Mais je ne doute nullement que Vous n'admiriez ce qu'il fait sur ce Xe. livre.

Puis que Vous voulez absolument qu'on laisse Votre preface comme elle est, je l'ai donnée ainsi à l'imprimerie, & on aura soin d'observer tout ce que me mandez.

[fol. 1v] Ne dit on pas la raison pourquoi Mr. Morel est si long temps enfermé: & ne sait on pas si cela doit finir bientot ou non?[3] A propos de Monsr Toinard: ayez la bonté de lui faire mes treshumbles recommandations: & de lui demander s'il ne me veut[e] faire achever son Specimen.[4] Il faut que j'advoue que je ne suis pas fort heureux à imprimer des Specimens. Je n'ai jamais sû le fascheux accident de Votre cuisse, & j'en ai asseurement beaucoup de chagrin.[5] Cependant le bon Dieu fait tout pour le mieux! C'est à lui que je Vous recommende de tout mon cœur! Je suis parfaitement

    & entierement à Vous,

H Wetstein

[No address]

[a]. me peut *originally written as one word, then separated by* /: me /peut.
[b]. cette derniere proposition *altered from* ce dernier *[illegible]*.
[c]. gueres *inserted*.
[d]. n'ayants *sic*.
[e]. veut *inserted*.

Wetstein begins with the problem of the frontispiece, and encloses a letter for Perrault; to Ménage he concentrates on the difficulties of paying for it, and the financial arrangements for Le Clerc's indices. He continues with an account of Meibomius's latest eccentricity – a bizarre belief that the entire Hebrew scriptures are written in verse – which is distracting him from the Diogenes. The letter again ends on more personal matters, relating to Morel and Toinard, and sympathy over Ménage's crippling accident, from which he has never fully recovered.

1 Wetstein's reply to Perrault is printed below as Letter 62A.
2 Meibomius had first adumbrated this novel theory in 1678, but worked on it extremely slowly and did not publish his most sustained exposition until 1698. See Wetstein's last letter to Ménage, of 8 May 1692, note 3.
3 See note 5 to letter of 4 September 1691 (Letter 60).
4 On Toinard, his book, and his slowness, see Wetstein's letter of 27 January 1684 (Letter 15), note 3, and also his last letter to Ménage, of 8 May 1692.

5 Wetstein's memory has failed him over Ménage's accident: see his expressions of sympathy in his letter of 19 May 1684 (Letter 16). His comment now strikes an almost Panglossian note, in which it is tempting – but probably wrong – to detect a note of irony.

LETTER 62A

Wetstein to Perrault. 20 September 1691

Je ne contredis à aucune chose de tout ce que repond Monsieur Perraut, qu'à son dernier article, où il dit que je suis chagrin de ce que ce dessein me coute 25 livres bien qu'il vaille dix pistolles. Sur cela je declare que nonseulement j'ai trouvé ce dessein tresbeau, mais aussi que tous ceux qui l'ont vû l'ont trouvé de méme. Je declare deplus que je ne refuserois jamais dix écus à quiconque m'en feroit un pareil, & qui me pût servir; & que méme je n'en plaindrois pas douze écus. Mon chagrin ne vient que de ce que je ne puis me servir d'un si beau dessein. Et quelque autre que j'en fasse refaire ici je n'en aurai jamais qui vaille celui-là. Voilà mon chagrin.

Monsr Perraut dit vrai quand il avance, qu'il n'y a point de graveur qui grave sur un simple crayon: Mais s'il faut reduire ce dessein au petit pied, nous n'avons pas méme de graveur assez habile par deça, qui puisse travailler sur ce plus grand dessein & le suivre exactement. Ainsi il faut que je le fasse refaire par un peintre tout comme si je n'en avois qu'un crayon. Sur quoi j'espere que Monsr Perraut me fera la grace d'avoüer que je n'ai rien avancé que de fort veritable, quand j'ai dit qu'un crayon m'auroit autant valu que le dessein que j'ai reçu.

Mais je dis encore plus. J'ai voulu faire reduire au petit petit le dessein: mais je m'asseure quand Monsr Perraut le verroit qu'il n'en voudroit point lui-méme; tant qu'il perd de sa beauté & de sa grace quand les figures en sont plus petites d'un 5 ou d'un 6me.

[fol. 1v] J'ai pensé à un autre expedient, en voulant reduire la ligne horizontale d'un 6me plus bas qu'elle n'etoit, pour conserver la grandeur des figures dans un moindre espace: Mais alors la plus grande beauté de cette perspective qui fait un si bel effect, s'en va.

Quand on a pris la grandeur du dessein sur l'imprimé que j'ai envoyé à Monsr Menage, on n'a pas songé que toute l'impression ne se fait pas sur de si grand papier, mais qu'il y en*a* de moins grand. Outre que par deça on ne fait jamais les taille-douces de beaucoup plus grandes qu'une page imprimée du livre. Je n'avois aucune pensée de recevoir autre chose qu'un crayon assez rude, & peut-etre méme une simple description. Si j'eusse jamais crû qu'on feroit faire un dessein aussi beau, j'aurois averti en temps & de la grandeur, & d'une place convenable*b* pour mettre le nom du livre, que nous estimons par deça une chose essentielle à un titre en taille-douce.

[No address, date, or inscription of any kind]

a. qu'il y en de *sic (a omitted).*   *b*. convenable *inserted.*

An interesting letter, in which Wetstein politely but firmly justifies his criticism of the picture sent for the frontispiece and discusses in some detail what might be done with it.

LETTER 63

Wetstein to Ménage. 1 October 1691

d'Amsterdam ce 1r. d'Octobre 1691

Si Vous n'avez pas payé les 120 livres portez par le billet de Mr. Le Clerc, n'en payez que les 95 livres parce que j'ai trouvé un honnete-homme de peintre qui pour une pistolle a fait en sorte que je pourrai me servir de la plus grande partie du frontispice que m'avez envoyé. Si Vous avez payé les 120 livres je Vous ferai rendre les 25 livres ou Vous les ferai bon d'une autre maniere comme Vous voudrez.

[space left in MS]

Revant ces jours passez à l'ordre de notre ouvrage, je songeois*a* s'il ne seroit pas plus à propos que Votre hist: mul: philos. suivit immediatement le texte de Diogene, & qu'on lui fit succeder Vos Observ. sur Diogene. En effet cela me paroit plus naturel, d'avoir les femmes philos. aprés les hommes, & de leur faire suivre les Commentaires sur celui-ci, que de couper ces*b* commentaires pour y mettre entre deux les femm: phil: Car si on met celles-ci aprés Votre Commentaire, il faudra lui faire succeder les Observ. de Mr. Kuhnius. Et par là il y aura ce me semble une incongruité qu'on pourroit eviter en mettant les femmes philosophes à la tete de Vos Observations. Je n'attendrai que Votre reponse pour mettre la main à l'ouvrage & pour faire imprimer l'histoire des femm: ph: Nous avons encore 12. ou 13. feuilles à faire à Vos Observations, & cinq tout au plus au texte du Diog. auquel M. Meib. fait des eclaircissemens extraordinaires. Mais aussi il nous traine horriblement. Je suis cependant Monsieur tout & entierement à Vous.

H Wetstein

[No address]

a. songeois *altered from* me *[deleted] followed by [illegible word].*   *b*. ces *altered from* les.

Wetstein has found a solution to the problem of the frontispiece, which also resolves the difficulty of paying for an unusable picture. The rest of the letter concerns undecided questions of fitting in the Historia mulierum philosopharum *and the other secondary material, and the general progress of printing. Wetstein often tempers his complaints about Meibomius with acknowledgement of the quality of his scholarship, as though to justify his perseverance with such a difficult collaborator; here he is more enthusiastic than usual in his praise ('des eclaircissemens extraordinaires').*

LETTER 64

Wetstein to Ménage. 18 October 1691

d'Amsterdam ce 18. d'Octobre 1691

Monsieur

Je Vous dois réponse à deux lettres du 26. du passé & 8e. du courant. J'ai reçû avec celle ci Vos augmentations à l'histoire des femmes philos. que j'ai rangées d'abord.

Je n'ai jamais eu autre intention qu'à me servir du frontispice que m'avez envoyé pourvû que je pusse le faire ranger en sorte que je pûsse m'en servir: ce qu'à la fin j'ai obtenu par un bon peintre pour une pistolle, comme je Vous l'ai mandé par cidevant.[1] J'espere de Vous en envoyer une epreuve dans peu.

Pour l'histoire des femm: philos. je la tourne & la retourne, sans lui trouver aucun lieu plus propre qu'au commencement du 2d tome. Je n'aurois aucune repugnance à la mettre à la fin du 1r. tome: mais cela me grossiroit trop ce tome à proportion du 2d. Et d'ailleurs je ne trouve aucun inconvenient à faire suivre l'histoire des femmes à celle des hommes: & par[a] aprés les annotations sur l'histoire des hommes. Hors delà je ne trouve aucun lieu à la[b] placer convenablement qu'aprés les tables: ce qui me paroit bien plus hors-d'œuvre qu'au commencement du 2d tome. Enfin j'en consulterai M[r]. Grævius & suivrai son sentiment. Je lui avois aussi ecrit touchant la medaille de Monimus.[2] Il me dit que les contorniates avoient presques toujours des inscriptions si ridicules, qu'on n'en pouvoit tirer aucun sens. Il ajouta, pour rire, qu'il n'y trouvoit que ce sens NUGas MAGnas CONatus est MONIMUS.

Je suis tres-aise de Vous savoir entre les mains une partie du Diogene, que je Vous ai envoyé par Strasb. Je m'en vai Vous en envoyer la suitte par la méme voye. Mais je suis tres-surpris que Vous n'ayez pas encore la precedente partie: j'en écris la ci-jointe, & Vous aurez la bonté de l'envoyer.[3] Surquoi j'espere qu'en aurez bientot des nouvelles.

Nous sommes au IXe. livre de Vos observations sur Laërce, & n'avons plus que pour onze feuilles tout au plus: du texte il n'y a plus que pour 3. feuilles. Cependant voila que M. M. s'en va faire un escapade pour 8. jours, je ne sai pas où, sans dire mot, [fol. 1v] sans nous laisser ni copie ni epreuve/[c] voila des pauvres ouvriers sans pain pour une semaine entiere/[d] enfin c'est une misere: je presse tant que je puis; & lui nous retarde tant qu'il peut. J'espere pourtant d'en sortir à la fin: s'il plaît à Dieu! & puis oncques n'y retourneray.

La 1e. partie du Diogéne se fait si grosse, que je serai contraint d'en mettre la table à la fin de la 2e. partie, avec la Votre. Nous verrons quand nous serons un peu plus loin. Cependant je demeure Tout à Vous

H Wetstein

[No address]

[a]. par *sic (for pas)*.
[b]. la *altered from* les [?].
[c]. / : *Wetstein's ρ mark.*
[d]. / : *Wetstein's ρ mark.*

Wetstein sends final reassurances over the frontispiece. He discusses further the placing of the Historia mulierum philosopharum: *interestingly, it is to Grævius that he is turning for advice, and he also reports Grævius's humorous comments on the Monimus image. Wetstein returns to the problem of sending packages safely: the parcel sent through Strasbourg to his brother in Basel has reached Ménage, but not the one sent earlier to Tournes in Geneva. Meanwhile Meibomius has vanished for a week without warning.*

1 Ménage's critical comments over the frontispiece must have been contained in his first letter (of 26 September), before seeing Wetstein's last of 1 October.
2 Wetstein had written to Grævius in August (see Letter 59). The picture of Monimus was included among the plates (Vol. I, facing p. 353), with its inscription 'NVG MAG CO N MONIMUS' (Plate 6). Grævius's joke about its meaning might be loosely translated as 'Monimus produced a great deal of rubbish'.
3 Wetstein encloses a letter for Ménage to send on to Tournes in Geneva (see Letter 66).

LETTER 65

Wetstein to Ménage. 5 November 1691

d'Amsterdan ce 5e. de Novembre *1691*
Puis qu'il n'y a point de cartier^a à atendre de Votre coté, & que Vous voulez absolument qu'on ne mette pas Votre histoire des femmes phil: à la tete de Vos notes, il faut se resoudre à les mettre à la fin & avant les notes de Mr. Kuhnius; bien que tout le monde demeure d'acord qu'elle seroit^b mieux au commencement. Mais puis qu'il faut vouloir ce que Vous voulez, il n'y faut plus penser. Il n'y en a encore rien d'imprimé, parce que je voulois auparavant avoir Votre derniere resolution. Nous sommes fort avant dans le 9e. livre de Vos notes: & il n'y a^c plus que 5. ou^d 6.e feuilles à faire en tout. Pour le texte nous sommes à la page 293. de l'edit. de Londres, & dans 2½ feuilles nous aurons le reste. J'en voudrois être dehors. Il y en^f a deja quelques pages de composées. Enfin avec peine & patience nous atraperons la fin. Les tables de Vos notes sont faites; s'entend des feuilles qui sont imprimées. J'ai traitté avec Mr. Le Clerc de faire celles du reste: à quoi il avoit bien de la peine à se resoudre: cependant en les faisant il se met aussi à faire des Observations, que je ne pourrai refuser de mettre à la fin de celles de Mr. Kuhnius.[1] Cependant nous y verrons: car je n'ai pas peut etre du papier pour tout cela; & il me fait croire que les tables iront à prés de dix feuilles. Kyrieeleison.[2] Car je ne sai presque plus où j'en suis. Cependant je fais tirer les portraits, & me mets en pieces pour avoir fait avant Noël. Mais c'est comme si tous les elemens avoient conspiré contre moi, pour n'avoir jamais fait; & plus je travaille, moins j'en voi de fin. Cepen-

dant me voilà 4000 ecus dont je ne puis tirer un double: ce qui n'est gueres agreable à un marchand, & qui a dix enfans à nourir. Mais tout cela ne me chagrine pas tant, que ce que je ne puis sitôt satisfaire à l'envie que Vous avez de voir cet ouvrage fini. J'espere pourtant que le bon Dieu nous en fera la grace, & dans peu. J'ai changé dans l'histoire des f. ph. les corrections que m'avez envoyé*g* dernierement*h*. Sur le titre du 2d. tome, aprés les mots Æg. M. in D. L. Notæ & Obs. je mettrai: accedit Historia mul. phil. eod. Menagio scriptore. Par ce que si je mettois accedit ejusdem: cet ejusd. feroit un double sens: ou plustot un equivoque.[3] Je suis entierement à Vous.

H Wetstein

[sideways up left side of this page]
Il y a tant de malades dans ces païs, que s'il en mouroit à proportion, ce seroit pis que la peste. Mais il en meurt trespeu. Ce sont des fievres qui Vous afoiblissent fort dans peu de jours: & on a peine d'en revenir. Le commun peuple & les artisans en patissent le plus. J'ai deja divers ouvriers malades: cependant aucun n'est mort encore. mais cela ne laisse pas de me retarder.
[No address]

a. cartier *sic (for* quartier*)*.
b. elle seroit *altered from* elles seroient.
c. a *inserted*.
d. 5. ou *inserted*.
e. ou 7. *[?] deleted*.
f. en *inserted*.
g. envoyé *sic*.
h. envoyé dernierement *originally written as one word, then separated by* /: envoyé/dernierement.

This letter, like most of the later ones from Wetstein, is a general review of the progress of the great work in its final stages: factual, occasionally exasperated, and constantly leavened with touches of humour. In a postscript he finds a new excuse for delays: sickness among the workforce.

1 In the event, Wetstein did not include a section of Le Clerc's 'Observations' in the edition.
2 Kyrie eleison: 'Lord have mercy on us!'
3 If Wetstein had printed 'accedit eiusdem Historia mulierum philosopharum' the potential double-entendre would have suggested that the women, rather than the history, were Ménage's – particularly unfortunate in view of the scholar's well-known affection for intelligent and literary ladies. In the event the title-page to the second volume reads: *In Diogenem Laertium Ægidii Menagii observationes & emendationes, hac editione plurimum auctæ. Quibus subjungitur Historia Mulierum Philosopharum eodem Menagio scriptore* ...

Wetstein to Ménage. 10 December 1691

d'Amsterdam ce 10. Decembre *1691*

Monsieur

J'espere qu'aurez reçû ma precedente, avec celle que j'y avois jointe pour Monsr de Tournes de Geneve.[1] Je serai bien aise d'aprendre en son temps qu'elle ait servi à Vous faire avoir les feuilles en question. D'autres amis m'ont fait des plaintes du méme personnage, pour n'etre pas trop ponctuel à s'acquiter des commissions qu'on lui donne. J'espere que nous n'aurons plus besoin de lui: & d'autre coté j'aurai soin de ne le charger plus de ces petits soins, qu'il dedaigne peutêtre; & que pourtant je souhaite qu'on execute exactement, ou qu'on ne s'en charge pas.

Cependant je Vous donne avis que depuis quinze jours ayant eu occasion d'envoyer quelque chose en Suisse, j'y ai joint un pacquet des feuilles Iiii. Kkkk. Llll. Mmmm. Nnnn. du Diogene Laërce: & depuis celle de q jusques à kkk. de vos notes, avec un exemplaire complet de tous les portraits qui entrent dans mon edition. J'en ai chargé mon frere le Professeur Wetstein à Basle, & il aura soin de Vous le faire tenir seurement comme le precedent.

Depuis nous avons achevé entierement & vos notes & l'historia mul. phil. qui finit à la feuille sss. On travaille aux notes de Mr. Kuhnius qui feront sept feuilles, & on en est à la 3me. On fait la feuille du titre, dedicace, preface, & de la lettre de Mr. Pearson, qui sera devant Vos notes, & fera le commencement du 2d tome. Oooo du Diogéne est composé, mais non pas corrigé. Il ne reste plus qu'une ½ feuille pour Pppp ou ¾.

Dieu nous en fasse trouver la fin: Car M. M. nous lanterne terriblement. Il m'a fait une autre piece. Mr. Gale de Londres,[2] un des plus honnetes gens du monde, & obligeant au delà de tout ce qu'on en peut [fol. 1v] dire, m'avoit prété son exempl. du Diog: qui étoit conferé avec & corrigé sur[a] deux beaux Manuscrits l'un de Cambridge, & l'autre d'Arondel. Il n'y a point de page où il n'y ait plusieurs var. lectt. Mr. Meib. s'en est servi & en a inseré dans son texte toutes les lectures qu'il a jugé[b] bonnes, sans dire le moindre mot du monde d'où il les a tiré, ni des Ms. ni du Dr. Gale. peut etre pour nous donner tout cela pour ses propres conjectures & corrections. Maintenant je travaille à extraire toutes ces Varr. lectt. de l'exempl. du Dr. Gale, que je mettrai aprés les notes de Monsr Kuhnius, cum honorif. elogio, que merite l'obligeant Dr. Gale.[3] M. M. en enrage, & voudroit qu'on obvint tout cela. Mais comme cela ne me semble pas dans l'ordre, je prendrai la peine de ne faire pas les choses à sa fantaisie. Tout cela me chagrine terriblement, & c'est comme cela qu'il en a toujours agi avec moi. Enfin je n'espere pas d'étre prét avant fevrier, ou il faudroit un miracle.

Je ne sai si je serai plus heureux avec notre frontispice. Deux habiles graveurs y ont travaillé depuis deux mois: cependant il n'est pas fait encore. Sat cito si sat bene.[4] Je l'espere. Dieu nous fasse la grace de voir bientot tout l'ouvrage fini. Je suis de tout mon cœur Votre treshumble & tresobeïssant Serviteur

H Wetstein

[No address]

ª. & corrigé sur *inserted*.   ᵇ. jugé *sic.*

The letter begins with the problems of sending large packages of proofs to France; Wetstein com-
plains of Tournes's inefficiency, and is sending another package via his brother. He reports on the
progress of printing, then relates the latest contretemps with Meibomius: he has appropriated as
his own work variant readings from two manuscripts in England, provided by the distinguished
English scholar Thomas Gale. Wetstein is himself sorting out the imbroglio, which has now
delayed completion until February 1692. Finally, the frontispiece is still not ready.

1 The letter for Tournes was enclosed with Wetstein's letter of 18 October.
2 Dr Thomas Gale (1635?-1702) was successively Regius Professor of Greek at Cambridge (1666-72), High Master of St Paul's School (1672-97), and finally Dean of
York. As Wetstein's comments suggest, he had an attractive personality and was celebrated for his generosity and his modesty. He maintained an extensive learned correspondence with continental scholars.
3 Wetstein did as he had promised. The title-page of the second volume includes: ...
Accedunt Joachimi Kühnii in Diogenem Laertium observationes, Ut & variantes lectiones ex duos
codicibus MSS. *Cantabrigiensi & Arundeliano, cum editione Aldobrandiniana collatis, quas nobis-*
cum communicavit Vir Celeberr. Th. Gale...
4 'Quick enough if good enough': *Dicta Catonis,* quoted in St. Jerome, Epistle LXVI,
§ 9.

LETTER 67

Wetstein to Ménage. 21 January 1692

d'Amsterdam ce 21e. Janvier *1692*
Monsieur
On est à la table des matieres. C'est à dire à la fin du Diogene. J'ai été obligé de faire
mettre toutes les tables à la fin du 2d tome. Ainsi aprés Votre hist. mul. phil. il y a les
notes de Mr. Kühnius, suivies par les Varr. lectt. de Mr. Gale, & les vieilles prefaces.
Aprés quoi j'ai mis index Auctorum quos citat Diog. Laert. qui est suivi par celui des
Autheurs de Vos Observ. le troisiéme est l'Index rerum & verbor. Diog. L. & de Vos
observ. que j'ai été contraint de mesler ensemble pour ne pas trop multiplier les tables
sans necessité. le 4e. sera la table des mots grecs de Vos Observ. que Mr. le Clerc a jugé
ne devoir pas confondre dans la table latine. Et voila tout. Reste à faire le titre, ma
Dedicace à l'Electeur de Brandebourg,[1] & la preface de Mr. Meib. avec la table des
philosophes,[2] le catalogue des editions de Diog. (: que je pourrois aussi mettre à la fin
du 2d tome, selon que cela viendra à propos) & la table de l'ordre de tout l'ouvrage. Ce
sera tout au plus pour la fin du fevrier. Ce qui etant fait je Vous enverrai les feuilles qui

Vous manquent encore, par la voye de Liege, & dont Monsr. Pellisson-Fontanier[3] s'est chargé de Vous les faire parvenir. La planche du titre est faite à peu prés, & sera préte dans trois jours. Elle me coute furieusement de l'argent, comme tout le Diogene: qui m'a si bien epuisé que je n'y saurois plus fournir, s'il chassoit plus loing qu'il ne fait. Il chasse tout juste la moitié plus que je ne pensois, & me coute le double de ce que j'avois crû. Dieu soit loüé que nous en[a] soyons là. [fol. 1v] J'ai mis la vie de platon écrite par Olympiodore, aprés les Prefaces de Meric Casaubon. Car j'ai evité avec soin de n'omettre pas le moindre jota, qui seroit dans l'edition d'Angleterre. Voila ce que j'ai crû Vous devoir dire. Et je ne doute pas que ma premiere que je Vous ecrirai aprés celle ci[b] ne Vous aprenne la fin entiere de tout l'ouvrage. Ainsi soit il! Je demeure toujours entierement à Vous.

H Wetstein

Depuis trois semaines j'ai[c] eu la douleur qu'un de[d] mes freres, Medecin, s'est noyé à deux lieües d'ici; & que depuis j'ai eu sept enfans grievement malades tous ensemble. [No address]

[a]. en *inserted*.
[b]. que je Vous ecrirai aprés celle ci *inserted*.
[c]. last letter of j'ai *altered from* u.
[d]. qu'un de *altered from* que m.

Wetstein writes what he hopes will be the final report on the last stages of the edition (although in fact there was one further drama to come from Meibomius). The completion date is now the end of February. Thanks to Ménage's intercession he has found a new route for sending packages to Paris, through Liège. The frontispiece is at last almost ready; as before, this gives Wetstein occasion to lament the expense of the whole enterprise. He ends in a postscript with a tragic item of personal news.

1 Friedrich (1657-1713), son of the Great Elector Friedrich Wilhelm, had succeeded his father as Elector of Brandenburg in 1688; in 1701 he was to crown himself King of Prussia. He was already celebrated as a patron of learning, and later was to induce Leibniz to come to Berlin as president of the newly-formed scientific academy.

2 The dedication and preface did not proceed as smoothly as Wetstein had foreseen, and Meibomius's preface was never written. The spectacular quarrel that ensued is described in Wetstein's next letter.

3 Paul Pellisson Fontanier (1624-1693) was an old friend of Ménage's. He had been a favourite of Fouquet and had shared his patron's disgrace, spending four years in the Bastille from 1661 to 1665, a time when Ménage was of great service to him. He was later fully restored to favour by Louis XIV, especially after he abjured his native Protestantism in 1670. He became a highly influential figure: he was named royal historiographer, and, in particular, was put in charge of the substantial funds used to reward (or purchase) conversions to Catholicism.

LETTER 68

Ménage to Grævius. 8 February 1692

A Paris ce 8.^a Fevr. 1692.

Etant votre serviteur au point que je le suis; vous honorant, vous estimant, & vous admirant comme je fais; & vous aïant autant d'obligations que je vous ay; vous ne doutez pas, Monsieur, que je n'aye pris toute la part que je dois dans la perte que vous avez faite de Monsieur votre fis;[1] & ce n'est, Monsieur, que pour satisfaire à la coutume que je prens aujourdhuy la liberté de vous écrire pour vous en assurer. Je vous prie de croire, Monsieur, que je m'interesseray de mesme dans toutes les choses qui vous arriveront. Je prie Dieu qu'il vous console.

Tout à vous à l'ordinaire

Ménage

[Address on fol. 2v (not M's hand):]
Hollande. / A Monsieur / Monsieur Grævius, Professeur / à Utrecht. / | / *A Utrecht.*
[Annotated *XII* in later red crayon]

^a. 8. *inserted, replacing* 10 [?] *deleted.*

A sad sequel to the end of Ménage's letter of 10 September 1691 (Letter 61): a note of consolation on the death of Grævius's son.

1 See letter of 10 September 1691, note 6. The young scholar had died at the beginning of the year, shortly after his appointment as *lector* in Utrecht. His father later saw his edition of Callimachus through the press. In his letter to Ménage of 13 March 1692, Bayle gave an indication of the scholarly abilities and promise of Grævius's son: 'Mr Gravius a perdu depuis le commencement de cette année son fils unique qu'il avoit deja fait créer Lecteur en Histoire et en belles lettres dans l'Université d'Utrecht et qui avoit un Callimache sous la presse. Mrs Broeckhuisen Franzius &c ont fait des vers funebres sur cette mort qui ont eté imprimez.' (Bibl. de la Sorbonne, Bibl. Victor Cousin, Collection d'autographes, v, no. 7, fol. 2r).

LETTER 69

Wetstein to Ménage. 6 March 1692

d'Amsterdam ce 6e. de Mars^a 1692

Monsieur,

Revenant d'un tour que j'avois fait par^b ces provinces, je trouve l'agreable Votre du 11e. du passé. Le Diogene est enfin achevé, excepté seulement les tailles-douces ou

figures du titre, auxquelles on n'a pû travailler par ce froid excessiv. On est aprés à les
tirer presentement. Et je m'en vai Vous envoyer incessament ce qui Vous manque à
parfaire Votre exemplaire. Mais je m'étonne que ne me dites rien du commencement
de Diogene, dont le Sr. de Tournes s'estoit chargé. Pour le dernier pacquet que je
Vous ai envoyé par Basle, il faillit à me couter 300 écus & plus. Je l'avois mis dans un
ballot d'etoffes à mon Beaufrere. ce ballot fut ouvert par les Imperiaux sur les frontieres
de la Suisse, qui y trouverent ce pacquet portant Votre adresse. On ne parla pas moins
que de confisquer le tout. Mon beaufrere en fut averti, y fit un voyage, & accommoda
l'affaire pour 3. pistolles, & 2 autres que lui couta le voyage. Je croi qu'à l'heure qu'il
est Vous aurez ledit pacquet entre les mains. Ce n'etoit pas mon dessein non plus de
joindre Votre table des matieres à celle du reste; mais Mr. Le Clerc jugea que Diogene
ne parlant d'aucune chose tant soit peu considerable, dont Vous ne parliez aussi, il
seroit trop embarrassant pour le lecteur d'en chercher à deux fois: & trop ennuyant
d'avoir deux indices des mémes choses; mais des mémes au pied de la lettre.^{c} Au reste
comme tout le Diogene m'a été une source fertile d'avantures, il n'a pas fini sans m'en
faire avec Mr. Meiboom: qui n'ayant aucun droit à la dedicace, outre un aveu en forme
de ne savoir personne à qui l'adresser, pretendoit me la disputer quand il voyoit que
j'en avois fait une à l'Elécteur de Brandebourg. Non qu'il pretendit la faire: mais que je
lui en devois ceder le profit s'il y en auroit: sans pourtant vouloir s'engager [fol. 1v] aux
frais qu'il faudroit faire. Et quand je me moquois de ses propositions extravagantes, il
crût m'y contraindre en refusant de faire la preface à moins que de les lui acorder. Je le
pris au mot; & a^d son defaut je fis & la dedicace & la Preface, dont les Connoisseurs
disent plus de bien qu'elles ne meritent; & quelques uns peut etre trop complaisants,
qu'ils ne voudroient pas que celle de M. Meib. fut à la place de la mienne. Mais raillerie
à part; je n'y songeois pas d'abord, comme je le vis aprés, que Mr. Meib. dans sa preface
n'auroit parlé que de lui-méme, ni fait d'autres eloges que le sien tout seul. Et moi j'ai
parlé de tout le tissu de l'ouvrage, & de ceux qui y ont contribué: comme Vous le verrez. Ainsi que je dois étre bien-aise que Notre Heros n'y ait pas touché: à qui pourtant
je fis vir ma preface avant que de la faire imprimer. Quand il vit qu'on n'avoit plus
besoin de lui, il jetta feu & flamme, & voulut tout abismer: mais sans m'en inquieter le
moins du monde, je fis imprimer fort tranquillement ma preface. Il me manda qu'il s'en
vengeroit, & je n'y repondis pas un seul mot; me contentant de considerer que quand il
voudra ecrire contre moi, je ne manquerai pas de plume, & que j'aurai une presse par
dessus le marché. Dieu merci je me connois, & ne pretens pas m'égaler à trente étage^e
prés d'un homme d'une telle erudition; mais je pretens d'etre beaucoup plus raisonna-
ble, & beaucoup moins bourru. Enfin à cela prés me voila hors de ses griffes. Adieu
Monsieur, je suis tout & entierement à Vous

H Wetstein

[No address]
[Beneath the date at the head of the letter is written in another, larger hand: 'L'Ep.
dedic. & la Preface sont de la façon de M. Wetstein. Il le mande à la 2e. page de cette
Lettre.' The phrase on fol. 1v, lines 4-5, 'je fis & la dedicace & la Preface, dont les
Connoisseurs disent plus de bien qu'elles ne meritent' has been underlined, presumably
by the same (early) hand]

ᵃ. Mars *written over* fevrier *[?]*.
ᵇ. par *written over* en *[?]*.
ᶜ. *This sentence is followed by a longer than usual space, before the next sentence continues on the same line.*
ᵈ. a *sic.*
ᵉ. étage *sic.*

Ménage must have written to express his pleasure with the look of the edition, in a letter alluded to by Wetstein. However the frontispiece is still not printed, because of the cold; Ménage has still not received his package of proofs from Tournes in Geneva; and Wetstein relates the dramatic adventures of the last parcel sent via Basel. The second half of the letter is an account, told with considerable humour, of the final 'avanture' with Meibomius ('Notre Heros'): a failed attempt at blackmail over the dedication and preface (both of which Wetstein wrote himself), followed by a spectacular tantrum.

LETTER 70

Wetstein to Ménage. 8 May 1692

d'Amsterdam ce 8e. de May *1692*

Monsieur

Je suis bien aise que les feuilles du Diogene, que le Sr. de Tournes avoit gardé prés d'un an, Vous aient été rendues à la fin. J'espere que depuis Vous aurez encore reçû le 2d. pacquet que j'ai envoyé par la voye de Basle, & peut-etre encore le reste des feuilles, que j'ai envoyé*ᵃ* par Liege à Mr. Pel. le 1r. d'Avril. Comme je n'ai point d'avis de Votre part que le 2d pacquet de Basle Vous ait été rendu, j'y ai écrit la sepmaine passée pour en avoir des nouvelles. Cependant pour obvier à tous les accidens j'ai fait envoyer depuis un mois de Francfort à Basle, un autre exemplaire tout complet du Diogene Laerce avec 12. exemplaires de Vos poesies, pour Vous étre envoyés ensemble par la voye de Strasbourg. J'espere que le tout Vous sera bien rendu.¹ Ce livre ne trouve par deça que des approbations: & on estime le livre aussi parfait, en toutes manieres, que quelque autre qui ait*ᵇ* esté imprimé depuis 50 ans. On Vous y donne toute la part que Vous meritez: & Vous meritez tout, ou peu s'en faut.*ᶜ* Je suis fasché de ne pouvoir envoyer des exemplaires à Paris. Les frais sont si horribles par la Suisse, & les risques si excessifs par mer, qu'il n'y auroit aucun moyen à s'y sauver. Mr. Meiboom & moi vivons en si grande indifference, comme si nous n'avions jamais rien eu à demesler ensemble ni en bien ni en mal: & s'il ne venoit quelquefois chez moi pour se plaindre de l'Imprimeur qui fait son Specimen biblicum, je ne le verrois aparamment jamais. C'est un homme à faire tourner l'esprit à tout le monde. Il y a 44 feuilles de fait de ce specimen (: qui est le livre dont Vous me demandez des nouvelles, où il veut prouver que tout le texte hebreu est ecrit en vers) il m'a fait rimprimer quelques feuilles deja par deux fois, & [fol. 1v] je ne sai pas encore où j'en suis. Il y a 5 ans qu'il est commencé. quelquefois on fait deux feuilles par semaine; quelquefois on n'en fait pas une en six mois. Enfin cela fait pitié.[2] Monsr. Toinard n'en fait pas mieux. Il y a quatre ou cinq ans, qu'il me fit imprimer 4. feuilles de son harmonie sur Josephe. C'etoit le texte qui devoit étre illustré par des belles notes etc. que j'attens encore au bout de cinq ans, & Dieu sait si elles viendront jamais.[3] Dieu preserve tout honnéte Libraire de rencontrer de tels autheurs. C'est le vrai moyen d'aller à l'hopital.[4] Vive Monsr Menage! qui envoit sa copie toute d'un bout à l'autre, sans se faire attendre. On me blâme de n'avoir pas ajouté Votre portrait à Votre ouvrage,[5] aprés en avoir tant fait graver pour le Diogene. Il me semble que ces gens n'ont pas tout le tort, & je les blame à mon tour de m'en[d] avoir pas fait souvenir plustot. Je suis parfaitement & entierement à Vous

H Wetstein

[Address on fol. 2v:

A Monsieur / Monsieur l'Abbé Menage au cloitre / N. D. à / Paris]

[a]. e deleted at end of envoyé.

[b]. ait inserted.

[c]. This sentence is followed by a longer than usual space, before the next sentence continues on the same line.

[d]. m'en sic (ne omitted).

The great work is at last finished. Ménage has finally received the parcel from Tournes, and Wetstein enquires about those sent by other routes; he has in any case now despatched a copy of the whole work complete. He has at last produced the 'chef-d'œuvre d'édition' promised nine years before: the edition has met with universal applause. We have a final picture of Meibomius, and the only role he now plays for Wetstein: that of a hopelessly slow and difficult author. Toinard is another. But: 'Vive Monsieur Ménage!'; and the letter, and the correspondence, ends with Wetstein's warm praise for the old scholar.

1 Ménage's comments on the work, as recorded in the *Ménagiana*, synchronise closely with Wetstein's letter: 'il y a près de neuf années qu'il est sous la presse, & je n'en ai reçu que deux exemplaires que M. Wetstein m'a fait tenir de Hollande par Strasbourg. C'est une route bien longue; mais la guerre est cause de ce desordre. Je suis bien satisfait de l'impression. Tout le monde la trouve belle. Je ne croiois pas voir cet ouvrage avant que de mourir'. An editorial footnote serves as a pendant to Wetstein's 'Vive Monsieur Ménage!': 'M. Ménage mourut environ un mois après avoir reçu ces exemplaires' (*Ménagiana*, I, 76). Ménage died on 23 July 1692.

2 See above, Wetstein's letter of 20 September 1691 (Letter 62), note 2. Meibomius's work eventually appeared six years later: *Davidis Psalmi duodecim, & totidem Sacræ Scripturæ Veteris Testamenti integra capita. Quæ novi speciminis loci Biblicarum suarum emendationum & interpretationum, prisco metro Hebræo restituit, & cum tribus interpretationibus adparere voluit Marcus Meibomius* (Amsterdam, H. Wetstein, 1698).

3 See Wetstein's letter of 27 January 1684 (Letter 15), note 3, and also his letter of 20 September 1691 (Letter 62).

4 'On dit fig. d'Un homme qui se ruine par les procez, par le jeu, ou par d'autres folles despenses, qu'*Il prend le chemin de l'Hospital*' (*Dictionnaire de l'Académie*, 1718).

5 A new portrait engraving was made of Ménage in the last years of his life, by Roger de Piles, because, as Ménage commented, he no longer resembled the well-known engraving by Nanteul made forty years earlier for his *Miscellanea* (Paris, Courbé, 1652). See *Ménagiana*, II, 173. See Plate 1.

BIBLIOGRAPHY

Works of Reference

Allgemeine deutsche Biographie, ed. R. Liliencron and F. X. Wegele, 56 vols, Munich, 1875-1912

Biographisch woordenboek der Nederlanden, ed. Abraham Jacob van der Aa et al., 21 vols, Haarlem, 1852-78

Biographie universelle, ancienne et moderne, ouvrage rédigé par une société de gens de lettres et de savants, 52 vols, Paris, Michaud, 1811-1828

Deutsche biographische Enzyklopädie, ed. W. Killy et al., 12 vols in 14, Munich, 1995-2000

Dictionnaire de biographie française, ed. J. Balteau et al., vols 1-19, Paris, 1933-

Le Dictionnaire de l'Académie françoise, Paris, Veuve de Jean Baptiste Coignard, 1694

The Dictionary of National Biography, ed. L. Stephen and S. Lee, 22 vols, Oxford, 1973 (first edition 1885-1900)

Neue deutsche Biographie, hrg. von der Historischen Kommission der Bayerischen Akademie der Wissenschaften, vols 1-20, Berlin, 1953-

Nieuw nederlandsch biografisch woordenboek, ed. P. C. Molhuysen et al., 10 vols, 1911-37

Nouvelle Biographie générale, ed. J. C. F. Hoefer and F. Didot, 46 vols, Paris, 1853-66

The Oxford Classical Dictionary, ed. M. Cary, J. D. Denniston et al., Oxford, 1957 (first edition 1949)

Manuscripts

This is far from a complete listing of Ménage's surviving correspondence. The manuscripts listed are those which are of particular relevance to the present edition.

Amsterdam, Universiteitsbibliotheek

MS G.k.64: letter from Nicolaas Heinsius to Ménage, 24 October 1679

MSS G.m. 8a-8ae: 30 letters from Wetstein to Ménage, 1683-1692

MSS III.E.8.59, E.9.64, E.10.63, 73, 131, 311: 6 letters from Ménage to Vossius, 1644-1682

Basel, Universitätsbibliothek

Autograph-Sammlung. Geigy-Hagenbach Nr. 1374: letter from Ménage to Nicaise, 15 June 1682

Copenhagen, Kongelige Bibliotek

MSS Thott 1263: 40 letters from Ménage to Grævius, 1679-1692

MSS Thott 1268: drafts of 4 letters from Grævius to Ménage

MSS Fabricius 104-123: draft of one letter from Grævius to Ménage

Other relevant correspondence with Grævius is found in:

MSS Thott 1250 (D. Elzevir), 1259 (Bouillaud), 1262 (Justel, Huet), 1263 (Huet), 1258, 1268 (Bigot)

Florence, Biblioteca Medicea Laurenziana

MS Ashburnham 1866. 1195-1414, 1420-1428: letters from Ménage to Huet, 1660-1692

MS Ashburnham 1866.208a: letter from Carpzovius to Ménage, 12 February 1690

MS Ashburnham 1866.208b: letter from Ménage to Huet, February/March 1690

MS Ashburnham 1866.1185: letter from Henricus Meibomius to Carpzovius, 21 December 1689
Cod. Laur. Rediano, 224, No. 44: letter from Ménage to Redi, 23 December 1678
Acq. e Doni 734: letter from Redi to Ménage, 5 February 1682

FLORENCE, BIBLIOTECA NAZIONALE CENTRALE

MS Magi. VIII. 362, fols 1-48: 26 letters from Ménage to Dati and to Magliabecchi, 1659-1691
MS Magi. VIII. 362, fol. 50: letter from Ménage to Cinelli, 25 January 1683

DEN HAAG, KONINKLIJKE BIBLIOTHEEK

MS 72.C.46, fols 4-15: 4 letters from Ménage to Cuper, 4 drafts of letters from Cuper to Ménage, 1678-1689
MS 135.A.28: letter from Bayle to Ménage, 4 April 1689

LEIDEN, BIBLIOTHEEK DER RIJKSUNIVERSITEIT

MSS Burm. F.8.: 26 letters from Ménage to Nicolaas Heinsius, 1645-1681
MSS Burm. F.8.: 2 letters from Nicolaas Heinsius to Ménage, 1650
MSS Burm. F.8.: letter from Pellisson to Ménage, 30 July 1659
MSS Burm. F.11.: 6 letters from Ménage to Vossius, 1644-1682 (copies in letter-book)
MSS BPL 291 I-II: *Ruana ou Memoires et Opuscules du Sr Rou*, 2 vols, containing copies and extracts of letters from Ménage (1688-1689), II, fols 80r-86r
MSS BPL 1886: letter from Bayle to Ménage, 10 January 1692
MSS BPL 1923. II. 140: letter from Bigot to Heinsius
MSS PAP. 7 (1-11): 11 letters from Ménage to Saumaise, 1644-1648

PARIS, BIBLIOTHÈQUE NATIONALE DE FRANCE

Fonds fr. 3930, fols 157-69: 8 letters from Ménage to Saumaise
Fonds fr. 9359: correspondence of Nicaise, including (fols 328-43) 8 letters from Ménage
Fonds fr. 15189, fols 41-69: letters from Ménage to Huet (19th-century copies)
Nouv. acq. fr. 1341: letters from Huet (and others) to Ménage (18th-century copies)
Nouv. acq. fr. 1343: letters from Bigot to Ménage
Nouv. acq. fr. 1344: letters from Tanneguy Le Febvre to Ménage
Nouv. acq. fr. 17270, fols 1-94: letters from Nublé to Ménage, 1645-1685
Nouv. acq. fr. 18248: correspondence between Mme de La Fayette and Ménage
Rothschild A. XVII, vols 1-13: many letters to and from Ménage, arranged alphabetically by the name of the writer

PARIS, BIBLIOTHÈQUE DE LA SORBONNE, BIBLIOTHÈQUE VICTOR COUSIN

Collection d'autographes, V, no. 7: letter from Bayle to Ménage, 13 March 1692
                              no. 22: letter from Huet to Ménage, 2 October 1689

PRINCETON, UNIVERSITY LIBRARY

John Wild Autograph Collection, V, 142: letter from Ménage to Toinard, 11 December 1683

REIMS, BIBLIOTHÈQUE MUNICIPALE

Collection P. Tarbé, Carton XV, 81-84: 4 letters from Étienne Foulques to Ménage, July-December 1688, about the printing of *Anti-Baillet*

UTRECHT, UNIVERSITEITSBIBLIOTHEEK

MS 7.c30: letter-book of J.-G. Grævius, containing a letter to Ménage of March 1690 (p. 58)

MS 6 k 12.30a: letter from Th. Jansson van Almeloveen to Ménage, undated, but late 1686 or early 1687

MS 995, II (5 k 9), fols 29r-30r: letter-book of Th. Jansson van Almeloveen, containing a copy of a letter to Ménage dated 18 March 1687

Editions of parts of Ménage's Correspondence

ASHTON, H. (ed.), *Lettres de Madame de La Fayette et de Gilles Ménage*, London, 1924

BANDERIER, GILLES, 'Une lettre inédite de Gilles Ménage', *French Studies Bulletin*, no. 87 (Summer 2003), 11-13 (p. 12)

BEAUNIER, ANDRÉ (ed.), *Mme de La Fayette: Correspondance*, 2 vols, Paris, 1942

BRAY, BERNARD, 'Les Lettres françaises de Ménage à Nicolas Heinsius', in *Mélanges historiques et littéraires sur le XVIIe siècle offerts à Georges Mongrédien*, Paris, 1974, pp. 191-206

DUCHÊNE, ROGER (ed.), *Madame de La Fayette: Œuvres complètes*, Paris, 1990

MABER, R. G., 'An unpublished letter from Gilles Ménage to Madame de La Fayette?', *French Studies*, 32 (1978), 147-51 (p. 148)

OMONT, HENRI (ed.), *Lettres d'Émeric Bigot à Gilles Ménage et à Ismaël Bouillaud au cours de son voyage en Allemagne lors de l'élection de l'Empereur Léopold Ier (1657-1658)*, Paris, 1887

PÉLISSIER, L.-G. (ed.), Lettres de Ménage à Magliabecchi et à Carlo Dati, Montpellier, 1891

PENNAROLA, LEA CAMINITI (ed.), 'Lettere inedite: Gilles Ménage a Pierre-Daniel Huet', *Quaderni del Dipartimento di Linguistica dell'Università della Calabria*, 3 (1986), 27-59

PENNAROLA, LEA CAMINITI (ed.), *Lettres inédites à Pierre-Daniel Huet (1659-1692), publiées d'après le dossier Ashburnham 1866 de la Bibliothèque Laurentienne de Florence*, Naples, Liguori, 1993

VILLEBOIS-MAREUIL, BARON DE, 'Correspondance de Gilles Ménage', *La Revue Angevine*, 3 (1896), 162-69, 194-201, 211-17, 259-64, 300-06, 393-400, 426-31, 492-502, 526-32

Works by Ménage

This is not a complete list, but includes the works and editions relevant to the present corrrespondence.

'Ægidius Menagius Guillelmo Menagio Proprætori Andecavensi Fratri Carissimo S.D.', in: Jean de Launoy, *Dissertatio duplex . . . Accedit Ægidii Menagii ad Guillelmum fratrem epistola*, Paris, E. Martin, 1650

Anti-Baillet ou critique du livre de Mr. Baillet, intitulé Jugemens des savans: par Mr. Menage, 2 vols, La Haye, Estienne Foulque & Louïs van Dole, 1688

------ , 2 vols, La Haye, Louïs & Henry van Dole, 1690

Dictionaire etymologique ou Origines de la langue françoise, Paris, Jean Anisson, 1694

Discours sur l'Heautontimorumenos de Térence, Utrecht, R. van Zyll, 1690

Histoire de Sablé. Première partie qui comprend les généalogies de Sablé et de Craon, avec des remarques et des preuves, Paris, Pierre Le Petit, 1683 [=1686]

Seconde Partie de l'"Histoire de Sablé", ed. M. B. Hauréau, Le Mans, Monnoyer, 1844

Historia mulierum philosopharum. Scriptore Aegidio Menagio. Accedit eiusdem Commentarius Italicus in VII. Sonettum Francisci Petrarche, à re non alienus, Lyon, Anisson, J. Posnel & C. Rigaud, 1690

The History of Women Philosophers, trans. and ed. Beatrice H. Zedler, Lanham, New York, & London, University Press of America, 1984

Juris civilis amœnitates, ad Lud. Nublaeum, advocatum Parisiensem, Paris, G. de Luyne, 1664

–, Paris, G. Martin, 1677

–, *Tertia Editio, prioribus longè auctior et emendatior*, Frankfurt am Main and Leipzig, Chr. Günther for the heirs of Friedrich Lanckisch, 1680

–, *Editio quarta*, ed. Tobias Gutberleth, Franeker, L. Strickius, 1700

Laertii Diogenis de vitis, dogmatis et apophthegmatis eorum qui in philosophia claverunt libri X, London, O. Pulleyn, 1664

Diogenis Laertii de vitis, dogmatibus et apophthegmatibus clarorum philosophorum Libri X. Græce et latine. Cum subjunctis integris Annotationibus Is. Casauboni, Th. Aldobrandini & Mer. Casauboni, Latinam Ambrosii Versionem complevit & emendavit Marcus Meibomius. Seorsum excusas Æg. Menagii in Diogenem Observationes auctiores habet Volumen II. Ut & Ejusdem Syntagma de Mulieribus Philosophis; Et Joachimi Kühnii ad Diogenem Notas. Additæ denique sunt priorum editionum Præfationes, & Indices locupletissimi, Amsterdam, H. Wetstein, 1692 [title-page of volume I]

In Diogenem Laertium Ægidii Menagii observationes & emendationes, hac editione plurimum auctæ. Quibus subjungitur Historia Mulierum Philosopharum eodem Menagio scriptore. Accedunt Joachimi Kühnii in Diogenem Laertium observationes, Ut & variantes lectiones ex duobus codicibus MSS. Cantabrigiensi & Arundeliano, cum editione Aldobrandiniana collatis, quas nobiscum communicavit Vir Celeberr. Th. Gale. Epistolæ & Præfationes, variis Diogenis Laertii editionibus hactenus præfixæ Indices Auctorum, Rerum & Verborum locupletissimi, Amsterdam, H. Wetstein, 1692 [title-page of volume II]

Ménagiana ou les bons mots et remarques critiques, historiques, morales et d'érudition, de Monsieur Ménage, recueillies par ses Amis. Nouvelle édition, revised and extended by Bernard de La Monnoye, 4 vols, Paris, Veuve Delaulne, 1729

Mescolanze d'Egidio Menagio, Paris, Louis Bilaine, 1678

–, *Secunda edizione, corretta, ed ampliata*, Rotterdam, R. Leers, 1692

Miscellanea, Paris, A. Courbé, 1652

Observations sur la langue françoise, Paris, C. Barbin, 1672

Observations sur la langue françoise. Segonde partie, Paris, C. Barbin, 1676

Les Œuvres de Monsieur Sarasin, Paris, Augustin Courbé, 1656

–, Paris, N. Le Gras, 1685

–, Paris, Veuve Sebastien Mabre-Cramoisy, 1694

Le origini della lingua Italiana compilate dal Signore Egidio Menagio, Paris, Sebastien Mabre-Cramoisi, 1669

Le origini della lingua italiana compilate dal Sre. Egidio Menagio, Gentiluomo Francese. Colla giunta de Modi di dire italiani, raccolti, dichiarati dal Medesimo, Geneva, J. A. Choüet, 1685

Ægidii Menagii poëmata. Quarta editio auctior et emendatior, Amsterdam, Ex officina Elzeviriana, 1663

–, *Septima editio, prioribus longe emendatior*, Paris, Le Petit, 1680

–, *Octava editio, prioribus longe auctior et emendatior, et quam solam ipse Menagius agnoscit*, Amsterdam, H. Wetstein, 1687

Les Poésies de M. de Malherbe, avec les observations de M. Ménage, Paris, T. Jolli, 1666

–, Paris, C. Barbin, 1689

Responce au discours sur la comedie de Terence, intitulée Heautontimorumenos, ou par occasion sont traittées plusieurs questions touchant le Poëme dramatique, Paris, Veuve Jean Camusat, 1640

Vita Mathæi Menagii, primi canonici-theologi andegavensis, Paris, Christophe Journel, 1675

Vitæ Petri Ærodii quæsitoris andegavensis, et Guillelmi Menagii advocati regii andegavensis, Paris, Christophe Journel, 1675

Other Primary Sources

Works directly referred to in the Ménage/Grævius/Wetstein correspondence are marked with an asterisk. Editions of texts are listed under the name of the editor where the editor's contribution is the principal focus of interest.

*ATHANASIUS, SAINT, *Sancti patris nostri Athanasii archiepiscopi Alexandrini opera omnia quae extant vel quae eius nomine circumferuntur, ad mss. codices Gallicanos, Vaticanos, &c. necnon ad Commelinianas lectiones castigata, multis aucta: nove interpretatione, praefationibus, notis, variis lectionibus illustrata: nova sancti doctoris vita, onomastico, & copiosissimis indicibus locupletata. Opera & studio Monachorum Ordinis S. Benedicti e Congregatione Sancti Mauri*, 2 vols in 3, Paris, J. Anisson, 1698

BASNAGE DE BEAUVAL, HENRI, *Histoire des ouvrages des sçavans*, 25 vols, Rotterdam, R. Leers, 1687-1709

*BAYLE, PIERRE, *Dictionnaire historique et critique*, 2 vols in 4, Rotterdam, R. Leers, 1697

BAYLE, PIERRE, *Dictionnaire historique et critique, troisieme édition*, 4 vols, Rotterdam, Michel Bohm, 1720

BAYLE, PIERRE, *Œuvres diverses*, 4 vols, La Haye, P. Husson *et al.*, 1727-31; includes *Nouvelles de la République des Lettres*

*BENEDICTUS, JOHANNES (ed.), *Luciani Samosatensis opera omnia in duos tomos divisa Iohannes Benedictus Medicinæ Doctor, & in Salmuriensi Academia Regia linguæ Græcæ Professor ... Editio purissima, cum Indice locupletissimo*, Saumur, Petrus Piededius, 1619

BENTLEY, RICHARD, *Richardi Bentleii et doctorum virorum epistolæ, partim mutuæ*, London, Bulmer, 1807

*BÈZE, THÉODORE DE, *Theodori Bezae Vezelii poemata varia. Sylvæ. Elegiæ. Epitaphia. Epigrammata. Icones. Emblemata. Cato Censorius. Omnia ab ipso auctore in unum nunc Corpus collecta & recognita*, Hanover, Guilielmus Antonius, 1598

BIGOT, EMERY (ed.), *Palladii episcopi Helenopolitani de vita S. Johannis Chrysostomi dialogus. Accedunt homilia S. Johan. Chrysost. in laudem Diodori, Tarsensis Episcopi. Acta Tarachi, Probi, & Andronici. Passio Bonifatii Romani. Evagrius de octo cogitationibus. Nilus de octo vitiis*, Paris, Veuve Edmond Martin, 1680

*BONA, CARDINAL GIOVANNI, *Rerum liturgicarum libri duo*, Paris, L. Billaine, 1672 (first published Rome, N. A. Tinassius, 1671)

BURMAN, PIETER (ed.), *Sylloges epistolarum a viris illustribus scriptarum*, 5 vols, Leiden, Samuel Luchtmans, 1727

*BURMAN, PIETER, THE YOUNGER (ed.), *Nicolai Heinsii Dan. Fil. Adversariorum Libri IV. Numquam antea editi. In quibus plurima veterum Auctorum, Poëtarum praesertim, loca emendantur & illustrantur. Subjiciuntur ejusdem Notae ad Catullum et Propertium nunc primum productae, curante Petro Burmanno, juniore . . . Qui Praefationem & Commentarium de Vita Nicolai Heinsii adjecit*, Harlingae, Folkert vander Plaats, 1742

BUSSY-RABUTIN, ROGER, COMTE DE, *Correspondance de Roger de Rabutin, Comte de Bussy*, ed. L. Lalanne, 6 vols, Paris, 1858-58

BUSSY-RABUTIN, ROGER, COMTE DE, *Correspondance avec le Père Bouhours*, ed. C. Rouben, Paris, Nizet, 1986

BUSSY-RABUTIN, ROGER, COMTE DE, *Correspondance avec le Père René Rapin*, ed. C. Rouben, Paris, Nizet, 1983

CAILLEMER, E. (ed.), *Lettres de divers savants à l'abbé Claude Nicaise*, Lyon, 1885

CHARPENTIER, FRANÇOIS, *Carpentariana ou remarques d'histoire, de morale, de critique, d'erudition, et de bons mots de M. Charpentier, de l'Academie Françoise*, Paris, Nicolas le Breton, fils, 1724

★Cujas, Jacques, *Iacobi Cuiacii . . . opera omnia in decem tomos distributa . . . Editio nova emendatior et auctior . . . cura Caroli Annibalis Fabroti*, 10 vols, Paris, S. & G. Cramoisy *et al.*, 1658

★Dacier, André, *Remarques critiques sur les Œuvres d'Horace, avec une nouvelle traduction*, 10 vols, Paris, D. Thierry & C. Barbin, 1681-89

★Dacier, André and Dacier, Anne, *Reflexions morales de l'Empereur Marc Antonin avec des remarques*, 2 vols, Paris, C. Barbin, 1690

Diogenes Laertius, *Diogenis Laertii Vitae philosophorum*, ed. Herbert S. Long, 2 vols, Oxford, 1964

Diogenes Laertius, *Lives of eminent philosophers*, trans. R. D. Hicks, with Preface and Introduction by Herbert S. Long, Loeb Classical Library, 2 vols, Cambridge, Mass., and London, new edition, 1972

Du Cange, Charles du Fresne, sieur, *Glossarium ad scriptores mediæ et infimæ latinitatis*, 3 vols, Paris, Edmond Martin & Louis Billaine, 1678

Du Cange, Charles du Fresne, sieur, *Glossarium ad scriptores mediæ et infimæ græcitatis*, 2 vols, Lyon, Ancillon, 1688

★Félibien, André, *Entretiens sur les vies et sur les ouvrages des plus excellens peintres, anciens et modernes*, 5 vols, Paris, P. Le Petit, S. Mabre-Cramoisy, J.-B. Coignard, Veuve S. Mabre-Cramoisy, 1666-88

Gassendi, Pierre, *Animadversiones in decimum librum Diogenis Laertii, qui est de vita, moribus placitisque Epicuri*, 3 vols in 2, Lyon, G. Barbier, 1649

Gassendi, Pierre, *De vita et moribus Epicuri libri octo*, Lyon, G. Barbier, 1647

Goss, John (ed.), *Blaeu's The Grand Atlas of the 17th Century World*, London, Royal Geographical Society, 1990

★Grævius, J.-G., *Johannis Georgii Grævii Orationes quas Ultrajecti habuit*, Leiden, J. de Vivié, 1717

Grævius, J.-G. (ed.), *Isaaci Casauboni epistolae . . . Editio secunda LXXXII. epistolis auctior*, Magdeburg & Helmstadt, Christian Gerlach & Simon Beckenstein, and Braunschweig, Andreas Duncker, 1656

★Grævius, J.-G. (ed.), *M. Tullii Ciceronis De officiis libri tres . . . Ex recensione Ioannis Georgii Grævii*, Amsterdam, P. & J. Blaeu, 1688.

Grævius, J.-G. (ed.), *M. Tullii Ciceronis Epistolarum libri XVI ad familiares ut vulgo vocantur*, 2 vols, Amsterdam, Daniel Elzevir, and Leiden, apud Hackios, 1676-77

★Grævius, J.-G. (ed.), *M. Tullii Ciceronis Epistolarum libri XVI ad T. Pomponium Atticum*, Amsterdam, Blaeu brothers and H. Wetstein, 1684

★Grævius, J.-G. (ed.), *L. A. Flori Epitome rerum romanarum, recensitus et illustratus a J. G. Grævio*, Utrecht, Ribbius, 1680

Grævius, J.-G. (ed.), *L. Annaei Flori Epitome rerum romanarum ex recensione Jo. Georgii Grævii cum ejusdem annotationibus longe auctioribus*, 2 vols, Amsterdam, G. Gallet, 1702

Grævius, J.-G. (ed.), *Hesiodi Ascraei quae extant*, 2 vols, Amsterdam, Daniel Elzevir, 1667

Grævius, J.-G. (ed.), *Justinus cum notis selectissimis variorum*, Amsterdam, Louis & Daniel Elzevir, 1669

★Grævius, J.-G. (ed.), *J. Meursii Themis Attica, sive de legibus Atticis libri II*, Utrecht, J. Van de Water, 1685

★Grævius, J.-G. (ed.), *J. Meursii Theseus, sive de eius vita rebusque gestis liber postumus*, Utrecht, F. Halma, 1684

★Grævius, J.-G. (ed.), *J. Meursii de Regno Laconico libri II, de Piraeo liber I, et in Helladii Chrestomathiam animadversiones*, Utrecht, G. Van de Water, 1687

Grævius, J.-G. (ed.), *C. Suetonius Tranquillus . . . Editio tertia auctior & emendatior*, Utrecht, A. Schouten, 1703

GRÆVIUS, J.-G. (ed.), *Syntagma variarum dissertationum rariorum: quas viri doctissimi superiore seculo elucubrarunt*, Utrecht, G. van de Water, 1702

GRÆVIUS, J. G. (ed.), *Thesaurus antiquitatum romanorum*, 12 vols, Utrecht and Leiden, F. Halma & P. van der Aa, 1694-1699

GRÆVIUS, J. G., and P. BURMANN (eds), *Thesaurus Antiquitatum et Historiarum Italiæ, Neapolis, Siciliæ . . . atque adiacentium terrarum insularumque*, 45 vols, Leiden, P. van der Aa, 1704-1725

GRÆVIUS, THEODORUS et al. (eds), *Callimachi Hymni, epigrammata, et fragmenta ex recensione Theodori J. G. F. Grævii cum ejusdem animadversionibus*, 2 vols, Utrecht, F. Halma & G. vande Water, 1697 [The second volume consists of Spanheim's *Observationes*, entered separately here]

*HARDOUIN, JEAN (ed.), *Caii Plinii Secundi naturalis historiæ libri XXXVII interpretatione et notis illustravit J. Harduinus . . . in usum . . . Delphini*, 5 vols, Paris, F. Muguet, 1685

HARDOUIN, JEAN (ed.), *Sancti Joannis Chrysostomi epistola ad Caesarium monachum*, Paris, François Muguet, 1689

*HEINSIUS, NICOLAAS (ed.), *Virgilius Maro, accurante Nic. Heinsio, Dan. Fil.*, Amsterdam, ex officina Elseviriana, 1676

*HENNIN, HEINRICH CHRISTIAN DE, *Henrici Christiani Henninii Hellenismos orthoidos. Seu, Græcam linguam non esse pronunciandam secundum accentus; dissertatio paradoxa*, Utrecht, Rudolf van Zyll, 1684

HUEBNERUS, H. G. (ed.), *Comentarii in Diogenem Laertium*, 2 vols, Leipzig, 1830-33

HUEBNERUS, H. G. (ed.), *Diogenes Laertius: De vitis, dogmatibus et apophthegmatibus clarorum philosophorum libri X*, 2 vols, Leipzig, 1828-31

*HUET, PIERRE-DANIEL, *Alnetanæ quæstiones de concordia rationis et fidei*, Paris, Thomas Moette, 1690

HUET, PIERRE-DANIEL, *Censura philosophiæ cartesianæ*, Paris, Daniel Horthemels, 1689

*HUET, PIERRE-DANIEL, *Petri Danielis Huettii … Censura philosophiae cartesianae, cum H. Meibomii praefatione*, Helmstadt, G. W. Hammius, 1690

*JANSSON VAN ALMELOVEEN, THEODORE, *De vitis Stephanorum, celebrium Typographorum, Dissertatio epistolica ad virum Cl. Joh. Georgium Grævium*, Amsterdam, Jansson and Waesberge, 1683

Le journal des sçavans, 2 fevrier 1688, Amsterdam, Wolfgang, Waesberge, Boom & Van Someren, 1688

LE CLERC, JEAN, *An account of the life and writings of Mr. John Le Clerc . . . to which is added a collection of letters, from J. G. Grævius, and Baron Spanheim, to Mr. Le Clerc. With a particular account of Dr. Bentley, and his two associates Gronovius and Burman*, London, E. Curll & E. Sanger, 1712

*LE CLERC, JEAN, *Bibliothèque universelle et historique*, 25 vols, Amsterdam, Wolfgang, Waesberge, Boom, and Van Someren, 1686-1693

LE CLERC, JEAN, *Bibliothèque choisie, pour servir de suite à la Bibliothèque universelle*, 27 vols, Amsterdam, Henry Schelte, 1703-1713

*LE CLERC, JEAN (ed.), *Luciani Samosatensis opera . . . ex versione J. Benedicti. Cum notis . . . J. Bourdelotti, J. Palmerii a Grentemesnil, T. Fabri, A. Menagii, F. Guieti, J. G. Grævii, J. Gronovii, L. Barlæi, J. Tollii, et selectis aliorum*, Amsterdam, P. & J. Blaeu, 1687

*LE FEBVRE, TANNEGUI (ed.), *Publius Terentius Afer. Diligenter recensuit et notulas addidit T. Faber*, Saumur, R. Péan, 1671

LONGUERUE, CHARLES DUFOUR, ABBÉ DE, *Longueruana, ou recueil de pensées, de discours et de conversations, de feu M. Louis du Four de Longuerue*, 2 vols, Berlin, [no printer], 1754

*MABILLON, JEAN, *Traité des études monastiques*, Paris, C. Robustel, 1691

*MEIBOMIUS, MARCUS, *Davidis Psalmi duodecim, & totidem Sacræ Scripturæ Veteris Testamenti integra capita. Quæ novi speciminis loci Biblicarum suarum emendationum & interpretationum, prisco metro Hebræo restituit, & cum tribus interpretationibus adparere voluit Marcus Meibomius*, Amsterdam, H. Wetstein, 1698

*Moréri, Louis, *Le Grand Dictionnaire historique, ou le mélange curieux de l'histoire sainte et profane*, Lyon, J. Girin and B. Rivière, 1674

Pearson, John, *Vindiciæ Epistolarum S. Ignatii ... Accesserunt Isaaci Vossii epistolæ duæ adversus David Blondellum*, Cambridge, J. Hayes, 1672

Perrot d'Ablancourt, Nicolas, *Lucien, de la traduction de N. Perrot, Sr. d'Ablancourt*, 2 vols, Paris, A. Courbé, 1654

*Petau, Denis (ed.), *Epiphanii ... opera omnia in duos tomos distributa. Dionysius Petavius ... recensuit, Latine vertit, & ... illustravit*, 2 vols, Paris, M. Sonnius, C. Morellus & S. Cramoisy, 1622

*Petit, Pierre, *Petri Petiti, philosophi & doctoris medici, Miscellanearum observationum libri quatuor, nunquam antehac editi*, Utrecht, Rudolph a Zyll, 1682

*Petit, Pierre, *Petri Petiti philosophi et doctoris medici, selectorum poematum libri duo: accessit dissertatio de furore poetico*, Paris, Jean Cusson, 1683

*Petit, Pierre, *P. Petiti ... Thea sive de Sinensi herba Thee carmen, ... cui adjectae F. N. Pechlini de eadem herba epigraphae*, ed. F. B. Carpzov, Leipzig, 1685

*Rancé, Armand-Jean-Baptiste Le Bouthillier de, *De la sainteté et des devoirs de la vie monastique*, 2 vols, Paris, F. Muguet, 1683

*Rivius, Joannes, *Castigationes plurimorum ex Terentio locorum, et in his obiter quidam explicati, per Jo. Rivium*, Cologne, J. Gymnicus, 1532

Rou, Jean, *Mémoires inédits et opuscules*, ed. F. Waddington, 2 vols, Paris, Société de l'Histoire du Protestantisme Français, 1857

*Sannazaro, Jacopo, *Actii Synceri Sannazarii ... Opera latina omnia, & integra. Accedunt notae ad ecloges, elegias & epigrammata. Item 3 fratrum Amaltheorum, Hieronymi, J. Baptistæ, Cornelii Carmina*, Amsterdam, H. Wetstein, 1689

Saumaise, Claude de, *Exercitationes de homonymis hyles iatricæ*, ed. Louis de Saumaise, sieur de St-Loup, Leiden, 1688

*Saumaise, Claude de, *Plinianæ exercitationes in Caii Julii Solini Polyhistora; item Caii Julii Solini Polyhistor ex veteribus libris emendatus*, 2 vols, Paris, C. Morell, 1629

Scudéry, Madeleine de, *Clélie, histoire romaine. Troisiesme partie*, Paris, Augustin Courbé, 1658

Sévigné, Mme de, *Correspondance*, ed. R. Duchêne, 3 vols, Paris, Gallimard, 1977–78

*Sirmond, Jacques, *Opera varia*, 5 vols, Paris, e Typogr. Regia, 1696

Spanheim, Ezechiel, *Ezechielis Spanhemii in Callimachi Hymnos observationes*, Utrecht, F. Halma & G. vande Water, 1697

Spon, Jacob, *Recherches curieuses d'antiquité contenues en plusieurs dissertations sur des médailles, bas-reliefs, statues, mosaïques & inscriptions antiques*, Lyon, Thomas Amaulry, 1683

Spon, Jacob, *Miscellanea eruditae antiquitatis*, Lyon, frères Huguetan, 1685

*Strauch, Johann, *Amœnitatum juris canonici semestre*, Jena, S. A. Müller, 1674

*Toinard, Nicolas, *Evangeliorum harmonia Graeco-Latina*, Paris, Cramoisy, 1707

Valois, Adrien de, *Valesiana*, Paris, F. & P. Delaulne, 1694

*Valois, Henri and Adrien de (ed.), *Ammiani Marcellini Rerum Gestarum qui de XXXI supersunt Libri XVIII ...*, Paris, A. Dezallier, 1681

*Vavasseur, François, *Observationes de vi et usu quorumdam verborum, cum simplicium, tum conjunctorum, in Multiplex et varia poesis, antea sparsim edita, nunc in unum collecta. Accesserunt ejusdem nondum editae Observationes de vi et usu verborum quorumdam latinorum*, Paris, veuve C. Thiboust and P. Esclassan, 1683

*Vossius, Gerardus Joannes, *Gerardi Joannis Vosii et clarorum virorum ad eum Epistolæ. Collectore Paulo Colomesio, Ecclesiæ Anglicanæ Presbytero. Opus omnibus Philologiæ & Ecclesiasticæ Antiquitatis Studiosis utilissimum*, ed. Paul Colomies, London, R. R. and M.C. for Adiel Mills, 1690

*Vossius, Isaac (ed.), *Caius Valerius Catullus et in eum Isaaci Vossii observationes*, Leiden, D. à
Gaesbeeck, 1684 / London, Isaac Littlebury, 1684
Vries, Gerard de, *Exercitationes rationales de Deo, divinisque perfectionibus*, Utrecht, F. Van de
Water, J. Ribbius, and F. Halma, 1685

Modern Critical Studies

a) On Ménage

*The great majority of critical studies on Ménage over the past forty years have been devoted to his linguistic
and etymological scholarship. With a few exceptions, such specialised studies have not been included here.*

Ayres-Bennett, Wendy, 'Dangers and difficulties in linguistic historiography: the case of Gilles
Ménage', in W. Hüllen (ed.), *Understanding the historiography of linguistics. Problems and projects*,
Münster, 1990, pp. 195-206
Ayres-Bennett, Wendy, 'Gilles Ménage (1613-1692): lexicographe, grammairien et annota-
teur', in *Actes du XXe Congrès International de Linguistique et Philologie Romanes, Zürich, 1992*,
Tübingen and Basel, 1993, IV, 23-36
Chauveau, Jean-Pierre, 'Ménage, lecteur des poètes', in G. Cesbron (ed.), *Les Angevins de la littérature*, Actes du colloque des 14, 15, 16 décembre 1978 organisé par le Département de Lettres Modernes et Classiques de l'Université d'Angers, Angers, 1979, pp. 93-107
Leroy-Turcan, I., and T. R. Wooldridge (eds), *Gilles Ménage (1613-1692), grammairien et lexi-
cographe: le rayonnement de son œuvre linguistique*, Actes du colloque international tenu à l'occasion du tricentenaire de la parution du *Dictionnaire étymologique ou Origines de la langue françoise*
(1694), Université Jean Moulin Lyon III, 17-19 mars 1994, Lyon, SIEHLDA, 1995
Maber, R. G., 'A publisher's nightmare: Ménage, Wetstein, and Diogenes Laertius', *Seventeenth-
Century French Studies*, 23 (2001), 165-77
Maber, R. G., 'Colbert and the scholars: Ménage, Huet, and the royal pensions of 1663', *Seven-
teenth-Century French Studies*, 7 (1985), 106-14
Maber, R. G., 'La Correspondance de Gilles Ménage', in W. Leiner (ed.), *Horizons européens de
la littérature française au XVIIe siècle*, Tübingen, 1988, pp. 27-34
Maber, R. G., 'Ménage, Nicaise, and Madame de La Fayette: the evidence of a newly-discov-
ered letter', *French Studies Bulletin*, no. 91 (Summer 2004), 15-17
Maber, R. G., 'Scholars and friends: Gilles Ménage and his correspondents', *The Seventeenth Cen-
tury*, 10 (1995), 255-76
Mouligneau, Geneviève, '"Nostre amitié ne finira que quand nous finirons", Madame de La
Fayette et Ménage', *Dix-septième Siecle*, no. 109 (1975), 67-91
Pennarola, Lea Caminiti, 'La Correspondance Ménage-Huet: un dialogue à distance', in
Suzanne Guellouz (ed.), *Pierre-Daniel Huet (1630-1721): Actes du Colloque de Caen (12-13 novem-
bre 1993)*, Paris, Seattle, and Tübingen, 1994, pp.141-154
Samfiresco, Elvire, *Ménage, polémiste, philologue, poète*, Paris, 1902

b) Selected general works

Berkvens-Stevelinck, C., H. Bots, P.G. Hoftijzer, and O.S. Lankhorst (eds), *Le Magasin de
l'univers: the Dutch Republic as the centre of the European book trade*, Leiden, 1992
Blok, F. F., *Nicolaas Heinsius in dienst van Christina van Zweden*, Delft, 1949

BOTS, HANS, and WAQUET, FRANÇOISE, *La République des lettres*, Paris and Brussels, 1997

BRAY, BERNARD, 'L'Enquête des correspondances', in *Le XVIIe siècle et la recherche: actes du sixième colloque de Marseille*, Marseille, 1976, pp. 65-78

DOOLEY, BRENDAN, 'Snatching victory from the jaws of defeat: history and imagination in baroque Italy', *The Seventeenth Century*, 15 (2000), 90-115

DOUCETTE, LEONARD E., *Emery Bigot: seventeenth-century French humanist*, Toronto, 1970

GIGANTE, MARCELLO, 'Ambrogio Traversari interprete di Diogene Laerzio', in Gian Carlo Garfagnini (ed.), *Ambrogio Traversari nel VI centenario della nascita*, Firenze, 1988, pp. 367-459

GRUYS, J. A., and C. DE WOLF, *Thesaurus 1473-1800: Nederlandse boekdrukkers en boekverkopers, met plaatsen en jaren van werkzaamheid*, Bibliotheca Bibliographica Neerlandica, 28, Nieuwkoop, 1989

GUELLOUZ, SUZANNE (ed.), *Pierre-Daniel Huet (1630-1721): Actes du Colloque de Caen (12-13 novembre 1993)*, Paris, Seattle, and Tübingen, 1994

HOPE, RICHARD, *The Book of Diogenes Laertius*, New York, 1930

JONES, HOWARD, *Pierre Gassendi, 1592-1655: an intellectual biography*, Nieuwkoop, 1981

LABROUSSE, ELISABETH, *Inventaire critique de la correspondance de Pierre Bayle*, Paris, 1961

LABROUSSE, ELISABETH, *Pierre Bayle, I: Du Pays de Foix à la cité d'Érasme*, The Hague, 1963

LABROUSSE, ELISABETH, *Pierre Bayle, II: Hétérodoxie et rigorisme*, The Hague, 1964

LAEVEN, A. H., 'The Frankfurt and Leipzig book fairs and the history of the Dutch book trade in the seventeenth and eighteenth centuries', in C. Berkvens-Stevelinck, H. Bots, P.G. Hoftijzer, and O.S. Lankhorst (eds), *Le Magasin de l'univers: the Dutch Republic as the centre of the European book trade*, Leiden, 1992, pp. 185-97

LANKHORST, OTTO S., *Reinier Leers (1654-1714). Uitgever en boekverkoper te Rotterdam*, Amsterdam, 1983

LEINER, W. (ed.), *Horizons européens de la littérature française au XVIIe siècle*, Tübingen, 1988

MARTIN, H.-J., *Le Livre français sous l'Ancien Régime*, Paris, 1987

MEJER, J., *Diogenes Laertius and his Hellenistic background*, Wiesbaden, 1978

MOMIGLIANO, ARNALDO, *Studies in historiography*, London, 1966

NELLEN, H. J. M., *Ismaël Boulliau (1605-1694). Nieuwsjager en Correspondent*, Nijmegen, 1980

POPKIN, RICHARD H., *The history of scepticism from Erasmus to Spinoza*, Berkeley, Los Angeles, and London, 1979

POPKIN, RICHARD H., and CHARLES B. SCHMITT (eds), *Scepticism from the Renaissance to the Enlightenment*, Wolfenbütteler Forschungen 35, Wiesbaden, 1987

DE QUEHEN, HUGH, 'Politics and scholarship in the Ignatian Controversy', *The Seventeenth Century*, 13 (1998), 69-84

ROCHOT, BERNARD, ANTOINE ADAM, ALEXANDRE KOYRÉ, and GEORGES MONGRÉDIEN, *Pierre Gassendi, 1592-1655: sa vie et son œuvre*, Paris, 1955

ROCHOT, BERNARD, *Les Travaux de Gassendi sur Épicure et sur l'atomisme, 1619-1658*, Paris, 1944

ROSTENBERG, LEONA, *Literary, Political, Scientific, Religious and Legal Publishing, Printing and Bookselling in England, 1551-1700: Twelve Studies*, 2 vols, New York, 1965

SANTINELLO, GIOVANNI (ed.), *Storia delle storie generali della filosofia*, 5 vols, Brescia, 1981- [?]

– Vol. I: F. Bottin, L. Malusa, G. Micheli, G. Santinello, I. Tolomio, *Dalle origini rinascimentali alla 'historia philosophica'*, Brescia, 1981

– English edition edited by C. W. T. Blackwell and P. Weller: *Models of the history of philosophy: from its origins in the Renaissance to the 'Historia Philosophica'*, Dordrecht, Boston, and London, 1993

– Vol. II: F. Bottin, M. Longo, G. Piaia, *Dall'età cartesiana a Brucker*

SCHALK, F., 'Von Erasmus' Res Publica Literaria zur Gelehrtenrepublik der Aufklärung', in *Studien zur französischen Aufklärung* (Frankfurt am Main, 1977), pp. 143-63

STEGEMAN, SASKIA, *Patronage en Dienstverlening. Het Netwerk van Th. J. van Almeloveen (1657-1712) in de Republick des Letteren*, Nijmegen, 1996

STEINBERG, S. H., *Five Hundred Years of Printing*, 2nd edition, Harmondsworth, 1961

ULTEE, MAARTEN, 'The Republic of Letters: learned correspondence, 1680-1720', *The Seventeenth Century*, 2 (1987), 95-112

WILLEMS, A., *Les Elzevier: histoire et annales typographiques*, Brussels, 1880

INDEX OF PROPER NAMES

174

[Wetstein *continued, sub* 'correspondence']*n.1*, 145 *n.3*, 148 *n.1*, 153 *n.3*; printing of *Poésies*: 4, 16, 79 *n.3*, 81, 83, 83 *n.2*, 84, 85, 89, 90, 94 *n.4*, 95, 97, 98, 99, 103, 104, 105, 106, 111; printing of *Diogenes Laertius*: 4, 16, 23, 24, 25, 26, 61, 62, 68 *n.4*, 73, 77, 80, 84, 85, 94 *n.4*, 97, 100, 101, 106, 110-11, 111 *n.2*, 112, 120-25, 129-49, 151-53; format of *DL*: 16-17, 82, 83, 84, 88, 89, 97, 100, 101, 102; costs of *DL*: 16, 89, 90, 102, 110, 140, 143, 146, 148, 149; illustrations for *DL* (see under Ménage, *Diogenes Laertius*); difficulties with *DL*: paper shortage: 18, 69, 70, 99-100, 110, 111, 111 *n.2*, 129, 130 *n.3*, 145; weather: 18, 67, 68, 100, 110, 124, 151, 152; illness: 18, 146; communications (see under War); English printers: 16, 71 *n.2*, 75; collaborators: 15, 16, 68, 69 *n.4*, 70, 75, 76, 77, 77 *n.5*, 81, 95, 100, 110, 111, 112, 113, 120, 121, 124, 125, 136, 140, 141, 143, 147, 148, 149 *n.2*, 151, 152, 153; complaints by Ménage: 15, 71, 72, 72 *n.1*, 77, 78, 79, 88, 89, 90, 93, 102, 103, 104, 105, 106, 107-08, 109, 145 *n.1*. See also: Paper; Meibomius; Ménage (*Diogenes Laertius*).

Wetstein, Johann-Rodolph II (father of Henrik): 14, 130 *n.2*.
Wetstein, Johann-Rodolph III (brother of Henrik): 14, 19, 129, 130, 130 *n.2*, 145, 147, 148.
Wetstein, M. (physician, brother of Henrik): 149.
Willems, A.: 50 *n.7*, 85 *n.2*.
William III, Prince of Orange: 12, 13, 30 *n.24*.

Xenophon: 135.
Xenophanes: 135.
Xenocrates: 122, 133.

Zedler, B. H.: 135 *n.2*.
Zeno: 122, 133.
Zeno Eleates: 135.
Zyll, Rudolph van: 20, 110 *n.1*, 113, 114, 118, 119.